Old Dog New Tricks

The Dogfather · Book Nine

roxanne st. claire

D1056823

Old Dog New Tricks
THE DOGFATHER BOOK NINE

978-0-9993621-5-0– ebook
978-0-9993621-6-7 – print

COVER ART: Keri Knutson (designer)
and Dawn C. Whitty (photographer)
INTERIOR FORMATTING: Author EMS

Critical Reviews of
Roxanne St. Claire Novels

Don't miss a single book in
The Dogfather Series...

And yes, there will be more. For a complete list, buy links, and reading order of *all* my books, visit www.roxannestclaire.com. Be sure to sign up for my newsletter on my website to find out when the next book is released! And join the private Dogfather Facebook group for inside info on all the books and characters, sneak peeks, and a place to share the love of tails and tales!

www.facebook.com/groups/roxannestclairereaders/

Chapter One

Katie Rogers tore out of the front door of her dorm, officially fifteen—no, *twenty*—minutes late for her date. She negotiated the front steps of Gillespie Hall while checking her watch, smoothing her hair, and adjusting the sweater she'd grabbed to throw over jeans, hoping it was nice enough for a Saturday night.

Oh well. She was late for a good cause. That phone call had been…amazing. And so, so tempting.

She closed her eyes and shook Nico Santorini's soft, sweet voice out of her head. Every time he whispered, *Come home to me, baby*, she shuddered. Every time he suggested she drop out of school and marry him, she weakened. Every time he said he loved her, she had to fight not to say it back.

Because she'd sworn to her mother that she'd *spread her wings* and *play the field* and *be a college girl* and everything else Mama had told her she had to do. She was *trying* to forget the high school

1

sweetheart she'd broken up with when she started her freshman year at Vestal Valley College in Bitter Bark.

She was trying so hard that she had another date with Daniel Kilcannon tonight, who was getting darn near to qualifying as her *new* boyfriend. They'd even invited two friends for a fix-up tonight, which was such a couple-ish thing to do.

Yes, Katie was doing what was expected—no, *demanded*—by her mother. She'd broken up with the grandson of Greek immigrants whose entire future would be running his family's deli in Chestnut Creek, and gone to college, unencumbered. So, according to Mama's rules, she could date a nice boy who was going to be a doctor or a lawyer or something else to impress her parents' friends.

Giving up Nico had been—and still was—awful. Dating Daniel wasn't so bad, though.

A few months ago, she'd walked into the kitchen at an apartment kegger and spied the tall, good-looking veterinary student nursing a beer and sharing pretzels with the host's dog. He wore a wry smile, as if the pup was more entertaining than the party, and turned out to be easy to talk to and even easier to kiss. In fact, when he walked her home, leaned her up against the brick wall of Gillespie Hall, and melted her with his mouth, she'd actually forgotten Nico for a moment or three.

Almost immediately, they started dating...and kissing. A lot. Their conversations were light, full of laughter, and he'd even taken her to meet his mom, dad, sister, and Irish setter, Murphy, who all lived at a place called Waterford Farm, not too far from campus.

Yes, she liked Daniel. She liked going out with him and *really* liked kissing him. The kissing escalated rather quickly to major make-out sessions that left them both hot, bothered, and wanting more. Then last Tuesday, when her roommate got sick and went home for a few days, Katie let Daniel spend the night in her dorm room.

At the town square, she slowed her step and swallowed hard, still not quite used to the idea that she'd gotten that intimiate with a man who wasn't Nico Santorini. And it had been...good.

Well, a little awkward in that skinny dorm bed, with some fumbling and actual tumbling when he put on protection, and certainly not as mind-blowing as it had been with Nico. But they'd stayed up late talking and laughing and did the whole thing over again on Wednesday night. She hadn't seen him since then, but when he called to ask her out for tonight and casually inquired if her roommate was back yet, she suspected they might go for round three tonight...if she wanted to.

Did she want to?

She walked a little faster, letting the chilly breeze lift her hair. It was as if she could hear Nico sighing with sadness over this. Guilt and regret and a bit of shame snaked up her belly. She still hadn't told Nico she was seeing someone else. If he found out she'd actually slept with another boy? He'd be heartbroken, even though they were no longer officially dating.

Oh, Nico. I'm sorry. I'm trying to do what I'm supposed to do.

She rushed across the grass and checked her watch one last time as she reached Bushrod's, taking a minute to catch her breath and get her head back in the present, not stuck in the past. No matter how great that past was.

"Hey, Katie. You're as late as I am."

She turned to see Daniel's friend Jimmy hustling toward her. "We're both late?" she asked. "I thought you and Daniel were coming together."

"Change in plans." He shrugged and looked past her through the doorway when someone walked out of the bar. "Is my blind date in there?"

"Anne Harper? I don't know. I just got here." She gave him a friendly elbow jab. "But I think you're going to like her."

He gave a nervous laugh. "Yeah, sure. I thought it was cool when Daniel mentioned you had a chick for me to meet. Is she pretty?"

She managed not to roll her eyes at the question, which was lame and shallow, and she'd bet the five dollars in her wallet that Daniel hadn't called Anne *a chick*.

"She's super pretty," she assured him.

That wasn't a lie, either. Katie had noticed the girl with thick auburn hair and big hazel eyes in her sociology lecture, mostly because she always had dirty boots and dog hair on her jacket.

When they got paired up on a group research project a few weeks ago, Katie found out Anne Harper volunteered at a local dog shelter and had few human friends because she was from out of state. Of course Katie wanted to help her make friends, and then Daniel said one of his buddies on his pickup basketball team hadn't met any girls—and the blind-date idea was born.

She looked around when they walked into the crowded bar, fully expecting to see six-two Daniel stand up and loom over everyone else to find her. The place was crowded, but not wall-to-wall yet, with no sign of him.

She scanned the tables, the dance floor, and finally her gaze landed on Daniel's dark hair and broad shoulders at the bar. He stood with a beer bottle in his hand, leaning close to talk to someone intently, and suddenly he threw his head back and belly laughed loud enough to hear over Stevie Nicks at full volume.

Then she realized it was Anne Harper who'd made him laugh like that.

"They must have found each other," she said to Jimmy, who followed her gaze.

"Oh yeah." His eyes popped. "Man, she *is* pretty."

And witty, since once again, Daniel gave a hearty laugh. In fact, Katie wasn't sure she'd ever heard him laugh quite like that.

As she got closer, and still didn't get noticed, Katie's gaze fell over the jacket Anne wore—complete with dog hair, of course—and the long waves of reddish-brown hair that fell down her back.

Daniel inched closer to deliver his next comment right in Anne's ear, and it was her turn to laugh at whatever these two complete strangers seemed to find hilarious.

"Move it." Jimmy nudged Katie from behind. "Before Kilcannon eats her up like she's dessert."

Katie wanted to shoot Jimmy a dirty look, but she was frozen, watching the two of them. She took in their direct eye contact, the subtle body language, and the way Anne's face tilted up and Daniel leaned down. She waited for a punch of jealousy because, hey, he was *her* guy.

But none came. The only thing that punched was a

5

memory of how Nico used to look at her exactly the same way.

Just then, Daniel looked up and blinked in surprise, like he'd totally forgotten there would be two other people involved in this double date, then he broke into his usual wide and genuine smile.

"There she is!" Instantly, he left Anne's side, arms out, to offer Katie a tight hug.

"I'm sorry I'm late," she said quickly. "I found Jimmy outside, too."

"It's fine," he assured her. "I've been talking to Annie."

Annie? "Oh, good," Katie said. "I felt bad about you sitting here alone when I found out Jimmy was late, too. How'd you know who she was?"

"I don't know. We just found each other." He gave a quick laugh as if that moment of meeting had some significance attached to it. "She's great. I don't think I ever met anyone who knows so much about dogs who isn't an actual vet."

Oh, of course. They'd bond over dogs. "She volunteers at a shelter."

"I know." His eyes lit up. "And she loves setters. Come on, I've got them holding a table for all of us." He put an easy arm around Katie and kissed her forehead. "Thought you might be standing me up," he added under his breath.

She looked up at him. "Why would you think that?"

"Because," he said softly, sounding deeply sincere, "I know you sometimes get a call on Saturday afternoons that makes you a little blue."

"Oh." The sound escaped her lips, a mix of surprise and a subtle appreciation that he'd remembered and

6

cared that Nico called her on the weekends. Maybe a little guilt, too. And here she'd thought he'd been flirting with Anne Harper when he'd been worrying about her talking to her high school boyfriend. "You're sweet, Daniel," she added, giving voice to her thoughts.

He winked at her. "Don't tell anyone."

They made the official introductions and got a booth in the back, the two couples sitting side by side. The arrangement seemed natural, but somehow Katie was facing Jimmy and Daniel was facing Anne and...*whoa*. They sure found a lot to talk about.

Like how devoted Welsh corgis were, and the keen intelligence of Australian shepherds, and was there anything greater than a French bulldog?

"Do all dogs come from another country?" Katie asked, and instantly Daniel did that headshake again, an apology easy to read in his clear blue eyes.

"Enough about dogs," he said quickly. "Were you able to get that humanities paper written?"

She appreciated that he remembered the paper was due on Monday, but the question came with no gleam in his eye. Sincere interest, like she might get from a brother, but no...spark. Not the way he looked at Anne...and not the way Nico looked at her.

She tried to push the thought away and keep the conversation light, but by the time they finished burgers and fries and a few more rounds of drinks, Katie was certain of three things: Jimmy and Anne had about as much connection as oil and water; Daniel enjoyed talking about animals more than most men liked sports; and Katie missed Nico in a way that left her aching from head to toe.

Once the bill was paid and everyone said good night, Jimmy and Anne shook hands but most certainly did not exchange phone numbers. Daniel and Katie headed back toward campus together, with almost nothing to say as they walked.

They were halfway across Bushrod Square before he reached for Katie's hand, and she already knew why it had taken so long. She couldn't help sneaking a look at him, wondering if she should say what they were both thinking and save him the embarrassment.

"So that was fun," he said, the attempt at conversation sounding a little desperate after he'd so easily chatted across the table all night.

"Yeah. I don't think our first try at a setup was a success, though," she said. "Anne and Jimmy hardly talked."

"Mmm." Even in the dim streetlights of the square, she could see his throat rise and fall as he swallowed. "Wrong guy for her," he said.

Poor boy. He was trying hard to cover something that simply couldn't be covered. Shouldn't be covered, really.

"Well, you two seemed to hit it off," she said with a gentle squeeze of his hand.

"Oh yeah, well, you know me. I get along with everyone."

She nudged him with her elbow. "You like her, Daniel."

"Well, I feel bad for inviting Jimmy, who was obviously not her type."

"I think *you* might be her type."

He slowed his step and glanced at her. "You're not jealous, are you?"

Sadly, honestly? She was not. But would it hurt him to know that? When she didn't answer, he came to a complete stop.

"Oh God, Katie. I'm sorry," he whispered.

"For what?"

He turned her toward him, squaring his shoulders and lifting his chin like he did when he was about to follow that unwavering moral compass of his. "Listen, I was trying to make her feel comfortable, and I thought I should talk about dogs, but..." His voice trailed off, and he closed his eyes. "I guess it was more than that."

She gave a teasing smile. "You're a sucker for a girl with dog hair on her jacket."

He cringed and grunted quietly. "Guilty."

"Don't feel bad." She looked him in the eye to make sure he knew how sincere she was. "Because I'm not the least bit jealous, Daniel."

"Not mad at me?"

"No, and I think that tells us a lot."

His blue gaze searched her face with a mix of confusion and hope. "Like...what?"

She reached her hands up, his sculpted cheeks warm and rough against her chilly fingers. "I can't stop thinking about Nico," she admitted. "Does that make you mad at me?"

"No, not at all. He was your boyfriend since ninth grade."

"Eighth." Actually, the summer before eighth grade to be precise.

"You have every right to miss him." Daniel closed his much-bigger hands over hers. "But I don't have any right to...to..."

"Flirt with a girl I fixed up with your friend?"

He shut his eyes, ashamed. "I didn't mean to flirt."

"You actually didn't," she said. "You connected. Like…" Like puzzle pieces, she thought with a smile. Just like Nico used to say they were. "Like Nico and I used to."

He scanned her face some more, obviously unsure where this was going. "Well, Katie, I'm so sor—"

"No." She put her hand over his lips to stop the apology he had no need to deliver. "Don't be sorry. Don't be sorry for me, and don't be sorry you clicked with Anne. You can't fight fate."

"Fate?"

What else could she call it? "I believe that there's a person for everyone, Daniel. A single human that is like the…" *Just say it.* "Like the puzzle piece God wants them to be next to in the great big jigsaw puzzle of life."

"The jigsaw puzzle of life?" He tapped her on the nose. "That sounds like something you would say."

Her heart shifted around, realizing that he might think that, but it was something Nico *had* said…and she and Nico had one mind and, on the best nights, one body. And one…puzzle.

"I mean there's someone for everyone," she insisted, unable to hide her passion. "A really, really *perfect for you* someone who makes you feel whole and complete and excited to wake up every day." With each word, her chest tightened a little as the truth and importance of what she was saying hit her.

"You're right," Daniel said slowly, considering her words. "Hopelessly romantic, but right."

"And I think…" She took a slow, shuddering

breath. "That Nico Santorini is my someone." Her voice cracked on the confession.

"Aw, Katie." He instantly reached to pull her closer in a comforting hug, letting her press her face into his jacket and wish it was Nico. After a moment, he drew back to look at her. "You should be with him."

"I know. It's all I want in the whole world. But my mother told me I shouldn't, and I always listen to her, but…"

"It's your life. It's your future. If he's the one you want, if he's your…your puzzle piece, then go for it."

She tightened her hug with a grateful squeeze. "You're right. You're so right." What was she doing trying to please her mother? It was Nico she wanted. It was Nico's dream of their future that felt utterly right to her. "You're amazing, Daniel."

He started to shake his head, but she wouldn't let him deny it.

"You're a great guy. Your heart is as good as anything or anyone I've ever known. You're cute and you're funny and you're kind. And you have so much love to give, but I…I…" She closed her eyes. "I'm in love with someone else. And if I sleep with you again, it'll be wrong. I don't want to be with anyone but Nico for the rest of my life. I'm sorry."

He added some pressure on her shoulders with his big, secure hands. "I'm not going to let you off the hook that easily, Katie Rogers. You can't break up with me without letting me take some blame. Ever since we left the bar—even before that—I've felt I had to tell you that…" He hesitated as if the disclosure would hurt, but being Daniel, he'd do the right thing.

Roxanne St. Claire

"There's something about that girl. I don't know what it is, but I felt something I never felt before. I can't stop wondering if she felt it, too."

"Why don't I give you her number so you can find out?"

His smile was slow and so, so sincere. "Would you?"

She nodded. "And if you'd be kind enough to walk me to the bus station, I can get the 1505 to Chestnut Creek and be with Nico in about three hours."

"You're going there? Now? Are you coming back?"

"I don't know. But I need to snap my puzzle into place tonight."

"I have a better idea." He tightened his arm around her shoulders, leading her forward. "Why don't you get some stuff from your dorm room and call Nico to tell him you're on the way? My car's parked in the vet school lot, and I can have you in Chestnut Creek in under an hour and a half. No stops, no bus fare, no problem."

"Oh, Daniel." She threw her arms around him again. "Thank you. And you know what?" She leaned back to make a point she fervently believed. "Something tells me you found your puzzle piece tonight."

"Something tells me you're right."

Chapter Two

Present Day

"It's the croissants, Annie girl, I swear." Daniel whispered the words into the chilly January air as he climbed out of his SUV and gave Rusty the nod that he could get out, too.

The old setter didn't leap to freedom as he usually would, but instead shot a look at Daniel that said he far preferred the open air of the Waterford Jeep to this Chevy Tahoe.

Daniel gave his shiny red head a rub of affection. "We'll get to the hardware store eventually," he said. "But I need a croissant. And you need one of Linda May's famous canine cookies."

He barked, which was the only response Daniel was getting that morning. The voice in Daniel's head, the sweet sound of his late wife, Annie, was uncomfortably silent. Usually when he talked to her—which was multiple times a day—he could hear her response as clearly as if it came from her own mouth and not his imagination.

He could hear that delicious laugh that started in her chest and made her shoulders shake with mirth. He could imagine her mesmerizing eyes that were a perfect balance of green and brown, widening with surprise at something he'd said. He could feel the silky touch of her fingertips on his arm as she added a witty comeback. All the things he loved for thirty-six years of the happiest marriage, until everything ended in a cold, antiseptic-smelling hospital room a little over four years ago. The day the heart that belonged only to him stopped beating.

But the voice in his head had been weirdly silent. And not just this morning, he mused as he and Rusty walked down Ambrose Avenue, taking in the wintry window displays in the brick storefronts that wrapped around Bushrod Square.

Fact was, Annie had been "quiet" after he'd talked with Cilla Forsythe for a solid hour after the Bitter Bark Beautification meeting. And again, when Shane brought the dog-show lady, Una, to the house for dinner, and she and Daniel had had such a spirited debate over a glass of Jameson's about what makes a dog a "champion." Annie had had nothing to say about the smile Daniel wore when he gave their guest a friendly hug good night that evening.

Then silence again today, on his run to pick up wood stain in a vain attempt to fix the worn spots on the living room floor that so sorely needed to be refinished.

But he needed his daily croissant first.

Or did he just need a pleasant conversation with the woman who *baked* the pastries? Truth was, he looked forward to Linda May's kind smile as eagerly as the first taste of her world-class raspberry croissants.

Guilt tapped its way up his chest and settled right next to denial, then leaned over to greet some lingering grief, and they all stared down a vow he'd made that he would never, ever break.

"Oh, who am I kidding?" he muttered to Rusty. Guilt, denial, grief, and four-year-old promises made during the worst moments of his life? Sure, maybe all that resided in him.

But so did a few hormones that were still mighty active despite the calendar reading sixty-one years of age. Not to mention a bone-deep need for the kind of emotional connection he'd enjoyed with a woman for his whole adult life. And, of course, there was something every one of his six kids and their significant others could see as plain as the silver hair on his head: loneliness.

Quenching his thirst for companionship didn't break any promises, did it?

Rusty slowed outside the bakery, looking up as if to tell his master, *You're walking right by the place.* Daniel stopped and let out a derisive snort. Way too much introspection for one morning. He had more important things on his mind than this kind of navel-gazing, damn it.

He was running the largest canine training and rescue facility in the state and still had a huge—if fully grown and partnered-up—family to think about. Those nephews and niece of his weren't making any progress toward the altar, so he'd have to work a little of his matchmaking magic that had been so successful over the last two years with his own kids.

And if anything would get Annie talking to him again, it was the subject of romance for their family. She'd led him straight to the right partner for every one of his kids.

Come on, Annie girl. Let's get to work on those Mahoney kids. Should we start with Declan, since he's the oldest? Or Braden, since he's had bad luck in love? How about Connor? Finding a woman to make that tail chaser settle down won't be easy. And who on earth could settle wild and wonderful Ella?

Once again, Annie didn't answer in his head.

Still, the idea of concentrating on a new match put a smile on his face as he pulled open the frosted glass door of Bitter Bark Bakery and braced for the sweet, buttery atmosphere that comforted him. Rusty led the way, of course, as dogs were as welcome in here as almost every other business in Bitter Bark.

He set his gaze on the short line at the counter and found himself looking for Linda May, but before he saw her, Rusty gave a quick bark and strolled over to a small table where two women were sipping coffee and sharing pastries.

"Rusty," he said, automatically reaching for the dog who normally never left his side.

He barked again, sidling up to one of the women who seemed to be inviting him over with a flick of her fingers.

"Sorry," Daniel said, snagging Rusty's collar and taking in the young woman's face, struck by something vaguely familiar. She wasn't a local, but hadn't he seen her recently? Hadn't he passed her on the street yesterday and nodded? And before that? Hadn't she been in the hardware store when he bought the wrong color of floor stain the other day? She wasn't someone you'd forget, but a remarkably beautiful, almost exotic-looking woman who might only be thirty. Rusty certainly remembered her.

Could this be the one for Braden? He had a weakness for brunettes, based on his last relationship, though he seemed a bit scarred by it. Maybe Connor. He had a weakness for *women*, but usually did the scarring.

"He only goes to people he knows and likes," Daniel said, easing Rusty back.

"Then he must like me." She reached out to pet the dog, but beamed up at Daniel. "Irish setter?"

He nodded, then glanced at the other woman at the table, who looked up and studied him with a strange mix of anticipation and uncertainty in her eyes.

Afraid of dogs, he decided instantly, getting a good hold of Rusty's collar. "Really, I'm sorry. He generally knows his boundaries."

A shaky smile lifted the corner of the second woman's lips, and another sense of familiarity seized him. She had to be the younger woman's mother, since the resemblance was apparent enough. Like her daughter, she had brown eyes, only they were softer, not as intensely dark. Her hair was deep brown, but not black, and cut short in a way that the ends brushed a delicate chin. But he'd seen her before, too. Not recently, but...he knew her.

Didn't he? She looked younger than he was, but definitely a contemporary, likely in her fifties, although there wasn't a thread of silver in her hair and only slight crinkles at her eyes. Maybe because she wasn't smiling, but searching his face as though she sensed that same familiarity.

A Waterford client? Someone he'd met at one of the zillion town committees he was on? Someone from his mother's church choir who'd come to the house? How did he...

"Daniel?"

It was her voice. Distinct, a little throaty, and utterly memorable. A chilly January night. A long ride in the dark. A lot of talk about...puzzle pieces.

"Katie? Katie Rogers?" His jaw fell as recognition hit him. "I don't believe it."

She sucked in a little breath and let it out as a soft "Oh!"

Instantly, she rose, and they hugged each other, their heads going the same way so they bumped, eliciting awkward laughs.

Katie Rogers. The girl who introduced him to Annie. "Wow," he muttered, closing his eyes, and in that split second, he could swear he heard his dearly departed wife's knowing chuckle.

Had Annie...

"I wondered if I'd see you around Bitter Bark," Katie said, giving him another light embrace, but leaning back to look at him the same way he was looking at her.

"Of course, I live here. I can't believe it's you."

"Old friend?" the other woman asked.

"Very old," Katie said, then instantly held up her hand in apology. "Not that you look old, Daniel. You look fantastic."

"So do you." That was an understatement. The compliment must have tumbled out with great

18

enthusiasm, since it earned a little snort of laughter from the younger woman.

"Oh, Daniel, this is my daughter, Cassie."

She stood and shook his hand as Katie introduced them.

"Honey, this is a...friend from that brief half semester I spent in college, Daniel Kilcannon."

He turned to her daughter, but it wasn't easy to take his gaze from Katie. She really looked amazing. Older, yes, but somehow the same. That pretty girl had bloomed into a beautiful woman.

"Hi, Cassie. So great to meet you." And then he was back to her mother. "I can't believe it, Katie. It's been what? Forty years? More, I guess."

She placed a pink-tipped finger to her lips. "Shhh. We don't admit to those numbers."

"You don't have to," he said. "You look...holy cow. You haven't changed at all."

She angled her head. "Then your eyesight has gone, but thank you."

"I told you, Mom. Nothing to worry about."

Katie was worried about her looks? Impossible. He turned to Cassie. "And I can see plenty of that same young woman in you."

"Really? 'Cause everyone says I'm a Santorini through and through." She gestured to the table. "Would you and your sweet dog like to join us?"

He glanced at Katie to make sure she was comfortable with that, and sure enough, there was an uneasy look on her face. Maybe she didn't want her daughter to know they'd dated? But he was dying to talk to her and catch up. Didn't she feel the same?

"I don't want to intrude," he said, even though he really, really did.

"I insist." Cassie whipped out an empty chair from the next table. "I love to meet Mom's old friends. Do you want coffee? Of course you do. And have you tried the raspberry croissants? They rock the foundation of the world."

He had to laugh. She was such a force.

"Cassie," Katie said softly. "He might not want to stay."

Daniel turned to her, drinking in the face of a woman he'd once cared for very much. Time really had been kind to her, with the years leaving nothing but a softness to her dewy skin and an elegance in the way she held her slender frame. She was maybe a year younger than he was and looked as if life had been very, very good to her. And that made him happy.

"I'd love to stay," he said honestly. "It's been so long."

Her expression relaxed a little, the sweetness he remembered about her visible in every fine feature. "It has been, Daniel."

Cassie put a hand on his shoulder and nudged him into the chair. "Sit. Talk. I'll be back with some refreshments. My treat." She took off toward the counter, leaving Daniel and Katie to ease back into their seats.

"She's beautiful, Katie," he said, the compliment bringing out a smile.

"She's, uh, not shy. Or subtle, I'm afraid."

Suddenly, he realized why her daughter might have been so encouraging for him to stay, and it felt extremely familiar. "I have a few like that myself."

She inched forward, took a breath, and said, "I'm sorry about Anne."

The words nearly knocked him back. "You know?"

She nodded, and her narrow throat moved with an awkward swallow. "It was in the Chestnut Creek paper because the same company owns the *Bitter Bark Banner*, and they run a lot of the same obits."

The explanation came quickly, almost as if she expected to be asked how she knew.

"Oh, I see. Well, thank you. We had a very happy thirty-six-year marriage." Except that he wanted thirty-six more.

"I'm sorry I didn't contact you," she added.

He gave his head a shake, surprised she'd think he'd expect that. They'd never seen each other again, not once, after the night he drove her to Chestnut Creek. He'd heard from a friend of a friend that she'd dropped out of Vestal Valley, and they'd lost touch.

"It happened while I was in the throes of Nico's cancer, and I had my hands full," she said.

Nico Santorini, the boy he'd taken her to see that night. "Cancer? Is he…"

She closed her eyes. "He passed two years ago."

"Oh man. Sorry." He put his hand on hers, surprised at how familiar it felt, despite the decades that separated them. "There's nothing worse."

"Nothing." She sighed and searched his face again. "But we have our families."

"Oh yeah." He felt his smile return. "I have six kids," he said. "Grown and either married or about to be. Three grandkids, too. How about you?"

"I have five," she told him, with a clear note of

pride. "Not one close to married. Four boys, and Cassie's the baby."

"I have four boys, too," he said, grinning at the unexpected connection. "They all live here in Bitter Bark and work with me, along with my two daughters. And you? Still in Chestnut Creek?" he guessed, since she'd mentioned the local paper.

"Yes, I'm still there. In a townhouse now."

Once again, she looked intently at him, as if sizing him up. Maybe wondering how he'd changed. Maybe wondering what might have been if they hadn't gone on that double date on January 17, 1976, which became one of the many anniversaries he and Annie liked to celebrate every year.

Meeting Day, Annie liked to call it, and they always went to Bushrod's and sat in the same booth and relived the electricity that had zapped them both that night. This year, he and Rusty took a long walk and had a good pity party.

"I hope I didn't miss anything important." Cassie returned and set a cup of coffee and a raspberry croissant in front of him. "Black with one sugar. The lady behind the counter says you're a regular."

"I am, and thank you, Cassie. Your mom tells me you're the youngest of five."

"Youngest, loudest, prettiest, and most opinionated." She lifted her coffee cup in a toast. "Just ask my big brothers."

"So like my family," he told them with a laugh, thinking of his youngest, Darcy, and all her spunk and confidence. "Are all of your sons in Chestnut Creek, Katie?"

"Two of them," she answered. "John and Alex,

they're my twins, live there and work in the family business. Theo's in the military, stationed in San Diego now. And the oldest, Nick, is…" She lifted a shoulder and added a shaky smile. "Somewhere…"

"He's a physician with Doctors Without Borders," Cassie explained. "He was home at Thanksgiving for a few days, then back to Africa. Internet is shaky there, so we can go weeks without hearing from him."

"Really?" Daniel looked from one to the other, seeing pride in the sister but something more like fear in Katie's eyes. Of course. She must worry day and night about him in dangerous situations. "Congratulations on such a terrific family."

"Thank you. They mean the world to me."

"I get that," he said easily. "And never more than when you have to go it alone. I'm sorry about your father," he added to Cassie. "I hope he didn't suffer terribly before he died."

The two women shared a look that he took to mean the man had indeed suffered. They all must have. A familiar sympathy caught in his chest, knowing that long or fast—the way Annie's shocking heart attack took her—it all hurt the same.

"Is this your only dog?" Cassie asked, deftly changing the subject he suspected was too tender to explore.

"Yes and no. In reality, I'm surrounded by so many dogs, I've lost count. I own a canine training and rescue facility outside of town."

"Very cool," Cassie said. "I keep telling Mom she should get a dog to fill the void."

Katie cleared her throat. "And I keep telling her I have a great job and a lovely family, but you don't know stubborn until you've met the daughter of a Greek man. All of my kids think they know exactly what I need."

Daniel let out a true and hearty laugh. "Trust me, my six are literally competing for who can best fix my life. Is your job also in the family business, Katie?"

"The deli?" Katie shook her head. "I'm not Greek enough to work at Santorini's."

"But she has redesigned both our locations," Cassie said. "Mom is a talented and successful interior designer."

It was his turn to lean forward, brows raised. "Really? That's awesome. Is that what brings you to Bitter Bark?"

Before she could answer, the two women exchanged lightning-fast looks, almost as though silently agreeing on what they'd tell him.

"Cassie is looking for possible space to open up another Santorini's."

"Oh, fantastic. Is it a restaurant or a counter deli?"

"It started as a deli," Cassie told him. "When my grandparents opened it in the 1950's. So, it's still called Santorini's Deli, but it's been a full-service restaurant for years."

"With top-quality catering under Cassie's direction as an event planner," Katie added, smiling at her daughter.

"All true," Cassie agreed with a saucy tip of her head.

"And you're thinking about expanding to Bitter Bark?" he asked.

"We have two locations in Chestnut Creek," Cassie said. "One in town, one in a mall, but business is booming, so my brothers and I think the time is right to grow. We're looking at Holly Hills and Crestview, too."

"I'm sure you've learned the real estate market is really tight here."

After another one of those nearly imperceptible shared glances, both women nodded.

"Yes," Cassie said. "We have."

"Bitter Bark is growing like crazy," he told them. "But we could always use more good restaurants." He narrowed his eyes, thinking about a thread of a conversation he'd heard at the last Economic Development meeting. "In fact, I think one *might* be coming on the market soon for rent or sale. I can make some calls for you."

"Oh, that's not—"

Daniel waved off Katie's comment. "I'm happy to help," he assured her. "But a word of warning. We spent a year using the name *Better* Bark to establish this town as one of the most dog-friendly places in America." He gestured toward a King Charles spaniel sleeping in the corner and a sheltie keeping watch next to another patron. "So you'd have to welcome four-legged friends."

"That wouldn't be a problem," Cassie said, looking down at Rusty, who'd curled up contentedly in the space between Daniel's and Katie's chairs. "I read about the Better Bark campaign and thought it was genius."

"It was actually my daughter-in-law's idea." He couldn't keep the pride out of his voice. "And, honestly, I think I somehow got roped into every committee this town ever dreamed up," Daniel told them. "So I can definitely get the inside scoop for you on real estate availability."

Cassie's eyes widened, and she looked at her mother, a not-so-subtle intensity in her dark gaze. "Isn't that awesome, Mom?"

"Yes, yes, it's great," Katie responded with a little less enthusiasm.

And then the secret language became crystal clear to Daniel. Good Lord, did all kids that age try to matchmake their widowed parents?

Smiling, he leaned closer to Katie. "My family is exactly the same," he said. At her questioning look, he added, "Wait until they start running a betting pool on who you should be dating. It's like the fantasy football draft with my social life as the team."

Her cheeks darkened with a flush, which somehow made her look even prettier. "They think they know everything."

"And we already *do* know everything," he said.

That made her laugh, a deep, sultry sound that lifted her shoulders and lit her eyes. In that instant, she looked exactly like the spontaneous, spunky girl he'd known in college. That memory must have been what gave him an unexpected jolt he felt right down to his toes. Something certainly…jolted.

"I have an idea," he said, leaning back to look from one to the other. "Why don't you both come to Waterford Farm for dinner tonight?"

Neither one answered, but both blinked in surprise at the invitation.

"It's really beautiful," he said, sensing that, for whatever reason, they needed a little nudge.

"I know," Katie said. "I've been there, remember?"

"Oh yeah." He exhaled, surprised that for the whole conversation, he'd been so wrapped up in who she was now, he'd forgotten who she'd once been. A girlfriend, more or less, and she'd had dinner with his parents and sister when they were dating. "Well, my mother's still around and as much a spitfire as ever, since she's now an eighty-seven-year-old blogging sensation. But Waterford Farm has changed a lot in the last four decades, and I'd love you to see it and meet my family."

"They all still live there?" she asked, sounding shocked.

"Oh, no. But it's Wednesday, and that means anyone who's in town comes to dinner."

She looked at him, not committing yet. But he wanted her to come. She was a connection to the past, and for some reason, he wanted that. And maybe she did, too.

"Why don't I make a few calls today and find out what local properties might be coming on the market?" he suggested. "You guys poke around town today and then drive out to Waterford around four or five. I'll give you a tour, and you can tell my family what you're looking for as far as space. If you get the Kilcannons involved, things will happen, I promise."

"I guess we could do that," Katie said, still nursing way too much hesitation.

"Oh yes, we'd love to." No hesitation from her daughter, though.

"Then it's decided." He put his coffee down and inched his chair back before she could change her mind. Rusty immediately stood to attention next to him.

"Are you sure it's not an imposition?" Katie asked, looking up at him as he stood.

In that split second, he saw the girl again. Young, fresh, wide-eyed and...and in love with another guy. Was that why she seemed a little reserved, or had the years and travails of life changed her?

"Not in the least," he said. "My family is going to go crazy to meet the girl who introduced me to Annie."

He could have sworn she paled. "Oh, that would be—"

"That would be perfect, and you will love meeting the whole family. In fact," he turned to Cassie, "a few of my firefighter nephews might be there, too."

Cassie gave a sly smile. "You think things'll get so hot we're going to need a firefighter?"

"You never know." He straightened and snagged Rusty's collar with one hand, reaching into his pocket for a card. "Here's my cell, Katie, and the address of Waterford. I'm really looking forward to seeing you again."

As if on cue, Rusty took a few steps closer to Katie, looking up at her with a plea for affection and attention, making them all laugh.

"My dog is doing his best to persuade you," Daniel said. And to be honest, so was he.

"Thank you, Daniel," she said, absently petting Rusty's head, but looking up at him. "I would like to...to talk to you. It's been so long."

"Too long." He held her gaze for a heartbeat or two, then Cassie reached her hand to shake his.

"So nice to meet you, Dr. Kilcannon. And you, Rusty. Bye!" She also gave the dog a pet on the head before Daniel stepped away, holding up his hand to say goodbye as he and Rusty headed out the door.

It wasn't until he was outside that he realized he'd never mentioned being a veterinarian, so why would she call him *Dr.* Kilcannon?

They must have both studied that obituary pretty closely four years ago.

A twinge of doubt tapped at him. Was that meeting *not* by accident?

Oh, these matchmaking kids. He chuckled as he walked toward the hardware store with a little more bounce in his step than had been there before. They needed to leave the setups to a professional. In fact...

He pulled out his phone to text Braden to see if he was off duty that night.

Yes, the Dogfather usually had a little more finesse in these situations, but the meet-up with an old friend had thrown him. Everything about Katie Rogers had thrown him, to be honest. Just giving her a hug had him...

Oh man. Maybe that encounter had been pure coincidence. Or maybe someone *else* was pulling strings.

He glanced up to the clouds. She wouldn't send someone who...

No. Not Annie. Right?

But like she had for the last few weeks, his late wife—and his imagination—remained quiet.

Chapter Three

"Well, that was a thousand times easier than you thought it would be." Cassie leaned across the table, her ebony eyes glistening. "Of course, that's because you totally buried the lead."

Katie looked away from her daughter, but her gaze shifted out the window just in time to see Daniel Kilcannon walking down the street with his trusty setter, looking as confident, handsome, and damn sexy as he'd been the first time she'd met him.

"I chickened out," she admitted. "But we're going there for dinner. I'll tell him tonight."

Cassie lifted a dark, perfectly shaped brow. "You better, because we're not seriously considering Bitter Bark for the next Santorini's, and the man's already making phone calls."

"You're the one who told me we should have a story for why we're here. He might remember seeing us in town the last few days."

"Only if he thought it was some weird coincidence that we're sitting in the very bakery he frequents every morning."

Katie let out a slow exhale, so long and deep she wondered if she'd been holding her breath since the minute Daniel had walked in and she'd had to act surprised. Acting didn't come naturally to her, but she'd fought to meet him this way.

If it had been up to Cassie, they'd have stormed Waterford Farm and demanded an audience.

"I have to say, he was really nice." Cassie lifted her cup and leveled her dark gaze at Katie. Her eyes were so much like Nico's, sometimes it hurt to look at her. Nearly coal black, soulful, and expressive and as Greek as Cassandra, the mythological princess she was named after. "He is very handsome. I mean, not as good-looking as Dad in his day, but I can see the silver-fox appeal. And he seemed really happy to see you, which is…"

Katie looked down at the remnants of the croissant he'd barely touched, closing her eyes against an unexpected burn.

"Mom?"

She shook her head quickly, working like hell to ward off the tears.

"Mom, don't cry."

"How can I not?" she asked. "My life is upside down and sideways. Nothing is what it's supposed to be. Nothing is real, nothing is right. *Nothing.*"

"Except this daughter staring back at you, who loves you and needs you and is your best friend. Also, your sons, who think you are capable of making the sun rise and moon move. *We're* right."

Katie merely swallowed. "What am I going to do?" she finally asked in a whisper.

"What you have to do," Cassie said simply. "And

we've completed step one by meeting him. The door couldn't be more open. Now you have to…"

"Not chicken out," Katie finished. "Although I wish I could forget everything and go back to the way it was."

Cassie squeezed her hand. "You know you can't do that. You can never do that. Every time you—"

"Can I clear this for you?" A woman in an apron stepped closer and brought the whispered conversation to a halt, hovering an empty tray over their table. "There's no rush if you want to stay," she added. "But I can take some of it."

"Sure," Katie said, glancing up at the woman whose white apron read *Linda May, Best Baker in Bitter Bark.* "Thank you."

"Can't believe he didn't eat the croissant," the woman mused as she gathered up the plate full of broken pieces of pastry. "Something's wrong in the universe the day Daniel Kilcannon passes on one of my raspberry croissants. He sure must have been distracted."

"Oh, well, we were talking," Katie said.

The other woman eyed her. "So you know him?"

She opened her mouth to answer, ready to say they'd once dated, but something stopped her. Maybe she didn't want anyone to know that yet. Maybe *he* didn't.

"They knew each other forty years ago," Cassie chimed in, never one to shy away from a conversation with a stranger.

"Oh?" Linda May lifted a brow. "Then you must have known his wife, Annie."

"As a matter of fact, I introduced them."

"Really?" Linda May regarded Katie with unabashed curiosity. "Well, you should have some kind of plaque in the town square, then." Without being asked, the baker dropped down on the chair Daniel had just been sitting in. "Have you stayed in touch with them over the years?"

Katie shook her head. "No. Actually, this is the first time I've seen him in more than four decades."

As if the news kept flabbergasting her, Linda May looked from Katie to Cassie and back to Katie again. "I guess I don't know whether to thank you or strangle you."

Cassie leaned closer. "Why?"

"Well, we can thank you for giving the world one of the greatest marriages of all time. Those two were…" She smashed her index and middle finger together. "Inseparable. Perfect. Storybook. And their family is exactly what you would think. One better, brighter, and more beautiful than the next. Not to mention that Daniel is known as the Dogfather, because of the strings he pulled to matchmake his kids into their own romances so sweet it would make a grown woman cry."

Katie stared at her, processing all this information that was so much more than Cassie had scraped together from her internet searches. All she knew was what anyone would know, that he was a well-known veterinarian with six children and that he ran a canine facility. And, of course, that he'd been a widower for four years.

But this love story? These beautiful children he helped guide to adulthood and then into their own marriages? His obvious respect from the townsfolk and place of honor in Bitter Bark? None of this was online, and it painted a portrait of a man who wouldn't want to have his perfect world shaken up, not one single bit.

"Why would you want to strangle her?" Cassie asked, hanging on the woman's every word.

"Because there's not an unattached woman over forty and under sixty-five who wouldn't like to slide into Daniel Kilcannon's life and arms and..." She waggled her brow. "Sheets."

Cassie snorted, but Katie felt heat rise to her cheeks. She'd been in those sheets—well, technically he'd been in hers. Twice, many years ago.

"But who could possibly follow in the footsteps of Annie?" Linda May continued. "I mean, she was just this side of a saint. No, she actually *was* a saint. And so's he." The woman leaned in as if it was her civic duty to share more information, even though each piece of it was starting to tear Katie to shreds.

His life was ideal. His world was established. His family loved him, and so did his friends and neighbors. So she shouldn't—

"It's never about him," the woman said, interrupting Katie's litany of truths. "Every move he makes is for his family, or this town, or, of course, the dogs. His kids think he walks on water, but none of that seems to affect him." She looked out the window in the direction Daniel had walked, making Katie wonder if this woman had gazed at him as he left, too. "He's just as good as gold, and what you see is what you get. And what you see is damn nice, isn't it?"

Across the table, Cassie gave her a long, meaningful look that Katie easily interpreted. But did her optimistic, fearless, problem-solving daughter really think it could be simple because Daniel Kilcannon was a *good* man? That only made this harder.

"Very nice," Katie agreed.

"He's invited us out to Waterford Farm," Cassie added, as if that underscored all that the woman was saying.

"Huh." Linda May gave Katie a much more thorough examination after getting that information. "Well, I'd take him up on it. Waterford's beautiful, even now in the dead of winter. And you never know what could happen."

Oh, Katie knew. And so did Cassie. Lives would be irrevocably changed.

Linda May stood slowly, still studying Katie with interest. "Maybe since you introduced him to his wife, you have a chance."

"I don't want a—"

"Linda May?" A woman who'd just walked in came over. "Sorry to interrupt, but have you seen my father-in-law?"

Linda May's eyes widened at the question, then she let out a belly laugh. "He just left, and we're still talking about him." She gestured for the woman to join them. "Come and meet the very woman who introduced him to Annie Kilcannon."

Katie's heart jumped into her throat. Father-in-law? She wasn't quite ready to meet members of Daniel's family. She was still reeling from—

"Really?" A beautiful blond woman with sky-blue eyes clapped her hands together as if being led to a national treasure. "Oh my gosh, that's exciting. I'm Andi." She reached out her hand and drew Katie from her seat to shake her hand. "I'm married to Liam, Daniel's oldest son."

The words almost knocked her right back in her seat along with a blinding smile. "Hello, I'm Katie Santorini, and this is my daughter, Cassie."

"Katie..." Andi frowned as if digging for a memory. "My husband's told me the story of how his parents met. I thought it was on a blind date. Daniel was fixing someone else up, and Annie was a friend of a girl he was..." Her voice faded, and her jaw slipped open, and she started to put two and two together and come up with...the woman she was staring at.

"She's the one," Cassie chimed in with a laugh.

"Wow, it's incredible to meet you. Liam said that the entire time he was growing up, his parents celebrated their wedding anniversary by sharing the story of how they met. It's a big family tradition. And you? Why, you're part of Kilcannon folklore."

Well, she was about to be even more so. "I'm honored."

"I didn't know Annie, but I can tell you she raised an awesome family," Andi gushed. "My husband is all heart and the best imaginable father, but he, of course, has his father as a role model."

"Of course." Katie pressed her sticky, nervous palms together. "I'm...so glad."

"I hope you'll come to Waterford and let the whole family thank you."

"We're going tonight," Cassie said.

"Oh, wonderful. We'll be there. Wednesday-night dinners are fun. But the real good time is on Sundays. Those gatherings are always a highlight for the family. We'll see you tonight, then."

"Sure, thanks." Cassie smiled and nodded, and for the first time, Katie noticed her daughter was a little paler since this new arrival had come. No surprise. What they were about to do was getting very, very real.

"Well…" Andi stepped back. "Linda May, if Daniel stops in again, ask him to run up to my office. He just texted me about Hoagies & Heroes."

"I heard the Shipleys might be retiring," Linda May said.

"They might, and they're trying to decide if they want to rent as is, or do some major remodeling and try to sell, which is why they contacted me. I suppose Daniel wants some insight for one of his many committees."

Or, Katie thought, he'd already made good on his promise to check on a property for another Santorini's. She glanced at Cassie, who returned the same guilty look.

"Before I call him back, I thought I'd check to see if he was in here getting his croissant du jour," Andi joked.

Linda May held up the plate in her hand. "He was so distracted by running into an old friend, he didn't even eat it."

Andi's brows lifted as she looked at Katie. "Seriously? That's quite a compliment." On an easy laugh, she waved goodbye and stepped out, then a customer stole the baker's attention, leaving Cassie and Katie alone and staring at each other.

"Let's go outside," Cassie said softly.

Katie lifted her bag from the chair and grabbed her jacket, but didn't bother to put it on. Her hands were shaking, and her head was light. The chilly air would help. Silent, she followed Cassie out the door and walked a few steps to a private spot on the sidewalk.

"Mom, it's only going to get worse," Cassie whispered.

Katie took a ragged breath. "I know. I didn't expect him to be so…revered. So loved. So perfect in the eyes of this town and his family."

Cassie stared at her. "You just met a woman who said she's married to his oldest son."

"I heard her." Katie could barely breathe the words.

"Look, I know you're scared. I know you don't want to believe it's true. I know your world has been shaken ever since the day I walked into your house with that envelope." Cassie got a little closer, all her sass gone from those Santorini midnight-black eyes. "And I'm sorry that I had to be the one to bring the news to you, but I thought I was doing something fun for our family. How would I know what we'd find out?"

"Cassie, so many people will be affected," Katie whispered. "His entire family. *Our* entire family. So much is at stake, Cassie. Your father's legacy, my life, and that man's whole world. And, honey, we're still not entirely one hundred percent sure."

Her daughter cocked her head. "Did you hear him laugh? Did you see the way he gestured? Did you even look at his smile? We're not talking eyes and hair here, but something subtle and undeniable."

"I am going to deny it until I have absolute proof," Katie said, clinging to that single strand of hope she had.

"Mom, Daniel Kilcannon has a right to know the truth. He has a right to know that Liam Kilcannon is *not* his oldest son and that he has seven children, not six. He has a right to know that he is Nick's father."

Katie swayed at the power of her words. "You know I agree. I'll tell him tonight, but not in front of his whole family. He has to be alone when he finds out. It's going to stun him. And then we can work out a plan for telling his family and your brothers."

"And Nick."

"Nick *is* your brother."

"Half," she said, a note of sadness in the single syllable.

"See? You already look at him differently."

"I don't, but, Mom, if I were the oldest Santorini, I sure as hell would want to know ASAP who my father is and that he's not buried in Saint Catherine the Great Cemetery in Chestnut Creek, but alive and well and running a dog farm. And, oh yeah, I have *six* more siblings."

Each word pushed her back, because Cassie was absolutely right. But crushing *two* families in the process seemed absolutely wrong.

"We don't know for sure," Katie said, knowing her flimsy hope was fading fast.

Cassie sliced her with a look. "Mom, four out of five Santorinis measured over seventy-five percent Greek and less than three percent Irish. That was switched for Nick. The likelihood that John, Alex, Theo, and I are full siblings was ninety-nine-point-eight percent. And Nick—"

"Was three percent. But not zero."

"Essentially zero."

"But there's a chance we're wrong, Cassie. A tiny, minuscule chance." Katie reached out to her daughter. "Don't you think I should be one hundred percent certain before I tell anyone?"

"Well, if you can figure out a way to get the man's saliva sample, I can figure out a way to get his DNA tested and see if it matches what we have for Nick. That takes time, Mom. At least eight weeks, and Nick will come home again in a few months. Don't you think you and Daniel would want to break the news to him together?"

She couldn't even fathom that conversation. Or the ones that would have to happen first.

"I'll tell him tonight."

"Okay." Cassie put her arm around Katie's shoulders and pulled her closer. "Now, come on, let's go shopping."

"For what?"

"For new clothes. We're meeting the whole family tonight, and we Santorini girls have to look a-*may*-zing."

Chapter Four

"I heard we have a new arrival." Daniel came around the corner of the kennels to the section they jokingly called Solitary, which was a large, gated room where the dogs who couldn't be around any others were kept while they were trained.

There, he spied his son Garrett, on his hands and knees, face-to-face with a mahogany-colored retriever who was currently sulking in a corner. Declan, Daniel's oldest nephew, leaned against the wall with his arms crossed, his gaze locked on the dog.

"Some of my men picked her up on a call today for a wellness check," Declan said, shaking his head as he looked at the dog. "Happy to say she's in much better shape than her owner, who went to the morgue."

Daniel made a face at that. "Anyone we know?"

"I doubt it." Declan shifted from one foot to the other. "We got a call from the postal service about a man who lived in a trailer way out past Goose Hollow Road who hadn't opened his mailbox or moved his car in a week, but they could hear the dog barking inside. Sadly, he passed of natural causes and left the dog behind. Sheriff was there, of course, and wanted to take her to county, but one of my men thought he could keep her."

"What changed?" Daniel asked.

"He's got four other dogs, and it was obvious the minute she got to the station that this one does not play well with others, since she 'bout tore Monty's head off," he said, referring to one of the dogs that lived at his fire station. "You know what that would mean at the county shelter."

Daniel huffed out a soft curse under his breath, language he generally saved only for shelters that routinely put down "unadoptable" dogs. "Thanks for bringing her, Dec."

"Of course."

"Has Molly seen her?" Daniel asked, knowing his daughter was the vet on duty at Waterford today.

Garrett nodded. "Full physical. She checked out fine." He pushed the food bowl closer, but she didn't attack it the way Daniel would have expected for a starving dog. "Unless you consider severe hatred of other dogs a disease, I happen to think of it as a daily challenge."

From flat on the floor, the dog moved only her eyes to follow the conversation closely enough that Daniel would have sworn she knew what they were saying.

"I take it you tried her in the pen?" he asked.

"Until she went after Lola and Ruby. So..." He inched down to look her in the eyes. "Sorry, but it's a nice big solitary unit until we have our way and train you, Miss Goldie."

"That's her name?" Daniel asked.

"I gave it to her," Garrett said and shot a teasing

42

look to Declan. "So no other noobs confuse her with an Irish setter."

Declan curled his lip at the friendly dig. "Sorry, but that dog looks exactly like Rusty to me."

Garrett and Daniel shared a look. "Not even close," Garrett said.

"An understandable mistake," Daniel added. "But that's a red golden retriever, and you can tell the difference by the waves in her hair and the shape of her tail."

"Well, knowing that's not my job," Declan said. "Which"—he looked at his watch—"starts in an hour. Thanks for taking this one."

"Oh, then you won't be here for dinner?" Daniel asked. "I've invited some guests, and I was hoping for a good Mahoney turnout."

"Sorry, Uncle Daniel. Both my brothers are on duty with me tonight, and Mom and Ella are in DC."

"Oh, that's right." He'd forgotten his sister and her daughter had gone to Pet Expo to check out new products for their business, Bone Appetit.

"Sorry to miss meeting your new friend," Declan added. "I heard she caused quite a stir at Linda May's today."

Daniel blinked at him. "Excuse me?"

"And that her daughter is pretty," Garrett said.

Daniel whipped around. "How do you know she has a daughter?"

"News travels fast, Dad," Garrett joked.

"News...what...*how*?"

At his stunned reaction, both men laughed, and Declan put a friendly hand on Daniel's shoulder. "No such thing as a secret in this family, is there?"

"It's not a…" He gave up. "We'll miss you tonight, Dec. And we're happy to take care of Goldie and get her ready for adoption."

"Thanks." He gave him a pat on the shoulder. "Good luck with your new lady friend."

"She's not—"

"New," Garrett finished. "They knew each other in college." At Daniel's look of sheer disbelief, Garrett added, "Andi met her, too. And she told Chloe, who told Shane, who told—"

"The free world," Daniel finished.

"Pretty much." Garrett laughed.

Daniel held his hands up in surrender. "I give up."

But he was still amused by the whole thing a few hours later when he looked up from the place settings he was carefully arranging in the dining room to find his mother tugging on the sleeves of a navy cardigan and eyeing the table with a look of amusement.

"The china and crystal, lad?"

"We have guests coming."

"And the everyday stoneware isn't good enough for a lass you wooed in college?"

"Is there anyone around here who *doesn't* know who's coming to dinner?"

"I know!" His youngest daughter, Darcy, blew into the dining room in her usual whirlwind fashion, blond hair flying, little Kookie tucked under one arm and Stella barking behind them.

"Me, too." Molly, his other daughter, popped through the other entrance, from the kitchen, still wearing scrubs from her day in the vet office.

"And I have a question." Pru, Molly's teenage daughter, was hot on their heels. "Does 'lady friend' mean an old girlfriend from the past, or is that a nice way of saying she's Grandpa's age? I'm confused by that."

Daniel snorted softly. "In this case, both."

"Oooh. The G word." Pru flipped her hand to offer Molly an empty palm. "Mom, you totally owe me a dollar."

"Not so fast, kiddo." Molly came closer as if an examination of Daniel's face was in order. "He said an *old* girlfriend, not a current one. Which is it, Dad?"

He didn't know whether to laugh or howl for help.

"You only have yourself to blame," Molly said, obviously reading his expression. "You set us all up in perfectly wonderful relationships."

"'Tis true, lad," Gramma Finnie chimed in. "They say, 'There's nothing quite as contagious as happiness.' And this family is positively buzzing with it these days."

"And that makes this father elated, but..." He walked around the table to do a mental head count. "As far as I'm concerned? You're all abuzz about nothing."

"But ye still brought out the best china, lad." Gramma Finnie straightened a knife and fork at one of the place settings. "*And* the Sunday silverware."

"Yes, I did," he said. "Because Katie is a special guest and an old friend—I mean one from way back. As I'm sure you've heard through the overactive rumor mill, she's the person who introduced me to Annie. I'd say she deserves the best we have." He picked a plate up and examined a slight chip on the rim. "Of course, these are forty years old."

"Wedding presents for you, as I recall."

He sighed, because like everything else in this house, even the plates had Annie's fingerprints on them. Staring at tiny cracks in the surface, a memory flashed in his head, an image of Annie turning from the china cabinet one day to say something when one of the saucers fell and shattered. Her only concern had been that the dog would step on a piece of broken porcelain.

"Dad." Molly's hand on his arm tugged him from the memory. "We're teasing you. You know that, right?"

He glanced down at her, forcing a smile. "I have no doubt that once my romantically charged offspring catch a glimpse of this woman, they will start the next betting pool on what day we'll get married."

Her eyes widened in surprise. "Really?"

"But that is not what this is about, okay?" He looked up from one to the other. "As the women closest to me in the world, could I ask you to remember that?"

"We only want to see you as happy as we are," Darcy said.

"I'm happy," he insisted. "Well, I'm content. And I've danced around six different women that you kids all thought I should date, and I'm done. Okay? I'm done with your fix-ups and betting pools."

"No actual money has exchanged hands," Pru said softly, an apology in her voice.

"Until that dollar you want from your mother."

She gave him a grin that revealed her good heart and a mouth full of braces. "You still didn't answer. Is she a girlfriend or not?"

He exhaled some frustration. "Katie Rogers—er,

Santorini—is coming here as a friend," he said. "An old friend who I share some nice memories with, including the night I met the *one and only woman I am ever going to love.*"

From the corner, Rusty lifted his head at the serious tone. Daniel must have been more forceful than he'd realized, because they all looked a little taken aback. But for crying out loud, what was it going to take to get it through everyone's head that he wasn't interested in dating anyone?

After a second, his mother held up her hands. "Aye, lad, you're right. We'll all stop the teasing."

"I'll tell everyone to chill, Grandpa," Pru promised. "It'll be an order from General Pru."

He smiled at his granddaughter. "Thanks, kid." Except he'd heard it all before, and it never did stop.

Once again, he looked from one to the next. In one way or another, these were the women—and a girl— who'd stepped in four years ago when his world was shattered, picking up whatever pieces of Annie's life they could.

Gramma had moved out of her townhouse and back to Waterford to pick up the household role that Annie had managed so effortlessly, whether that was making the bread pudding or remembering every birthday. Molly never failed to be the unofficial hostess at any event, always ensuring guests and friends felt comfortable at Waterford. Darcy kept things light and fun, spreading her inimitable warmth and brightness even in the darkest moments, exactly as Annie had. And Pru? Well, she was Annie's voice of common sense—and reminded him more of her every day.

He knew all they wanted was a little more love

around here. And he needed a way to get the heat off of him and onto someone else. As an idea occurred, he leaned over the table and narrowed his eyes at them.

"But I will let you in on a secret, so you can start placing bets on a new romance."

"What is it?" they asked in almost perfect unison and breathless anticipation.

"It's her daughter I have my eye on."

"What?" Pru choked.

"Are you crazy?" Molly exclaimed.

Darcy looked at him like he'd grown another nose, while Gramma Finnie sucked in a low, noisy breath of raw disapproval.

"Sweet Saint Patrick, I'll not be havin' any of that nonsense, young man. Or should I say *old* man?"

He started laughing, and every time he looked at the horror in their expressions, he laughed harder.

"Dad!"

"Grandpa!"

"Daniel Seamus Kilcannon."

"Not for *me*," he finally managed to say between burst of laughter. "She's barely thirty years old. But have you forgotten I'm the Dogfather? I'm not done matchmaking this family. Colleen has four kids, and they all need Uncle Daniel's help."

A collective sigh of relief practically rocked the room, followed by an instant barrage of questions.

"For Braden?"

"No, Declan's the oldest. Wouldn't he be first, Grandpa?"

"Connor could use some settling down, don't you think?"

He lifted a shoulder. "I'm thinking Braden."

Darcy shook her head. "Ella said he's not over Simone."

Simone *Schimone*. Braden was ripe for the picking. "Don't mention this to Ella," he said to Darcy, who rolled her eyes because she and her cousin barely breathed without consulting each other first. "None of the Mahoneys will be here tonight, so your job, ladies, is to get to know Cassie and help me decide who we should set her up with."

"Is that how you do it, Grandpa?" Pru asked. "I thought the Dogfather went on raw gut instinct."

"I do," he replied, acknowledging the compliment. "But that was before I had a committee of experts working with me. I'm relying on your second opinion."

Darcy crossed her arms, clearly intrigued. "So, what's she like?"

"A spitfire," he said, using the first word that come to mind.

"Perfect for Braden," Molly said.

"And very attractive."

"That would be Connor's top requirement," Darcy said wryly. "Possibly his only one."

"But she struck me as intelligent and kind."

"Exactly what my Declan needs," Gramma announced.

"See?" He gave a light laugh. "I need you to help me on this one. Can I count on an assist?"

"Absolutely." Molly reached over and high-fived Darcy.

"We're your team, Dad," Darcy assured him.

"Only if I can do a blog about it," Gramma said. "I'd like to have something ready for Valentine's Day, so can you work quickly?"

They all laughed as Pru took out her phone. "I'll start a list of questions and notes, then we'll all meet and give you our recommendations. Sound like a plan?"

"Sounds like I put the right person in charge."

"Dad."

He turned to see Shane filling the door behind Molly, just in from the kitchen. "Yes, son?"

"She's here." A huge smile broke across Shane's face, and his eyes twinkled with the next joke. "I'm revising the pool and putting all my money on this one."

"Did I tell you?" He glanced at Molly, Darcy, and his mother for some help, but they were cracking up or—God help him—agreeing. "Bring him in on the new plan, will you? I'm going to greet our guests."

He stopped at the kitchen window to see a small group gathered in the driveway and quickly spotted Katie and Cassie, already talking to Garrett, Aidan, and Trace, surrounded by a few dogs.

His gaze immediately locked on Katie, taking in how little she'd changed in all these years. Her dark hair still had a saucy swing when she moved her head, and she had maintained a lean figure that looked both elegant and feminine in a creamy white sweater and gray slacks, her jacket slung over her arm. She smiled at something one of the dogs did, but then she glanced to the house, and that smile flickered and faded and turned into a look of...fear?

He could have sworn he'd seen the same expression that morning in the bakery, but what the hell did she have to be afraid of?

Maybe all this gossip and whispers of romance had gotten past his family and back to her. Of course she'd be scared. She didn't want to replace her late husband any more than he wanted to replace Annie.

Sometime this evening, he'd have to get her alone and assure her of that. Until then, his job was to make her feel welcome and remind her she was in the home of an old friend who had her to thank for every day of happiness he had for thirty-six years. Annie had been very close to leaving Vestal Valley College that semester, she'd been so lonely. If they hadn't met that fateful January night, he might never have known she lived on this earth.

Oh yes, he owed Katie Rogers a great and profound debt of gratitude. For that, he would do whatever was necessary to make her feel comfortable in his home.

Chapter Five

T he first hour—and what felt like a hundred introductions—passed in a blur. Not only did Katie have to take in the impact of Waterford Farm in all its glory, but she had to meet the family who'd once lived and now worked there. And finally, she had to look Daniel in the eyes every few minutes and know that, soon, she'd change his life completely.

So Katie tried to concentrate on the first two things instead.

In some ways, Waterford Farm had completely transformed in the decades that had passed since Katie's one and only visit. Back then, it had been little more than a comfy clapboard house surrounded by lots of land, tucked deep in the foothills of the Blue Ridge Mountains. And while she certainly remembered Daniel had a dog or maybe two, it had been nothing like this, with dozens of dogs, trainees, and kennels all bustling, barking, and happily improving lives, both canine and human. Even the sweet and unassuming farmhouse had been updated and upgraded to a sprawling three-story manor with a wraparound porch and three chimneys puffing smoke.

But in other ways, Waterford was the same. The commanding view of rolling hills would always dominate the landscape, taking her breath away in winter even as it had when she'd seen it bathed in autumn's most stunning colors. The air was still crisp and clean, and the smell of pine and earth permeated everything. And family—from the much smaller one back then to the seemingly endless one now—remained the life's blood of this magical piece of paradise.

And then, as today, a small, spirited woman somehow stood as the heart center of it all. Daniel might have been the man of the house for most of his life, but it was his mother who seemed to sprinkle some sort of fairy dust on the place. She now went by the adorable moniker of Gramma Finnie and looked much older than the last time she'd greeted Katie.

Her hair had grayed to a soft white puff, her body had shrunk a few inches, but her Irish brogue was still as endearing, and her touch still held an underlying strength that no doubt guided her through whatever unexpected curveballs life threw at her.

Like the one Katie was about to fling at the family.

Surely this tiny woman with a massive heart would be forever rocked by the news that she had another grandson.

They all would. Like the bubbly blonde named Darcy who instantly slid her arm into Cassie's and welcomed her as if they were long-lost cousins. And the warm and lovely Molly who so proudly introduced her new husband, Trace, and their daughter, Pru, and announced there was another on the way. All Katie could do was look from one set of hazel eyes to the other and notice how much Molly and Pru looked like Anne Harper. Pru's hair was darker, but Molly's was a replica of Anne's auburn mane.

And all these young ladies were about to have their worlds shaken and broken and changed.

Then there were the sons and their significant others. She met the youngest, Aidan, tall and good-looking and so very humble when his father heaped praise on him for the service he'd given to the country. A handsome man named Garrett whose wife, Jessie, looked like she could deliver yesterday and be past her due date. Yet, even with that concern, Garrett was talking about a retriever who'd been brought in when her owner had passed away and left her behind.

She met a charmer named Shane who made them laugh and instantly put her at ease, warning them about the water since his wife was in her first trimester of pregnancy, which gave Katie an unexpected twinge of jealousy. Daniel had three *more* grandchildren on the way?

And she hadn't even met everyone, since Daniel and Anne's oldest, Liam, had yet to show up and was bringing his son and baby daughter, whose very name made Daniel light up.

All of them, every one, would feel betrayal, pain, shock, frustration, disbelief, and anger. Jealousy, maybe. Resentment that their world had been changed by a stranger. Maybe a bone-deep disappointment in the father they loved, or fury with her for not realizing sooner that the son she was carrying when they rushed into marriage shouldn't have been baptized Nico Matteo Santorini Jr. and called Nick his entire life.

When the introductions ended and small talk dwindled, Darcy whisked Cassie off to see the grooming studio, and Daniel suggested a quick tour of the canine part of the property, starting with the kennels, which were at the center of the whole operation.

They walked around a large fenced-in pen, with his dog, Rusty, trotting close behind. They were alone, Katie realized, but the kennels didn't feel private enough to talk, and she hated to start with her news. Better to wait until after dinner, she decided.

Chicken.

She shoved the truth away and looked around the cheery hallways, taking in the rows of large cages, each outfitted with food, water, beds, and, of course, dogs.

"This is more like a hotel than a shelter," she noted.

"It's a refuge," Daniel said as they passed a few sleeping dogs, one on his back with four legs in the air, dead-bug style. "When Annie and I were dreaming of the design, long before this place became a reality, she'd been to a similar farm out in Virginia and had seen kennels like this. You see the door each kennel has in the back? We train them to go back there and do their business, which of course we can hose down a few times a day. It was important that the individual kennels stay clean and bright." He pointed toward the roof. "That's why we have so many skylights in here."

Even this late in the afternoon, sun poured in, warming the whole maze with a golden glow. "It must have been quite an adventure, building all this and raising six kids."

"Oh, the canine business is only four years old." He slowed his step and looked at her. "I decided to start this business the day after I buried Annie."

"Oh." That was a surprise. "I figured this was all her, since she loved dogs so much."

"She fostered, and over the years, the boys and I built small kennels, very rudimentary compared to what we have now. At the most, we'd have five, maybe six dogs on the property at a time, and our Irish setter in the house." He glanced at Rusty with a smile. "But when Annie and I were raising kids, I was a full-time vet in town, and she had her hands full with six kids all born within about twelve years, so we never did more than that."

Katie nodded. "And I thought five in twelve years was some kind of a record. And two were twins. That really must have been a challenge for you two."

"*One* kid is a challenge when you take parenting seriously," he said. "But they all grew up and moved out, so we started dreaming about running a dog refuge. And you're right, it was her dream first, but I loved the idea of a place to train people how to manage their dogs. You'd be shocked at how many people get a dog and are completely clueless at how much this pet will change their lives and have no idea how to train one."

She studied him as he talked, lost for a moment in how the timbre of his voice changed when it was a subject he was passionate about. She could easily see the young vet student she remembered, now matured and mellowed by age, and pick up that same undercurrent of something she used to think of as fierce kindness. A serious, focused, driven man with a good heart and an unwavering need to help people.

Exactly like Nick.

"You look surprised at that," Daniel said, reminding Katie that she'd never been very good at hiding her thoughts and feelings. Nico used to say he could walk in the door, take one look at her face, and know exactly what kind of day she'd had. And then he made it better.

"No, no," she said quickly, trying to tamp down her thoughts. What had he said? She rooted around for his last sentence. "I think it's wonderful that you made it happen after she passed away. A tribute to her, in a way."

"In a way." He eyed her for a moment, making her wonder if she'd done a poor job of covering what she was really thinking. "It was also a not-so-secret ploy to get my kids to come home and fill the void."

"Really?"

He shrugged a shoulder that was no less broad than when she'd last put her arms around him. More so, in fact. "I woke up that morning after the funeral, and I looked out my bedroom window. I saw them all out here, the six of them. They were a far-flung pack then. Aidan in the military overseas, three of them on the West Coast working for Garrett's dot-com company, Darcy flitting about the globe. And I wanted them here. Home. In Bitter Bark. And Annie sort of whispered the answer to me."

"Build it and they will come?"

That made him laugh. "More like suggest it and *they* will build it and never leave."

"Then it worked."

"Like a charm."

They turned a corner to a cage that was easily four times the size of the others. Instantly, the dog inside lifted its head and growled, making Daniel stop and look from the penned area to Rusty, who was right next to him.

"Whoops," he whispered. "I forgot our newest arrival isn't socialized."

"Oh, is this the dog your son mentioned? Goldie?"

"Yes, and she's..." He hesitated, watching as Rusty went closer to the gate. After a second, Goldie stood up, stared at Rusty, and took one step toward him.

After a beat, she stopped growling and stared, and her silky tail swooshed. Rusty's did the same. "Whoa." Daniel gave a soft laugh. "Maybe she's more socialized than we realized."

Katie studied the dog behind the gate. "Maybe she thinks they're related," she suggested.

"You might think that," he said, "but they're not the same breed."

"They're not?" It was astonishing. "They look so much alike."

"Goldie's a red golden retriever, and he's an Irish setter, and they..." Each got a little closer, still staring. "They don't hate each other."

"That's good, right?"

"Always."

Goldie looked up at Daniel, then at Rusty, then back to Katie with a gaze so pure and honest that it made her heart slip around a little.

"She thinks you brought Rusty," Daniel explained, putting a hand on her shoulder. "I could be wrong, but I think she just said 'thank you' in dog language."

Katie laughed and crouched down next to Rusty. "You like this boy, Goldie?" she asked through the wire mesh. "I bet he'd be your friend. I will, too."

Goldie barked once, turned in a circle, then resumed staring at Rusty, wagging her tail with a contented tick-tock.

"So what's going to happen to her?" she asked.

"Not what would have happened at the county shelter," Daniel said, the edge in his voice unmistakable. "My sons will train her, and we'll get her adopted."

She stayed eye-to-eye with Goldie. "How old is she?"

"My guess is under five, but I don't know for sure. She's surely a little brokenhearted after what she's been through."

She looked up at him, frowning. "What has she been through?"

"Her owner passed, and the firefighters and sheriff discovered him on a wellness check. Goldie was alone in a trailer with the man."

"Oh. How sad for her." She straightened slowly as the impact of that hit. "She watched her owner die?"

Daniel put a hand on her back. "She'll be okay, I promise."

Okay? Maybe. But never the same, Katie thought. "Can I go in and pet her?"

"Yeah, but..." He angled his head and reached for the latch. "I'll stay here with Rusty. She's definitely an unknown around other dogs, but she's fine with people."

As the door opened, Goldie finally tore her attention from Rusty to focus on Katie, looking up like a small child who really needed and wanted affection.

"Oh, love," she whispered, bending over to pet her. "You've been through a trauma, haven't you? I know."

Goldie lowered to sit, holding her head up for the affection Katie offered.

"Oh, Daniel, my heart."

Behind her, she heard a soft, knowing laugh. "You can give her a treat from that container on the wall and pretty much seal the deal that she'll love you forever."

His voice was so tender, Katie's heart nearly folded in half. She snagged a brown cookie-shaped treat and let Goldie eat it out of her hand, getting rewarded with another spin and happy tail.

Delighted, Katie clapped her hands and cooed at the dog. "Good girl, Goldie. You're a good girl." Turning, she looked at Daniel. "You're positive someone will adopt her, right?"

"Now that I've seen her with Rusty, yes. She's obviously trainable, as most retrievers are."

"Did you hear that, Goldie? You'll have another home. You'll see." She gave her head a good pet again, but Goldie walked by her to the gate to stare at Rusty some more. "I think she's more interested in a four-legged friend than me."

He carefully opened the gate to let Katie out but leave Goldie in. "She knows she's got you," he teased.

"She surely does," Katie agreed. "How did that happen?"

"It's dog magic. They get into your heart with one look. There's like a connection that's almost instant."

"Love at first sight?"

He laughed. "I've heard it called that. You look at them, they look at you, and *wham*. Don't even have to touch, but the connection is made. I just saw it with you and Goldie. You'll think about her all night, I promise. And you'll want to come back. Even if you know you can't have her, you'll care about her." He shook his head. "I've seen it so many times."

"So have I."

He turned to her, surprised. "Really? You have?"

"With you." She smiled at his confused look. "And a girl named Anne Harper."

"Oh." He exhaled the response, almost laughing, almost sighing. "Yeah. I guess that happened to us."

"It did, and I'm glad I was there to witness it."

They shared a long look and a smile, the single crossover of their history like a sweet connection no one could take away from them.

Except it wasn't the only crossover of their history, and Katie had to remember that.

"So you've seen everything except the house," he said, leading her out and holding the door for her. "But I get carried away when I show off our dog business."

"As you should. You've done an amazing job with this place, Daniel."

"Team effort." He looked around, but Rusty wasn't there. "Where did he go?"

"I think he stayed with Goldie."

He gave her a surprised look. "That would be a first." He whistled a four-note tune into the kennels, and almost immediately, they heard the patter of his paws on the tile. "He really is smitten."

"Goldie has that effect," she said lightly.

"Or he wants us to be alone," he added. "Because Rusty knows what my kids don't."

She stopped midstep and stared at him. "Which is?"

"That you're not here to, uh, change my life."

She felt a slow flush burn her cheeks. *Oh yes, I am, Daniel Kilcannon.*

"Don't let it embarrass you," he said quickly, putting a light hand on her back. "They've all fallen head over heels in love over the past two years, so they seem to think it's my turn. So I hope you can handle the ribbing and not-so-subtle hints that will be flung your way all through dinner."

Things would be flung her way before the night was out, but they might not be hints. "The only thing I heard is them crediting you for all their happiness."

He shrugged it off. "Nah. I did a little nudging. A bit of schedule changing here, a suggestion to attend a meeting there."

"It worked."

"My wife used to say, 'You're only as happy as your least-happy child.' So I did what I thought would make them happier, and it worked." He studied her for a moment. "Wouldn't you do that for your kids?"

"I have, but with exactly zero success."

"Maybe you need some advice from an expert," he joked.

"Maybe I do," she volleyed back, holding on to the lighthearted moment. The laughter would be gone as quickly as that peach sunset fading over the hills when she made her confession.

Was this the right time? This moment? Should she suggest they follow that picturesque path down to the lake and find a quiet place away from family where they could talk?

Looking up at Daniel, she tried to imagine how he'd take the news.

Would that strong jaw lock in anger? Would those blue eyes taper to disbelieving slits? Would he be hurt? Scared? Horrified or crushed? Because when Cassie had come to her house with the Bloodline.com paperwork that day a little over a week ago and announced that there was something very wrong and weird with Nick's DNA results, Katie had felt all of those things.

And a million more since then.

"So are you looking for help?" Daniel asked. "Because I have to confess I've already got Cassie and my nephew Braden engaged in my head."

"*What?*"

"Just kidding." He winked at her. "Kind of. He's on duty at the station tonight, so you can relax."

How could she tell him that that was the last—the absolute *last*—level of emotional complication they needed? She couldn't, not until she told him about Nick.

"I seem to recall you enjoyed a good setup back in the day." Daniel smiled as they walked, the poor man utterly oblivious to the sledgehammer she was about to use on his heart.

"I do, but...my kids and your..." Oh Lord. *No.*

"Nephews. Not my kids. You're too late for that, I'm afraid. Come on. I'll show you through the front of the house so you can really see it, though no one ever uses this door." He urged her toward the house. "Just think about it. Might be the right thing to do."

Was he talking about Cassie and Braden or which door to use? Who knew? Her heart was slamming against her chest, and her palms were actually damp.

"That's always guided you," she said, seizing the last thing he'd said, because she actually couldn't think straight. "I remember you're a man whose life decisions are dictated by right and wrong."

"Can't see any other way to live."

Then she should do what was right...right now.

Just say it, Katie. Say it. There's something I want to talk to you about, Daniel. Where can we go that's private?

She swallowed, felt the words form in her mouth, took a breath, and...nothing came out.

"How about a glass of wine or a drink? Crystal should have dinner ready in about forty-five minutes."

A drink would be...*perfection*. Maybe two. Maybe six. "Crystal. Is that another Kilcannon I haven't met?" Did her words sound as stupid and thick as they felt in her throat?

"Oh, no. Crystal's our housekeeper." Daniel didn't seem the least bit fazed by what she was going through. "She's here on weekdays to help out with feeding the staff and any trainees we have and makes dinner most nights. Always Wednesday, when anyone who can make it comes to dinner. There could be anywhere from four to fourteen on any given Wednesday, depending on what's going on."

Small talk. Keep making small talk, Katie. "Your daughter-in-law said you do the same on Sundays, too."

"Sunday dinners are more sacred and set in stone. Sundays aren't for work. That's a family day that

Kilcannons have had since I was a kid. The Wednesday dinners started around the time we began to build the business, mostly as a way to get everyone in one room and have an ad hoc staff meeting."

With every word, she felt...not ready. She wasn't ready to tell him, not here, not now, not yet.

"Let's stop off for that drink in the living room," he suggested. "If we go in the back kitchen door, they're going to be all over you to get *your* version of what happened the night I met Annie. Then my time alone with you will be over."

Along with her opportunity to wreck his life.

"My version wouldn't be any different than your version," she said. "No hard feelings, no jealousy, no ugly breakup so you could run off after another girl. They know that, right?"

"They know everything."

Not...*everything*. Only she and Cassie knew everything.

He brought her around to the front of the house, which faced the long, curved driveway and more manicured lawns and trimmed bushes. "We rarely use this door, though some guests might. Life at Waterford takes place on the other side of the house, as you just saw. But Annie liked to keep the front kind of formal. And over there, behind that gate?" He pointed to a section of yard closed off by thick bushes joined at the front by a small wrought-iron gate. "That was her garden, purposely separated from everything. But now it's..." He shook his head. "I haven't done a great job of keeping it up."

"Makes you sad to go there?"

He gave her a smile and didn't answer for a long

beat. "You know what's great about this, Katie?" he finally asked. "You *get* it. You know exactly what I'm feeling. You had a strong, healthy marriage, and you know what grieving feels like."

"I did and I do," she agreed.

"That's the real reason I don't date, but my kids, who think they've inherited the matchmaking gene, don't get that."

She blinked at him, a little surprised by the segue.

"All I really want to do is talk about Annie. All day, all night, all the time. Makes me the worst date."

She laughed, shaking her head. "I know what you mean. I've gone for coffee or lunch now and again, and the entire time, all I want to do is share a story, or tell them about my awesome husband."

"Guaranteed no second date," he quipped.

"You know it."

"Well, you are welcome to talk all night about Nico," he said. "I'm so happy you had a great marriage, too."

She gave him a wistful look. "My marriage was..." What word could she use to describe the love and laughter, the connection and teamwork, the good times and the bad? The healthy, youthful days that somehow became sick, weak, incapable days? Through it all, there had been love. "Perfect," she whispered. "I know it's a cliché, but our marriage was perfect."

For a moment, she thought Daniel's eyes welled up as he swallowed hard enough that she almost heard it. "That's why you get it. And you see that garden?" He notched his head toward the hedges and gate. "Like falling on a bed of nails for me."

"Same way I feel when I go anywhere near Nico's workshop or the kitchen of Santorini's," she confessed. "Even more than our bedroom. The places that were his are the hardest."

He nodded, taking her hand to lead her to the front door. "Oh, I get that. For Annie, it was her garden and the old kennels. And..." He opened the front door and led her into a wide marble-floored entryway and gestured toward an oversized formal sitting room to the left. "The living room. She loved that room, and now hardly anyone goes in there but me. We have Christmas in there, so it is ground zero in December. It's great for entertaining and a party, too, but...no one uses it. Oh, and I'm trying to fix that discoloration in the hardwood floor and maybe do something to the furniture. I haven't figured it out yet, because..." He laughed. "I don't care enough, I guess."

She took a few steps into a wide arched entryway and onto worn wood, taking in the wing-backed chairs, the heavy drapes, the paint in a perfect shade of...2003. But she could imagine Daniel and Annie sitting side by side by the fire, maybe sharing a glass of brandy from a decades-old bar cart, or reading or talking about their days or the kids.

She could feel the love in the room, the stability and permanence. She could breathe the sense of family and forever. She could understand why he didn't care about how outdated the room was. It was home and comfort and a place to live in a happy past.

"She decorated this," he said, probably sensing that she was sizing up the colors and style. "Every room in the house, really. It's all her."

Looking up at him, she searched his face. "And you don't want to change a thing," she guessed.

He stared at her for a long time, reminding her that he never answered without thinking first. Nico, an emotional, passionate Greek, had rarely given a moment's thought before replying to anything. But Daniel always considered his words.

Exactly like Nick.

"Are you asking as a fellow widow or a decorator?"

She smiled. "Both."

Their gazes locked, and suddenly she remembered with crystal clarity that moment they'd stood in Bushrod Square and admitted they both had feelings for other people.

"Let's take the easy course," he said. "What would a decorator change in this room?"

Everything, but he probably wasn't ready for that. "Have you ever heard of the concept of memory tags?" she asked him.

"Why do I think that's not something I can cut off and risk the penalty of law?"

"It's a risk, all right. But there is a way to save the tag in your memory and let go of the item it belonged to."

He frowned, considering that. "Okay. And does that apply to pictures?" He gestured toward a solid wall jam-packed with framed photographs, a few canvas portraits, and at least six collages, all featuring dozens of smiling faces and captured moments. In the middle was Daniel and Annie's wedding photograph, which looked like it had been taken at the bottom of the stairs in the entryway.

"That's an amazing collection," she said, choosing her words carefully.

"But it's a hot mess."

She laughed at that. "It's...a..." Decorator's nightmare.

"Annie called it her 'wall of fame.' She kept adding to it and adding to it."

"It could be beautiful."

"How?" he asked.

She'd actually seen worse and had come up with some creative ways to streamline family photographs before. "I'm not sure, but the solution would be to have the actual people in the room as the focal point, not the two-dimensional pictures on the wall. They're a testimony to a lovely past."

A slow smile broke on his face, and his expression looked a little...astonished. "She sent you," he whispered.

"Excuse me?"

"I don't know if you get these feelings about your husband, but sometimes I can't help thinking that things happen, or people show up, and it's Annie's hand in the process. Like she can guide fate from beyond. Do you think that?"

"Sometimes," she admitted. "It's impossible not to imagine them as angels, although I'm not sure it works that way."

"Well, I think it does. And I think she sent you to help me." He took her hand and gave it a squeeze.

She opened her mouth to answer, but behind them, someone cleared their throat noisily, making Daniel and Katie automatically inch apart in surprise and turn to see who it was.

"Sorry to interrupt."

"Oh, Liam. Come on in." Daniel put his hand on

the shoulder of a man who looked to be about forty, with dark eyes and hair, but everything else was a carbon copy of Daniel. "Liam, this is Katie Santorini, a very dear friend from my college days. Katie, this is Liam Kilcannon, my oldest son."

She looked up at him, automatically taking the hand he extended, not sure if she trusted her voice. She swallowed first and attempted a smile. "Hello, Liam."

"Katie. It's great to meet you. Let me be the first of about eighteen people who are going to thank you for introducing our parents to each other."

Oh, no, Liam. You are not going to thank me when you find out you are not your father's oldest son.

"I have a feeling you're going to have to tell that story whether you like it or not," Daniel said to her.

She wouldn't mind telling that story. It was the one that had begun a few nights earlier that she was dreading.

After dinner, Katie. After dinner.

Chapter Six

Daniel had forgotten one very, very important thing about Katie Rogers.

He *liked* her. Yes, that easy friendship and undeniable attraction had disappeared like a wisp of smoke when Hurricane Annie blew into his life. And time had dimmed his memory of Katie to little more than a person who'd played an important, if fleeting, role in his life's history.

But sitting at this table, watching her navigate the personalities of his family, amused and interested in every one of them while letting her pistol of a daughter add color and humor, he remembered she'd been a very easy girl to like.

There'd been a gentleness he'd admired in young Katie that had developed into a gracefulness that he found very attractive. She listened closely, far more guarded than Cassie, and when she gave her attention to someone, there was no one else in the room.

More and more, he wanted that attention directed at him, thinking about how quickly dinner would end so they could get a chance to talk again—about their past, about their losses, about anything, really.

He understood why he'd been drawn to her in college and how easily she'd become a friend, a confidant, and...a lover.

Holy hell.

He shifted in his seat, taking a drink of water as the thought hit him, a little embarrassed that he hadn't even remembered that until this moment. But yes, they'd had one, maybe two, rather awkward—but pretty sweet—nights in her dorm room all those years ago. And if he hadn't met Annie, there probably would have been more. But once he'd fallen under Annie Harper's spell and into her bed, any woman who existed before or after paled in comparison.

But nothing about this woman was...pale.

"Maybe we should make Dad leave the room for that," Molly said, pointing to him with a tease in her eyes, dragging him back to the conversation.

He answered with a slight frown he hoped didn't give away that he'd been thinking about nights in dorm rooms and not whatever they were talking about.

"No, all witnesses have a right to hear the testimony," Shane quipped.

Liam rolled his eyes. "Always the lawyer."

"Oh, no, let Dad add the color commentary," Garrett said.

"But we want every single detail." Darcy leaned toward Katie. "Because to hear our parents tell it, the heavens opened and angels sang the night they met."

Katie shot Daniel a sideways look that was sweetly conspiratorial and a smile that enchanted everyone at the dinner table. Including him.

"Were those angels singing?" she asked. "I thought it was Fleetwood Mac on the jukebox in the bar."

"It was the seventies," Daniel agreed. "Best music ever."

The comment elicited a big laugh and a lot of eye rolls from the kids. "I was ten before I knew the Bee Gees weren't modern music," Garrett said.

Liam turned to Daniel and shot him a warning look. "Don't."

Daniel chuckled, remembering the time he'd mortified his son by sharing the fact that he'd been conceived to the soundtrack of *Saturday Night Fever*. But the rest of the table were still making seventies-music jokes, so Liam's secret was safe.

"Well, that sounds familiar," Cassie joked. "Although my dad was more into heavy metal, so we were raised on Black Sabbath and Aerosmith."

"Now *that's* music," Shane said.

"Who cares about the music?" Darcy chimed in. "We want deets. Don't leave a single thing out, Katie."

"Because we'll know if you do," Molly added. "We've heard the story three dozen times."

"Some stories get better with age, lass," Gramma Finnie said. "I know mine do."

"But this one never changes," Liam said. "Every anniversary, at this table, same story."

"Did your family do that?" Darcy asked Cassie. "The family anniversary dinner thing?"

"Family anniversary?" Cassie snorted. "We were handed over to Yiayia and Papu, my Greek grandparents, and Mom and Dad rolled off to some secret location for a whole weekend."

"Cassie." Katie looked down at her plate as a soft flush rose on her cheeks.

She didn't need to be embarrassed, Daniel wanted to tell her. He understood better than anyone at the table what those secret weekends were all about, and it only made him like Nico Santorini more for loving Katie the way Daniel loved Annie.

"It's true, Mom. You two were always like that...I mean, before..." Her voice faded, and the table grew quiet. "We did do a family thing for one anniversary," Cassie added. "And I'll be honest, it was one of our best Santorini moments." She hesitated and looked around the table. "We gathered around my father's hospice bed for their fortieth, which was their last."

A few of his kids shared sympathetic looks, because that, they understood.

Katie held up her hand to deflect anyone's response. "No sadness tonight," she said. "Just happy memories."

But Cassie's words lingered in Daniel's head. Their *fortieth*?

He did some quick math to be sure he'd heard that right. Whoa, they'd gotten married quickly after Katie left Bitter Bark. They must have been even more in love than Daniel and Annie, who didn't get married for almost two more years, and only because Liam was on the way. But he'd had vet school. Katie mustn't have even finished college.

"Happy memories like how your parents met," Katie continued, using that innate grace and class to guide the talk back to something lighter. "But if what I say conflicts with what your father has said, blame it on time and old age."

"Or the fact that my son got my storyteller gene

74

and embellished it over the years," Gramma Finnie quipped. "You've got the floor, lass."

Her dark eyes widened as she became the center of attention, a place Daniel suspected Katie didn't relish. But she cleared her throat, twirled the stem of her wineglass once, and looked up at him to tell the story.

"I was running very late that night, so I only had myself to blame for leaving the two of them alone. But…" She slid a loving glance to Cassie. "I had been on the phone with the man I would marry a few short months later."

"Whoa, that never made it into Mom and Dad's version," Shane said.

"But we knew the part about you showing up late," Darcy added. "Because that's when Dad and Mom famously sat on the same barstool at exactly the same moment. And Mom said her name was Anne, but that only the people who truly loved her called her Annie—"

"And Grandpa thought, 'I want to be on that list!'" Pru called out, reciting words Daniel must have said, well, thirty-six times when they told this story on their anniversary.

Katie turned to him and gave a sweet smile. "I knew it was love at first sight," she said softly.

"I guess it was," he acknowledged.

"So what happened then?" Chloe asked.

Shane leaned closer to his wife. "Dad launched his secret career of matchmaking, that's what happened."

Katie shrugged. "There's not much more to tell," she said. "He was clearly smitten and so was your mother, and my heart was far away."

"Not that far," Cassie added. "Since the night

ended with you in Chestnut Creek with my dad, and you never spent another night apart for forty-plus years."

"Really?" several of them asked in unison, since the Kilcannon version of the story ended there, but obviously the Santorini family saw things differently.

"That's true," Katie said, giving her daughter a look that fell somewhere between warmth and a warning. Maybe she was embarrassed that she'd gone from a date with Daniel to another man, but was also grateful that her daughter wanted this family to know how much her parents loved each other. Daniel still couldn't quite read the silent messages between these two women.

"In fact, Daniel drove me there that night," Katie said. "And he saved me time and money and got me right where I belonged—with Nico."

"I never heard that part," Liam said.

"So you parted on a good note." Molly sighed. "I'm so glad to hear that."

"Right?" Darcy nodded. "I always wondered how you felt about losing your boyfriend to a person you'd set up with his friend."

"I felt…" She looked at Daniel, her gaze direct and unwavering. "Grateful that we were instrumental in helping each other live our lives with our soul mates."

"Oh my word." Gramma Finnie tapped the table. "I might have to write a blog about that. Would you mind, lass?"

"Oh, maybe." Katie turned to her, her smile fading as that look Daniel could describe only as fear crossed her fine features again. "Do a lot of people read your blog?"

"Not so many."

Pru's jaw dropped. "Not so many, Gramma Finnie? Did you check the stats last week? You had thousands of hits."

"Thousands?" The word seemed to catch in Katie's throat. "Oh, I don't think I'd want that story to go…around."

"It's so cute," Darcy said. "Gramma's readers would love it."

"No." Cassie leaned forward, all teasing gone from her dark eyes. "We're a very private family."

"Of course," Gramma agreed quickly. "'Twas just a thought."

Cassie nodded and pretended to sip her wine, shooting one more of those nanosecond-fast looks at her mother that was rich with secret communication. Not grief this time, but…something he couldn't begin to understand that was definitely bubbling under Cassie's surface.

"That's enough reminiscing," he said, pushing his dish away as if that would officially end dinner.

On cue, Rusty sat up from where he'd fallen asleep under Katie's chair.

Molly put her hand on Cassie's arm. "I don't think you had a chance to see our puppy kennels, did you?"

"I didn't even know there was such a thing," Cassie replied. "Are they as cute as they sound?"

"Even more so," Molly assured her. "And I'm the vet on duty tonight and have to check on a litter that was born a few days ago. Come with me?"

"I'd love to."

"Oh, I don't think I saw puppy kennels earlier," Katie said quickly. "Can I go, too?"

"You stay, Mom," Cassie said, giving her a direct look. "Talk to Daniel."

"I would like to talk a little more," Daniel said, putting his hand on Katie's shoulder.

She glanced over her shoulder to see Cassie and Molly making their way toward the kitchen. "Cassie," she said, getting her daughter to turn.

"Mom, really, you don't need to come with us," she said, a little more forcefully. "Go. Talk to Daniel. Really...*talk* to him."

He chuckled a little and nudged her toward the door. "They all think they're matchmakers now," he murmured to her under his breath. "I think it's that story."

She looked up at him, and her eyes flickered, and this time, he couldn't deny it. She was afraid of something.

But what? Being alone with him? That the matchmaking might work? That their decades-old attraction would rekindle?

That wasn't what he wanted, and he needed to tell her that. But if he did, would she disappear forever? Because he didn't want that, either.

Right then, he didn't know what he wanted except to wipe that look of fear out of her eyes and replace it with the look of hope and happiness he remembered from the night she climbed out of his car and disappeared into another man's arms.

Katie had no doubt at all that Cassie fully expected this conversation to be *the* conversation. But as she walked toward the center hall, Katie was already trying like hell to think of ways to delay.

"Could I see the whole house, Daniel?" she asked. "It's such an extraordinary place."

"It is, isn't it?" He threw her a smile. "It's always good to see this home through someone else's eyes. Makes me realize how special it is."

She kept a hand on Rusty's head, who'd come along, as if he could somehow give her moral support.

"There's a lovely, family feel to this house," she said, slipping into decorator mode because it was natural and felt easy. And took up time. "It has the most amazing bones for that farmhouse chic that's so popular now."

He gave a soft laugh. "Not sure what that is, but it sounds…feminine."

"Not necessarily. It can be very rustic and masculine if you do it right."

"And it also sounds time-consuming and expensive." He led her toward a grand staircase that stood as the very center of the entire house.

"Not if you use a good decorator." She ran her finger along the worn wood banister. "Someone who knows how to preserve the spirit of the home, but still bring it all into the twenty-first century."

He snorted. "Is that your extremely classy way of saying my house needs a facelift?"

She grinned up at him. "Something many beautiful women think about getting when they hit a certain age."

"Not you," he quipped, tapping her nose. "But it's a nice analogy since this house was born in the 1950s."

"Like all good things," she joked, ignoring the flutter in her chest at his compliment and attention. Instead, she held on to the sound of his laugh, because soon, very soon, she wouldn't hear it anymore.

He led her around a wide second-floor landing, gesturing to the doors off the hall. "The kids' rooms have morphed into overflow guest rooms, more or less. There's a room here that used to be for them to do homework, and it's sort of become a catch-all."

He opened the door to a room with a wall of desks and bookshelves. A rarely used stationary bike stood in one corner and, under the window, a settee.

"Pretty uninspiring," he said.

"Uninspiring?" She certainly didn't see it that way, her designer brain kicking in at the first sight of the huge window. "The light is fabulous. It could be an amazing exercise room. Maybe put a craft table in that corner. It could even be a playroom for all those grandchildren you have on the way. This room could be anything, and wonderful."

"Hmm." He looked around as if seeing the space for the first time. "An exercise room? I hadn't thought of that."

They stepped out, and he showed her two adjoining rooms, very girlie and a little dated.

"After Molly had Pru, she moved back home and studied vet medicine at Vestal Valley," he said. "Pru slept in there, and often still does. I love when she's here, as you can probably tell. She's a great kid."

"I envy you the grandchildren," she confessed.

"I can work on those kids for you." He put a light arm around her. "I won't even charge a matchmaking fee."

She laughed, warmed by the idea and his touch and wishing desperately that things were different. She wanted just to be friendly with him, to joke about their kids' futures, and share their lives and pasts. Being this close to him, talking to him, made her ache in a wholly different way. She honestly hadn't realized how lonely she was.

Well, too bad. Daniel Kilcannon would not be supplying lighthearted companionship when he found out what she had to tell him.

She glanced down the hall to a set of closed double doors. "The master?" she guessed.

"Yep."

She looked up at him. "May I?"

"As long as you don't suggest any changes," he said simply, leading her in. "But you're welcome to look."

The windows were huge, the fireplace dreamy, and she completely understood that the space was packed with meaning and memories for him. To her, it was bursting with the potential to be a showstopper.

"I think it's pretty nice," he said, a note of defensiveness as if he, too, could see that it missed the mark for greatness. "I mean, I spend most of my time in here with my eyes closed, so who cares how it looks, right?"

"It's very nice."

"Which translates into 'Wow, this place needs work.'"

Laughing, she shook her head. "Not much, but have you ever thought of putting the bed over there? Maybe getting rid of the big four-poster to open things up?" She pointed to the wall where a well-loved and woefully old sofa took up premium space. "Maybe switch out that sofa for a streamlined console table?"

Rusty marched right over to it and jumped up on the most worn cushion.

"You can see what my dog thinks of that," he joked.

"I know, but you'd wake up and see that view instead of having it at your side."

He let out a sigh and shifted from one foot to the other. "I always had a wonderful view in here when I woke up. And I doubt seriously I'd ever get rid of that bed."

The ache in his voice twisted her heart. "Of course. I'm sorry."

"Don't be, it's just..." He looked around, slowly, as if looking at it through her eyes. "I guess I could paint it. But...that sunny yellow is..."

"Annie's favorite?" she guessed.

"She always loved it."

"Totally get that." She smiled up at him. "If you ever think about changing it, the room would look fabulous in a cool gray, maybe with some deep-green tones. You could change out that earth-tone area rug, too. A simple, inexpensive change that would really make a difference."

His eyes widened like she'd suggested switching out one of his kids rather than an old-school might-have-been-shag-once rug.

"Or not," she added.

He laughed at that. "Annie and I went to Charlotte to get that rug and drove home with it hanging out the back of the truck, laughing like loons when it almost fell out on the highway. Then we'd dragged it up here and..."

She touched his arm. "Keep the rug, Daniel."

"No, no…" He swallowed and walked closer to the area rug, deep in thought as he put a large booted foot on it as if testing the temperature of water. "For argument's sake, what would you put in its place?"

She considered the room, imagining it before answering. "I think something like faded tapestry would look good on this hardwood, but as I told you, some things have memory tags, and it sounds like this one is massive. Deep. Long." She gave a soft laugh. "However memory tags are shaped."

"They are shaped like knives that cut your heart out."

"Oh." She closed her eyes, feeling the statement as well as hearing it. "I get that."

"Sorry."

She put a gentle hand on his arm. "I'm sorry for going all house designer on you. Show me another room, and I swear I won't say a thing about the decor."

"Then come to my office downstairs," he said. "It's *never* changing."

He led her out and closed the doors with enough of a forceful click for them to both know he'd never change a thing in that room, and she honestly didn't blame him.

Downstairs, he walked her to the spacious room in the east wing where she suspected he spent much of his day running the business of his life.

The oversized office included a sitting area with a classic burgundy leather couch, a small bar with decanters and glasses, and one deliciously comfortable chair in front of a fireplace.

"Definitely a man cave." She turned to the large mahogany desk with enough paper clutter to know it wasn't for show. His desk chair backed up to a picture window with a commanding view of the hills and mountains in the distance.

Next to his desk, a huge cushioned bed became Rusty's next stopping place. It was nestled in a corner, under a wall of framed pictures of dogs. Each and every single one *could* have been Rusty, except that the backdrops and coloration told her these were different Irish setters from over the years.

"Remember Murphy?" He came up right next to her, pointing to a dog in front of the version of this house she remembered from her first visit.

"Yes, I met him once, but I would swear that's a picture of Rusty. Or my new pal, Goldie."

At the sound of his name, Rusty got up and stood right between them, angling his head one way, then the other, as if to ask them both for a head rub. And they obliged, their fingers brushing as they touched the dog.

"You can't see the difference between the setter and the golden retriever like I do. But yes, Rusty looks like Murphy because they're grandfather and grandson," he explained. "All the setters who've lived here descend from the same couple, named Fergus and Enya, who lived in County Waterford with my father when he was very young."

"All from the same dogs?"

"The same lineage. Fergus and Enya had Corky, who my parents brought with them when they emigrated to the States back in the 1950s." He pointed to a sepia-toned picture of a very young Gramma

Finnie, her distinctive features easy to recognize even as she was dressed in a dated dress that looked like something Cassie would buy at a vintage shop.

"My father bred setters, so Corky had Laddie." That dog was featured in a color photo with a boy and a girl who looked to be around ten or twelve, obviously Daniel and his sister. "Colleen and I loved him so much. He went blind in his later years, but still, a great dog. He was the father of Murphy, who fathered Buddy, and then Buddy fathered Rusty."

"Who has fathered…"

He shook his head slowly. "I didn't breed dogs after my father died. Rusty is the last of that great line of true setters who come from Ireland, and he'll be the last dog to call me master."

"Why?"

He shrugged. "There'll never be another like him." He turned and smiled. "I bred kids, not dogs, and I have a wild and wonderful collection of granddogs who are all enough for me."

"Granddogs?" She laughed, but almost instantly her smile faded as the words hit her heart and she remembered her mission. He'd fathered…more kids than he knew. She swallowed and inched away from the pictures and him, knowing the time had come.

"Your whole family is just…" She shook her head. "Amazing."

"Credit to Annie," he said, walking toward the bar. "How about a nightcap? One little Jameson's, so we can toast…" He waited a long moment, then turned to look right into her eyes. "Our new relationship."

For a moment, she felt herself sway. This was it.

This was the time. "Our...relationship is about to change," she whispered.

"I sure hope so." He angled his head, quiet long enough for her to actually feel her knees weaken and her heart punch her ribs. Long enough for her to realize something was changing in that moment, and she hadn't yet mentioned Nick.

"You...do?"

He put his hands on her shoulders, inching her imperceptibly closer. "I have a proposal for you."

"You do?" she repeated, her voice even higher this time.

"I'd like to hire you."

"Oh, Daniel, I—"

"Nope, hear me out. Not to do the house, which I couldn't even fathom. But while we walked through and I heard your ideas, it really got me thinking. I'd like to try this...this change business."

"Change...business." Oh, she was bringing change, all right.

"We could start small, with one room." He started talking faster, as if he sensed she needed convincing. "The living room. It needs the most work, and I think I'm ready to try it. New paint, floor, furniture, drapes. With your help and guidance. We could do it together. It could be fun."

"Fun." She stared at him and swallowed.

But he just gave his easy laugh. "Don't look horrified, Katie. I'm willing to do some work myself and learn about those...what did you call them? Memory tags? How long would something like that take?"

Long enough for her to prepare better. To break the news in a way that maybe wouldn't wreck him or his family. It might even give them a chance to become friends, to work out a way that they could tell their children with minimal damage.

This gave her the one thing she craved—time. "A few weeks at the most," she said. That's all she needed, right?

"And there could be more," he added.

"More?" She felt the blood drain from her face. "Are you suggesting more than…decorating?"

He took a step closer and reached for her hand, enclosing it in both of his much larger, much stronger ones. The warmth of the sudden contact shocked her, along with the incredibly sincere look in his eyes. "I am."

She managed a slow, shuddering breath, sensing where this was going. And wishing the situation were different. Because if she hadn't had a bombshell to drop on him, this was the first and only time she could imagine even considering a date with another man. Not too much more, but someone to go to dinner with, someone to talk to, maybe, just maybe…kiss good night.

A sudden longing gripped her, constricting her throat and stomach, shocking her with the force of it. She was so hungry for this, she could practically taste that first kiss, and if that wasn't the stupidest, craziest, most wrong thing in the world, she didn't know what was.

Nico had been gone only two years, but he'd been sick for almost four years before that. It had been so, so long since someone…

No. Never. Not with Daniel, not with anyone, not with this ticking bomb hanging over her head. "I'm not ready for that."

He added some pressure to her hand. "I'll never be ready, Katie. I'll never, ever be ready to let go and try again."

"Then what are you asking? Because something tells me you want more than new paint and furniture in your living room."

He smiled. "As I told you, I'm the world's worst date. All I want to do is relive every moment of my marriage, from day one to the last."

She couldn't help letting out a soft, understanding laugh. "In painful detail. I hear you. That's my go-to topic, which I imagine would turn off every man."

"Every man except me."

She frowned. "You want to talk about Nico?"

"And Annie. At great length. In excruciating detail. Because I'll listen to *every* word you have to say about him, and I know you'd do the same. No expectations, no disappointments."

"So what exactly are you proposing?"

"I'm proposing we redecorate one room and spend the time together with a simple rule: There's no limit to the talk of our dearly departed spouses."

For a long moment, she didn't say a word.

"Should I sweeten the deal?" he asked, lifting his brows. "You can spend all the time you want with Goldie."

That made her drop her head back and laugh. "You drive a hard bargain, Dr. Kilcannon."

"It's a win for everyone," he said. "I get a new room that I can see I desperately need, and we both get the sympathetic company we also desperately need."

But best of all, she'd get a few more weeks, to develop a trusting relationship with him and let him see into her past, so that when she did gently and tenderly tell him about Nick, he'd understand why it happened the way it had.

He broke into that slow, sweet smile she remembered so well from college. "You're thinking about it," he said.

"Seriously thinking about it."

He let go of her hand and took one step back to his bar, turning to let her stand there and decide. While she did, he poured two small shot glasses of amber-gold liquid with great but simple ceremony. After putting the glass topper back on the decanter, he lifted the two glasses and offered one to her, a questioning look on his face.

Still silent, she took the glass and held it while he tapped the crystal and made it ding.

"To jigsaw puzzles."

She frowned, a wisp of a memory pulling at her chest. "Jigsaw puzzles?"

"When we are done, I'll have a new living room. And I will have the full picture of the puzzle that was your life with Nico, and you will have mine with Annie. You remember telling me that people had certain puzzle pieces they belonged next to in that great big jigsaw of life?"

"Yes, I do. Nico said that."

"I never forgot that," he told her. "And now my puzzle is complete, and so is yours, and this way, we can sit back and admire each other's handiwork. And that room can be cleared of memory tags, and you have a new client. What do you say?"

"I say..." Not what she'd come into this room intending to say. But she wasn't ready. She needed time. Just a little more time. "Here's to jigsaw puzzles."

They toasted again, and each tossed back the shot, the hot, smooth liquid numbing her throat and silencing the secret she would keep for a little bit longer.

Chapter Seven

Pinterest? "What fresh new hell is this?"

Rusty didn't answer Daniel's muttered question. In fact, he barely lifted his head from the living room hearth, regardless of the fact that it was too early in the day for Daniel to start a warm fire. It was also too early in the day for Daniel to learn a new app on his tablet.

He perched on the edge of the sofa, squinting at the instructions on the screen, angling the device as if better light would explain how to open an account he didn't want. Couldn't she tear pictures out of a magazine? Wouldn't that be easier than…Pinterest?

He tapped the first button he saw and suddenly the page filled with pictures of sofas, bookshelves, and quaintly painted furniture. And a wedding dress. And a Christmas wreath. And…was that a dog on a sled?

"God, I hate technology."

"You sound like an old man, Dad." Darcy's voice floated into the room right before she did, with little Kookie steps behind. Without so much as a *good morning*, his youngest daughter took the tablet out of his hands with that air of authority that anyone under forty had when it came to technology. "What do you need?"

"A teenager or my mother, the only people I know who use…Pinterest."

She looked from the screen to him, brows drawn. "Pinterest? You looking for new recipes for Sunday-night dinners? And stop the rotation of pot roast, meat loaf, and baked ham?"

"You joke about my lack of cooking skills, but I notice you all show up to eat it."

"We're here for the Bloody Marys and good company." She grinned and plopped onto the sofa, studying the tablet while Kookie cuddled up next to Rusty by the fireplace.

"Katie wants me to open an account so she can share ideas with me on my…board. Do I have a board?"

She gave him a totally unsubtle side-eye. "Ideas for…" She lifted her brow. "Or don't I want to know?"

"Decorating," he said simply, knowing her overactive imagination wouldn't stop at that even if he tried to convince her otherwise.

"Oh. I see." She smiled and returned to the screen. "You somehow managed to get on Gramma Finnie's account. Let me set one up for you." She put her feet on the coffee table and started tapping.

Happy to relinquish the task, he sat on the sofa next to her, picking up his coffee cup and the list he'd been making for his lunch and day of shopping with Katie.

"Okay, you need a password." She held out the tablet. "I won't look."

"I don't care if you know the password. Just make it something I can remember."

"Like…Katie and Daniel *decorate*?" She gave a dirty laugh.

"How about 'jigsaw puzzle' but no space? I'll remember that."

"Jigsaw puzzle? What does that mean?"

"It's an inside joke I have with Katie."

"An inside joke, huh? Now I see."

"No, you don't, but I can wait while you tear out of the house and over to the kennels to share this tidbit with your siblings."

She grinned. "I'll tell them later."

Oh, he bet she would. He could already hear it.

They have an inside joke!

It must be serious.

I bet they're doing more than decorating the living room.

"What's so funny, Dad?"

"Am I laughing?"

"The low secret Dad chuckle," she explained.

He looked over at her, letting his gaze rest on his youngest, and some might say fairest, offspring. Although he couldn't possibly play favorites, each of his kids had something special, unique, and dear to him. Darcy cracked him up. "You always make me laugh, Darce."

"But I didn't say anything funny." She narrowed her eyes, skeptical and intense. "Maybe you're *happy*."

"Do I have a Pinterest account? Can you find something called a board? That'll make me happy."

93

Smiling, she nodded. "You do. DSKilcannon6, password jigsawpuzzle with no space." She tapped the screen again. "Anything else?"

"Find a secret or private shared board with Katie? Does that sound right?"

She bit her lip and looked up at him. "That sounds *promising*."

He shook his head, reaching for the tablet. "Thank you for the tech assist."

She didn't give up the device, though. "One sec and I'll find it." She tapped the screen some more and studied some pictures, her smile fading fast. "You're not really thinking about doing this, are you?"

"Doing what?" He came closer to look over her shoulder.

"This…farmhouse flair with a twist of coastal chic." She scrunched up her expression and gestured to the room. "In here?"

"Well, I don't know." Taking the tablet, he scanned the pictures Katie had promised to send. Everything was very…soft. Casual. Blue and easy and clean. "I kind of like it, don't you?"

"If you're planning a big reveal on HGTV."

"What's wrong with that? Isn't a makeover the whole idea of hiring an interior designer to update a room?"

She looked back at the tablet. "And what's this file that says 'other rooms' on it?"

"She said if she saw things that made sense for the guest room or even my bedroom, she'd put them in a file, but we're only going to do the living room for now."

She threw her arms over the back of the sofa as if

she could physically prevent it from being moved. "You're not really going to change this, though, are you?"

"Weren't you listening when I told you I hired Katie?"

"We all figured it was a ruse to cover your obvious attraction to the woman."

"A ruse? Do you know me? I don't *ruse*."

"No? What do you call it when you suggest I rent a certain apartment with the world's hottest landlord? Or that Liam offer up his favorite dog to the woman he's crushed on for years? Or that Aidan and Beck figure out a way to 'share' a dog? Dad, you're a master of the ruse."

Maybe he was. "Well, this isn't anything like that. We are redecorating my living room."

"Why?"

He gestured with two hands, as if taking one look around would speak for him.

"It's perfect the way it is," she insisted.

"It's out of date, faded, clumsy, dark, and...there's no focal point."

"Excuse me while I roll my eyes."

"Roll all you want, but you know what's really funny? That it's fine if you think we're cooking up some hanky-panky, but if she actually wants to change out the furniture, you have an issue."

"Hanky-panky? Who says that?"

"The same people who say 'ruse.'"

She laughed. "Just call it dating, Dad. And we—your children, I mean—are one hundred percent behind you having a nice lady to have dinner with and maybe breakfast, if you catch my drift."

He felt a slow heat in his chest and narrowed his eyes. "I'm still your father, Darcy Kilcannon. And that drift is not welcome."

Her eyes shuttered at the chastisement, and she nodded quickly. "Sorry. But this room? You can't change the living room. It's like a…"

"Museum," he finished.

"Of memories."

He sighed, knowing exactly how she felt. "Some of them, not all, need to go."

"Go where?"

"To…wherever old things go to make room for new ones."

She searched his face, silent for a long time, letting their joking stop as her expression grew serious. "Mom decorated this room," she finally said.

"She decorated every inch of this house," he replied. "Some of the furniture is fifteen or twenty years old. That coffee table you just casually put your feet on, for instance, was purchased when Pru was born because its predecessor had sharp corners that could hurt our first grandchild's mouth."

"*Exactly.*"

"Exactly what, Darcy?" he asked. "We can get a new baby-friendly coffee table that isn't fourteen years old."

"But I don't think you should change it too much," she said softly, looking away to study the wall of family pictures and portraits. "Mom loved this room. I remember when I was little and I couldn't sleep, I would come down here at ten or eleven o'clock at night, and you'd be sitting right there, reading the *AJVR* or some nonsense."

"Nonsense? The *American Journal of Veterinary Research* is not nonsense."

"And Mom would be on the other side of the fire, making lists or petting a foster dog or planning one of our birthday parties, and..." Her voice cracked, along with Daniel's heart.

He took her hand and pressed it between his. "Darcy, I feel those same things, and they are..." How could he explain it without hurting her? "Holding me back."

She exhaled slowly, her shoulders sinking with the breath. "From what?"

"Living." The word came out before he gave it any thought. "And they are, in some weird way, making me lonely. Lonelier."

"Oh. Dad." She squeezed his hand. "Nobody wants you to be lonely."

"So let me paint and get some new furniture."

"Okay, okay." She stood slowly, smiling down at him. "I get it, Dad. I do."

"Thank you, honey."

"And I have to go." She gave a little clap for Kookie. "Let's go, Kooks. We're working in town today, and we're late."

Daniel set the tablet to the side and stood, his six-two frame towering over his petite daughter. "Darcy, listen to me."

She finally met his gaze, surprising him that there was a hint of dampness in her usually clear blue eyes. "Yes?"

"I have no intention of getting 'unlonely' to the point of wiping away Mom's memory. You understand that, don't you?"

She swallowed hard and nodded, then looked at Kookie. "Why won't she get up?"

He turned to see the little Shih Tzu had climbed higher and was tongue-bathing Rusty's chest and chin, but the old guy snored right through it. "She's always had a weakness for Rusty," he said, only half joking. "She thinks she can have her way with him while he sleeps."

That was enough to make Darcy smile and walk over to scoop up her pup. "Come on, kiddo. Let sleeping dogs lie, as they say." She lifted Kookie easily, then paused, leaning over Rusty. "Is he okay?"

"Our morning walk tired him out, I think," Daniel said, taking a few steps closer to Rusty. "We old guys tucker out easily."

She gave him a playful smile. "Maybe not when it comes to, uh, *decorating*."

"Go," he said, giving her shoulder a nudge. "If you hurry, you can catch Molly before she starts her rounds, and you can update the betting pool on my dating life."

"We're not..." She closed her eyes. "Yeah, okay. I may do that."

A laugh rumbled in his chest as she walked out. His...what had she called it? *Low secret Dad chuckle.* And she'd also called him *happy*.

For the first time in a long while, he kind of was.

"Mom! I'm in the kitchen drinking your coffee. Don't come down naked or anything."

Katie chuckled at the greeting that floated up her stairs as she slid on earrings and did a last check of her outfit. Her daughter frequently popped in unannounced, using her own key to the townhouse Katie had moved into last year, but she had a feeling Cassie had an agenda this morning. She knew where Katie was headed and had come to deliver a pep talk.

"Be right down," she called back. "Fully dressed."

Normally, she loved nothing more than coffee with her daughter if it happened to be morning, or a glass of wine at the end of the workday. But they'd been avoiding each other—and the unavoidable topic—since they'd left Waterford Farm on Wednesday night.

Cassie had claimed she understood Katie's decision to get more time with Daniel before telling him about Nick, because the night with the Kilcannons had shown her just how much damage the news could do to the strong and healthy family. But they had different definitions of *more time*.

A few minutes later, Katie stepped into the kitchen to find her daughter holding a mug, staring out at the tiny backyard patio, a million miles away.

"I'm not changing my mind," Katie announced, tempering the news with a hug from behind and a kiss on her daughter's dark, sweet-smelling hair. "But I love that you won't give up."

"I'm not here to tell you what to do, Mom." She turned, a wry smile lifting her lips. "As out of character as that would be."

"You always were the bossiest little thing," Katie teased.

"Someone had to push those four beastly brothers around and show them who was in charge." She took her coffee to the table and slipped into a chair. "By the way, John is super interested in that property in Bitter

Bark that Daniel told us about at dinner the other night. The sandwich shop the owners are putting up for rent or selling? How's that for complicating things?"

Katie didn't answer, rinsing out the cup she'd left in the sink earlier and trying to imagine how that could or would complicate things.

"How do you feel about that?" Cassie pressed.

"You three own the business," Katie said. "If you want to open another Santorini's in Bitter Bark, the fact that I know someone who lives there shouldn't matter at all."

She snorted softly. "*Know*...like in the biblical sense."

"Cassie." She whipped around, narrowing her eyes. "It's not funny."

"If we don't find some humor in this, I'll go crazy." She dropped her chin into her hands, letting her elbows clunk on the table. "I'm sorry, but it was a little weird to meet a guy you slept with before Dad."

"The only guy," she clarified. "Before and after. Plus, it was only twice."

"But clearly he shoots loaded bullets with magic sperm."

Katie closed her eyes and sighed. "I told you we used a condom."

"And then you had sex with Dad and didn't."

She dug deep for patience. Cassie was blunt, honest, and in this case, absolutely right. "I know this is hard for you to fathom, honey, but it was 1976." She turned from the sink to face Cassie. "The whole 'condom for disease protection' hadn't really become a cultural thing. We wore rubbers, and yes, that's what we called them, to prevent pregnancy. Your father and I didn't want to prevent pregnancy, as you know. Getting pregnant was our ticket to a marriage that neither family approved of."

"Grandma Diane didn't approve of the marriage until the day she died. She's probably dissed Dad in heaven every time she sees him."

If she's there. "That wasn't for lack of me trying to convince her I'd done the right thing. And you had Yiayia."

"And won't Yiayaia be happy to find out Nick isn't Greek?"

"It could cause the next Trojan War," Katie joked. "But can I just say that spending time with that little Irish grandma could make me believe in leprechauns? How cute is she?"

"She's adorable, but don't change the subject."

"Right. Condoms. Me and...my men."

"Both of them."

"Cassie." She stepped closer to make her point. "It's really important that anyone who knows about this realizes that I did—*Daniel and I did*—do the smart thing on those two nights together. And that I went straight to your father, which is why I've always assumed that—"

"Did it break? With Daniel, I mean."

"I don't know." She shook her head, the memory so incredibly fuzzy. "I honestly don't recall much about it except that there was quite a bit of floundering with the package. He sort of slipped off the bed."

"Smooth."

101

"It was a dorm bed, and he's over six feet tall. They're only ninety-eight percent effective, you know. We thought we did the right thing."

"You were thinking about Dad?" She sounded almost scared to hear the answer.

"We were raging with hormones, but yes, I do remember feeling a lot of guilt because I was in love with someone else." More guilt than satisfaction, come to think of it.

"Then why did you sleep with him? Just because he was good-looking?"

Katie sighed. "Do the words 'Grandma Diane' mean anything to you?"

"Grandma Diane told you to have sex with boys at college?" Cassie snorted. "I find that difficult to believe."

"She told me to spread my wings and…and…" Katie laughed softly. "Marry well. You think *I'm* old-fashioned? My mother thought college had one purpose for a young woman—getting an MRS, not a BA. Preferably to a doctor. I'm not even sure she'd have been happy with a vet, but at least he wasn't a Greek restaurant owner."

"God forbid," Cassie said dryly.

"No, but my mother did. You understand that, right? My parents insisted I break up with your father, and in those days, kids actually did what their parents told them."

Cassie tipped her head. "I do what you want. I didn't make any grand announcements on Wednesday." She sighed and closed her eyes. "Which is why I do kind of understand your decision."

"I'm not chickening out. I want to do it right."

"You have to," Cassie agreed. "That family is rock-solid. White bready Irish, but hey, not everyone can be Greek, as Yiayia likes to say. But I'm seriously afraid this could crack them."

"And us," Katie added. "Plus, I keep clinging to the hope that what if that DNA mail-in test was wrong? You know, I read that sometimes they get sent back for not being able to find enough DNA in the saliva, because the sample was too small."

"It's rare. Like, one in ten thousand. Or 'ninety-eight percent effective' as some might say."

Katie ignored the comment, still clinging to hope. "Or what if they got his results mixed up with someone else? Or what if the gene dice rolled differently, and that's why he was three percent Greek and seventy-two percent Irish. I might have Irish in me. There are other explanations, Cass."

Katie had had no interest in taking the test when Cassie had first persuaded her brothers to participate over Thanksgiving. But after the results came in? Katie took it the next day, hoping that might explain the inconsistencies. Nick was listed as a "possible distant cousin," not a sibling to any of them. And since none of the Kilcannons had ever registered with the site, none had shown up. But her results wouldn't show up for many weeks, and—

She frowned at the distant digital melody. "Is that my phone? Hang on."

"Yeah, it might be your new client, *Dr.* Kilcannon." Cassie followed Katie into the laundry room where she'd hung her purse. "Grandma D'd be so proud of a doctor boyfriend."

"Stop it." Katie pulled out her buzzing phone to read

"unidentified caller" on the screen. "Probably one of those dumb marketing calls," she said to Cassie.

"Oh, let me answer it." Cassie grabbed the phone. "I love to tell these people what's what when they call." She cleared her throat, then touched the screen and hit the speaker button. "This better be good, because I am a very busy woman."

"It's good, Cass, and you're not Mom."

"Nick!" They both shouted his name at the same time in the same high-pitched excited voices.

"I guess I hit the mother-daughter jackpot."

"Are you okay?" Katie seized the phone as if that were a way she could actually touch her son. "You never call in the mornings."

"I'm fine. Still in CAR," he said, referring to the country of Central African Republic, where he'd been for months. "I've been running the mobile clinic in Kolaga, but a little trouble broke out down in Bangui, so we're headed there to take care of some people."

The names of places so foreign that Katie had a hard time finding them on a map faded away, because all she heard was *a little trouble.*

She shared a worried look with Cassie, who was already gnawing at her bottom lip. It was constant war and death, and no matter how hard Nick tried, he couldn't save everyone. But he'd never stop trying. It was who he was.

"We hit a spot on the road with the rare cell service, so I thought I'd call."

"Oh, that's wonderful, honey."

"How you doing, bro?" Cassie asked, her voice soft and full of love. She adored all her brothers, but Nick was on a pedestal above the rest. He was the ultimate firstborn—a fearless leader, a protector, the best big brother to his siblings.

"I have never been better," he announced, making them look at each other with wide eyes of surprise.

"That's...great." Katie didn't want to say what she was thinking...that *never been better* was a huge improvement over the miserable man who'd been home for three days last Thanksgiving and deeply in the "angry" stage of grief over losing his father.

"Does that mean you're coming home?" Cassie asked.

He laughed. "No, it means I'm in love."

"*What*?" The question came out with laughs of shock and disbelief in perfect unison again.

"You?" Katie asked. "My confirmed bachelor?"

Cassie's jaw hung open. "Dude. I gave up on this hope years ago."

He laughed again, but Cassie's words reflected Katie's thoughts. At forty-two, Nick was committed to one thing: his job with the organization Médecins Sans Frontières, also known as Doctors Without Borders. In his sixth year with the organization, he lived a lifestyle that defied settling down, marrying, or having children. It defied anything "normal," but that was exactly the way her intrepid, risk-loving, doctor son liked it.

"Well, I'm still a bachelor," he said. "For the moment."

"Wow, that's fantastic, Nick," Katie said.

"Details, please," Cassie added. "Who is she? How did you meet?"

"She's an MSF anesthesiologist," he said. "And, man, does she numb my pain."

They laughed at that, but Katie's smile quickly faded when she thought about how severe that pain had been. Of all her children, Nick had taken Nico's illness and death the hardest. Not only had Nick and Nico shared a name and an extremely close bond, Nick was a man who literally lived to heal, but he'd been unable to help his own father beat cancer.

"Tell me more," Cassie urged. "What's her name? Where's she from? When will we meet her?"

"Her name's Lucienne Dumonier, and she's from a little town outside of Paris."

"Oh, *oui, oui*! A French girl," Cassie teased.

"Woman," he corrected. "She's thirty-eight, but on her first tour with MSF. I met her on her first day here, right after I got back from the States, so I'm not sure if she'll be coming home with me anytime soon. She doesn't have much vacation accrued yet."

"But...you'll come without her, right?" Katie asked. "In May? Like you said?"

He hesitated long enough for her to feel the first pinch of disappointment. "I'll try, but I'm not sure about the clinic, with the move and everything."

Katie and Cassie exchanged another glance. If he didn't come home in May, Katie had more time to figure things out with Daniel. A little welcome relief rolled through her, mixed with some shame that she was such a coward.

"You do sound happy, Nick, and that's all that matters, really," Katie said.

"Yeah, I am. I think you'll love her. Dad would have loved her."

She heard the hitch in his voice, and her eyes shuttered for a moment as guilt crawled up her chest.

How could she ever break his heart again? When she sat him down to tell him that his hero, his best friend, his namesake was *not* his father, would he go back to square one with grief? She moaned a little at the thought.

"It's okay, Mom," he said, misinterpreting the sound. "I can talk about him now. Lucienne's helped me so much."

"That's good." Because this woman would have a lot more work to do in that regard. "Tell me about her."

"Well, she's beautiful, of course. And funny. And a genius. Oh, and she wants kids."

"Really?" Her voice rose with hope she didn't even try to contain as she reached to grab Cassie's arm and give it a squeeze. "Well, that would be unexpectedly wonderful."

He laughed. "Listen, I'm glad I got you both, because I want to know about that DNA test thing you did at Thanksgiving, Cassie. Did you get the results yet?"

For what felt like an eternity, neither of them moved. They just stared at each other in absolute shock and speechless silence.

"You still there?" Nick asked.

"Oh…yeah." Cassie's voice cracked as she took the phone back and waved it through the air. "I thought we lost you for a minute. Nick? Are you there?"

Katie scowled at her.

"What else can I do, Mom?" she mouthed. "We can't tell him like this." No sound came from her lips, but Katie read every word. And with each passing second, her head felt lighter.

"Am I losing you guys?"

"We're here," Katie said, her own voice sounding thick in her pulse-pounding ears.

"Well, did you get the results?"

"Not yet, no." Cassie stepped closer to the phone, cringing like she had as a child when she'd told a fib. "They said it could take many weeks, maybe months. I've read about people not getting results for six months or more." She said the last sentence quickly and closed her eyes as if the lie hurt to say.

"Oh, really?" He sounded genuinely disappointed.

"Is it that big a deal?" Cassie asked. "As I recall, you couldn't scoff enough at the idea."

"I know, but Lucienne is really interested in seeing if I have any French in me. She says that kind of thing is important to her family." He gave a dry laugh, but Katie reached for the coat hook on the wall to steady herself. "I knew you'd understand that, Mom, since Yiayia put you through the wringer for not being Greek."

She blew out a breath, not sure what to say.

"So, yeah," Nick said into the awkward silence. "I guess you can deduce that since we're talking about families, it's pretty serious."

"How serious?" Cassie asked.

He was quiet for a moment. "She's the one," he finally said. "We have to figure out life, but...oh damn, I gotta go. They want me back on that bus ASAP. Listen, tell John and Alex I said hey. Is Theo okay?"

"Yes," Katie said. "Still in San Diego."

"Of course he is." Nick laughed. "World's luckiest guy. Hey, listen, don't worry about the DNA thing,

Cass. I'll do my own if it becomes a deal breaker with Luci's family. I think once they meet me, they won't care that I'm a Greek god." He gave a dry laugh that was so much like Daniel's, Katie had to grab the wall again. "Love you guys."

"We love you, too," Cassie said.

"Be careful, Nicky," Katie added.

The line went dead, leaving them to stare at each other in silence.

"I'll tell him today," Katie finally whispered.

Cassie shook her head.

"No? I have to, Cassie. You heard—"

"I lied to him," she said, her voice cracking. "I hate myself for that. Now I'm complicit in this thing. I've deceived my own brother."

"Oh, honey." She reached for her and wrapped her arms around Cassie's slender body, holding her close. "You are doing nothing but trying to protect the ones you love. The only person complicit is me." She inched back. "I give you my word, I'm telling Daniel today. I'll ask him to take the same test and see if Nick shows up as a possible relative."

"But what if Nick does his first and finds this out?"

That would be…the worst possible scenario. "Even if he can get the internet access needed, it could take a long time. But not forever. I won't wait. I can't wait, now. Daniel has to take the test, so I'll tell him today. We were supposed to go over sofa fabrics and paint ideas, then have a nice long lunch. I'll tell him then."

Cassie nodded and added a hug. "You can do it."

"I know. In some weird way, I'm glad Nick forced my hand. I'm not sleeping well knowing I'm being deceptive. Daniel has a right to know. They both do."

Cassie gave her one more squeeze. "Mom, you're the strongest woman I know. You've been through way worse. You're doing the right thing."

She leaned back and smiled at her. "I knew you came over here to give me a pep talk."

"Of course I did." She hugged harder. "I love you."

She clung to the words and the dear daughter who delivered them. They would be her strength during what was going to be one of the worst conversations of her life.

But now she had to protect Nick from finding out first. When her children's happiness was at stake, her own fears didn't matter.

Chapter Eight

Daniel leaned across the table, watching Katie pick at Ricardo's tiramisu as if the dessert he'd suggested for her tasted like mud instead of the heaven he knew it was. For the twentieth time since they'd started lunch a little over an hour ago, she let out a noisy sigh, looked out the window, then at Daniel, then back at the window, then her food.

"I'm going to venture a wild guess," he said, resisting the urge to soften what he was about to say by touching her hand. "This whole 'you talk about yours and I'll talk about mine' isn't working for you."

She lowered her fork without taking a bite. "I like hearing about Anne."

"You can call her Annie."

"That's only for people who really love her, remember?" Her smile was vague. "I sure can tell you do."

"But you haven't offered much in return. To be fair, you've barely talked since we got to the restaurant."

She looked at him, then swallowed.

"It's not a date," he reminded her gently. "No expectations, no need to be 'on' or anything. Would you prefer we go back to the fabric discussion?"

"A subject you hated," she teased.

"I didn't hate it, but I can't get too excited about it. I'm looking forward to our trip to High Point to pick out new furniture." He waited a beat, then added, "Mostly because I thought I'd get to know more about Nico and your forty years of happy marriage."

She took a slow breath and abandoned the dessert altogether. "It *was* happy," she said, almost a little defensively.

"And you beat us by a few years," he added. "You must have gotten married not long after you left Bitter Bark. And you were young, as I recall. Barely eighteen."

She lifted her gaze, and in that one instance, he saw that look again. Every once in a while, she had that trepidation and uncertainty around her eyes.

"We had to get married," she whispered.

"Oh." He nodded, understanding. "We did, too," he admitted. "And Annie's parents were so furious about it, they didn't even come to our wedding, which was at Waterford Farm."

She searched his face for a minute. "Daniel, I have to—"

"Well, there you are! Who told Dr. K he could change his weekly hours and take long lunches?"

They both turned at the woman's voice, and Daniel immediately recognized Bella Peterson, a client and one-time date—thanks to Garrett—coming toward them. He started to stand to greet her, but she waved him down.

"No worries, I don't want to interrupt." She shifted her attention to Katie, openly scrutinizing her. "I simply wanted to express my disappointment that you canceled your office hours this morning. I brought Buttercup in for a checkup, and you know how much she likes you."

"She's in good hands with my daughter," he assured her and then gestured to Katie. "Bella, this is my friend Katie Santorini. Bella holds the distinction of being the proud owner of eleven—"

"Twelve," she corrected.

"Twelve cats."

Katie smiled up at her. "Hello, Bella."

Bella made a joke about being a crazy cat lady, but Daniel's attention was on Katie, still trying to figure out what was going on with her. She was different today than she'd been on Wednesday. Instead of interested and animated, she seemed distant and troubled.

And all he really wanted to do was draw her out of that, hear her laugh, and yes, give her a chance to walk down memory lane like they'd agreed they would do when they were together.

"So, are you a dog-owning patient of Daniel's?" Bella asked. "Or a trainee at Waterford?"

"I'm the client," Daniel said, purposely not getting into the whole *we knew each other in college* backstory. That would make Bella linger and ask questions, and he didn't want that at all. "Katie is an interior designer giving me some help at Waterford."

"Oooh." She drew the word out with some satisfaction, as if a professional relationship was far preferable to a personal one. "That's so nice. But don't change too much," she added. "We like Daniel exactly the way he is."

How could Garrett ever think he'd be attracted to this woman? The cats were okay…but the claws were not.

Rusty nudged his ankle under the table, as if he, too, wanted Bella to leave, so Daniel absently reached down to pet him and glanced at Katie again, hoping their visitor got the message that she was interrupting.

To her credit, Bella backed away. "Well, then, I'll let you two talk business," she said. "Nice meeting you, Katie. Now, Daniel, next time you switch office hours with Molly, you be sure to put a note on the website."

Daniel gave her a quick smile and nod, which did the trick, but when he looked at Katie, he saw a little confusion in her eyes.

"Did you change your hours to accommodate me?" she asked.

"Yes." Why lie? "I usually work in town on Fridays, but it was no problem for Molly."

"Thank you." She glanced in the direction of Bella's table. "I'm flattered, considering what high demand you're in around here."

"It's my kids," he explained. "They've tried to match me up with half the single women in Bitter Bark."

"You can't blame them for wanting you to be happy," she said, taking her napkin off her lap and folding it. "It's payback for how happy we made them."

Sensing the first chink in her unexpected armor, he seized the topic. "Tell me about your kids," he said.

"Start with Nick. The oldest. The doctor. He sounds great. Is he married?"

And all that warmth evaporated instantly. "Yeah...no." She shook her head as if she didn't know where to start or what to say.

"You don't want to talk about your kids, either," he deduced. "Katie, is something wrong?"

She eased back into the leather booth, looking at him intently. "You've always been incredibly sensitive," she said. "You're so empathetic. Always in tune with what other people are feeling."

He didn't know what to make of the compliment, so he let her continue, sensing there was more.

"Nick is that way," she said.

Oh...okay. It was a roundabout way to talk about her kids. "That's probably what makes him a good doctor."

"One of many things. He's smart. Excelled at chemistry." She added a look that made him think he would appreciate that. "I remember you were good in chemistry."

"It probably helped him in med school," he said.

"He's kind. Thoughtful. Has an easy sense of humor and always puts the family first." She put enough emphasis on the words for him to know they carried great weight for her.

"He sounds terrific," he said, encouraged that she was finally talking. "Do you have a picture of him?"

She exhaled and looked toward the diners at the next table and the sound of Bella laughing a few tables away. "Daniel, could we go outside?" she asked suddenly. "Take a walk maybe? In the square?"

"Of course. I think Rusty would love you for it," he added, feeling another push from his dog's nose. "He's been pestering me, and he's usually quiet in here. Let me grab the check."

She reached for her bag and jacket. "I could use the air."

He held up his hand to catch the server's attention, but studied her. "Are you sure you're all right, Katie?"

"Yes, yes," she answered far too quickly. "I just like the idea of talking outside."

As soon as Daniel slid to the edge of the booth, Rusty got up, giving him a plaintive look like he was as anxious as Katie to leave. Daniel snagged the leash he always had on hand in a restaurant like this and handed the end to her, clipping it on Rusty's collar. "Here you go. I'll meet you in two minutes."

"Thank you." Taking the dog, she moved through the tables with more speed than he'd expected, leaving him to wonder what was up while he paid the bill.

Not three minutes later, he stepped outside and spotted her waiting at the corner to cross the street and head to Bushrod Square. He hustled to beat the light and reach her first.

"Are you running off with my dog?" he teased.

Instead of laughing as he'd expected, she looked up at him. "It's quiet in the park. Let's go there and talk. I want to tell you something."

"All right." He put a light hand on her back to guide her across the street and also offer a comforting touch that she obviously needed. Something about Nico? Their past? The job he was hiring her to do?

He had no idea, but he stayed close as they made their way into the square. It wasn't exactly deserted at two in the afternoon, but it was a brisk day and overcast enough to keep the dog walkers, joggers, and baby strollers to a minimum.

They didn't talk until they reached the sidewalk in the square and stayed silent while Rusty stopped and sniffed the grass. Daniel kept his gaze on Katie, though, watching and waiting to see where she was taking this and if there was anything he might do or say to help her.

But long, uncomfortable seconds ticked by until she finally murmured, "It's about Nick."

Her son? "Yes, you were going to show me a picture of him. Do you have one? On your phone?"

She exhaled again, slow and deep. "I have... something." She looked left and right, as if someone might help her. Or maybe she was seeking privacy.

"Want to sit down here?" He pointed to a bench under a tree a few feet away.

Without answering, she walked there, still holding Rusty's leash. When they sat, Daniel automatically reached over and unclipped it, giving the dog some freedom to roam a familiar place.

After a moment, she reached into her bag, pulled out her phone, and started scrolling the screen. Daniel waited, assuming she was looking for a picture of her son or family.

"He called this morning," she said softly. "Right before I left."

"Is that unusual?"

"Yes. He doesn't have cell service very often in Africa, working at a mobile clinic."

Daniel gave a light whistle of admiration. "That's a seriously respectable career choice," he said. "It takes

117

a very strong and dedicated medical professional to work like that. Will he stay much longer?"

"I don't know. He's met a woman he cares about. An anesthesiologist from France."

"Really? That's fantastic. Is it serious?"

She didn't answer, but stared at her phone for a long, long time. "What I'm about to show you isn't a picture," she finally said, looking up at him. "But it is a...snapshot, of sorts."

He frowned and glanced down at her hand, noticing that it was trembling. "Katie, what's wrong?"

She shook her head and made no effort to hide the tears that sprang into her eyes. Instantly, he moved closer.

"What's the matter?" he asked, stroking her hair gently.

"Everything." She barely whispered the word, and still her voice cracked.

"What is it?" He reached for the phone, knowing that whatever was on that screen was the root of her troubles. And all he wanted to do was make them go away. "Can I..."

She relinquished the phone, and he looked at it, blinking at what looked like a picture she'd taken of a piece of paper. There were names of countries and bar graphs next to them, making him squint, but without his reading glasses handy, it was difficult to make sense of the small print.

"Last Thanksgiving, Cassie had this idea."

He gave up on figuring it out and studied Katie as she talked.

"She wanted to do that...that DNA ancestry thing and trace our family. Bloodline.com."

"Okay..." He drew out the second syllable as the confusion of the moment deepened to something like pressure on his chest.

"And it revealed that..."

He tried to swallow, but his throat was suddenly dry and tight.

"That Nick, my oldest son..." She looked down at the phone, then back at him, blinking so that one lone tear trailed down her cheek.

He stared at it, following the path it took along her nose, settling on her mouth, forcing his brain to think about that tear and not what she was saying. Because...his whole body started to hum with confusion and shock. Maybe fear.

Yes, it was that same fear he'd seen in her eyes. That fear of...something he wasn't capable of putting into words.

"None of his results match his siblings'," she said. "He's only three percent Greek. And seventy-two percent Irish. He wasn't even included as one of their siblings, but possibly a distant relative."

He literally couldn't breathe. Or think. Or let the reality of what she was saying hit him as she stared at him and let him put two and two together and come up with...

"Oh God."

"I didn't know, Daniel," she insisted, her expression carved with misery. "I had no idea. I thought I got pregnant the night you took me to Nico. I never doubted that. We didn't use...anything. But when I saw those results...I think I must have already been pregnant when I left Bitter Bark."

The whole world swirled around him, darkness licking at the edges of his sight as his stomach clenched and the hot sensation of adrenaline and shock spurted through his veins.

"Nick...is...*mine*?"

"I'm not one hundred percent certain, but—"

"Hey, is that your dog?" A man's voice punched through his consciousness, and Daniel turned to the sound like a man moving through water. "Looks like he's sick."

He blinked in the direction the stranger pointed, seeing Rusty sprawled on the grass with a heap of vomit in front of him. Without a word, he shot up from the bench and launched toward him, putting a hand on his head to guide him away from the mess. "Hey, bud. What's going on?"

His voice sounded like he was underwater, too, drowned out by the pounding of his pulse, deafening in his ears.

I must have already been pregnant when I left Bitter Bark.

The words echoed like the *rat-a-tat* of gunfire, ringing in his head, taking aim at his heart.

Katie was next to them in a second. "Is he okay?"

"I don't know." Daniel eased the dog toward a clean stretch of grass and sat down next to him, waiting to see if he'd be sick again, silently noting the quickness of his panting and a slight tremor that shook his body.

I know exactly how you feel, buddy.

Katie dropped to the ground next to him. "What's wrong with him?"

"He's...sick."

I must have already been pregnant when I left Bitter Bark.

"Something he ate?"

He rooted deep for his training, his cool, his legendary calm in the face of chaos and a sick animal, lifting his gaze to meet hers. "Why didn't you tell me?"

"I just did."

"Sooner."

"I had no idea sooner. You thought I should walk up to you in the bakery and drop this bomb? Or maybe at the dinner table? Share it with your whole perfect family?"

Her voice rose with frustration, the same kind that was still ricocheting through him.

Rusty whimpered, turned, and threw up again, his gaze confused and broken, his back leg spasming like he might be having a seizure.

"Holy hell." Daniel leaned over him, holding his flank and neck, forgetting he was a vet for one minute and wanting only to give comfort to—and get comfort from—a creature he loved and trusted and needed so badly.

"Should I get my car?" Katie asked. "I can pull it up to the gate, and—"

He shook his head, silencing her, finally getting a thread of common sense in his addled, stunned brain. "My vet office is on the other side of the square." He straightened and started to stand. "I'll carry him there."

"Okay, let's go."

"No." The word came out much too sharply, but for once in his damn life, he didn't care how someone else felt. He was the one who'd been blindsided, deceived, and cheated out of a child.

No, no, that was ridiculous, but...*was it*?

"Just let me go," he said, getting his balance.

"Let me help you."

He finally looked at her, wishing he could care about the pain in her eyes, the streaked mascara, and her deathly pale skin. Someday—soon—he'd think about how this affected Katie Santorini. And her family. And his. And...him.

But right now, all he could do was wonder how in God's name was this possible, and what the hell should he do about it?

"Please, Daniel. Let me help you."

But he simply couldn't deal with her right then. With anything.

Rusty stayed collapsed on the ground, his muscles twitching, his gaze faraway. It didn't take his degree to know this dog was having a seizure. Bending over, Daniel slid both hands under his belly and hoisted him up with a grunt. "My dog is sick. That's all that matters to me right now."

But even as he walked away, carrying a trembling, whimpering Rusty, he knew that was a lie.

What mattered was the fact that somewhere in Africa, there was a kind, empathetic, talented forty-two-year-old doctor who'd spent his entire life loving the wrong father.

Chapter Nine

"Dr. K! Is that Rusty?" Elise, the trainee tech covering the front desk that day, shot up from her chair as he walked in, instantly opening the door to the back office.

"Which room is open?" he demanded.

She blinked in surprise, probably because she'd never heard such a gruff tone from him. Once again, he ceased caring about anything except the last line to sanity he had, who was fighting a seizure in his arms.

"Two's open, but a patient just left. Let me clean the table and—"

"I got it. Is Molly free?"

"She can be in a minute." Elise stepped aside to let Daniel and the dog pass. "I'll get her."

Exam Room Two was less than three steps from the waiting room, but it took Daniel only two, then he used his foot to kick open the door, and letting out a grunt, he put Rusty on the table.

"It's gonna be all right, boy. I promise."

But would anything ever be all right again?

He huffed out a sigh and went to work, booting everything out of his head but the examination he'd done a thousand times. Check the gums for signs of shock and CRT. But the blood returned quickly when he pressed on the pink flesh. Look at the pupils. Not dilated. Check the heart rate. Increased, but not dangerously so.

I must have already been pregnant when I left Bitter Bark.

Daniel bent over as the blow hit him again. He let out a long, sorrowful moan.

"Dad!" Molly flew into the room, reaching for him with one hand and Rusty with the other. "What happened?"

"Possible seizure. He vomited. Collapsed."

She moved closer to Rusty, easing Daniel aside as she started the same exam. "How long did it last?" She lifted his lips and pressed on his gums, then angled his face, slipping a penlight from her jacket pocket to shine the beam into Rusty's big brown eyes.

"It lasted..." *A lifetime. He'd missed Nick's entire lifetime.* "I'm not sure. A few minutes. He's calming down now, but..."

"But you're not." Molly looked up at her father with concern in her eyes as she used both hands to gently palpate Rusty's belly.

"It scared me," he said softly.

Molly frowned as if the very idea of him being scared sounded wrong to her, saying nothing as she popped her stethoscope in her ears and placed the bell on Rusty's heart. "Nothing to be scared about," she said after a moment.

There was everything to be scared about. His family, his life...his world just got drop-kicked onto its side.

"Could he have been exposed to a toxin?"

He forced his brain to function like a vet. Toxin? "Not that I noticed. He was under my table at Ricardo's."

She looked a little relieved. "Maybe he ate an olive, Dad. They make him puke. Or maybe Ricardo's night help left some pest control under the table and he ate a pellet? Is that possible?"

"Anything's possible." *Including the fact that I have seven children.*

Molly pulled a thermometer from her other pocket, turning to Daniel as they waited for the digital beep. "You're honestly in worse shape than he is."

"Yeah." He tore his gaze from Rusty's face to look at his daughter, the truth bubbling up inside him. He needed help. He needed someone to talk to. He needed time and clarity and...*Annie.*

Oh dear God, *he needed Annie.*

"No fever," she said, snapping the device back into her pocket. "Cordell is the vet tech on duty, and Elise will send him in here any second. He'll carry Rusty to the back, and we'll start blood work and scans."

"No, I'll do all that," he said, staring at her, but not really seeing his grown, competent daughter. Instead, he saw Annie's hazel eyes and auburn hair. Laughing. Caring. Knowing exactly what to do in this horrible, impossible situation.

You have another son, Daniel? Why, you sly dog. When can we meet him?

Oh, now he could hear her. Loud and clear.

"Dad?"

He literally shook the voice out of his head. "I'll take Rusty back," he said, turning to the table, but Molly grabbed his arm.

"No, you won't," she insisted. "You're too upset. Your dog is the patient, and you are not the doctor in this situation."

He blinked, clearing his vision. "I don't know what I should do," he muttered, the honesty too close to the surface.

She scowled at him. "You're going to leave this room and wait like any other dog parent we have in this place. You can't work on Rusty, because you're too emotionally involved."

"I'll let you do the blood work, Molly, and take him into the back for a full work-up, but I'm not leaving him. Not for one minute."

She lifted her chin and narrowed her eyes in defiance and, in that one move, looked more like her mother than ever. "Who did you come with?"

"Alone."

Her brows tugged to form a tiny crease. "Wait. You changed your schedule today so you could spend the day with Katie Santorini. Where is she?"

He lifted a shoulder, not trusting himself to even talk about her in that moment.

"In the waiting room?" she suggested.

"She left." At her incredulous look, he added, "We drove separately to town so she could head back to Chestnut Creek after lunch."

"Oh, so she wasn't with you when Rusty got sick?"

"Yes, she was, but..." *She detonated my life with an unfathomable announcement.* "She left," he repeated.

"Dad, really? She left after Rusty..." She huffed out a disgusted breath. "Then she's not the lady for you."

No kidding.

Afraid he'd give away too much and not ready to share this bombshell with anyone, he turned to Rusty, who rested on his cheek, lightly panting, eyes at half-mast. "We'll get through this, old boy." He leaned over and pressed a kiss on his soft red head. "We've been through worse and survived. Right?" He stroked his neck and fought another punch of emotion. "So much worse."

Molly put her hand on Daniel's shoulder and gently eased him away from Rusty. "I'm calling rank now. You're not on duty, which means I'm currently the best working vet in this county, or so you've said a million times. Let me handle this."

He said nothing, then accepted defeat when the victor stared him in the face. "I'm scared," he admitted softly.

Her eyes shuttered, and she nodded. "He's old, but he's never been sick a day in his life," she said. "He hasn't shown a single symptom of epilepsy, heart issues, or cancer. Nothing ever more serious than a little arthritis and a tendency to overeat."

Just then, someone tapped on the door and opened it, revealing a tall, beefy vet tech with the body of a linebacker and the heart of an angel.

"I hear Rusty's sick," Cordell said, stepping inside.

At the sight of him, Rusty lifted his head a little, giving Daniel the first glimmer of hope he'd felt in a few minutes.

"Happier now that you're here." Daniel stepped aside to give Cordell access. "I think he can walk, though."

"No need." Cordell scooped him up with far more

ease than Daniel had. "Come on, my boy. Let's start your tests." He gave a questioning look to Molly.

"The works, Cordell. Full blood panel, CT scan, ultrasound on the torso, check for viral, bacterial, or parasites. I'll be right back there as soon as I escort my father out of this office."

"It's cool, Dr. K," the big man said as Molly opened the door for him. "We got your boy. You relax."

Daniel smiled at him. "Thanks, Cordell."

After he walked away, Molly kept the door open and stepped into the hall. "Out, Dad. I'm going straight to the back to take care of Rusty."

He just stood there, staring at her, feeling the adrenaline dump that left him numb. "I don't know what—"

"Oh." Molly looked toward the receptionist's desk and smiled. "Looks like you have a friend." She gestured for him to step out and follow her gaze.

There was Katie in the waiting room, perched on a chair, her face still streaked from tears.

"And it looks like Rusty's illness upset her as much as it did you." Molly gave him a light nudge in that direction. "Maybe she's not the wrong lady for you after all, Dad."

But Daniel stayed rooted where he was, a whirlwind of emotions roiling through him at such a speed he couldn't stop and grab a single one. Anger. Frustration. Disappointment. Disbelief. There was even a thread of hope, but that came and went before he could seize it.

Mostly, he wanted to be as far away from Katie Santorini as possible.

"Dad." Molly's whisper was as probing as her gaze. "What's wrong with you?"

"Nothing. I...don't want to go through this with her."

"Through 'this'?" she fired back, her color rising. "Do you mean Rusty being sick?"

"Worse."

She inched closer. "It's not worse."

Oh yes, it was.

"He probably has a little gastroenteritis, but you're acting like it's the end of the world."

Daniel closed his eyes, not wanting to speak the truth and certainly not wanting to look at the woman in the waiting room who'd brought it to him.

But Molly misunderstood all that, squeezing his arm. "Whatever he has, why would you—why *should* you—go through it alone? Even if it's the worst possible outcome, why would you endure that alone?"

The worst possible outcome? A one hundred percent positive DNA test. Would that be the worst possible outcome?

"Look, I think Rusty is fine," Molly continued. "But the next few days might be tough on him and you. Sitting right out there is a lovely woman who is obviously as worried about your dog as you are." She leaned in. "I know she's not Mom, but she's a good woman, a mother in her own right."

A mother of...*his son.*

"You have a shared, long history, and she's right there, waiting for you."

Molly's words finally penetrated, sliding through his haze of emotions to reach somewhere deep in his soul.

They did have a shared history and, quite possibly, a shared child. No, he shouldn't go through this difficult journey alone.

"It's what Mom would want," Molly said softly, adding a little pressure to her touch. "I know it is."

He finally looked at her, and all the anger evaporated like a fog lifting over Waterford on an October morning, leaving everything as clear as Molly's green-brown eyes. She was right. She was absolutely right. Maybe for the wrong reasons and about the wrong cause, but the news that he might have another child wasn't something he could or should go through alone.

"You're so smart," he said softly, sighing hard enough that his shoulders fell.

"Learned everything I know from you."

"From Annie," he corrected, but Molly shook her head.

"You don't give yourself enough credit, Dad. You raised me, too."

"Someone did a good job."

She beamed at him, inching up on her tiptoes to plant a kiss on his cheek and whisper, "She can be your friend."

"She can be…" *The mother of my son.*

"Just start with friend." She gave him a firm nudge toward the door. "And see where that takes you, Dad."

He knew where it would take him. To Nick. Not anywhere else. But if that man was his son, he wasn't going to lose the next forty-two years. And the only way to get there was through Katie Santorini.

Chapter Ten

Katie looked up to see Daniel and his daughter on the other side of the arched doorway, straightening as she made eye contact with him.

Would he send her away? Demand more proof? Or be the man she knew he was and figure out how to handle this in the best possible way?

She waited for a moment, still but for her thumping heart, and held his gaze as he walked to her.

"How is he?" she asked before he said anything.

"He's being tested."

She stood slowly, silent, studying his expression, aching to know what Daniel was made of.

"I think we all are," he added under his breath.

Exhaling with the softest sigh of relief, she nodded.

"Do you want to go be with him?" she asked. "I'll wait. However long it takes, I can wait right here."

"I thought you left."

She angled her head. "Seriously?"

His smile, the first since they'd left the restaurant, was wry, but real. "That's kind of what Molly said when I told her you'd left."

"Because even after only meeting me once, she knows better than that."

"But I told you to leave." He closed his eyes as if a slap of shame had hit him. "I'm—"

She stopped the apology before it came, lifting her hand. "I understand the heat of the moment and the shock of…" She glanced around, and so did he, both aware that the receptionist was not three feet away and two clients with cat carriers sat flipping through magazines.

"Come on, Katie." He took her hand and led her to the door. "Let's find somewhere else to wait."

She closed her fingers around his much larger hand and squeezed. "Okay."

On the street, he didn't let go of her hand, which made her heart feel like it might melt into a pool on the sidewalk. Instead, he clung to her, staying close, walking in silence. After a few minutes, he paused and looked to his left at the darkened window of Bitter Bark Bar.

But she knew the locals still called it Bushrod's. And she remembered it well as the location of their last date in college.

"This feels appropriate," he said. "And let's be honest, we both could use a drink."

She managed a soft laugh. "No argument here."

Inside, it was dimly lit and nearly empty at three in the afternoon. A few tables along the right side had late lunchers finishing up, and a heavy-set man behind the bar was the only sign of an employee. He looked up from the cash register and gave a smile to Daniel.

"Yo, Dr. K. Lunch is over, but I can get you guys something cold."

"Just a drink, Billy." Daniel gestured to a secluded table near the window, guiding her there and pulling out her chair. "What would you like, Katie?"

"Whatever you're having."

"Jameson's. Straight up."

"Sounds perfect."

He helped her scoot her chair in and then put a hand on her shoulder, standing behind her. "I'll be right back." His voice was still tight, not warm like it usually was, but at least they were talking. They'd come a million miles since the horrible moments in the square. She clung to that thought until he returned, setting two glasses of golden liquor on the table and taking the chair opposite her.

"I texted Molly and told her we were here," he said. "They'll call the minute I can go get Rusty. Until then…" He lifted the drink to her, but she stared back at him as she waited to know what he was thinking. "Here's to surprises," he finally said.

She huffed out a breath and took a deep drink, letting the welcome burn hit her throat.

"No one was more surprised than I was," she said as she set the glass down. "Except maybe Cassie."

He frowned. "I'm trying to remember what you said out there. She did tests? The bloodline DNA things?" Suddenly, his eyes widened. "Do they all know? Does Nick?"

She shook her head vehemently. "And neither do we," she added. "Not for certain. You'll have to take a test."

"A paternity test?"

"I don't think that's necessary, nor would it be very easy with Nick on another continent. I thought…" She swallowed and looked up from her drink. "You could just take one of the Bloodline.com tests and send it in for analysis. It takes about six weeks, but it'll come back with your full ancestry and distant relatives and...close relatives. If Nick is on that list, then we know."

He searched her face, a hundred questions in his expression. But he didn't ask any, only took another drink of his whiskey.

"I found out about ten days ago when Cassie brought me the results. The minute I saw them, I...knew. You're the only other man I've ever been with, and—"

"We used protection," he said softly. "I distinctly remember that it was..." He lifted his brows. "Not my most graceful moment in the bedroom."

She had to laugh, warmed by the tiny bit of humor, and maybe the drink. "But we did use it. Both times."

"I didn't think you could use a condom wrong, but we were young and inexperienced, so maybe..." He lifted a shoulder. "What does it matter now? It happened." Then he scowled again. "Is it possible he's not yours or mine? That he was switched at birth and your son is somewhere else?"

"No," she said, putting a hand over his to calm the sheer terror in his voice. "He's definitely related to my other kids. But not as closely as they are to each other."

He sighed with relief.

"I swear to you, Daniel, the thought that Nick was not Nico's son never—not once in forty-two years—occurred to me. Unlike us, Nico and I didn't use protection. We knew both our families were against our union and believed that if I got pregnant, they couldn't stop us from getting married. So, of course, when I realized I was pregnant two months after leaving Bitter Bark, I never dreamed he wasn't Nico's son."

He took one more drink, nearly draining the glass. "Can I see his picture now?" he asked, his voice a little thick with emotion.

"Of course." She reached for her bag, taking out her phone to click through the photos and get to the ones she'd taken last Thanksgiving.

She found the one of Nick on her sofa, his arms spread over the back, a rare smile—those few days, at least—on his face. She stared at it, not quite ready to hand it to Daniel. Would he see himself in that image? She didn't. Even knowing what she knew, she didn't see the resemblance. Not in his face. Other, deeper, less obvious ways, but not in his face.

"Here he is," she finally said. "Nico Matteo Santorini Jr."

"Oh. I didn't realize he's a junior."

"Yeah. Ironic, huh?"

He didn't seem too amused as he took her phone, turned it, and angled for the best view. Then he stared at it for what had to have been a full minute. He pinched the screen and spread the image with two fingers, no doubt zeroing in on every facial feature, looking for that…connection.

She examined Daniel's face as carefully as he examined Nick's. Watched to see if his jaw tightened or his eyes tapered or his blood drained from his face. But none of those things happened. After a while, he put the phone down, pressed a fist into his palm, and leaned on his knuckles, staring at the table.

"Daniel?" she said softly. "Do you see any resemblance?"

"To Liam. Maybe Garrett, too, around the mouth."

"Yes, I could see that, having met them. But not super strong."

"Definitely something familiar about him." He closed his eyes for a moment. "I can't believe it."

"Sometimes I don't believe it, either," she said, making him look at her again. "But I think it's more that I don't *want* to believe it. Still, we need final proof before we tell anyone. I need you to take that test, Daniel. With Nick in their database, it will immediately show if you're related."

He tipped his chin toward her phone. "Can I see those results again?"

"I have the original in my bag." She pulled out the envelope that Cassie had brought over to her house less than two weeks ago. Handing it to him, she leaned back and picked up her drink. "They're all there. The results for all five kids. I didn't take the test when Cassie had them do it at Thanksgiving, but I have since then. I should have my results in a little more than a month. But they won't tell us much. Obviously, I know I'm his mother."

As he opened the envelope, he gave her a curious look. "Then why take it?"

"To see if I have an unexpected amount of Irish in me that maybe I didn't know about. That might explain Nick's results. He's not zero percent Greek, but...well. You'll see."

She sipped her drink while he read each results page with the same intense focus she remembered he used to have when poring over a chemistry study guide. In some respects, it was like no time had passed at all. She could see that young vet student right in front of her, despite some lines on his face and silver hair. He was still broad-shouldered, proud, intelligent, and incredibly soft-hearted.

And the fact that they were sitting here, quietly having a mature and calm conversation, was testimony to that.

Finally, he looked up. "What are we waiting for? He needs to know as soon as possible. They all do."

"Not yet." She shook her head a few times to underscore that this wasn't negotiable. "I know I might only want to believe this is wrong, but mistakes happen. We need to know for sure before I tell him and put him through that particular hell."

"Hell?" Daniel inched back. "I'm not exactly the devil."

"You're not his father," she replied, then held up her hand as if she understood the technicality. "He was very, very close to Nico. As long as there is even a shadow of a doubt, I can't tell him or anyone else. Please, Daniel."

"Then I'll take the test."

"Thank God," she breathed on a ragged sigh. "Because if—"

"On one condition."

She lifted her brows. "You have a condition?"

"I want to know everything about him. Everything. Every memory, every single moment you can conjure up. I want to see every picture, video, yearbook, award, report card, and detention slip. I want to know what kind of friends he has, what sports he's played, what pets he's loved, what girls he's dated, what med schools he applied to, what places he's traveled. Everything. And I'm not waiting six weeks for that."

She stared at him.

"I want to know what I missed, Katie. I need to know what we missed."

"What *you* missed," she corrected. "He *had* a father. He and Nico were best friends. They were closer than any others in our family. Nico's passing gutted Nick."

Daniel winced, as if he felt Nick's pain.

"I'm sorry, but you can't swoop in and demand to be his father just because…because a condom failed forty-three years ago." A mix of anger and frustration welled up, along with a new fear. "He has a father already. Yes, he's dead, but you cannot replace Nico Santorini. I won't let you do that."

He shifted, reaching into his pocket to pull out a phone that must have vibrated. Looking at it, he nodded. "Rusty's test results are back. I'm going over there."

"Did you hear me, Daniel?"

"Of course I heard you. Did you hear me? I'll take the test if you'll allow me to know…my son."

"He's not…" But maybe he was. And she had to find out for sure. If those were his conditions, she'd meet them. "Okay. Fine. Then I have a condition, too." She stood, looking hard at him, placing her hand on his forearm to elicit the promise she wanted before he stood, too. "You can't tell anyone, not a single, living soul. When we reveal this to our families, it will be together and in the most loving way possible."

"I couldn't agree more." He eased his forearm

through her fingertips, slowly standing and taking her hand in his again. "Thank you, Katie."

"For…"

"For telling me."

"I wanted to tell you in the bakery, then again on Wednesday. But I was so scared."

She braced for his disappointment, or even a reprimand for waiting, but he only nodded with understanding, which just about turned her heart into a bowl of mush.

"I can imagine," he said. "It would have been tempting to hide this."

"Tempting, but impossible. For one thing, my conscience would have wrecked me. For another, Cassie would have told Nick. Or he'd have done a test himself. He's the first out of the four brothers to even ask about the results. People can't hide these things anymore."

"True." He drew her a little bit closer. "But more time could have passed. Hell, I could have passed. No one knows better than us how fleeting life can be."

She looked up at him, searching his face, feeling his pain. "My only consolation in this has been that Nico never knew. He'd have killed you."

"Really?"

"Or himself. I'm sure he couldn't have lived on an earth where Nick wasn't his biological son. Put yourself in his shoes. What if someone sat you down and told you Liam was the result of a faulty condom and a dorm-room liaison that your wife had with another man?"

He actually paled at the thought. "I see your point."

"I'm sure your wife wouldn't have loved it, either."

He considered that, cocking his head. "Annie? By now, she would have organized a joint family reunion, with get-to-know-you party games and nicknames for everyone." He gave a sad smile. "Annie was a the-more-the-merrier type, including kids. Especially kids."

Katie sighed, holding tight to the belief that no woman, not even Saint Annie, would have liked the idea that her husband had a child with another woman...and that woman was already pregnant the night they were introduced. No, no one would like that.

"Well, we have enough family to deal with," she said. "When we're both ready."

"And not a minute before," he promised, holding the door open for her.

"What's the word on Rusty?" she asked as they stepped into the cool air.

"I don't know. I'm going to find out now."

She slowed her step and tugged his hand lightly. "Do you want me to go home now?"

He turned to her, looking down to hold her gaze. "No." He sounded a little surprised at that. "I don't know what the night holds, and I'd rather not be alone. Would you stay?"

She should say no. She should go home, hash this out with Cassie, and start gathering the memories of Nick he wanted.

But the truth was, now that he knew, she wasn't quite ready to leave Daniel's side. And it had been a long time since anyone had needed her company.

"Of course."

Chapter Eleven

At the sound of Katie's footsteps, Daniel looked up from where he sat next to Rusty, who was rolled into his favorite bed in the den.

"I hope this was a good idea, bud," he whispered to his sleeping dog. "She thought maybe you needed company. It's helping me, so maybe it'll help you."

Rusty's only answer was a deep sigh and a flip of his head to face the doorway, which was sad, because normally he'd be up to investigate anyone who came into the house.

"We're in the den," he called to Katie. "Did you get her?"

"I sure did." He heard paws tapping on the kitchen floor as they came closer. "She came right to me, no hesitation, and only barked a little when I brought her out."

Katie appeared in the doorway, still wearing her coat, with Goldie right next to her.

"How's our patient?"

"Resting right here. Bring her over slowly."

She did, bending to slide her hand into the collar. "Nice and easy, Goldilocks," she whispered as they walked in.

At the sight of Rusty, Goldie froze for a moment and barked once. Rusty didn't lift his head, but his tail rose and fell and swished a few times. That was good enough for Daniel.

"Hey there, Goldie," he said, using an inviting voice to get her closer. "Come see your pal."

With Katie still holding her collar, Goldie came closer, getting up right near Rusty's face, but not making a sound. She sniffed his nose and neck, turned in a complete circle, sniffed again, then settled down with her belly facing his bed.

"Oh my gosh. She loves him," Katie said, folding next to the two dogs. "Isn't that the sweetest thing?"

He smiled at them both, and her. "Good call, Mrs. Santorini. What made you think of that?"

"Sick kids," she said without hesitation. "John always had something as a boy, so I sent Alex or one of the others in to watch TV or play a game."

"You didn't worry about spreading germs?"

She shrugged. "They spread anyway, but a sick kid gets better faster with a friend to cheer him up." She leaned over and stroked Rusty's head. "Isn't that right, big boy?"

Rusty didn't move, except to blink, then close his eyes. She looked up at Daniel, searching his face with the same tenderness she had for the dog. "And how are you feeling? Worried about him?"

"A little," he admitted. "The blood work was inconclusive. Molly just texted to say that John Rudolph, the radiologist I trust most, is out of town until tomorrow night, so I can't make any definitive guesses about the scans. It's quite possible Rusty has some gastroenteritis, not anything serious. We'll know in a day or two. Still, it was a tough day."

"Are you hungry?"

He thought for a moment, then realized he'd gone way beyond hungry. "Ravenous."

"Want me to make you dinner?"

"More than life itself, but I don't know what you'll find out there. We could order out."

She made a face. "What's in your pantry and fridge?"

"Your guess is as good as mine."

"Do you have lettuce, tomatoes, and maybe a cucumber, an olive or two, and a box of spaghetti in that kitchen?" she asked.

"I'm pretty sure you'll find most of that in there. But you'll also find menus for every restaurant in Bitter Bark that delivers."

She pushed up, and Goldie instantly rose, too, looking at her.

"You stay here, Goldilocks. You stay with Rusty."

After a second, the dog settled right back down, getting a pet of praise. Then Katie held her hand out for Daniel. "And I shall make you dinner."

He pushed himself up, but didn't let go of her hand. "I can't think of anything I'd like more than a kind and beautiful woman making me dinner." He cringed as soon as he said it. "Oh God, does that make me sexist?"

"Does it make me ageist for getting a little thrill out of the 'beautiful' part?" she volleyed back, turning to the kitchen.

He followed her. As if he could do anything else. "Surely you know it."

She lifted a shoulder as she opened the fridge. "I feel good and healthy for my age, but you know what's sexist? That you can be a silver fox, and I have to cover up my gray."

"Then don't. Grow it in. You'd still be beautiful. See anything good?"

"Plenty." She started pulling things from the produce drawer, handing them to him. "Including a man who thinks I'm beautiful and wants me to cook for him."

He laughed. "Katie, I have no doubt your husband thought you were beautiful."

"He did, but I rarely cooked for him. It would have been like painting for Rembrandt." She gestured to the counter. "Can you get me a cutting board, knives, a bowl, and whatever pasta you have on hand? Then, relax."

He'd already relaxed, he realized. So he followed instructions, loving her squeak of delight when he produced a box of spaghetti.

"Would you normally make yourself dinner on a night like this?" she asked as he lined it all up on the island for her.

"Nothing is normal about this day or night," he said, getting a wry, knowing smile in return. "Most Fridays, I eat in town because I've usually spent the day at the vet office. Then, if my mother needs a ride, I'll bring her home from choir practice and church dinner. If you weren't here, I'd likely grab a drink and sit in the living room for a one-sided conversation with Annie."

She angled her head, obviously touched by that. "Best I can do is some spaghetti and a two-sided conversation."

"That's perfect." He studied her for a moment, noticing the straightness of her shoulders, the sureness of her knife skills, the slight jut of her chin. "You know, you're stronger than I realized," he mused.

"You thought I was weak?"

"No." He considered his answer as he walked to the wine rack. "But you've been through hell today and show no signs of wear."

"Trust me, I'm worn to a frazzle on the inside."

"Then how about a glass of wine?"

"None for me. I'm driving back to Chestnut Creek after we eat, and I had Jameson's earlier. But don't let me stop you. What makes you think I'm strong?"

Once again, he deliberated the right answer, digging the corkscrew in but looking at her. "You could have run today, for one thing."

"And left you with a sick dog and a shock to your system?"

"I'm a vet," he reminded her. "So's my daughter. Sick dogs are what we do."

"It's different when it's your own. And there was the shock."

Which was slowly wearing off and becoming a whole new way of thinking. He popped the cork and poured a healthy glass, setting it on the island, close enough that she could share. "Help yourself, if you need a sip. Plus, you're welcome to stay here tonight in the guest suite."

"I'll go home after dinner." She picked up a

tumbler of water she'd already poured and held it up in a toast, so he took the wine. "Cheers."

"Let's drink to your strength," he said. "It's evident in how you've lived your life, how you managed this turn of events, and how you handle that knife."

She snorted. "Turn of events. There's the euphemism of the year. But thank you, Daniel. I'm going to hold on to that compliment for a long time."

He clinked the glass, but looked at her face. "You didn't know you were strong? A widow? A mother of five? A successful businesswoman? How could you feel like anything but a superwoman?"

She rolled her eyes a little with a scoffing laugh, but didn't answer, cutting carrots with precise strokes instead.

The silence intrigued him as the first sip of wine rolled around his tongue. "Is this a lifelong confidence issue, or is this a recent development? Because I remember you as a spunky and lively and maybe a little fearless eighteen-year-old."

"Years of taking care of a dying spouse wears a person down. Then years of picking up the pieces, only to have…"

"Some of them break again," he finished when she couldn't.

She looked up, a little pain around her eyes. "It does feel like my world cracked. Like the foundation isn't what it was. Like…I could lose another beloved family member."

"You won't lose Nick, will you? It's not like you kept him in the dark for years, or that he was denied a relationship with a father, if not his biological one."

She didn't respond right away, finishing the salad by tossing the greens and vegetables with a set of salad utensils he hadn't even known he owned. "The only thing Nick loves more than helping people is his family."

The words tapped his heart a little. "I get that."

"He's an amazing son, brother, and doctor."

Daniel felt a smile pull, tamping down pride he really had no right to feel. Nick could have learned all that from his own father, rather than inheriting such genes from Daniel. "Then I think you shouldn't worry about losing him, Katie. He'll need some time to get used to the idea, but then…"

Her look was sharp. "I don't think you understand how close Nick and Nico were, or that you don't get *used to the idea* that everything you know about yourself is wrong. You've gained a son, Daniel, but he's lost a father."

"Only if you let him look at it that way."

"He's a grown man. I don't tell him how to look at life anymore." She gave a dry laugh. "Not sure I ever did. He's been an independent thinker since the day he was born."

"Tell me about that," he said, lifting the wine glass for a drink he knew he might need. "Every detail."

"He's always thought for himself, that's all."

"I meant the day he was born. Tell me about that. Labor, delivery, everything." He heard the longing in his heart echoed in his voice. But he couldn't help it. He'd missed so much—starting with that day.

Again, she waited a long time before answering, "It wasn't pretty. Twenty-six hours of labor, and he was born with a broken collarbone."

"No."

"It's common, actually, from hard labor. Fixes itself, too."

"Weight and height?"

"A strapping eight and a half pounds and twenty-one inches. Full head of dark hair, which we thought was thanks to his Greek heritage."

"You have dark hair," he noted.

"So do you. Can you tell me where to find a pot I can boil pasta in?"

He took another swig of wine and slipped off the counter stool, heading to the cabinet. "Slept through the night?"

"At about a month."

He pulled out the pot. "First step?"

"One day shy of ten months."

"Whoa." He lifted his brow as he handed the pot to her. "Early."

She closed her fingers over his, pressing his palms against the cool metal edge of the pasta pot. "Don't make me go through every milestone, because it'll get repetitive. Nick was—*is*—perfect. Charming, well loved, respected, high-achieving, brilliant, and deeply caring about others. He did everything earlier, better, faster, and with more style than anyone. Oh, and he's drop-dead handsome. Don't make me spell it out."

He looked at her for a long time, tucking all this new information into a mental box he could open later and think about. But for now, she couldn't just stop with a sweeping assessment and no details.

"You promised," he reminded her.

"But you can't take credit for all of that."

"I'm not trying to. I'm trying to learn about him."

She pressed his hands harder. "I see the look in your eyes. Comparing him to your own sons. To yourself. Feeling smug."

"No," he replied firmly. "I'm trying to get a handle on who he is and who he's been. No comparisons, no smugness. I've already met Cassie, so I know the Santorini gene pool is swimming with greatness. I assume your other three sons are, too." He slipped one finger out from under to tap her hand and make a point. "Don't assume you know what I'm thinking or feeling, Katie."

Tipping her head in acknowledgment, she headed to the sink to fill the pot. "I feel like I'm betraying him," she said, so quietly he barely heard it over the water flow.

He stepped closer to lean against the counter. "You're betraying Nick? How so?"

"I'm betraying *Nico*," she clarified. "He's not here to prove some of that wonderfulness came from him, not you. He's not here to claim his influence over Nick. He's not here..." Her voice cracked, and she closed her eyes. "And it would kill him all over again if he was."

Without even thinking about it, he put his arm around her, pulling her into him as she turned off the water. "Stop, Katie. None of this should make you feel bad or like you're betraying Nico."

She let out a soft breath, but didn't look up at him.

"Hey." He put one finger under her chin and turned her face toward him, tilting it up to meet his gaze, ready to demand she tell him more. Everything. But then he saw that look again. It wasn't fear—the scary stuff was over now that he knew. No, it was pain, and he had no right to put that there with his demands. "Why don't we take a break from the Nick conversation?" he suggested.

"I thought you wanted to know everything."

"I do, but I also want to talk about something else that doesn't make you look far away and sad."

"I'm not far away or sad," she said. "I care about my family—those still with me and the husband who is gone—more than I care about taking my next breath."

"That caring is one of my favorite things about you." The admission slipped out without him really thinking about it, making her look up at him with an indecipherable look in her eyes. Maybe a warning. Maybe a question.

"You shouldn't have favorite things about me," she said.

Okay, a warning. "Why not?"

"Because we're already in dangerous territory. Favorite things and compliments and how close you are right now will really muck up some mucky waters."

He blinked in surprise, but didn't draw back. "How close…I'm standing?"

She took her finger and tapped his chest, then hers, then his. "Less than six inches."

"There's a distance rule?" He closed some of that air between them to make his point.

She merely looked at him, pinning him with those dark chocolate eyes flecked with gold. Had he ever noticed those gold flecks before? Because they were pretty.

Probably not the best time to mention that.

"Katie, we can be six or three or two inches apart. We share a bond few people have, and honesty is the only way we're going to figure out how to deal with it. Not only that, I'm sixty-one years old. I do not play games or mince words or walk on eggshells around people. I call it like I see it."

He watched her throat rise and fall as she listened, silent.

"And didn't we agree we'd be friends and have no expectations and spend a few weeks redecorating a room and sharing details of our respective wonderful marriages?"

She nodded, still silent.

"That hasn't changed. The only thing that's changed is…"

"Everything changed when I told you about Nick."

"Not everything. We're still—"

The kitchen door popped open, and they instantly separated, maybe a little too fast and guiltily, based on the flicker in his mother's eyes as she stepped inside the house.

"Oh, hello, lass," she said with a sweet smile. "I wasn't sure you'd still be here, what with Rusty and all." She set her big grandmotherly handbag on the table and looked at Daniel. "How is he?"

Rusty. Damn it all, he hadn't even thought about Rusty for the last ten minutes. Or Annie. Or anything. Just…Katie.

"He's hanging in there," he said quickly. "Nothing showed up on the tests. Not much of an appetite, though. Sleeping in the family room. Katie had the brilliant idea to bring Goldie in for company."

His mother's brow lifted as her gaze shifted past Daniel. "Really? It looks like they're up and about now, or were you too busy to notice?"

He tamped down a soft curse and turned his attention to the two dogs, standing side by side as if they'd been there all along, listening to the conversation. He bent over to pet them both.

"No dinner after choir practice tonight, Gramma?" he asked.

"No, the pastor's wife drove me back when three of the sopranos bailed. One hip failure, one arthritis flare-up, and one great-granddaughter's dance recital." When he rose, he caught his mother winking at Katie. "'Tis the way when your 'girlfriends' are all in their eighties."

Katie laughed. "I'm making pasta and salad, and you are more than welcome to join us, Mrs. Kilcannon."

Gramma Finnie gave a pretend scowl from behind her bifocals. "Not when ye call me that, lassie."

"But that's what I called you when I met you, remember?"

"Aye, I remember you. Came for dinner once and didn't eat a bite."

"I must have been nervous."

"Must have been Seamus who scared ye, lass. I'm the least frightening person in the world." She slipped out of her coat and hung it in the mud room off the kitchen, coming back in and rubbing the cold off her hands. "I'll go wash up for dinner. I'd love to join you, but you'll call me Gramma Finnie like every other living creature on this earth, includin' my own children."

After she left the room, Katie and Daniel shared a long look, both of them silent for a moment before she picked up the pasta water. "I'm glad she's going to join us," Katie said.

"Me, too," he said. Because a whole evening alone and things could suddenly get a whole hell of a lot more complicated. And while that might have been tempting a day ago, they couldn't risk anything more complicated than the hand they'd already been dealt.

For the next few minutes, he helped her finish dinner, set three places at the kitchen table, and eased them all into light conversation while they ate.

"Tell me about your plans for the living room, lass," Gramma said. "I'm a fan of that decoratin' channel on TV."

Katie grinned. "Me, too, except sometimes the houses all start to look too much alike. This home has so much personality and history, so I'd give the living room a fresh, clean look with new sofas, some shutters, a pretty new color on the walls. I do think the floors could be refinished." She glanced at Daniel. "That's what you thought this morning."

Was that only this morning? Daniel mused. It felt like a hundred years ago. One new son, one sick dog, and a hundred years. "I'm pretty much writing the checks and saying, 'Whatever you think.'"

"And you're painting," Katie reminded him.

"It sounds divine." Gramma beamed at her. "The Irish say, 'The best way to honor the past is to live well in the present.' Sometimes things need to change."

"Which isn't always easy," Katie said. "About a year after my husband died, I made the decision to move out of the large home where we'd raised the family. It was difficult sifting through all those memories and deciding what belonged in a three-bedroom townhouse and what belonged in the attic, with the kids, or at a charity. And whoa, my kids had opinions."

"Don't they all," Daniel mused, thinking of his conversation with Darcy.

"Tell me about your wee ones," Gramma Finnie said, putting a hand on Katie's arm.

"Well, not one of them is wee, that's for sure," she replied with a laugh.

"Do you have pictures?"

She hesitated for a moment, almost looking at Daniel, but then pushing up. "I do, on my phone. I'll get it now that we're done eating."

Daniel picked up his plate and Katie's, not anxious to look at Nick again, not with his mother's keen eyes on him. "You show them while I clean up," he said.

When she got her phone, she also grabbed her jacket and bag. But she tossed them on the counter and sat down next to Gramma Finnie to show her pictures.

"Oh, a Navy man," Gramma cooed when shown Theo, her youngest son. "Very handsome in that uniform."

"He is," Katie agreed, with pride in her voice he'd heard a thousand times in Annie's. "He's considering SEAL training, but hasn't decided yet. Whatever he does, it will turn out well. Theo was born under a lucky star."

"How old?"

"Thirty-three. And that's John, in the glasses, and his twin brother, Alex. They're both thirty-six."

"Sweet heavens, there are two of them."

"Identical twins that really are hard to tell apart if you don't know their personalities or John doesn't wear his glasses. But, believe me, in many ways they couldn't be more different."

"How so?" Gramma asked.

"John is a left-brained number cruncher who'd rather read a spreadsheet than a book, and Alex is a creative, passionate chef who lives for his next recipe discovery. They're both in Chestnut Creek and, along with Cassie, run the two Santorini's locations. Alex cooks at the downtown location and supervises the smaller, mall-based site."

"Are either of these handsome catches married?"

"None of my kids are yet."

Gramma looked at Daniel over the glasses that had slid down her nose. "Sounds like a job for the Dogfather," she teased.

"Well, at least he could give me some advice," Katie said. "I've tried to steer Cassie a few times, but none of the young men she's dated are Greek enough to suit her, and if they do come from the small, tight-knit Greek community in Chestnut Creek, she doesn't consider them wonderful enough."

"She has high standards," Gramma said.

"She had Nico as a father, and I'm pretty sure all she wants is a man exactly like him." Katie sighed. "But they are few and far between."

"Ahh." Gramma patted her arm. "The Irish say, 'To live in hearts we leave behind means that we never die.'"

"I like that," Katie said, staring at the phone, then clicking to the next picture. "Here's a shot of all of them together."

"Aye, a beautiful crew. Is that your oldest? Nicholas, is it?"

Daniel's stomach clenched as he turned on the faucet to rinse a plate.

"Just Nick. Actually, his name is Nico, like his father."

Not his *biological* father. Daniel stuffed the plate into the dishwasher, bending over to make sure he didn't give a thing away with his expression. But Gramma was staring hard at the screen.

"Is that the only picture? He's the doctor, right?"

"Mmm." She nodded. "He is a doctor and a very good one."

"That's a little blurry, though. Do you have another?"

Daniel watched as Katie slid her finger off the phone, her color deepening ever so slightly. Only he would notice that, or the fact that she sort of shook her head as if going through a thousand pictures wasn't worth it to find one.

She shouldn't be scared to show his picture to anyone, he thought, a tiny bit of irritation and pride tweaking. "Show her the one you showed me, Katie. From Thanksgiving."

"Oh yeah," she finally said. "Thanksgiving. Here it is."

Daniel paused in midrinse, watching his mother scrutinize the phone screen, angling it one way, then the other as she squinted at the image. He knew exactly what she saw on that screen. He'd glanced at it for only a few seconds, but the image of Nick Santorini was burned in his brain. The tilt of his head, the distinctive angle of dark brows, a set of dimples that were like two slashes at the side of a broad smile that lit his whole face.

The day with Rusty had turned things upside down, but he'd think about that picture a lot later tonight. Maybe Katie could send him a copy.

Or maybe she'd make him wait until he'd taken the test and proven his right to carry that photo.

"Oh, 'tis another fine lad," Gramma finally said. "Definitely a handsome one. How does a lad that good-looking stay single at… How old is he?"

"Working around the world and around the clock," Katie said, deftly answering one question but not the other, with a quick glance to Daniel. "But he's met someone, he says. So maybe not single for long."

Of course, his mother knew what year they'd dated, and she could do math. There'd be no way for her to know that Katie's wedding to Nico had been rushed, or any of the other timing details. Best to keep them all vague.

Daniel shook off his hands and came around the island. "Remarkable job, working for Doctors Without Borders. Not only do you have to be a great practitioner, you have to be a fearless adventurer."

"He is that," Katie said, reaching for the phone that Gramma reluctantly let go.

"You better hit the road if you're driving all the way to Chestnut Creek tonight," he said, reaching for her hand to guide her up. "Although the offer still stands. Guest room may not be decorated to your liking, but it's comfortable and clean."

"Thank you, but I have work at my office tomorrow and plenty to order for this job. I'll be back with samples and ideas, and once you've picked some you like, we'll head over to High Point to shop." She looked down to see Goldie had come over to give her leg a nudge. "Goodbye, my sweet girl. You take care of Rusty now."

"Looks like he went back to sleep," Daniel said. "And I should take Goldie back to the kennel."

She gave him a look that he instantly knew—he'd seen it on Annie's face a hundred times. "Unless you want to take her home with you," he said.

For a split second, she seemed to consider it, then shook her head. "I wouldn't know where to begin, but maybe she should stay with Rusty tonight."

He laughed softly and shared a look with his mother.

"And so it begins," she said in a singsong voice as she pushed up from the table.

"And so what begins?" Katie asked.

"A little something called foster failure," Gramma said, giving her a hug. "Thank you for a fine dinner, lass. I can't wait to see what you do with that room."

"I'll walk you to your car," Daniel said, leading her out to the drive with a light hand on her back.

Outside, it was clear and crisp, with a few hundred stars and a sliver of a moon.

She took a deep breath, putting her hand on his shoulder in a way that told him that was a steadying breath, not a head-clearing one.

"Are you all right?" he asked.

"That was harder than I thought it would be," she whispered. "She had no idea she was looking at her

grandson. I mean, maybe. *Probably* her grandson."
She gave him a pleading look that he fully understood.

"I'm going to arrange to take the test tomorrow,
and I'll contact Bloodline.com to see if I can pay a
premium to rush the results."

"Good, because…" She looked up, her eyes misty.
"I felt like I was lying to her without saying a word. A
lie of omission, if you will. When she finds out, she'll
wonder why I didn't tell her then and there."

"Because it's not something you casually drop into
conversation," he assured her. "We'll get the
confirmation and tell everyone then. No more lies, and
we'll get this done in as short a time as possible."

"How will she feel if she finds out I showed her
that picture and didn't tell her?" she asked. "She'll
despise me."

He shook his head. "My mother isn't capable of
hate. It's not in her nature. She is the very definition
of unconditional love."

Katie sighed and closed her eyes. "I've never had a
mother or mother-in-law like that."

"Well, now you have one," he said, making her
eyes flash. "I mean, with Nick as her grandson, my
mother will bring you into this family and make you
Irish by association."

Her smile was wistful. "You make it sound easy.
But people are not going to be happy."

He turned her slightly and put both hands on her
shoulders, adding some pressure that he hoped was
comforting. "Katie Rogers Santorini, listen to me."

She looked up, her eyes wide, her lips parted as if
she wanted to say something, but couldn't.

"You are not to blame for the way this happened. I

was there in 1976, and I know the timing, and I know how you could make the very simple and safe assumption that Nick is Nico's son. And when we get unassailable confirmation, if this website is accurate and dependable, we'll figure out how and when to tell everyone, including Nick, together."

She bit her lip. "We will?"

"I wouldn't make you go through this alone."

She leaned closer, letting her forehead bump his chin. "Thank you. I'm so grateful for your attitude today."

"My attitude?" He inched back and gave her a *get real* look. "I was a complete jerk in the square this afternoon."

"You were in shock, and then Rusty got sick."

"Don't forgive me that easily. I shouldn't have pushed you away. You proved that today by showing up in my office."

She gave a soft half smile. "I hope Nick has inherited your ability to forgive."

"I hope he's inherited yours."

They looked at each other for a few seconds as the distant sound of barking from the kennels carried on a clean, light winter breeze. In that moment, Daniel felt something shift in his heart, like a little tectonic plate moving when he'd thought it would always stay exactly where it'd been.

True forgiveness for the years lost with a son? Maybe. Hope that they could heal the hurt that would happen because of this news? Yeah, that, too. But maybe it was his heart, opening a little.

"Uh, Katie," he murmured, looking down at the space between them. "This is less than six inches apart."

"Yeah, that's…bad."

Except, right then, under the stars and in the cold Carolina night air, it didn't feel bad at all. He leaned forward and brushed her cheek, hoping for a casual, friendly non-kiss goodbye, but when their cheeks touched, there was nothing casual about it. A little electric. A little surprising. And way too complicated.

They both separated at the same instant, as if she must have had the exact realization.

"Watch that Pinterest board," she said as he reached for the handle to open her door.

"The modern-day equivalent of 'I'll call you,'" he joked, making her laugh as she slipped behind the steering wheel and he carefully closed her door.

When the lights of her car finally disappeared down the drive, and the chill of the night penetrated his thin shirt and jeans, he let out a sigh that probably sounded as confused as he felt.

Just his luck. He finally met a woman who intrigued and attracted him, and she came with impossible baggage: a son that carried his DNA.

Walking back to the house, he pulled open the door and stopped short at the sight of his mother standing with her arms crossed, her lips pursed, and her eyes…filled with tears.

"What's wrong? Rusty?" A white-hot flash of horror hit him as he looked down for the dog and found him curled under the table with Goldie next to him. "What's the matter?"

His mother swallowed, clearly having a difficult time speaking. "I need to show you something."

"Okay."

She uncrossed her hands and held out a piece of paper—no, a photograph. Old as the hills, probably from the 1950s, based on the tone and trim, giving it to him without a word of explanation.

"What is this?"

"Look at it."

A slow, hot tendril of worry curled up his chest as he tried to breathe, but couldn't. "Who is it?" He frowned at the picture, which was a little blurry. "I need my reading—"

She handed them to him. "I knew you would say that. Look at it, Daniel."

The insistence in her voice kicked him as he slid the glasses on and easily saw the image of a young man with dark hair and a wide smile. He had two deep lines for dimples and brows that framed his eyes in a singular, distinctive way.

"Who is this?" he asked, his voice thick.

"'Tis your uncle Paddy. My oldest brother, Patrick Brennan."

He tore his gaze from the picture, knowing exactly where this was going. Exactly. How on earth could he ever underestimate Finola Brennan Kilcannon?

One more piece of evidence that there was no "maybe" about Nick.

"Sit down," he said gently, putting a hand on her shoulder.

She bit her lip. "So it's true?"

"She didn't know," he said, the need to defend Katie shockingly strong. "She just found out. Don't hate her."

"Hate her?" Her eyes flashed as she pressed her brother's picture to her heart. "I have another grandson.

'Tis a miracle, I tell you. An absolute miracle. I can't ever remember bein' so happily surprised." She blinked a tear down her wrinkled cheek. "I love him already."

He looked at her for a long time, realizing that she'd put all his feelings into words. "That makes two of us," he whispered.

Chapter Twelve

Kate picked up her phone, stared at it, checked messages, stared at those, then put the phone down, hating the thud of disappointment that hit her stomach.

Was she literally watching the phone and willing a man to call? What was wrong with her?

Or was something wrong with Daniel?

She leaned back in her office chair, closing her eyes and thinking about those last few minutes that took place on Friday night.

Had she been imagining…things? Feeling chemistry where there shouldn't be any? Seeing attraction and interest in his eyes when he should be consumed with anger, frustration, and even fear? Both of them leaning into an awkward hug because…it seemed to be more right than wrong?

The questions had plagued her, waking her up in the middle of the night or dancing through her thoughts when she tried so hard to think about something else. She longed to talk to someone about it, but Cassie was her go-to girl for any and all emotional issues, and she'd have a cow if she even suspected Katie was feeling…things.

Things. What did that even mean at their age? In their incredibly unique situation? With eleven kids between them?

And why hadn't he called since Friday?

He'd seen the images she'd added to the Pinterest board, but no text or message or phone call. There was no reason he would or should, but she wanted him to. Which was wrong on so many levels.

What was going on with Rusty? With Goldie? With *them*?

Pushing back from her desk, she turned to look out the window, seeing a bleak winter sky over the small backyard behind her condo. She left the office and wandered through the rooms of her small but perfectly appointed townhouse, the shelter that once seemed like the ideal way to escape the memories of the home she and Nico had shared for so many years. Where they'd raised kids, celebrated Christmases, drank coffee on Sunday mornings, and then…faced years of illness.

Those were the memories she had needed to get away from when she moved out of the house and into the condo. Here, she'd made everything bright and clean and white and new…letting go of long nights and hospital beds and dreary dealings with the inevitable death of her beloved husband.

She'd tossed all the memory tags of sickness and death, replaced them with hope and happiness. And still that hadn't filled or healed the hole in her heart. Sometimes, only family could do that.

She grabbed her bag, jacket, and keys and headed to the garage to drive to town. Instead of soothing her, the fifteen-minute trip through the windy, tree-lined hills of western North Carolina gave her more time to think. About Daniel. About Nick. About Nico. And back to Daniel again.

In the heart of downtown Chestnut Creek, she parked behind the red brick building where she'd spent some of the best years of her life. Santorini's Deli, arguably one of Chestnut Creek's most popular restaurants, sat one block away from Central Avenue. Large plate-glass windows welcomed anyone passing by to come in, slide into a red leather booth, and dive into some creamy spinach spanakopita or tender, grilled souvlaki.

The food was great, but the main restaurant floor held little interest to Katie, who'd only worked there part time when they were in a jam after Nick was born. By the time Yiayia and Papu retired, she had four children and no time to work at Santorini's, and they'd moved to the house.

It was the second floor where Katie had her best and happiest memories with Nico. Climbing out of her car, she glanced up to the old casement windows that lined the two-room apartment. Behind those windows, a young married couple had lived, laughed, and loved so damn hard, it hurt to think about it.

No, their marriage hadn't been perfect. They'd fought, like most couples. Nico had had a flashing, quick temper, but had apologized as easily as he'd angered, and when Alex and John had been born five weeks premature, they had had some terrifying days up there. But mostly, it had been solid and healthy and she'd give her right arm for one more day and night in that little apartment.

But that was not to be. Now, the apartment was used as the business office, where John worked ordering supplies, running payroll, and managing the restaurant business like the well-oiled machine Nico had built it to be.

Alex was usually down in the kitchen, supervising the menu or planning a catering job. Cassie was often out meeting with an event client, but would breeze in with exciting news of what she had planned and a demand that her brother make her dolmades, because she lived for his stuffed grape leaves.

Using a key she'd carried for as many years as she and Nico had been together, Katie unlocked the side entrance and slipped up the back stairs, each footfall a soft assault on her heart.

Talk about memory tags. They'd kissed in this very stairwell the night Daniel had dropped her off to see Nico, who'd lived alone upstairs. They'd cried happy tears at her decision to defy her mother and stay with him. And they'd made love...with no protection and every hope that they were making a baby.

She paused for a moment, digging deep for the memory of that night, that reunion moment, that blissful surrender that nearly cost them both their families, but gave them a lifetime of love. Clinging to the handrail, she let herself fall into the past, conjuring up Nico's face and seeing...nothing.

She squeezed her eyes tight and forced her brain to cooperate. Eyes as black as a starless sky. That prominent nose, long lashes, and sweet smile.

None of it would come to mind. All she saw was the darkness of her lids and...

"Oh God, no." She wasn't ready to replace that memory with a new man. She wasn't—

"Mom?"

With a gasp, she popped her eyes open and stared at Alex, who had Nico's dark good looks and the ever-present slightly stained apron.

"Wow, it's so great to see you." Without hesitation, he took a few steps up and wrapped her in his strong, secure arms, his clipboard stuffed with handwritten notes on recipes pressed against her back. "You never come here anymore."

She eased back and looked at him, stroking the soft beard exactly like the one John had. They both started growing a beard the day Nico died. They kept them short and trimmed, but refused to shave in honor of their bearded Greek father.

"It's never easy to come here," she admitted.

"Mom." He hugged her. "We love when you do. And you're just in time for a management meeting. Come on up."

Above them, a door swung open. "Any day, Alex." Cassie's voice came down the stairs, followed by the sight of her face as she swung out to look down. "Oh, Mom! What are you doing here?"

"Rumor has it there's a management meeting."

"There is, and man, could I use some help on the side of reason. Come on." She waved her up, then turned toward the door. "John, Mom is here, and I am no longer a minority of one."

Alex led her up, a hand on her back.

"You think I'm going to run away," she teased him.

"It happens."

"I'm sorry," she whispered to her son. "I know I should come here more often and take more of a role in your business."

"Our family business," he corrected, adding slight pressure. "We don't want you to do anything that makes you sad, Mom, but we love when you're here. Also, you can talk some sense into your daughter, who is acting nonsensical today."

"About what?"

"Bitter Bark."

"What?" Her heart hitched.

"We're zeroing in on the next location, and that email you forwarded to us from your friend had some really encouraging numbers."

"Like what?"

"You know I don't do numbers unless they're in a recipe, but John is crowing. Come on."

Her first thought when she entered the apartment was that she shouldn't have stayed away so long. For one thing, it took true imagination to see the rooms as anything but a work space. Every shred of furniture and function as a home was gone. Desks, file cabinets, storage bins, and supplies lined the walls, and at some point, someone had painted the rooms a beautiful shade of sage. And ripped out the carpet to replace it with laminate—and good stuff, too, that didn't look fake.

"I didn't know you redecorated up here," she said, rounding the desk to give John a hug.

He looked up from his calculator, adjusted his glasses, and gave her a crooked smile that looked exactly like the one she'd just received from Alex. "We did that two years ago, Mom. After Dad died."

"I've been here since then," she said.

"But you were in a fog." He stood up and hugged her. "Maybe you're out of the fog now."

Maybe. She tightened her hug, then came around to sit on a sofa she swore she'd never seen before, next to Cassie, who gave her a smacker on the cheek and whispered, "You sure you want to be here?"

Katie nodded. "I do. I'm sorry it took so long."

"What inspired you?"

She shrugged. "I needed to get out of the house and see you guys."

"This'll inspire you," Alex said, producing a plate with a shiny, flaky piece of baklava in one hand and a steaming cup of heavily creamed coffee in the other. "I made the baklava an hour ago. It's as close to flawless as I could get."

She took the plate and nodded her thanks when he set the coffee on the table in front of her. "You're sweet."

"That's sweet," he corrected. "I'm glad to see you here."

She settled in and took a bite of Alex's creation, not able to stop herself from moaning with pleasure, getting a smug, secret smile from him.

For a moment, she let the contentment of the flavor and the moment warm her, looking at three of her five children with a sudden and surprising ache of love as they started up a conversation.

Alex, who showed his love with food, like his father. John, who masterminded business, like his father. Cassie, who ran on emotion and passion, like her father.

Missing was Theo, a born protector, like his father.

170

And Nick...the healer, the doctor, the empathetic caretaker...like his *biological* father.

"So, doesn't that sound like a great deal?" John asked, forcing Katie to mentally play back what they'd said while she was musing.

"It's not a great deal," Cassie answered for her. "Yes, the rent on this Hoagies & Heroes property in Bitter Bark is lower, but county taxes there are higher. And it's a smaller town, which limits the hiring population. And there are several established restaurants to compete with for catering."

"But look at the numbers." John tapped his laptop screen and turned it as if they could all read his minuscule spreadsheet. "We'd break even much faster there than in Holly Hills or Crestview."

"I love the Crestview location," Cassie said. "It's on a nice side street—"

"Less foot traffic," John interjected.

"And there's already a chain deli one block away in Crestview," Alex added. "Too close and too competitive."

"Your food will blow a chain out of the water," Cassie said.

"Not to mention this property is a sandwich shop, so the food setup is there," John said. "If they're willing to do some reno, we could expand and turn it into a real Santorini's, and the lease has an option to buy."

"To buy?" Cassie nearly choked. "You want to own property there now?"

"What do you have against Bitter Bark?" John asked her. "I know it wasn't on the short list, but the demographics are impressive, and that guy, Mom's friend who's on the Economic Development

Commission? The growth numbers he supplied are impressive. That town is booming, and there really isn't direct competition. The location is central, and the price is right."

Cassie threw Katie a look that hung somewhere between a plea for a lifeline and *I told you so*.

Was Daniel the reason Cassie was so opposed to Bitter Bark? Didn't she realize that once this all came out, he'd likely be a part of their lives in one way or another?

"I like the town," Katie said when they all looked at her for a fourth opinion. "It's a lot like Chestnut Creek and has a nice, homey feel to it, but still attracts a lot of tourists. It's close enough to the mountains to have great views and year-round activities, but they aren't a ski town like Chestnut Creek, so they don't live or die by the weather, like we do."

"There's still a place in Holly Hills," Cassie added, obviously sensing she was losing this argument. But why was she arguing at all? The money, location, and demographics sounded very smart, and if Cassie was anything, she was a shrewd businesswoman.

"One bad Christmas season in Holly Hills and you're DOA." John shook his head. "I don't want a town that's built on one thing, and they have an elf parade, for crying out loud."

"They'll make me add Christmas gyros to the menu."

"They'll make you add *bark*lava in Bitter Bark," Cassie said. "Did you run the cost of that special insurance for businesses that allow dogs in? Because you'll need it to compete in that town."

"It's a nominal amount, far offset by the break on the rent and increase in foot traffic."

John turned to Katie. "I think that friend of yours had something to do with getting us that price. The architect on the project is his daughter-in-law."

"Small-town graft and corruption," Cassie mumbled under her breath.

They all turned to look at her, and Katie added a warning glare.

"You know that's not true," Katie said. "You met Daniel Kilcannon and his whole family, including the architect, who happens to be an extremely talented professional. They're not the graft-and-corruption types."

"Seriously." John leaned over his desk, his dark eyes pinned on his sister. "What's up with you, Cass? I can normally count on you being the voice of reason in big decisions."

She took a slow breath, sliding her fingers into her thick black hair to pull it up and off her face as she often did when she didn't have a witty comeback or rapid-fire response. Again, her gaze landed on Katie, almost challenging her to say something.

Good God. Here and now? Katie looked right back at her and stayed silent. They'd agreed not to share this with anyone yet.

"It's that Daniel guy," Cassie finally said. "He...and Mom...have a history."

John's head whipped up from the calculator, and Alex leaned forward. "A history?" they said in perfect unison, like the identical twins they were.

"Ancient history," Katie said quickly, but the blood surged to her face, warming her cheeks, making her look like a liar...since she kind of was. But she sure as heck couldn't blurt out the truth. Not yet. Not until she knew for sure. And even then, Nick would have a right to know first.

"Wait. Wait." Alex's dark brows pulled in a frown. "Are you like…is this guy… Don't tell me you're dating, Mom."

"I'm not—"

"Oh, no wonder we're getting a deal." Alex puffed a quick breath. "No, thanks. I'm not selling my mother for some lecherous old—"

"Alex! He's not lecherous or old, and you're not *selling* me." She choked on the word, not sure if she should laugh or cry.

"You should have told us you have a vested interest." John's cool monotone was the opposite of his brother's, but Katie knew that meant he was just as hot on the subject. "And that he's more than a friend."

"He is *not* more than a friend." Katie sat up straighter to make her point, glancing at Cassie for support, but her daughter nibbled on her lower lip and pretended to concentrate on pulling a thread from the man-made hole in her ripped jeans.

The truth was, Daniel *was* more than a friend, but certainly not in the way they were presuming. Clarifying that now wasn't an option, but it probably wouldn't hurt to start laying the groundwork for the real fireworks.

"We dated during those few months I went to Vestal Valley College."

"Dated…how?" John asked. "Briefly? Casually? Meaningless or serious?"

She stared at him, trying to decide how to answer. Briefly, yes. Casually, kind of. Neither meaningless nor serious, but a child might have been the result. Oh Lord.

She pushed up to leave, the need to run from the problem pressing hard. "This has nothing to do with your business decision," she said. "I didn't mean to barge in—"

"No, Mom, wait." John was up as soon as she was.

"I'm sorry," Alex said. "I was out of line."

"Don't go." Cassie reached for her, too, her gaze softer now. "Nobody meant to make you take off."

She looked from one to the other, the genuine love in their eyes easy for a mother to see. For anyone to see. "You're just being protective," she said quickly. "But it's not necessary. I've never loved anyone but your father and never will."

Alex's dark gaze relaxed, and John actually sighed with relief.

"So, our picking this Bitter Bark location wouldn't be a conflict for you?" John asked.

"A conflict?" Katie smiled. They had no idea what was about to hit them. She rooted around for the right answer, but didn't know what to say.

Cassie stood and came next to her. "I think John means if anything were to happen with Daniel Kilcannon, anything at all, and it didn't go, you know, well...no one would want you to have to go to Bitter Bark on a regular basis, or even for us to be there, if it would be awkward."

Katie searched her daughter's face, grateful for the save and clearly understanding the subtext of Cassie's words.

"I don't have to frequent any of the satellite locations," she finally said, sliding her bag onto her shoulder. "But you should all make the best decision for the business and leave me out of it."

"Well, could you tell us what you think that decision would be?" John asked. "Maybe what you think Dad would have thought of this town full of dogs?"

"And this ex...beau?" Alex added, throwing a look at Cassie. "Didn't they call them that back then?"

Cassie rolled her eyes. "Yeah, if Mom was in college in the 1870s, not the 1970s."

The boys laughed, but Katie was still thinking about John's question. What *would* Nico want from this awful situation? "I think..." She considered her answer for a long moment, looking from one face to the next.

But suddenly, the one she saw in her mind's eye was different, older, and still familiar.

Keep them close.

Nico had made the request a thousand times in those last few months. He didn't want his children to drift apart as adults, or lose the great Greek family bond they shared. He asked for very few things on his deathbed, but he wanted that, and he wanted the business to always be owned and run by a Santorini.

And he wanted her to find love again.

"Your father would want you to make the decision that you all agree on, so there's no internal battles, and he'd want you to work together to make it succeed."

"Non-answer," Alex accused, but he added a smile to let her know it was a partial tease.

"Well, I don't know how to help you, then," she admitted. "And I'd really like to. I wish I had more to offer for this business decision."

"I have an idea." Cassie stood next to her. "Why don't you help by spending a little more time over there, since you're doing some work for him anyway? Eat at Hoagies & Heroes, do a little snooping around about how their business is doing, see if there are any catering opportunities, and report back?"

Katie searched her face, trying to psych out Cassie's motive for the suggestion, but she saw only love, concern, and honesty on her daughter's face. Cassie knew how Daniel had taken the news, since they'd talked about it at length on Saturday when they'd had lunch together.

"That's a good plan," John said.

"Just don't spend *too* much time with the guy," Alex added with a teasing smile.

She angled her head in question. "Why not, Alex?"

"Because..." He stood and put his hands on her shoulders. "I'd have to kill him if he hurt you."

She laughed. "You are your father all over again."

"Thank you," he said. "There is no higher compliment." He pulled her in for a quick hug. "We all love you, Mom. You deserve to be happy after what you went through with Dad being sick. You never gave up. You never ran away. You stuck with him through the worst times, and we all know that. You should be happy."

"Happy, but not...with anyone else?"

He searched her face for a long time. "Would that make you happy?"

She suddenly realized how much she wanted them to like—to really care about—Daniel. Wouldn't that make this whole situation easier when the truth came out? But it wasn't something she could force.

"Right now, seeing you kids working together, thriving, making the business grow is all I need to be happy." From the side of her handbag, a noisy melody announced a call, and she couldn't help how quickly she grabbed her phone. And tried not to show a flicker of disappointment when the caller ID read the name of a furniture store.

"Oh, and a call that tells me the sectional I want is in stock makes me happy. Gotta take this." She blew a kiss to all of them. "Get back to work, kids. I'll see you soon."

She slipped out and was halfway down the stairs and ready to tap the phone to take the call when Cassie caught up with her.

"Mom. Wait. Please."

On a sigh, she let the call go to voice mail and turned to her daughter. "What's wrong?"

"Everything, judging by the look on your face. Is he still taking the test? Being cool about it? What's the status? I haven't heard much from you since we had lunch."

"I haven't heard anything. In fact, not a word from him since I left his house on Friday evening."

Cassie frowned, her ink-black eyes scanning Katie's face for a tell. "And you're disappointed about that?" she guessed.

Oh yes, she was terrible at hiding her feelings, especially from someone who knew her as well as Cassie did. "I suppose I really liked the idea of not being alone in this whole thing."

"You have me."

"You're not quite as invested in the outcome as Daniel and I are," she said. "And frankly, you're right.

We do have a history. We share a timeline, of sorts. I didn't hate the idea of going through this with him, not as distant acquaintances, but as friends. I really like the idea. Don't take this the wrong way like your brothers did, but I really like *him*. As a friend," she emphasized again. "So I'm a little sad I haven't heard a word from him."

The moment the admission was out, she felt better. At least, she felt like she'd nailed the cause of her restlessness and the ache in her chest.

"Then call him."

Katie widened her eyes. "I don't really have a legit business reason to yet. That sectional is worth a look, but I really should wait until—"

"Call him, Mom. Pick up the phone and tell him what you just told me. Not about the sectional, about being friends through this."

She let out a sigh and shook her head. "I'm from a different generation."

Cassie let out a soft hoot. "The girls-don't-call-boys generation? Yeah, long dead. But you're still alive and kicking, Katie Santorini. And if you need him to be your pal during this time, then call him and tell him that." Cassie reached into Katie's bag and grabbed the phone. "Want me to dial?"

"What would I say?"

She shrugged. "Hello? How are you? Did you spit in the tube yet, and do you want to see the sectional, and can we go hang out at Hoagies & Heroes, so I can check it out for my kids?"

Laughing, she took the phone and gave her daughter a nudge back upstairs. "You make it sound so easy."

"It can be easy," Cassie assured her, leaning in to give a kiss, but as she did, Katie took her shoulders so she could look right into Cassie's bottomless black eyes.

"I love you," Katie said softly. "And I would be lost without you."

"I love you, too, Mom. We all do. We want you to be happy. And if that means this guy is your friend through all this, then you need to call him."

"Okay."

With one more kiss, Cassie took off upstairs, leaving Katie in the stairwell. After a moment, she walked outside, stared at her phone, and hovered her finger over her contacts list.

Of course she could call Daniel and not feel like a teenage girl chasing a boy. Of course he'd be warm and receptive to her call.

But if she was entirely honest with herself, she was scared that *friends* wouldn't be enough for her with Daniel Kilcannon. And it *had* to be.

As long as she remembered that, she should be fine. Taking a breath, she tapped his name and made the call, not surprised when he answered almost immediately.

"Hi, Katie." Of course his greeting was warm and genuine. They were friends. "I've been thinking about you."

And just the way he said it, her stomach got a little fluttery. *Come on, Katie.*

"Same," she replied. "In fact, I wondered if you were ever going to call me again."

He hesitated a few seconds, long enough for her to know the answer wasn't going to be completely casual and off the cuff. "Of course I was. I needed a few days to gather my wits."

Her heart bounced around in her chest a little. "And did you?"

"Yes," he said simply. "What are you doing this afternoon?"

Oh boy. "Nothing urgent. Why?"

"You're in Chestnut Creek?"

"Smack dab in the middle of downtown, as a matter of fact."

"I'm home. Are you familiar with Elk Knob State Park?"

She laughed at the question, already walking to her car with a bounce in her step that had definitely not been there on the way in. "I think I've taken my kids on at least ten hiking field trips there, so the answer is yes."

"It's halfway between us. Meet me at the western entrance near the Beech Tree Trail. Is it too cold for you to hike and eat outside?"

She squinted up at the sunshine, bathed in the warmth of a rare sixty-degree day and rays of hope she couldn't deny. "I love that idea," she said.

"I'll bring lunch and see you in about an hour?"

"That sounds wonderful." She tried to keep the happiness toned down, but might not have been too successful. "Can you bring Goldie?"

He laughed. "I have to if I'm bringing Rusty. They hate to separate."

"I can't wait to see her." *And you.*

"Oh, and Katie?"

"Yes?"

"Just a word of warning. My mother guessed after one look at Nick's photo."

She froze midstep, and all that bounce and happiness oozed out of her like air from a balloon. "What?"

"Evidently, Nick's the spitting image of my uncle Paddy from Ireland."

Which erased that last shred of hope that this was a big mistake. "Oh." The single syllable came out a little strangled.

"My mother can be trusted with your life and every secret."

"Does she hate me?"

He laughed out loud. "No. But her reaction really made me think, and that's why I needed a few days to get my head together, as we used to say in the good ol' 1970s."

"What was—"

"I'll tell you in person. See you at Elk Knob."

"Okay. See you soon." She tapped the phone and stood stone-still in the sunshine, but despite the warmth, she suddenly felt a little cold and scared inside.

Chapter Thirteen

The beech trees that lined Daniel's favorite trail in Elk Knob State Park were so bare that the sun streamed right through them and onto the hard ground plastered with dead leaves. Cool, clean, mountain air, a temperature a few degrees shy of fifty, and a complete absence of any other hikers, dogs, or schoolchildren combined to give Rusty and Goldie the two-mile hike of their dreams.

They trotted along, side by side, one stopping when the other did, their matching red coats gleaming in the sunshine.

Daniel had zero complaints as well. But that might have had a lot to do with the fact that, like Rusty, he had a friend to walk with. Next to him, Katie kept the pace, her hands deep in the pockets of her parka, and her brown suede hiking boots moving at an easy clip. Since they'd met and started their hike a few minutes ago, she hadn't pressed to continue their phone conversation. Mostly, Katie seemed to take in the beautiful setting, thanked him for the invitation, and made a fuss over Rusty.

"He's really bounced back," she said as they watched him trot a few feet in front of them.

"He's himself again," Daniel assured her. "We still haven't found the underlying reason for him to have had a seizure, since none of the scans or tests showed anything at all."

She looked up with a slight frown. "Is it possible it's just because he's a senior dog?"

"Possible, but I look for a clinical issue that might have caused it. If it doesn't happen again, then he probably ate something that seriously disagreed with him. If it does, we'll take him to a specialist."

"I think he found his specialist," she said, pointing to Goldie.

"Not sure what's going to happen when she's ready to be adopted," he said.

"You'd actually let her go once she trains?" She sounded flabbergasted. "You'll break his heart."

He threw her a look. "Maybe you should take her."

"I…" She shook her head. "I've never had a dog. Turtles, hamsters, and a snake once when Theo was going through a stage, but I don't know a thing about dogs."

"You're a natural, Katie. She comes to you first."

"Second, after Rusty." She studied Goldie's mahogany-colored tail as it tick-tocked with happiness. Every few steps, Goldie leaned over as though she were going to whisper in Rusty's ear, then nudged him with her nose, or gave him a lick. "No, I don't think I could do it."

"You sure?"

She nodded, silent. He knew from a lifetime of experience that people had their reasons for not wanting a dog, and often they were private. He respected that.

"I get it," he said. "Anyway, we're struggling with her."

"How so?"

"An aggressive golden retriever is very rare. One that can't be trained easily is also rare. She must have had a trauma with another dog at a very young age, and no one properly socialized her. So, having her at Waterford, even if she was in the house, is a problem. Among my six kids, I think there are at least nine family dogs, and they treat my home as if it's theirs. Shane's been working with her, but he's a little frustrated. If that dog whisperer can't fix her, she can't be fixed."

"So what will happen to her?" She sounded scared to even ask the question, and he put a reassuring hand on her back.

"Oh, Garrett will find someone, I promise. But they can't have other dogs, and they have to be able to work with her for those times when she's around dogs. It's a very strange idiosyncrasy for a retriever, I have to say. But she's been through something."

"She watched the person she loved the most die," Katie whispered. "That changes you."

"No kidding." He didn't really want to say more on that subject, because it was sure to ruin a bone-deep happiness that had resided in his chest for days, and that's what he really wanted to tell her today. He wasn't sure how she'd take it, so he was waiting for the perfect moment.

"Did you come here with Annie?" she asked.

"To be honest, we didn't, no. Only with the kids

when they were little, and like you said, I think every one of them had a hiking trip with school or scouts at some point. But Rusty has plenty of trails at home to walk. I only started coming here after she died, mostly because my pre-dawn walks with him at Waterford Farm are too heavy with memories. This is a place I came to escape and...mourn." Bawl his eyes out was more accurate. "And Rusty loves it here, so it's become one of our favorite places to come and think."

"Think about..."

"Things," he said.

"Like this thing with Nick?"

He laughed. "We're going to have to give it a better handle than 'this thing with Nick' or 'this turn of events' or 'our little problem.'"

"I never called it 'our little problem,'" she replied. "It's not little."

"And it's not really a problem."

She slowed her step and looked up at him. "Well, it's not exactly a happy surprise."

Except...it was.

Ever since Daniel had talked into the night with his mother, he felt great about being Nick Santorini's father. Not only had the resemblance to his long-dead uncle feel like the only real confirmation he needed, his mother's unabashed enthusiasm about a new member of the family had been infectious—and absolutely right.

The minute he'd stopped fighting the shock and disbelief, Daniel had had a hard time wiping the smile off his face or managing not to tell everyone he encountered.

I have another son.

He couldn't stop saying those words to himself. But he knew he'd have to tread carefully with Katie. "The truth is," he said, "I'm kind of excited about it."

"Excited?"

"Yes." And he wasn't going to be shy or coy about that, just careful. "How could I not be excited about the prospect of getting to know another son?"

She blinked at him. "What if he doesn't want to get to know you?"

He hated the punch in the gut that came with that question. "We'll cross that bridge, as they say."

"When we know for sure."

"Katie. After seeing my uncle's picture, I think we know."

"You *think* we know. And honestly, I think so, too. But a seventy-year-old photograph is hardly the solid confirmation I'd imagine a doctor and man of science would demand before lives are upended."

"Would you like to see the picture?" he asked.

She stopped and closed her eyes. "Do I want to?"

"If you want to continue to cling to that kernel of hope that this is all a mistake, then no. You're welcome to wait until we have the results from the test I took, which we could have in a month."

"It really takes longer than that."

"I spent a lot of time on the phone with the highest-level executive I could get to at the company, and she really did promise to expedite the results, considering the situation."

"You told her?"

"I had to make the company understand how important this was, and she assured me that ours wasn't the first case like this. In fact, they have a small division that personally handles situations like this. Cassie could call them and get a private representative to assure her that Nick's results are not a mistake."

Her jaw opened. "Did you do that, too?"

"I did, and the woman I talked to, Hannah Stavos, was confident the results are correct."

Katie gave a dry laugh. "A Greek, too. She'd know how important this is to us."

"It's important to everyone," he said. "They have a small department of specialists for NPE cases."

She gave him a questioning look.

"Not parent expected," he explained. "It's a thing now, with these DNA testing sites. So she asked if I wanted her to reach out to your family, to you or your daughter, and I told her I'd ask you first."

"My, you've been busy."

"I promised you I'd make it a priority. I know you want that, and I know the picture won't be enough."

"Can I see it?"

He stopped and reached into the inside breast pocket of his leather jacket, giving a quick whistle to Rusty to keep the dogs close by.

"Here's Uncle Paddy," he said, sliding out the envelope his mother had put the photo in. "The oldest son of the Brennan family of County Wexford, Ireland."

He handed over the picture with the reverence it deserved, not just as a family heirloom, but also as evidence.

She treated it with the same respect, keeping her fingertips to the side. For several seconds, she stared at it, then squinted and angled it toward the sun.

He watched her shoulders rise and fall with a sigh, and a soft moan came from deep in her chest.

"So?" he finally asked, impatient for her to look up and confirm she felt as he did, even though he was basing his opinion on one or two photos of Nick he'd seen and she knew him in the flesh. Maybe he was wrong. Maybe he was—

"That sound you hear?" She looked up with misty eyes. "My kernel of hope just hit the ground and disappeared forever."

Without thinking, he reached for her, hugging gently. "I get that, Katie. I do. But you have to listen to me." He tipped her chin so she had to look into his eyes. "I will not ever, *ever* try to take Nico's place in Nick's life or heart or head. I completely honor, respect, and understand their relationship."

She stared at him, silent. The only giveaway was that flicker of fear he'd noticed the first time he'd seen her in town. He wanted that gone. And he wasn't going to stop until it was.

"You asked me to put myself in Nico's shoes, and I have," Daniel said. "Long and hard. I also imagined how he'd feel if he were still alive."

She winced as if the very idea hurt. "I can't even think about it."

"Well, I can. I have four sons, and I know what each of those relationships means to me. If I found out Liam wasn't mine, I...I..." He shook his head, unable to put into words what it would do to him. And Liam. "It would hurt," he finally said. "But I wouldn't stop loving him. I wouldn't look at him differently. And I certainly wouldn't prevent him from knowing whoever that biological father was."

"You're speaking in hypotheticals," she said. "Nico isn't here, and Liam is your son."

"Hypotheticals are all we have, Katie. But I swear to you, I will not try to be Nick's dad."

She closed her eyes, and when she opened them, he could have sworn a little of that fear had softened. Not disappeared, but he had hope.

"Then what will you be?"

"His friend? His sounding board? His second opinion, if he needs one. But I don't expect even that much. Hope for it, but don't expect it. My only request is that the truth is out and open."

"Now? When?"

"Once we have that final, concrete confirmation, we tell Nick with that in hand."

"How? He's in Africa."

"We'll figure that out. But once he knows, I want everyone in both families to know, and that we can talk about it and repair the cracks this will cause in both the Santorini and Kilcannon foundations."

She stared up at him, processing his speech for quite a few heartbeats. Finally, she nodded. "I understand you wanting that. After all, you've missed forty-two years of his life."

It was a small victory, but enough for him to ease her an inch closer. "I'm trying not to think too hard about that," he assured her. "I've had my own sons and daughters. It's not like I've been denied fatherhood."

Silent for a moment, she looked hard at him. "I'm starting to remember…"

"Remember?" he asked when she didn't finish.

"What I liked so much about you."

He couldn't help smiling. "I'm sorry you forgot."

"It's your sense of right and wrong," she said, speaking slowly, as if the words were just landing in her brain. "You have that calm, logical goodness about you that is quite..." She swallowed. "Yeah. It's goodness. Like Nick, I have to say. He has a fundamental goodness about him."

"Thank you. I assume your husband had those qualities, too."

She angled her head, thinking. "Well, he definitely had a sense of right and wrong and was as fine a man as you could find. Calm? Never. Nico was Greek down to the last strand of his DNA, and he was driven by passion and emotion. All of the kids have that hot blood, especially Cassie and Alex. And Theo."

"And Nick?"

"He has a temper, but it's a slow burn. For the most part, he's level-headed and rational, unless he doesn't have control of a situation. Then he gets a little testy." She was quiet for a moment, still searching his face and processing the conversation. "I guess I can see why you're happy about this."

"I am," he said. "And that's why I didn't call you for a few days."

She drew back. "Because you realized you like the idea of Nick being your son?"

"I didn't know how you'd take it. You seem more comfortable with it being a problem than an opportunity. So I held back." He leaned his shoulder into hers. "It killed me, to be honest. I must have picked up the phone twenty times."

That got him a warm smile, one that lit her eyes and gave him a kick in the gut. "Funny. I must have looked at mine twenty times."

He chuckled to hide the zing of satisfaction that gave him. "You should have called me."

"My daughter tells me the girls-don't-call-boys generation is dead." She gave a shrug. "But some of us are just 'of a certain age.'"

"That's crazy. Call me anytime, day or night." He put his arm around her shoulders because it felt natural, and good. And because they'd crossed a huge hurdle, or at least it felt that way to him. "There is no reason for us to go through this whole thing alone."

"I agree. Since we're confessing thoughts we've had over the last few days, I have to tell you that I realized how much I need a friend in this. A calm, rational friend who has an equal interest in the events ahead unfolding in a way that hurts as few people as possible. Someone who understands what being a parent means." She reached up and touched his face. "Truth is, I need you."

A new wave of relief and contentment rolled through him. "Then let's make a promise right now that we won't hesitate to lean on each other while we're waiting for that confirmation, and after we get it. Especially then."

She was silent for too long, making him turn her in his arms so they could look directly at each other. "Daniel Kilcannon." She sighed his name with a wistful smile.

"That's what they call me."

"I guess if this was going to happen with any man in the world, I'm glad it was you."

"So, is that a promise?"

She closed her eyes and whispered, "Yes."

Suddenly, he was transported back in time, four

decades...a lifetime ago. To a college dorm that smelled like incense and lilac perfume. To lips that tasted like late-night coffee and all-night pleasure. To a girl who made him laugh and think and ache low in the gut every time they were together.

"Katie."

She opened her eyes, probably at the unexpected gruffness of his tone. "What is it?"

For a second, he didn't answer. He was still hovering in the past, and back then, the only answer to that question would have been to pull her closer and kiss her.

But that was then, and this was...breaking another promise he'd made.

"Why are you looking at me like you want me to promise something else?" she asked.

"I don't want anything." Except to kiss her. Right that minute, in the sunshine and cold, he wanted to lower his head, put his lips on hers, and kiss her right back to four decades ago.

Before Annie...

And that *was* wrong.

He quickly separated them. "But let's not forget our original plan. The one we had before..." Before *kissing* entered his brain.

"To decorate your living room?" she guessed, with a slight frown of confusion.

"Yes, yes, that. And to spend our time talking about the two people we miss the most and everyone else is sick of hearing about."

"Nico and Annie."

"Exactly," he said, maybe a little too forcefully. "Nico and Annie. They are..."

She smiled, almost as if she understood exactly what he was thinking. "They are our puzzle pieces," she whispered.

Yes, they were. And he couldn't forget that.

Driving behind Daniel's Tahoe on the curved road that took them to the picnic area, Katie tried to list all the safe subjects she would cling to over lunch. The decorating plan. Rusty's improved health. The restaurant in Bitter Bark. And, of course, their happy, happy marriages.

Not the fact that they had been one inch, one second, and one single breath away from kissing back on that trail.

Kissing.

"What was I thinking, Nico?"

She could have sworn she heard her late husband laugh, so her imagination was certainly playing tricks on her.

"But you wanted me to love again. You said it over and over those last few months."

Not this guy! Not this impostor with a claim on Nick!

She could hear Nico's voice, raised in frustration and disgust. Yes, it was easy for him to say she should love again, but this wasn't what he'd meant. He was thinking of some faceless, nameless, vague concept of "another man" he didn't think could ever compete for Katie's heart.

He wasn't thinking of a big, strong, wonderful, kind, thoughtful, handsome, sexy, funny hero who was *Nick's biological father.*

Safe subjects, Katie. Safe friendly *subjects.*

After they'd parked and Daniel retrieved a cooler from the back of his SUV, Katie launched into the safest topic she could think of.

"Once we have the sectional chosen, the rest of the living room will be a breeze," she said as they walked to the picnic tables. "When's a good day to go to High Point?"

If he noticed her effort to segue to something entirely new and different, Daniel was far too cool to call her on it. "This whole week is light for me, so you name the day."

"Okay, and while we're at it, we should pick paint, a new rug, and, oh, did you look at the shutters and window treatments I sent?"

He gave her a sideways look and a half smile. "Window treatments? I thought windows were treated with glass."

She laughed. "I'll pick them." She slid onto the bench and reached down to rub Rusty's and Goldie's heads, always side by side, when they came over to nuzzle her and sniff for food. "And we can bring these two sweet things to High Point."

"Sure." Daniel set a large water bowl on the ground, and they both instantly headed for it. "Water for you guys and subs for us. I hit Hoagies & Heroes on the way out of town."

She opened the cooler and saw the logo for the sandwich shop. "The kids are very interested in this place," she told him. "Thanks for sending those demographics and rental estimates to Cassie. They were meeting about it when I left Chestnut Creek."

"It's a great shop in an ideal location," he said. "Won't be available for long."

Katie settled onto the bench and opened the paper of her sandwich, already more comfortable than on the trail. The intensity of his gaze had lessened, and the rhythm of their conversation had returned to what two friends would talk about.

"I think they want to go over to Bitter Bark and do a walk-through," she told him. "They can meet with the owners. It's a change in plans, but John really thinks it's a great option."

"How is it a change in plans?" he asked. "Cassie said Bitter Bark was on their short list for new locations."

She made a face as she looked at her sandwich.

"You don't like turkey?" Daniel guessed, looking at her.

"I don't like lying." She bit her lip and dove into the truth. "We actually didn't have Bitter Bark on that short list for new locations. But Cassie and I wanted to have an excuse ready for why we were in town, other than stalking you, which we were."

He laughed easily. "Not sure I've ever been stalked."

"You probably have, if what Linda May at the bakery told me was true."

"Which is?"

"You're a hot commodity, Daniel." She slowly unfolded the napkin he'd supplied, reminding herself that every time they got into this personal talk, they risked...intimacy.

"You want to know what is a hot commodity? Retail space in Bitter Bark. If they're interested, let's get them in as soon as possible." Of course he deftly took them back to where they should be.

"Do you think that's a good idea?" she asked.

"Why wouldn't it be?"

She took a bite and chewed while considering how to answer. "We have this huge unknown...situation. Cassie is a little worried that if things go south with...this Nick issue, then..."

"This Nick issue?" He looked skyward at that. "We really do have to come up with something that doesn't sound like a euphemism for a fatal disease. But why are you worried about your family being in Bitter Bark, Katie? Because it's..."

"Enemy territory."

He snorted. "I was thinking more like 'my home.'"

"But what if, hypothetically, we tell everyone the truth and it goes very poorly?"

"What if, hypothetically, we tell everyone and it is, over time, a wonderful thing that brings together two families?"

She put her sandwich down and looked up at him. "You are so optimistic about this."

"Realistic," he corrected. "I know my family and what they're made of. You know yours. Honestly, what we're looking at is one big match that could end happily." He added a grin. "I happen to be *very* good at that."

"At matching two people, not two families."

"Why should it be any different? There's an art form to matchmaking, you know." He leaned a little closer as if sharing a secret. "There's kind of a guaranteed outcome, if you really know what you're doing."

She looked at him, smiling. "I wish I had the talent for it that you do. I told you I tried with Cassie, but she only wants a Greek man exactly like her father. When she meets one...*pffft*." She made a little explosion with her hands. "It fizzles fast."

"Maybe she *thinks* she wants a Greek man, but what she really wants is someone with passion and intelligence and a big heart, which she thinks is 'Greek' because her dad had that."

He was exactly right.

"You have to go about the matchmaking strategically." He polished off half his sandwich, wiped his mouth with a napkin, and looked out at the foothills, sipping his water and deep in thought. "But we're on to something, Katie."

Suddenly, he turned to her, swinging a leg over the picnic bench to face her. "I mean, in essence, we're matching two big, happy families that might, through some shared genetics and a huge surprise, become, well, one big, happy family."

She felt a smile pull. "You think you can orchestrate that? Wow, the Dogfather *is* very good."

"I'm six for six."

"And you made every one of them happen?"

"Well, I'm pretty sure I had some help from above." He looked skyward and laughed. "Divine intervention, a little guidance from their mother, and really lucky timing, but yeah. I did."

"So what are the secrets to success?"

He thought about that, taking another deep draw on his water. "So much of it is organic, you know. Just done by feel. When Jessie showed up, I instantly saw the change in Garrett. Like, the very first hour she was here. She almost left and abandoned her assignment to interview him, but I encouraged her to stay, and that was really all it took. Shane was a little more of a surprise to me, since I was trying to get Liam and Andi together, but Shane jumped in and met Chloe. But then I managed to convince Liam to give Jag to Andi when she needed protection. And of course, they got 'married,' but it wasn't real…" He grinned. "Until it was."

She laughed heartily. "And Molly? Darcy? Aidan?"

"Oh, they were all putty in my hands. Molly didn't know I knew the truth about Trace, but she should have realized Annie told me everything. I wasn't sure Aidan would fall for Beck, but I suspected her similarity to his best friend would attract him, and I was right. Darcy, well. I honestly didn't set out to fix her up with Josh, but after she met him, I knew we had a winner, and I merely encouraged her."

"You must have something that tells you the match might work."

He considered that, nodding. "The trick is to put them in the right place at the right time, then give them a mutual cause." He reached down and rubbed Rusty. "And a dog."

"A dog?"

"Every one of those romances happened because of a dog." He beamed at her. "But we already have a mutual cause with these two families."

"Nick?" Her brows rose.

"The restaurant in Bitter Bark. Your family wants to turn Hoagies & Heroes into the next Santorini's. My family can help. We need to get them together, convince your kids that the place is perfect, and mine will jump in to do whatever is needed to help transform it. Construction, word of mouth, an event. By the time it opens and has a line out the door, they'll be fast friends."

"You think it's that easy?"

"It could be." He scooted a little closer. "Listen, Hoagies & Heroes closes after lunch on Sunday. That's a perfect time for the Santorini clan to do a walk-through and sit down with the owners, which I can easily arrange. Then, since you'll all be in Bitter Bark, everyone comes to Sunday dinner at Waterford. Then we have everyone together, talking about a mutual cause. Easy-peasy."

Until it wasn't. "And when we announce that we kept this very important piece of information from them?"

He shook his head, taking her hand. "Don't think of it that way, Katie. We're not telling anyone until we know for sure. And then we're telling Nick first. We're not withholding anything."

"*We*?"

"We," he said, with no hesitation or doubt. "We're in this together."

"That does make it easier," she admitted, curling her fingers into his.

"Yeah." He looked down at their joined hands for a long moment and visibly swallowed. "Easier...in some ways. A little difficult in others."

"What do you mean, Daniel?"

"I mean that I *do* like being in it together. I like it a lot." He blew out a soft breath and looked away. "Maybe...too much."

She put her hand on his chin and turned his face

back to her. "Because you almost kissed me back there on the trail?"

He closed his eyes. "I thought maybe you…"

"Didn't notice? I was not, as the calendar will so wretchedly prove, born yesterday."

He smiled, but his expression grew serious again. "Katie, it's been a long, long time of being alone."

"And that's why you wanted to kiss me? Because you're lonely?"

"No." He shook his head. "I've had enough opportunities not to be lonely in the past few years. What I meant to say is it's been a long, long time since I've *wanted* to kiss anyone. Never thought I really would again, to be honest."

She swallowed, realizing that despite the bottle of water, her mouth was dry. "And you do now?"

Very slowly, he nodded. "And it scares the crap out of me," he admitted in a husky voice.

"Makes you feel like a cheater, a traitor, and a bad spouse?" she guessed.

"Like I'm breaking a vow." He ground out the words, obviously cut by them.

"I'm pretty sure part of that vow was 'until death do us part.'" She leaned closer. "Our marriages didn't end in divorce, Daniel. We lost people we loved wholeheartedly, and both of us think our dearly departed other halves are watching right now."

He let out a sigh. "It's the other reason I didn't call you for a few days."

"Because you wanted to kiss me?"

"Because I've been thinking…things."

Oh. That changed things, didn't it? "I've been thinking about those things, too."

"You have?"

"How could I not?" she admitted on a nervous laugh. "I was attracted to you the moment I laid eyes on you at some party in an apartment more than forty years ago. I wanted to kiss you five minutes after we started talking. And I was still in love with Nico then, like I am now."

He regarded her for a long time, holding her gaze long enough to make her pulse beat faster and her breath quicken.

And long enough for every cell in her body to want him to kiss her.

"Why don't we just get it out of the way?" she suggested in a soft whisper.

"Once we kiss and know that it's not…"

"Not what we're used to," she finished.

"Yeah, yeah. That should be enough to, you know…"

"Make us stop thinking about it."

He angled his head. "You think it works that way, Kate?"

She didn't know if it was the intimacy of the shortened name or the closeness of his mouth or the sunshine or the air or some long-dormant hormones that suddenly decided to spark up her body, but something made her lean closer.

"I don't know," she whispered. "Do you?"

"Not sure. But I think it's worth a try."

For a long, long time, they both stayed perfectly still. The only sounds were the blood thrumming in her head and Rusty's soft snore. She could smell the clean, woodsy air that clung to a man inches away and feel the heat of his thighs straddling the bench and close to her body.

She could see the flecks of dark blue in his eyes and the tips of his lashes when he closed his eyes and moved slightly closer. She could feel his breath then, and that made her eyes slowly close.

And then he was gone.

Up and off the bench so fast, she felt the air move.

"Let's not do this," he said.

The rejection hurt, but she nodded, standing slowly and wrapping up the other half of her sandwich. "Okay." But it wasn't. It really wasn't okay at all.

"I can't," he said.

"You *could*," she corrected. "You don't want to."

He gave a sharp laugh. "Oh yes, I do."

Turning to her, he squared his shoulders and raised his chin, the posture taking Katie back to a chilly January night in 1976. It was Daniel's do-the-right-thing pose, the body language that said he didn't exactly relish the direction his moral compass was sending him, but he'd go anyway.

"We should be friends, Katie. Just friends. Nothing more, nothing less. We're in this together, but...we need to make this as easy as possible on the people we love."

"In other words, if we kissed, everything gets a new layer of complicated?"

"Many layers. If we can't be friends, then we're back in this thing alone, and neither of us wants that. So we can't. We can't do that again."

They hadn't *done* anything, but she didn't want to drive that point home. They'd felt the same things, wanted the same things, and were terrified of the same things. But on Friday night, he hadn't seemed quite so opposed to those things. Maybe the time he'd had to think about Nick had helped build a wall where she was concerned, and she certainly understood that.

"Then we won't." She started packing up the food, cleaning the table for something to do with her hands, because putting them on Daniel's rough cheeks and telling him he was wrong about that didn't seem like an option.

"You understand, right?"

She turned and looked up at him. "Fully. Completely. And I agree."

White lie, but it was really the safest way to go.

Chapter Fourteen

"**S**o when are you breakin' the news, lad?" Gramma Finnie looked up from buttering her toast, meeting Daniel's gaze moments after the last of the Kilcannons and staff left the kitchen to begin a busy Friday at Waterford.

"In time."

She cocked her head. "I'm pushing eighty-eight, son. Don't take *too* much time."

He narrowed his eyes because she knew he didn't find jokes about her age funny. "No worries, Gramma. We have plans."

"And can I know them? Or is it only you and the lass in on your top-secret private plans?"

"Just us, for the moment. But the plan kicks off on Sunday when we have Katie and three of her kids here for dinner."

Her blue eyes widened behind bifocals. "Saints and angels, Daniel Seamus. When were you going to tell me? Sunday's young Ella's birthday celebration, and all the Mahoneys will be here, plus our crew. We're lookin' at nearly twenty people, and that's too many for the dining room, assuming Jessie hasn't gone into labor, which could be any day."

He stared at her for a moment, his mind a thousand miles away. Well, about fifty miles…in Chestnut Creek. "A buffet is fine," he said. "It's not about eating."

"With twenty hungry people in this house, it is." She put her knife down and leaned forward. "So you're making the announcement then? I sure hope so, since I canna hold it in a whole lot longer, lad. When I'm alone with Molly or Darcy, I all but burst with the news."

"Please." He gave her a stern warning look. "We still have to get the results from Bloodline.com, and if they are what we think they are, then Katie wants Nick to know first, and I couldn't agree more. We're a month away from anything like that."

"I know." She held up her hand and nodded, since they'd had this very same conversation every time they'd been alone in the past week. "But why didn't you mention the dinner sooner?"

He shrugged, knowing the real answer was he was preoccupied. Thinking about Katie when he shouldn't have been. Considering how they might tell Nick. Powering through his plan to be friends, while plagued by an age-old male frustration so foreign, he'd forgotten what it felt like to go to sleep hot, bothered, and second-guessing what he knew was *right*.

"Daniel?"

"I should have mentioned it," he admitted with an apologetic tip of his head. "I know you worry about where people will sit, but what's important is that we meld these families before we break the news. We thought it would help make the whole thing easier for them, and us, if everyone knows and likes each other. We're sort of matchmaking the families."

He expected that to amuse her, but her gray brows shot up. "Got pigs in your belly, lad?"

"Excuse me?"

"We...we...*we*. Didn't take long for a 'we' to emerge from this."

"Well, *we* are kind of in this together." Not as together as they could be, but as together as they *should* be.

"Truth is, you're 'kind of together' more than you're apart lately."

He'd fended off these comments—some subtle, some like a brick to the head—all week from his kids. "Not that much," he mumbled, turning to take his cup to the sink.

"Half a day on Tuesday."

"To pick furniture in High Point." Which hadn't taken long, but they'd turned it into a day trip and a wonderful drive with the dogs. They'd talked, laughed, and somehow managed not to even touch each other, but that hadn't stopped the electricity that seemed to hum when he was around Katie.

"And then here in town Wednesday."

"Had to get all those paint samples, and she wanted to stop in at Hoagies & Heroes." And they'd tested Goldie in the park, which hadn't gone well, so they'd brought her back here and ended up hanging out in the living room talking about what he might do with the furniture. And she'd told him wonderful stories about Nick, which he thought about all the time when he wasn't thinking about her.

"And yesterday?"

He blew out a breath, calling on a lifetime of respect for his mother even when she took things a little too far. "Katie wanted to take me to a model home she'd decorated out in that new development south of Holly Hills to see some of her ideas."

"Uh-huh."

He turned from the sink. "It's not what you're insinuating," he told her.

"I'm not insinuating anything."

"We're friends," he said. "Friends with much in common and a big...issue ahead." Hadn't he proven that with a quick hug every time they said goodbye? No more, no less. What friends did.

"And today?" his mother asked.

"Today, I'm meeting with some new Waterford clients, going into town for lunch with the Spring Festival Planning Committee, and then the boys are going to help me haul the living room furniture either into storage or onto a truck to go to Goodwill, so Katie and I can paint on Saturday."

"And then Sunday is the dinner."

"Buffet," he corrected with a wink.

"And you saw her on Monday, if I recall correctly."

"Have you ever *not* recalled correctly, Gramma?"

"So, six out of seven days? Is my math right?"

Really? That many? No wonder he was as frustrated as a teenage boy on a first date. He opened the dishwasher to slide the cup into a slot, pushing a little too hard. "I'm not counting." Except the hours until he saw her again. Those, he was definitely counting. "But yes, your math is correct, though your assumptions are not."

"I'll tell the troops. There's a buzz of speculation so loud I can barely hear myself think."

He rounded the counter, planting a kiss on her head, anxious to end the conversation and get his mind on anything else. "Let them buzz, but you keep the secret. You promised."

"And my word is good." She straightened the toast she'd yet to start eating. "So what do you two talk about all this time?"

"We talk about Annie. And Nico," he added when she gave him a look. "That's what's so great about being with her. We can talk to our heart's content about our late spouses, and the other one never gets bored."

She lifted a brow, looking both dubious and amused.

"I'm serious," he said. "It's a relief to be with a woman who *wants* to hear about the one and only person I'll ever truly love."

"And you want to hear about her husband?"

"Very much. Nico was a colorful character, and a good man. And we talk about Nick." He leaned close to whisper, "He was valedictorian of his high school, graduated first in his class at Duke, and got into five medical schools before picking Johns Hopkins."

"Oooh," she cooed, her eyes bright with the pride he heard in his own voice. "Isn't he the smart one."

"And he cares about people so deeply," he added, thinking about the volunteer jobs Katie told him about.

"So do your other children."

He drew back, blinking at the admonishment. "I know that."

"Just don't forget about them with your new shiny...son."

"Shhh." He frowned at her, but not for the use of the word. Because, as always, his mother got the truth of the matter.

"It's not a competition," he told her. "I'm sure there's some Irish saying about how we can make room in our hearts for one more, no matter how many there are."

"Not that I can think of, but I bet I can make one up."

He smiled at her. "You do that and give me a little breathing room, okay? I'm sixty-one."

"And whistlin'."

"Excuse me?"

"You've been whistlin' a lot."

He coughed a laugh. "And that means..."

"You're happy?"

Was he? At least he wasn't lonely. "Maybe I am."

"About Nick."

"About...life. And you don't have to worry about the rest of my crew. You don't have to let go of what's in one hand to hold on to something in the other."

She made a face, drawing back in astonishment. "Daniel! Did you pull that out of thin air?"

"Yes. You're not the only pithy one around here."

She flicked him away and reached for her laptop. "Go on with you now. I've got a blog to write."

"Topic?" he asked.

She lowered her glasses on her nose and leveled her aging gaze at him. "All I'm going to say is thank you for the inspiration, Danny boy."

He laughed at the nickname she probably hadn't used on him in fifty years. Cheered by it, he gave her one more kiss and left the kitchen to head to work, but all day as he went from tasks to meetings to training time with Garrett and Shane in the pen, he heard the brogue of his mother's voice in his head.

But it wasn't about Nick and the other six kids he already had. Frankly, he knew he could make room in his life for another son and make it work with his family.

But…another woman? What did the possibility of another woman in his life mean to the one he would forever hold as the one and only?

It didn't matter—he couldn't. And he wouldn't.

The sound of her door chime yanked Katie from a thought so lost and deep that she hadn't even realized she'd watered the amaryllis plant and the patio *and* the bottoms of her shoes.

Lost. That was the only way to describe herself lately.

"Hang on," she called, kicking off the sneakers and padding to the front door in her socks. Halfway there, she saw the tall figure, black hair, and broad shoulders of one of her favorite people on earth. "Alex," she whispered with a smile, opening the door. "What are you doing here on a Friday morning?"

"Trying to catch you between, uh, clients." He reached down and gave her a hug with one arm and held out a foil-covered paper plate with his other hand. "Something to make you say 'opa!'"

She inched back, giving him a look. "You know I don't say 'opa' or anything Greek. Every time I tried, Yiayia reminded me of how bad my accent is."

He lifted one broad shoulder and shook back some long, black hair. "Yiayia accepts you, and that is the most you could expect." He leaned closer. "More than your mother ever did."

"So true." She brought him in and closed the door, taking a sniff of the plate. "Butter crescents?" she guessed.

"Kourabiedes." Of course, he pronounced it perfectly, matching the way Nico had said it. "Which I happen to know are your favorite, because on his deathbed, Dad told me to give them to you whenever I wanted to *butter* you up for something. Get it?"

She smiled at him. "Or you could just ask. What do you need, Alex?"

He didn't answer yet, moving through the undersized entry and living room with grace and familiarity, his long, lanky frame filling the small space along with the faint scent of the kitchen that seemed to cling to him.

"Coffee," he said.

"Is that why you came bearing butter-me-up cookies?"

"No, it's a process, you know? Food, coffee, small talk, and then the request. Humor me."

Intrigued and delighted by this complicated male, as she always had been for the past thirty-six years, she followed him into the kitchen and went straight to the Keurig. "Regular or flavored?"

He lifted a dark brow.

"Of course. Regular. Strong. Black. I can pull out the espresso maker, if you like."

Shaking his head, he took a seat at the kitchen table and put the cookies down. "Not necessary, thanks. So how was the Heroes & Hoagies place?"

"You know that I went there?"

"Cassie Santorini dot-com, all the family news that's fit to share."

Not all of it, she hoped. "It was nice, actually. A little small, needs some investment, but the location is incredible. Right in the heart of town."

"Sounds good."

"It is." She poured more water into the coffeemaker and glanced over her shoulder, still thinking about Cassie. On one hand, she totally trusted her daughter. On the other, she had never been good at keeping a secret. "What else did Cassie say?" she asked.

"That we've all been summoned for some kind of Irish wake after we meet with the owners on Sunday."

"Irish *wake*?" She snapped the top of the coffee machine closed with a little force. "Alex, that's not the right attitude. Is that what you wanted to ask me?" She turned to meet his gaze. "You want to skip it?" Disappointment squeezed, mostly because she knew Daniel would be disappointed. "I really want you to go, but if—"

"Mom. Coffee. Cookies. Then the request, remember?"

She nodded in agreement, walking his cup of steaming coffee to the table to join him. "There's the coffee. Gimme a cookie. Then hit me with what you need."

213

He gave her a wry grin, his smile bright white surrounded by the dark facial hair that somehow looked poetic on him and professorial on his identical twin. "You really aren't a drop of Greek, are you?"

Heat crawled up her cheeks at the statement, which never would have bothered her before. Her non-Greekness had gone from a source of contention with her in-laws to a family joke with her kids and husband. But now, with Nick...somehow it was anything but funny.

Except, if Nick had inherited *all* of her genes, then—

"It's a joke, Mom," he said, taking the foil off the cookies to reveal his latest masterpiece. "Here. Comfort food the way Dad taught me to make it."

She smiled and grabbed a napkin from a basket on the table and picked up the delicate pastry, tapping off some excess sugar. "He was good at comfort food," she agreed.

"At all food," Alex said, taking one for himself.

"It killed him not to be able to cook those last few years."

"Killed him?" He smiled. "Ironic on purpose, or just a questionable choice of words?"

She managed a soft laugh. "I wasn't thinking. But he hated when he couldn't go to the kitchen anymore. He hated it so much."

"I remember."

She took a bite, closing her eyes at the sweet, soft deliciousness. "God, you're talented."

"Ehh." He polished off the cookie and the compliment, frowning as he finished chewing, his thick lashes brushing together as he narrowed his eyes in critical thought.

"If you think this is less than the best kourabiedes ever made, Alex Santorini, then Cassie is right and you really do have a hang-up with perfectionism."

He snorted. "Now our reporter is the family shrink. I have hang-ups with pistachio. I should have stuck with walnut."

"It's perfect."

Leaning forward, he shook his head. "There's no such thing as perfect, Ma." He grinned as he always did when he used the nickname she didn't love, except it was his secret name that for some reason only he could get away with. "But that doesn't stop me from trying to achieve it in all aspects of my life, which brings us to my request."

She eyed him, curious, but a little scared. What exactly had Cassie been telling her brothers? "Am I going to need another bite of this comfort cookie?"

"No. All you need is to slide out that sweet and wonderful heart of yours and forgive me."

She inched back, totally lost. "For what?"

"For what I said the other day when you were at the office."

"I don't even remember what you said." At his one lifted brow, she dug deep enough to recall the words. "You mean something about selling me to a lecherous guy?" The very words made her smile. "That was...you being passionate, opinioned Alex."

"That was me being a...jerk." His eyes flickered with the fact that they both knew he probably had a much worse word in his head than *jerk*. He'd picked up his father's penchant for swearing in the kitchen when he was about fifteen and had never lost it, except around her.

215

"Well, you're sweet to apologize, but it wasn't cookie-worthy." She picked up another. "But since they're here…"

He locked his inky dark gaze on her. "I think you should go for it, Mom."

She stared at him. "The cookie or…"

"The man. Who probably isn't lecherous."

Not at all. "There's nothing to 'go for,' honey."

"That's not what Cassie says."

"Oh, for crying out loud." She pushed back, dropped the cookie, and gave in to a punch of irritation and worry. "*What* does Cassie say?"

"Just enough, you know, between the lines, for me to guess this isn't casual."

She searched his face, not seeing him, but the sister who had the same distractingly dark eyes, trying to imagine what Cassie could have said. "She's implying that, what? There's more to this than friendship?" Because there was, but not like he was guessing.

"She says you have a 'history,' and I assume that means your relationship was…" He lifted a shoulder as if he didn't want to—or couldn't—say what that meant.

"Sexual?" she supplied.

Behind his dark whiskers, he paled. "Whatever you guys called it back in those days."

"Oh, we called it sex," she said. "Just like today. And it's still none of your damn business."

He flinched at her rare curse, knowing exactly what it meant. "Sorry, line crossed," he said. "But, Mom, I know that comments like the one I made—which was stupid and thoughtless—could keep you from being…fulfilled."

"Fulfilled?" She almost laughed, except that he was so sincere.

"What I mean is that you shouldn't let your kids stop you from doing anything. Staying overnight, going on a trip, even, you know, letting him come here."

She leaned back again, trying to wrap her head around the conversation and failing spectacularly. "You're giving me your permission to have sex."

He angled his head. "I know you, Mom."

"It would seem you think you know me a little too well."

"I mean that you probably think it's a crime or a sin or some kind of shocking scandal if you want to, you know..." He leaned forward and put his hands over hers. "What I'm saying is you don't have to marry the guy. That, we don't need. Just..." He shrugged. "Live like most people do. I mean, don't advertise it, but feel free to be. You know?"

She dropped her head into her hands and closed her eyes, not sure if she wanted to laugh or cry or throw her hands up and tell him the truth.

"Are you saying," she asked, looking up, "that you would prefer I sleep with a man than marry him?"

"Passion is a good thing, Mom. It drives me."

"Well, it doesn't drive..." *Daniel.* "Me."

"Are you sure?"

"No. Not of anything." She folded the paper napkin in front of her, thinking. "And what does John think? Or do I really want to know that you two actually converse about my private life?"

"John is a numbers guy. He wants to be sure the dude isn't after your fortune."

"My…" She choked a laugh at the idea of Daniel on a money-hunt. "For one thing, Daniel Kilcannon is about the most straight-up 'dude' you'll ever meet." She added air-quotes and a teasing smile. "For another, he doesn't need money. One of his sons sold a company to FriendGroup, and they all owned stock. Plus, Daniel's a successful veterinarian in his own right. He's invested wisely and has no interest in my little savings account."

"I told John you were too smart for anything like that. The guy's interested in you because you're smart, talented, and very attractive, Mom."

"No one is 'interested' in anyone," she said. "We are merely friends, Alex. Friends getting through something that…" She closed her mouth and cursed herself mentally.

"What?"

She stared at him, blanking out for a moment. "Widowhood," she finally said, relieved that it was true enough to make perfect sense. "We're getting through the deaths of our spouses."

"It's been two years, Mom."

"And four for him. We're both still grieving."

"Well, if that's all it is, but Cassie said…" He shook his head.

"Cassie said what?"

"Cassie said we should be ready for change in the family. Big change."

Oh, that *girl*. "She likes drama."

"True, but she's also closer to you than anyone else, and she's met the guy and his family."

"And she's…" *Not supposed to breathe a word of this*. "Seeing things that may or may not be there."

He looked intrigued. "So tell me the truth. Do you like the guy?"

So much. Too much.

"I do," she admitted, unwilling to lie any more than the situation had forced her to. "We have a lot in common, and he's a good man. Solid. Smart. Caring." And every time he touched her, something went haywire. Hormones she hadn't thought she had anymore decided to dance around. Body parts melted in ways she hadn't dreamed possible again. And every night, she went to bed taut and tense and remembering…sex.

"Holy cow, you do," he said. "That's a serious blush, Mom."

"Stop it."

He dipped his head to force her to look at him. "Just remember you're a big girl, and if you want to act like one, then no one's judging. That's all."

"And if I happen to…rock the family boat?"

He looked at her for a long, long time and finally gave a tight smile. "Then we'll get a little seasick and survive."

She stood as he did, both of them stepping into a long, warm hug. "Thank you, Alexander the Great," she whispered, using her own nickname for him.

"You bet, Ma." He gave her a squeeze, and when he left a few minutes later, Katie had a low-grade sense of hope she hadn't felt in a long time, and a whole lot to think about.

Chapter Fifteen

D aniel stood in front of the wall of fame and stared at a picture of his late wife holding a baby wrapped in pink. Molly? Darcy? God, no. That was—

"Grandpa?"

"Pru." He turned to greet his first grandchild, always a little taken aback at how tall and grown-up she seemed lately, and eons from the baby in the picture. "I was just looking at you as an infant."

"The picture with Grannie Annie?" She came to stand next to him and smiled at the framed shot. "I always love that because she looks so much like my mom."

"Well, your mom looks like her. That's the way genetics works, kid." He put an arm around her. "What has you here on a Friday night? No big date or party?"

"A date? Hah." She dropped to her knees to love on Rusty. "My dad told me I can't date until I'm thirty-five. Or at least until my braces come off."

He chuckled at that. "Isn't that soon?"

"March sixteenth at three thirty in the afternoon," she said. "The day before Saint Patrick's Day. We should have a party."

His smile disappeared at the thought. They'd tried to keep every tradition alive since Annie died, but no one had seemed to have the spirit or desire to pull together the Kilcannon Saint Paddy's Day party without her.

"Maybe," he said, turning back to the pictures.

"I'd really like it," Pru said. "I remember the ones we used to have when Grannie Annie made me green Sprite and Gramma Finnie told everyone about her big brother, Paddy."

Who looked like Nick. Well, Nick looked like him. Hadn't he just explained genetics to his granddaughter?

"Weren't they fun parties, Grandpa?"

Saint Patrick's Day had lost its luster for him. It was one of those days…like Meeting Day, First Time Day, and Blue Stick Day when two college kids' lives changed forever. All those "Annieversaries," as he used to call them, all those secret celebrations exclusively for the two of them.

Saint Patrick's Day was the first *I love you*, and while the rest of the clan was pounding down green Sprite—and beer—and celebrating their heritage, he and Annie were remembering that night they said those words for the first of a million times.

"And I'd get to show off my new teeth to everyone," Pru continued, taking out her phone. "Oh, it's a Sunday. Perfect, right?"

"Could be," he said vaguely. But his gaze shifted to a picture from one of those parties, and his heart—

"I have a month to plan it," she said. "You won't have to do a thing."

At the same time her words landed in his brain, Shane's big footfall hit the hallway. "How many Kilcannons does it take to move furniture from the living room?"

"I think almost everyone is coming to help," Pru said. "Except my two pregnant aunts, and Andi's at home getting ready to go out with Liam, because I'm babysitting, so that makes ten? I think."

"Ten." Shane strode into the room without missing a beat. "Nine to move the furniture and one to take care of the Jameson's." He lifted a bottle from a glass-topped server. "Please tell me you're not giving away this rolling bar thing. It's been part of my life since I was five. Garrett used to think I couldn't see him under it when we played hide-and-seek."

The bar cart? "Katie said it's got a real 1970s vibe," Daniel said.

"So do you, Dad." Shane put the bottle back. "And the wingbacks?"

"Donating them to an assisted-living home in Chestnut Creek."

"Really?" Pru threw herself into one. "I love these chairs. Remember that time you hired Santa to come to the house because I had strep throat? I sat in his lap right here. Best Christmas memory ever."

"Not true." Daniel's youngest son, Aidan, blew in next, his broad shoulders and big personality taking up a good bit of room space, his lovely fiancée, Beck, at his side. "The best Christmas memory was when I got leave from Afghanistan and surprised you."

"Oh, that was good," Pru agreed. "I'll never forget

the look on Grandpa's face when you came in holding that little Jack Frost."

"Hey, guys," Molly said, right behind him, with Trace's arm draped over her shoulders, both of them still wearing the glow of their recent winter wedding. Darcy and Josh weren't far behind.

"Trace and I have a hot date, so can we do this furniture thing fast?" Molly asked. "I mean, you're not moving everything out, are you, Dad? Just that hideous whiskey-on-wheels eyesore?"

"Ugh." Shane grunted and punched his chest. "You kill me, Molly."

"Everything goes." Daniel took the kiss and hug hello that Molly offered, smiling as Rusty trotted over to greet her and show some love to his favorite Kilcannon offspring. "Liam's coming, and Garrett, if everything went okay at the doctor today."

"She's two centimeters dilated," Molly said, reminding Daniel that Jessie and Molly were childhood friends and still very close. "But we'll stay, because I'd never miss the dismantling of Mom's..." Molly caught herself. "Of the living room."

Daniel shook his head. "I'm not dismantling anything." Except, he really was. And he could tell by the looks on their faces that they thought he was destroying a room their mother loved, and doing it for another woman. "I'm just..."

"Doing exactly what needs to be done." Darcy shot forward, away from Josh and her brothers, to stand next to Daniel in a show of solidarity. "He's...living."

All eyes shifted down to petite Darcy's level, but the attention made her square her shoulders and look up at Daniel, and instantly he remembered the conversation they'd had the day she helped him with his Pinterest account, and he understood why his support had come from this surprising corner.

"There's nothing wrong with updating this room and bringing it into this decade." She faced off with the whole lot of them, with a straight spine of fearlessness that made Daniel's heart break with love for this young woman. "I, for one, think it's a good idea."

Garrett arrived then, but obviously had heard enough of the talk. "But do you have to get rid of everything?"

"I want a clean slate."

"The pictures, too?" Liam asked.

All eyes moved to Annie's precious wall. "You know the people in the room should be the focal point, not pictures on the wall," Daniel said.

"What are you going to do with them?" Shane asked.

He cleared his throat before answering. "Katie said she's worked with picture collections like that and might be able to come up with something better."

They were all dead silent.

"I bet it'll be beautiful," Molly said after a beat. "I looked up Katie's work on her website, and she's really talented."

Daniel nodded his appreciation for the vote of confidence. "She is," he agreed. "And I trust her to give this room a much-needed redo without losing the..." What had she called it? "The spirit of the home."

"You mean Mom," Shane mumbled. When the attention shifted to him, he added, "Mom is, you know, the spirit of the home."

"Our *family* is the spirit of this home," Daniel said, making no effort to soften that response. When he had all their attention again, he took a step forward, letting go of Darcy's shoulder to make his point. "That hasn't changed, nor will it."

Except...the family would get larger, but not the way they expected.

They all stared at him, and not a single man, woman, or child in the room had the nerve to contradict him. Knowing he had that attention and respect, he decided to make a few things clear.

"At this time in my life," he said, quietly enough that they had to stay still to hear him, "I plan to make some changes. Some will be small and inconsequential, like changing those drapes to shutters or painting the walls something Sherwin-Williams appropriately calls Comfort Gray."

That made Molly's lips lift a little and Shane's big shoulders drop. Liam crossed his arms and gave the slightest nod, too.

"But other changes might be bigger."

Garrett's eyes flickered, and Darcy looked up at him, biting her lip, but everyone stayed silent.

"Like, I might add some people to our circle of life."

Liam shifted from one foot to the other, and when he did, Daniel saw his tiny mother standing in the center entry hall, on the outskirts of the small gathering, as riveted as the rest of them.

Daniel took a slow breath and continued. "A very wise person once said that you don't have to let go of what's in one hand to hold something in the other," he said.

"Ten bucks it was Gramma Finnie," Pru muttered.

"You'd lose that bet," Gramma called out.

Daniel nodded. "The point is, I can change this room and still treasure the memories it holds." Just saying it made the idea possible, and seeing a few of them nod slowly gave him even more confidence. "I can live a new kind of life and know that the years that preceded it made me exactly who I am."

"And who we are," Liam added softly.

Daniel gave him a quick smile. "Exactly. And..." He looked down at Pru, who gazed back with unabashed admiration, making his heart squeeze with love. "I can celebrate special days even if they are difficult for me."

Her whole face lit up. "Really? I promise I'll plan everything, Grandpa! You don't have to do a thing. It won't be difficult."

He reached down to brush her head with his knuckles, touched by her misunderstanding of why a Saint Patrick's Day party would be difficult. "I know you will, General Pru," he whispered, before looking back up to the other faces around the room.

He knew they were going to take the next statement differently than he intended, but that was okay. He was laying the groundwork for the hard road ahead, and as their father and leader, he had to do that.

"I can also bring good people into this home and family and still deeply and totally love the ones that are, or were, in it."

"Oh." Molly let out a little whimper and let her head drop onto Trace's shoulder.

"Dad." Darcy whispered his name on a sigh.

Shane gave a slow, honest smile, and Aidan

struggled to swallow. Garrett nodded in agreement, and Liam held his father's gaze with a look of support and approval.

True, they all thought he was talking about Katie, but the principle was the same. He would bring a new person into the family soon, and they needed to be mature and graceful enough to accept it.

"We're starting on Sunday," he announced, getting some surprised looks in response.

"She's coming for Sunday dinner?" Garrett guessed. "I hope Junior hasn't been born yet."

"If he has, we'll celebrate his birthday," Daniel said. "But yes, Katie, two of her sons, and Cassie are coming after they spend the afternoon at Heroes & Hoagies—"

"They must really hate your cooking," Shane joked under his breath.

"They're thinking about renting the space and turning it into a Santorini's, like the two they have in Chestnut Creek. And if they do, they'll need our help. Maybe some muscle, maybe some construction work, maybe some marketing and word of mouth. Some catering business would be good."

For a moment, they were silent, processing that, glancing at one another. Then Shane held up his hand. "I'm sure you can count on Chloe for the marketing, and I'll help them build."

"I'm happy to help with construction, too," Trace chimed in. "We can do what we did for Friends With Dogs."

"You did a great job transforming a travel agency into my grooming studio," Darcy said. "And I could offer discounts to my customers, and we could put flyers at Bone Appetit," she added, referring to the dog-treat business his sister, Colleen, and niece Ella owned.

"I'm sure we could do some kind of reciprocal marketing with my uncle's pizza parlor," Beck said, looking up at Josh. "He's been looking for an opportunity like that."

"And they could cater our Saint Patrick's Day party!" Pru added with a clap of delight. "Two birds, one stone. I love it."

Daniel took a step back from the sheer force of what happened every single time the Kilcannons put their heads together to solve a problem. He didn't even have to answer them as the ideas flew, along with jokes and chatter. Every drop of tension evaporated in the face of a challenge.

"Okay, awesome," he said, but they were all talking, planning, and scheming ideas. "I really appreciate the enthusiasm," he added with a laugh to a roomful of people basically ignoring him.

He looked past them at his mother, who leaned against the doorjamb, her gnarled knuckles wrapped around the collar of her cardigan, her eyes dancing with the truth that only she knew.

Pru stood up and looked from him to her great-grandmother, gasping softly, but staying silent.

Daniel's heart kicked up, and his mother's smile instantly disappeared. He'd forgotten those two had some kind of bizarre mental telepathy. If Gramma knew something, it was only a matter of time before Pru did, too. And Gramma was *itching* to share the news.

"I need your help, General," he said in an effort to

distract Pru. "This group forgot why they're here. Help me?"

She gave him a metal-mouthed smile. "I got this." She raised both hands and snapped her fingers, making Rusty stand up and bark, but no one else even noticed. "At least one of you pays attention," Pru lamented, looking up at Daniel. "Whistle for me, Grandpa?"

He put his fingers in his mouth and brought them to complete silence with the same ear-piercing whistle he'd used when he wanted to call a bunch of Kilcannon kids in from the lake or the fields for dinner.

Pru giggled into the sudden silence. "I gotta learn how to do that."

"Just run this show, General."

She gave him a playful salute and stood up on a small footrest in front of one of the wingbacks to get close to even with the tall men in the room. "Attention, Kilcannons! Chairs and sofa to the truck for donation. Rolly drink cart?"

"Donation also," Daniel said.

"You heard the man. Bookshelf gets emptied. Pictures go into those bins?" She glanced at Daniel, and he nodded. "Everything else...Grandpa will tell you."

And they were in motion, picking up chairs and taking down books and carefully unhooking the pictures, leaving empty pale yellow squares and circles on the wall.

"There better be beer at the end of this," Shane ground out through clenched teeth as he and Garrett hoisted the big sofa.

"There better be *food*," Garrett shot back.

"I'll order pizza," Gramma said as she came over to Daniel and slid her arm through his, her gray head barely reaching his chest as the years made her tinier and tinier. But when she looked up at him, he saw nothing but strength in those eyes. "Well done, lad."

He tipped his head in acknowledgment of the compliment. "We've got a long way to go."

"Not really, Grandpa." Pru set a framed picture in a plastic bin. "We'll have this room ready for painting in no time."

But he shared a look with his mother, who knew that they did, indeed, have a long, long way to go. As he looked at his sons, daughters, and extended family in action, he knew he had the best team possible on his side.

Next, they had to work on the Greeks.

Chapter Sixteen

Katie stretched out on the painting tarp, using the edge of her brush to get the curved edges of the baseboard a pure, bright white. The position was made a little more complicated by the fact that Goldie and Rusty decided the canvas made a perfect bed, and they were both lined up next to her.

When they moved, her brush slipped.

"Be still, kids," she whispered as she dragged the brush. "Or Mommy's gotta do this twice."

"Mommy?" Daniel, looming above her on the stepladder with the roller, snorted softly. "And she says she doesn't want to adopt a dog."

She glanced up at him, stealing her third—fourth?—look at the way his slightly paint-splattered T-shirt fit over his broad shoulders as he moved the roller. "I thought you said she could only go to someone special."

"You're special," he replied without hesitation. "And you don't have other dogs."

"Or a yard."

"Is that what's stopping you?"

She sighed and pushed up, rubbing her shoulder. "Fear of the unknown, I guess."

He looked down at her and smiled. "You've splattered enough Comfort Gray in your hair to make you look like me."

She laughed, reaching up to touch her hair and making a face when she hit some paint.

"It's on your cheek, too."

She wrinkled her nose and looked around for a clean cloth, but there was none. So she pushed up to a stand. "I think I need a cleanup break."

Rolling out a crick in his neck, Daniel nodded. "And I need a coffee break. Also a massage, Jacuzzi, and a couple of Advil."

"Amen to that."

He started down the ladder. "Old people painting."

"Speak for yourself, old man. I can do coffee and a cookie. Will that work?"

"Not as well as the massage, but I'll take it."

She narrowed her eyes in a tease that had become familiar and comfortable this past week. "Friends don't give friends massages."

He lifted a brow, and for a split second, she thought he might reconsider his stance, but then he nodded. "Point taken."

"I'll be right back, and after our break, let's tackle that last wall."

He shot a quick glance at the one solid wall with the ghostlike shadows of at least thirty frames. It wasn't the first time that day she'd seen a slightly uneasy expression on his face when it came to the wall. But it disappeared quickly when he nodded and slid the brush out of her hand. "Sounds like a plan."

"You want to come with me, Goldie?" She snapped her fingers twice, like she'd seen Daniel and others around Waterford Farm do, but Goldie sidled up to Rusty, who was not moving from his nap position. "See?" she said to Daniel. "She prefers him to anyone."

"I know," he said. "I just wish Rusty could teach her how to get along with everyone that way."

A moment later, after using the powder room in the hall and getting rid of the paint on her face and lashes, Katie headed toward the kitchen, taking in the serenity and comfort of the oversized farmhouse.

She rounded the corner that led to the kitchen, coming to a complete stop as she almost plowed right into tiny Gramma Finnie.

"Oh!" Their exclamations of surprise came out in perfect unison.

"I didn't realize you were here," Katie said, suddenly feeling like a prowler in the woman's house.

"I came home a wee bit early and was on my way to the living room to check on your progress." She slipped off an overcoat, revealing a deep purple sweater that had a stunning effect on her white hair. The outside air had put a pink tone in parchment-soft cheeks that crinkled when she smiled. "Didn't the Kilcannon clan do a magnificent job of cleaning out that room for you, lass?"

"They did," she agreed. "All we have to do is paint, and as you can see..." She held up her hands, which were still a little splattered despite the soap and water she'd used in the bathroom. "We're working on that. But taking a coffee break," she added to explain her presence in the kitchen.

"I'll make your coffee, lass." She gestured for Katie to come all the way in. "Sit a bit while I do."

"That's not necessary," she said. "You just got home."

"But I need a private moment with you."

"Oh, okay." They hadn't yet had one of those, and they should. "I'd like that."

The older woman's face slipped into a smile that easily reached her blue eyes, which might be dimmed by her bifocals, but were as sharp as the day Katie had met her so many years ago.

Gramma guided her to a seat at the island counter with a featherlight touch that belied the strength Katie knew the older woman had in spades.

"Daniel likes his coffee strong," Gramma commented. "Will that work for you?"

"The stronger the better," she said on a laugh. "Oh, and I brought these cookies." She gestured toward the Tupperware she'd left on the counter. "They're called kourabiedes. Greek butter cookies."

"How wonderful. Did you make them?"

"My son Alex. He's the master in the kitchen in our family."

"Like his father," she said, pouring the water into the coffeemaker with a steady hand.

"Yes, he definitely inherited a love for food, especially anything Greek."

"I'm looking forward to meeting the lads tomorrow." Gramma Finnie turned from the coffeemaker after hitting the start button, taking a few tentative steps closer to Katie. "All of your family, really."

Katie held her gaze for a beat and made a quick decision. This wasn't a woman to be coy with, or a moment to pretend they both didn't see the elephant in the room. "I don't know when you'll meet Nick," she said.

Gramma nodded, listening like her son would before jumping into a response.

"Or if you'll ever meet him," Katie added on a sigh. "I have no idea how he'll take this...news."

"Oh, lass." As if the ice broke, the little old woman's face crumbled, and she came around the counter with both arms outstretched. "He'll accept it." She folded Katie into her narrow body, squeezing gently.

Katie eased back with a shaky smile. "I'm sorry to do this to your family, Gramma Finnie."

"Hush! Another Kilcannon is never anything but a cause for celebration."

"He's not a Kilcannon," she said softly. "He's a Santorini. They're as proud of the name as you are of yours."

"It's a beautiful name," Gramma said. "I've seen pictures of the city by the same name."

"Nico's grandfather was born there and came here as a child," Katie told her. "Actually, their last name was something else completely, but when they arrived at Ellis Island, the person who registered them couldn't pronounce or spell it, so he used the name of their home city on the papers. They were too scared to change it back, so they kept Santorini, and that's how it became the family name."

Gramma's eyes twinkled. "Why, what a lovely story. My parents and brothers came through Ellis Island as well, though I wasn't on the same boat myself. Seamus and I came later." She leaned in and gave Katie's arm a squeeze. "One of these days, I'll take you aside and tell you the whole story. The *long* version."

An unexpected warmth rolled through her, along with equally unexpected tears.

"Oh, no cryin', lass. Ask any Kilcannon. The long version means I like you."

She had to laugh. Otherwise, she'd cry. "I'm not used to...this. To you."

Gramma's gray brows lifted. "I'm like any other old lady, only not scared of technology. Or history."

"You're not, though," she said. "You're not like my mother, who literally died mad at me, or my mother-in-law, who actually once told me she liked me, but didn't love me because I'm not Greek."

Gramma looked a little horrified. "My love has no strings, lass."

"Which is amazing."

She smiled, crinkling her face. "'Tis normal around here, I promise. So ye got nothin' to worry about. It'll all work out as it should. Surely you know that by now, lass."

"I realize that, but..." She squeezed Gramma's tiny shoulders. "Please don't expect perfectly smooth sailing. This will be hard for Nick, and for all my kids. It's life-changing."

"And how boring life would be if it never changed." She finally stepped away, letting out a sigh.

"But not everything is meant to change," Katie mused. "Not your DNA. Not your parents. Not your family name."

"You just told me about a family name changin'," Gramma reminded her. "No harm nor foul."

Katie smiled. "I hadn't thought about it that way."

"I can think of worse families to wake up and find out you're part of," Gramma Finnie said, taking two cups off hooks near the coffeemaker.

"I couldn't agree more, but any family that isn't the one you were raised being part of is going to be a..." *Shock* seemed like a ridiculous understatement. "Game changer."

Gramma Finnie didn't answer for a moment, but busied herself pouring three cups of coffee and getting some cream and sugar on the counter. She moved with remarkable grace and agility for a woman her age, her rubber-soled shoes squeaking on the wood with each step.

She got a plate and opened the Tupperware, taking some cookies out of the container and lining them up in a neat semicircle that would make Alex proud, then put the plate, the coffee, and the cream and sugar on a tray.

The quiet seemed natural, as they both sat thinking about what lay ahead.

Finally, she looked up at Katie with nothing but sincerity in her eyes. Based on all Daniel had told her about this woman, she expected a pithy proverb that would offer sweet, but useless, advice.

"What would you have done if you had known the child you carried was Daniel's?" she asked.

Katie blinked, not expecting the deeply personal question. "I don't know."

"Would you have left your Nico? Risked losing that wonderful life and the family you ultimately made? Would you even have told him, considerin' that things like this weren't so easy to discover back in those years?"

Katie considered the brogue-laced question, turning it over in her mind, thinking back to the early days and their love. She remembered the bone-deep joy she and Nico had shared that night when he'd come up from the kitchen and she'd wrapped pink and blue pipe cleaners all over the apartment. It was one of the best nights of their entire lives.

And it wasn't his baby.

"Nick was our personal victory," she said. "Because of him, we beat the four parents who opposed our union so vehemently. Nick brought them around the altar with us, where we knew we were destined to be."

"So you wouldn't have left Nico?" The question came from behind her in Daniel's deep voice, making her turn with a quick intake of breath. "I didn't mean to eavesdrop, but I caught the end of that on my way to see what was taking so long."

She looked from him to his mother, still pondering the real, hard truth of what she would have done if the timing had been different enough that she'd realized the baby was Daniel's.

"I wouldn't have left him," she finally said.

"Then we'd have had a problem," Daniel said. "Because I would have insisted on marrying you."

The realization of that hit her like a punch to the solar plexus. He would have, of course. He was Daniel Kilcannon, and *do the right thing* was the motto that drove his every breath.

"Then both our families wouldn't exist." And didn't he see how wrong that would have been?

Gramma came back around the counter. "The Irish say that what is meant for you won't pass you by." She patted Katie's arm. "Your lives and your families were worked out long before you two ever set your sights on each other or your wonderful spouses. The fact is, you had no control over this big plan, and we all know it. Together, we can help all our lads and lassies understand that, too." She waited a beat, then added, "Liam, in particular, will struggle, though he'll never show it."

Katie looked at her. "He seems so strong."

"Aye. But he's the eldest, and in an Irish family, that's a place of honor that no boy will give up easily."

"We'll make it work," Daniel assured them both. He came closer and wrapped his arms around them, pulling them into his big chest for a reassuring group hug. "I promise we will."

"And my son doesn't break promises," Gramma said, easing out of the hug. "Now go on and paint yer livin' room. It's my nap time. Will you be here for dinner, lass? I'm afraid Saturdays are leftovers, but we have plenty."

"I..." She glanced at Daniel, uncertain about his plans.

"I hoped we could go out and celebrate being done with the painting," Daniel said. "And since you have to drive back to Bitter Bark tomorrow, you might as well stay in the guest suite."

She'd thought of that and packed an overnight bag. "That would be easier for me than the round trip."

"Good, it's settled, then." Gramma Finnie gave her one last hug. "You have an ally with me, lass. For what that's worth."

"I have a feeling that with this family, it's worth a lot."

He'd have married her.

Daniel was still a little stunned by the thought—the first time he'd actually realized it—after they settled down on the living room floor and gave the dogs a few treats so they didn't come sniffing at the cookies.

He'd have *married* her.

He still couldn't wrap his head around that.

"Your mom's really something," Katie said after taking a sip of coffee. "I honestly never dreamed a mother figure could be so loving. It's like she's not real."

"Oh, she's real."

"Not opinionated."

He almost choked on a sip of coffee. "Yes, she is. But she gets her message across in cute little sayings."

"Yiayia prefers a good thump to the head. Preferably with a gyro."

He smiled at that, eyeing her, taking in this woman who sat in streaming afternoon sunlight now that his sons had taken down the heavy drapes that Annie had once called her Scarlett O'Hara drapes, which Daniel still wasn't sure he understood.

They'd been pretty, but this light was glorious, and he had to admit he loved Katie's idea for shutters. Plus, the golden glow made her look bright and beautiful.

He would have married her.

"You look a little shaken up over that conversation," she said.

"I am," he admitted. "Life could have easily been so different. Some might say it *should* have."

She searched his face. "Who would say that? Not our spouses. Not me or you. Nick?"

He lifted a shoulder, sure of nothing. "Does Nick know he was your 'victory,' as you put it?"

"I think so. We were honest with the kids about how much we wanted to get pregnant at that young age and how much we didn't think they should follow in our footsteps." She gave a dry laugh and brushed some sugar off her cookie. "We didn't mean forever, though."

"The grandchildren will come," he promised her.

She nodded, her gaze still far away in the past. "Maybe wanting a child that young was dumb, but you have to understand the forces that were against us. My parents hated Nico with an intensity that's hard to describe. You know there's a small, tight-knit group of extremely wealthy people in Chestnut Creek, and my family was at the heart of it. The Santorinis were low-class Greeks who owned a 'grease pit,' as my mother lovingly called the deli."

He cringed and shook his head at that injustice. "Your dad, too?"

She rolled her eyes. "He did what Mama said, but frankly, his full attention was on Adam, my brother, who could do no wrong. I was the girl—and an afterthought, at that." She added a wry smile. "First born boys in *many* cultures have distinct advantages."

"Are you close to Adam?"

She shrugged. "Christmas and birthday calls, and I flew out to California for his granddaughter's christening a while back. My 'family' was—is, really—the Santorinis. Yiayia and Papu got over the fact that I wasn't Greek because the kids are half Greek." She sighed. "Most of them, anyway."

He let the comment pass, more interested in her extended family. "How do you think your mother-in-law will take the news?"

She looked up with raised eyebrows. "I'm sure they'll hear her roar all over the retirement community. She'll be happy that Papu isn't around to feel the pain. So Yiayia is just another person I care about whose heart I'll be breaking."

He so wanted her not to look at the situation that way, but her perspective was different, and he understood that.

"What about when you and Annie found out she was pregnant before you were married?" she asked, then waved her hand as if to say she already knew the answer. "No doubt, the world's sweetest mother showered you in Irish wedding blessings and Claddagh rings for luck."

That's *exactly* what his mother did, right down to the ring that Molly now wore.

"But not so on the other side," he told her. "Annie's mother didn't even come here for our wedding, and I don't think they were here a dozen times in the thirty-six years we were married."

"Really? What didn't they like about you? You're perfect."

"Hardly. They didn't like the fact that she got pregnant before marriage. They were extremely strict Catholics, and even my mother's assurances that she was, too, didn't matter a lick. In particular, they were never kind to Liam, and it hurt Annie so much."

"I guess it's those kinds of slights and pains that made us all work so hard to have happy families," she mused.

"You're absolutely right." His gaze automatically shifted to the wall that had, for so many years, been the representation of all things Kilcannon.

"You put all those pictures in bins for me, right?" she asked, obviously following his train of thought.

"They're in the storage unit outside. Airtight. I don't know what else to do with them."

She turned and looked at the wall for a long time, narrowing one eye in thought and then sucked in a breath. "I have an idea."

"What?"

She was silent for a moment, then turned to him, a gleam in her eyes before she reached for him, closing her hand over his. "I have an idea. A great one. Can I surprise you with it? Would you trust me?"

He didn't answer right away, instead enjoying the warmth of her touch and the hope in her question.

"I trust you," he promised, his voice thick with emotion.

She tapped her finger on his arm. "Then tell me what you're really thinking."

He inched back. "I did."

"Something in the conversation we just had with Gramma threw you off your game," she said. "I wish you'd tell me what it was."

He didn't know what he liked more, the directness of the question, or the fact that she could read him so well. "I would have married you."

"But, Daniel, I would *not* have married you."

"I'd have convinced you."

"Then Nico would have killed you."

He laughed. "So, basically, things could be worse."

After a *minute*, she gave in to a slow smile. "Much."

But he would have married her, he had no doubt. He'd have won the battle, given up Annie, even charmed her horrible parents if he'd had to. He would have married Katie Rogers because she carried his child, and…it wouldn't have been awful at all.

Deep inside, he knew that's what stunned him the most. Wasn't Annie the *only* one?

Chapter Seventeen

Painting the wall hadn't been so bad, but the ceiling took forever, and Katie and Daniel were so sore and tired by evening that they decided to have Chinese food delivered and ate it at the kitchen table.

Gramma had taken some to her room and retired for the night, after admiring their hard work and fresh paint.

As they ate fried rice and cashew chicken, Daniel shared the details of every one of his kids' love stories, each one a little more fascinating and romantic to Katie than the next.

"So Christian actually used a sacred relic to fix a loose board on the playground structure?" She choked with laughter, even though the story itself, and the danger the child had been in, wasn't funny.

"I don't think he'll appreciate the historical significance of that until he's older, but it's great family lore. And, of course, Liam gives all the credit to Jag for being the real hero."

"Your kids have so many beautiful stories with happy endings. I especially love Molly and Trace's story." She sipped some wine and thought about the proposal he'd described. "I can't believe he found the very minivan."

"I can't believe my daughter got pregnant in the back of that minivan."

"It all turned out so well. You're clearly enamored with Trace and Pru."

"Trace is another son to me and living proof that a man can go to prison and come out better and stronger. And that little general is the greatest thing that ever happened to this family." Still smiling, he shook his head. "You should have seen her at the wedding. Trace insisted they all get introduced to the church as one family."

"Oh, that's so sweet."

"God, I love orchestrating some romance. We have to do more." He focused on her. "Who can we fix up next?"

If he noticed the fact that they had just turned into a "we," then he didn't even flinch. "We're matching two families over dinner tomorrow, remember?" she said. "I'm praying that it's good."

"It will be." He had such faith in his family, and hers, that it touched her. "I've met Cassie, and she's terrific. I'm sure Alex and John are, too. And I still think this is a very smart way to prepare everyone before..." He angled his head. "D-Day."

"DNA Day," she corrected with a wry look. "You can't imagine how badly I wish I had a crystal ball to know what will happen."

"Well, we have these." He pushed up and headed to the counter, reaching into the bottom of the brown bag from Tang Wang, Bitter Bark's one and only

Chinese takeout restaurant. He pulled out two plastic-wrapped fortune cookies and brought them back to the table, sitting next to her on the bench instead of across the table where he'd eaten. "You choose first."

She let her hand hover over both, moving back and forth. "I'll take…this one."

"Okay. This is it. Our peek into what's going to happen."

They opened each with great ceremony, breaking the cookies, but neither looking at the folded paper inside. Instead, they looked into each other's eyes, and as it had all day long, Katie's heart tripped around her chest and her very next breath got imperceptibly tighter.

He was so close, she wanted to inch closer and give in to the sensations that constantly brewed when they were together. The pull of attraction, the ache to get a little closer, the full-body tingle of electricity every time they accidentally touched.

He held her gaze with one as unwavering, his summer-sky-blue eyes locked on her as if he felt that same buzz.

"I'm a little scared," she whispered, waving the fortune, but meaning something else entirely.

"Don't be." He flicked the edge of his paper with a blunt-tipped nail, drawing her gaze to his hands. It wasn't the first time she'd studied them, counting paint drippings on his knuckles and noticing how long, lean, and strong his fingers were. The hands of a man who did hard work. The hands of a man who could…

"You first," he said softly.

She looked back up at him, wishing the invitation had been to kiss him. Because she would have. Right then and there, on the lips, and with all the pent-up frustration she'd been taking out on the wall paint all day. But instead of aching muscles and a sore back, she'd have…pleasure.

"Okay." She unfolded the slip of paper, hoping her hands didn't tremble like her insides did at the moment. He leaned closer, his broad shoulder pressed against hers as he read out loud.

"'Be mischievous and you will not be lonesome.'" He chuckled. "Mischievous, huh? Doesn't sound like a word I'd associate with you."

Really? 'Cause right at that moment, *mischievous* sounded exactly right. "Maybe you don't know me."

He stayed so close she could see every shade of blue in his eyes and the hint of salt-colored whiskers in the hollows of his cheeks. "Maybe I don't."

They didn't move at all, still and close long enough for her brain to be aware that she was flirting and her body not to care.

"My turn," he said, using his thumb to unfold the fortune. He inched back so she couldn't see the words, clearing his throat to make an official reading. "'Accept defeat.'" He frowned and pretended to look a little horrified at the thought. "'It will only make you stronger.'"

"Defeat?"

Daniel let out a snort of disdain and gave his head a hard, negative shake. "I'll accept no such thing," he announced. "We're not going to be defeated."

"Maybe the fortune cookie is talking about something else," she suggested. "Maybe your next matchmaking effort won't work. Which of your nephews did you have in mind?"

"Braden." He lifted his brow. "And Cassie."

"Yep. Accept defeat. He's not Greek enough for her."

"But it's a good idea, isn't it?"

"Good heavens, Daniel, aren't things messy enough between our families?"

He didn't answer right away, but studied her face for a few seconds, then looked away when Rusty loped over and flopped his big tail a few times. "He needs to go out, and I want to do a final run through the kennels. And we should take Goldie back home."

"Home? The kennel isn't her home. Can she stay in the guest room with me?"

He tipped his head as if he was considering that, then gave a negative shake. "I'm not sure that's a good idea."

"Why not?"

"First of all, she'll sense Rusty in the same house and will probably cry at the door all night. You wouldn't like that."

"I'll comfort her."

"And then she's going to get very attached to you and wonder why you leave. If you can't commit to taking her, you'll break her heart, and she's been through enough. The next person she should get attached to should be her forever person."

She closed her eyes and let the truth bubble up. "For four years, I was responsible for a sick man. Not that I minded," she added quickly. "We made that vow, and I did what any wife would do. But it wore me down. I have a little PTSD, which I don't like to talk about, and the last thing I think I want is to be responsible for anyone on a long-term basis."

"I understand," he said. "It's a huge commitment to take a dog, and we counsel people not to even consider it if they aren't in it for the long haul."

She gave a nod of thanks, and they cleaned up and headed to take the dogs out, with Rusty moving as slowly as if he'd been the one painting all day.

Outside, Katie paused to take a deep inhale of clean night air, filling her head with the smell of winter in the woods. The occasional dog bark echoed across the yard and pen from the kennels, but mostly Waterford Farm was silent, still, and bathed in moonlight.

"Do you ever get used to how beautiful this place is?" she asked.

"When I do, I kick myself."

They walked slowly, letting the dogs sniff and stop until they reached the gate that led to the large training pen and the kennels. She'd been out here only in daylight, but now it felt different. A little more mysterious and seductive.

Or maybe that was the effect of the man walking next to her.

At the pen, Rusty headed toward a spot in the back, moving so slowly, it almost looked like he was limping, or maybe that was because Goldie, so much younger, was actually running.

She looked up to mention it to Daniel, but froze at the way he was staring at her.

"What's wrong?" she asked.

He shook his head quickly, silent. Then, "Can you stay here with Rusty while I take Goldie in? I'll be right back."

She nodded and bent down to give Goldie a kiss

and got nothing but a sad look in return. While he was gone, she listened to the increased barking—mostly Goldie at the other dogs—and leaned against the fence with a mess of confusion tangling her heart. She squinted in the moonlight to watch Rusty walk across the pen, but must have imagined that limp.

"We're both a little guilty, you know," Daniel said as he came back out.

"Of falling for Goldie, but not committing to her?"

"No, of holding back."

She turned, not understanding. "What are we holding back?"

"We promised we'd share our lives and marriages, remember? You're not talking about the toughest times, and I'm not..."

She waited, uncertain where this could be going.

"I'm not telling you everything, either," he finally said.

"You've told me a lot of stories, and each has been more entertaining than the one before it." She nudged him. "Must be the Irish in you."

But his expression remained serious. "But I'm not telling you the real stuff." He was quiet for a moment, leaning on the fence, thinking. "I guess that's harder than I thought it would be."

"Still hurts to talk about her?"

"No."

The answer surprised her, especially because it came with zero hesitation. "Then why would it be difficult?"

"Because..." He swallowed and stared at the darkness, this time obviously choosing his words with care. "It's intimate."

"You don't have to share the intimate details, Daniel. I wouldn't want to hear them."

"Our life was intimate," he replied. "The moments I miss aren't the big ones, not the major trials and memories that might appear in the family Christmas letter. The ones I miss are the little ones, the secret ones, the conversations in bed when we'd wake up at three a.m., or the days when I'd come home from having to put a dog down and she knew just what to say."

Katie sighed in agreement. "The things that make a marriage tender and real. And for me, there are details of carrying my husband through to his last breath that I don't want to share with anyone."

She tore her gaze away from the dog to look up at Daniel, a little taken aback by the intensity in his gaze. It was hot, direct, and battled with her already-shaky emotions to make her legs feel weak.

"What's wrong?" she asked, sensing that something was. Something big. Something serious.

"Everything. Nothing."

She almost smiled. "Am I staring at a man in the middle of an existential crisis?"

He closed his eyes and sighed out a breath.

"Katie." His voice was gruff. "I have to tell you something."

She could barely breathe. "What?"

"Let's go somewhere else," he said. "Somewhere safe."

She blinked at him. "This isn't safe?"

"Somewhere safe for me," he muttered. "A place where I can only do one thing. The right thing."

He took her hand and led her away, and with each step, Katie sensed he wasn't going to hold back anymore.

And she didn't know if that thrilled or terrified her.

Chapter Eighteen

After taking Rusty back into the house, Daniel decided to have this conversation in Annie's garden. It was the safest spot he could think to go. For one thing, it was outside, so there was no real risk of getting too close, comfortable, or cozy on a sofa...or bed. But the real reason Daniel took Katie to the small, hedged-in space was that his late wife's spirit was there. That alone would remind him that he needed to put the brakes on the longings that had him tight, tense, and thinking about things that he'd sworn he never would think about again.

Hell, if he gave in to the urge—the constant, staggeringly powerful urge—to kiss Katie, surely Annie's voice would ring loud in his head again, insisting that he *stop*. It could go only one place, and that was a place he'd vowed he would never go.

But as he pushed open the creaky wrought-iron gate and stepped into the moon shadows of a piece of Waterford Farm that had always belonged to Annie Harper Kilcannon, he knew he still wasn't safe, not even here.

"Oh, everything is...dormant," Katie said, taking a

few steps along the stones that Daniel had laid after Shane was born and Annie wanted somewhere to put a playpen in the sunshine. On summer days, this garden had been green and vibrant, shaded by trees and cluttered with tools and toy John Deere tractors and trucks. In the winter, she'd kept it raked and clean and ready for spring planting.

It had been a humble garden, since Annie's focus was always the kids and the foster dogs. But this place had been a source of joy for her, a way to nurture and connect with the earth, and a refuge. Now?

"It's dead," he said. Just like she was.

"No, not entirely," Katie replied quickly, turning to take in the green wall of podocarpus that formed the perimeter and the four rows of railroad ties he and his father had lugged in here to make raised vegetable beds. She stopped at a bare tree and snapped a tiny twig, angling it toward the moonlight. "There's a sliver of green in here. There's life. You could coax these back, you know, if you start now."

"Coaxing them sounds…daunting."

"I'm not a vegetable gardener, but I'm pretty good with flowers and plants. I'll give you some advice as spring comes." She stopped, obviously reading the expression on his face that said he didn't want advice or help. Not about trees, anyway. "Or not," she added.

"Katie." He reached for her hands and instantly knew it was a mistake, since they were small and comforting and fit so nicely into his. "I didn't bring you here for gardening tips."

"I know. You have to tell me something, and you want to do it in a place that is imbued with the essence of your late wife."

He flinched at the dead-on accuracy. "How did you know?"

"Lucky guess." She notched her chin toward the bench a few feet away. "Should I be sitting down for this pronouncement?"

"Maybe." He kept one of her hands in his and walked there with her. "Because I want you to be comfortable."

She perched on the edge of the bench, looking anything *but* comfortable, thinking for a second until her eyes flashed and a soft gasp passed her lips. "Is she buried here?"

"No, no." He squeezed her hand. "Way out near the perimeter road. With my dad and my uncle."

She nodded, visibly relieved. "Okay. So tell me."

"I should have told you sooner," he started, looking straight ahead, but feeling her gaze on him. "I should have told you the first time I…" *Wanted to kiss you.*

"Just tell me now," she said, putting a gentle hand over his. "I'm right here."

Yes, she was. Right here, so close, and in one moment he could put himself out of his misery by pulling her into his arms and giving in to what he knew in his heart they both wanted. But…then what?

He turned to her, taking both hands to steady himself. "Yes, you're here, and you are…"

"Waiting," she teased after five long seconds ticked away.

"You are beautiful," he finished, hating that it sounded shallow and cliché when it was so, so true. "You are beautiful and graceful and charming and so…so…" He closed his eyes to try to put his feelings into the right words. "So *good* on my heart. Do you know what I mean?"

"Not exactly, but I like the picture you're painting."

He squeezed her hands. "You make me feel... unbroken."

"I'm glad, Daniel. I feel the same way. Like that black hole of loneliness finally has a light in it."

"Yes, yes." She got it. Good. "But that's not all you make me feel." He held her gaze. "It goes deeper and more...physical."

The hint of a smile curled her pretty mouth. "I know that."

He lifted his brows in question. "Are you feeling the same thing?"

She gave a quick laugh, sounding surprised he even had to ask. "Pretty much...constantly."

"So you understand that I want to be with you in a way that..." Euphemisms. God, he hated them. "I want to hold you. All night." Just saying the words tightened everything in him. "I want to sleep with you."

She let out a ragged sigh and a simple, "Yes."

Which made his whole body heat up and hurt more. "But I can't," he said.

She eased back, searching his face, clearly confused by the confession. "They have pills."

He laughed. "I *can*. Believe me, I can. If the way I've woken up every day for the past week is—"

She put her hand over his lips. "Then why not?"

"Because I..." He closed his eyes and whispered the rest. "I made a vow."

"I know. We just painted over the faded shadow of the wedding picture, remember?"

"Not that vow," he said. "I made another one. The

day Annie died. She was in the ICU, and I was outside…lost. I swore right then and there that if she died, I would never, ever make love to another woman."

She looked a little horrified. "Why? You're not old. You're not done. You're not dead."

He closed his eyes and dropped his head. "I was dead without her. So I made the promise that I would be alone until the next time I see Annie."

"I don't understand why you'd do that, especially if she didn't ask you to. Was it something you'd talked about?"

"Never. We planned to live until we were a hundred and die within weeks of each other and get buried next to each other." Each word was like an iron nail across his chest. "My mother says that's the kind of thing that makes God laugh."

"I don't know if He laughs," she said. "I imagine more of a smile of amusement and a wry shake of His head. Then comes the bolt of lightning from out of the blue." She leaned into him. "Or a woman you want to sleep with."

He looked at her and knew she was that woman. "No one else has ever remotely tempted me," he admitted.

And it was true. The ache for her was palpable, rolling through him, making him want like a starving man facing a gourmet meal. The temptation to disregard that four-year-old promise literally made his blood burn.

"I've been regretting that vow since…" He looked skyward with a laugh. "Since the day I walked into that bakery."

She blinked at him. "Your first thought was…that?"

"Not my first," he said. "And not a conscious thought, really. But the desire was under the surface, as real and powerful as the day you walked into a kitchen and asked if that dog was my date."

"We've always had chemistry," she agreed, sounding a little wistful.

"It's more than that." He stroked her knuckles with his thumb. "And that's what really scares me."

"That it's more than chemistry?"

"Don't you see?" he asked. "I could break my vow, give in to what we want, and then…"

"You're worried about what will happen when the truth comes out about Nick?"

If only that were all. "I'm worried that once I wake up next to you, I'm going to want to do that again. And again. And again."

"That doesn't sound awful," she whispered with smile.

"It sounds like…" *Love.* And that was something Daniel Kilcannon would never feel for anyone but Annie Harper. Never, ever. "An attachment I'm not sure I can have."

She gave a rueful laugh at that, which he totally deserved for using a stupid, meaningless phrase because he was scared to say the real word. But didn't she feel the same way? After Nico? Didn't the idea of loving someone else terrify her? Didn't it feel every shade of wrong?

"Don't you think this is something we should fight?" he asked.

"No," she said simply. "But then I *did* talk to my husband about this. We had many months knowing

259

that the end wasn't too far away. We talked at length about this."

"Really?"

"It was one of Nico's favorite subjects."

He backed away, making a face. "You being with another man?"

"My being satisfied and whole and not sexually deprived."

"That's not very…romantic."

"I disagree," she said. "They were some of the most romantic conversations we ever had." She closed her eyes, and he saw her fight a wave of grief, the sensation so familiar he could ride that wave with her.

She looked down for a moment, gathering her thoughts, and then met his gaze again, her eyes damp and dark. "He not only begged me to love again, he asked me to promise I would, which I did."

"So you made the opposite promise?"

"Yes, and I made it in a haze of grief and fear and knowledge that he likely wouldn't live to the end of that week." She drew a line in the dirt with the toe of her boot, lost in thought for a moment. "For the years he was sick, it became a little running joke. At first, a way to bring humor to the cancer situation. Like, if we joked about it, then we'd never have to face it. Especially in the beginning, when we had hope. With each new attempt at chemo, with each slight improvement, he'd tease me about how I wouldn't get a chance to take a lover or find a second husband."

Her voice cracked, and he stroked her hand, listening.

"As the years went by and cancer became our life, the idea of him dying became a reality, then my future was less of a source of humor. He wanted everything lined up, so I would be secure, and spent hours with John making sure the deli would always be a source of income for me."

"A wise and good man."

"He was." She clasped her hands in front of her chin, thinking. "A few days before he died, when he was briefly lucid, he made me promise that I wouldn't be alone. He made me take his hand and put it over his heart and..." A tear dribbled as a sob choked her.

"Katie."

She shook her head, not wanting to be stopped. "He made me swear I would love again. Made me promise—I'm not making this up—that I would have sex again. It was important to him, because our life in that regard died long before he did. So he made me take an oath that I would not go to my grave without..." She gave a wistful smile. "Well, you get the idea. He used...personal words."

The secret language of lovers. He knew it so well. "That was amazingly heroic of him, and not something many men would do. He obviously loved you with his whole heart and soul."

"He did. So I promised. I mean, what was I going to do? Deny a man his dying wish?" She wiped a tear. "So I've spent the last two years healing and growing and finding my independence."

He took her chin in his hand and turned her to face him. "And you're ready?"

"Completely." She held his gaze with one so beautifully dark and intense, it shocked him. "I would love to keep my promise, and I would love for that to be with you. I'm sure that's a little forward of me, but it's true. I would make love to you in a heartbeat."

Low in his gut, down to his toes, a slow, unfamiliar heat burned through him, pushing him closer, making his pulse pound, drying his mouth so that he couldn't swallow. Or breathe. Or think about anything but how they were inching closer and closer.

A heartbeat. Like the one pounding in his chest that very minute.

So much for his safe place in the garden.

"And you, sir..." She placed her hand on his cheek, a gesture that should have been tender, but suddenly felt as intimate and sexual as if she had raked her nails over his bare chest and kept going. "You have probably never broken a promise in your life, even one you made to yourself."

"I don't know, Katie." He let his gaze drop to her mouth, already tasting the sweetness of it. "Is it even a promise if it's only made to yourself?"

"No one heard you?" The hope in her voice was tender and adorable.

"I told Rusty later, and he's up in my room right now, waiting for me."

"He'll never know if you spend a few hours in the guest room."

His gut clenched as he stared at her. It would be so easy. So. Damn. Easy. He let his eyes close, felt himself lean in, slid his hand up under her hair...and kissed her.

Lightly at first, barely touching, but as the surrender took over, he pressed into her mouth, which was soft and sweet and tasted of that indescribable flavor of woman and pleasure and intimacy.

Her lips parted, her breath caught, and her hands slid up his arms to pull him closer. Fire licked up his back and into his chest, burning away any regrets, second-guesses, or hesitation.

He wanted this kiss. He wanted this moment. He wanted this woman.

They both turned toward each other, deepening the kiss and angling their bodies to hold each other closer. He gripped her shoulders and slid his hands down the silk of her down jacket, already aching to push it off her shoulders and get it out of the way.

She whimpered and sighed, and he curled his tongue around hers, then used his thumbs to lift her chin so he could press his lips on her jaw and throat.

Ancient, primal, long-forgotten sensations whipped through him, shocking him with their intensity, punching him with need, and taking his breath away as effectively as this powerful, perfect kiss.

"Daniel." She sighed his name, her hands moving from his hair to clasp his neck. Her palms were damp, her arms shaking. "Do you remember that night? After the party where we met?"

The question threw him from a blissful present to a blurry past, to a night he remembered only vaguely, but pleasantly. "Sort of," he admitted, very slowly pulling away to look at her, his arousal kicked to the next level at the flush in her cheeks, spark in her eyes, and parted lips he wanted against his again. "Why?"

"When you kissed me that night, I was…thrown."

He smiled. "You just said it. We have chemistry."

"That's not what threw me," she whispered. "I was thrown because I still loved Nico."

"You never stopped."

"Exactly. I loved him fiercely, and yet I let you press me right up against the wall outside of Gillespie Hall and kiss the holy hell and common sense out of me."

"You seem to bring that out in me."

"But I loved Nico."

He raised his brows. "Your point…"

"We have the kind of connection that allows for us to be physical and share pleasure, but not stop loving that…puzzle piece, whether it's next to us or not."

He stared at her for a moment. "Is that possible?"

"Obviously, yes."

"And that's what you want?" he asked. "Essentially, sex with the knowledge that we're both in love with other people, even though they're gone?"

She let out one long, shuddering sigh. "Well, when you put it that way…"

"It's the only way to put it." He inched away as a slow, icy, far more familiar numbness crawled over his skin, dousing the heat they'd just built. He knew this feeling, had learned it as a kid, lived with it his whole life. His gut instinct. His moral commandments. His foundation, taught to him by wise Irish parents who lived a simple life guided by knowing the difference between right and wrong.

Getting pregnant before marriage wasn't wrong. Skipping church on Sundays wasn't wrong. Pulling a few strings to be a matchmaker at romance wasn't wrong.

But making love to a woman while still loving another one?

"It feels wrong," he said simply.

"You always did have a helluva code of ethics."

He closed his eyes. "Not usually a fault, but yes, I live by a simple creed of doing what's right and walking away from what's wrong."

He felt her whole body slump ever so slightly. "I know that. I really like that about you."

"Then you have to accept that if I change that, if I go south when my compass tells me to go north, then…"

"You'll be lost."

He sighed with relief that she understood. "I'm afraid so."

For a long time, she sat very still, not touching him anymore, not even looking at him with that sexy, irresistible promise in her eyes. He prayed he hadn't hurt her, but didn't want to say anything as he waited for her response.

She just smiled and stood, the only noise the swish of her jacket-covered arms brushing her sides when she dropped her arms.

"You want to go in?" he asked.

"I'm going to get Goldie," she announced. "I'm going to bring her with me to the guest room tonight where she can sleep on the rug or at the bottom of the bed. If she needs comfort, I'll give it. If she offers company, I'll take it. If she gets too attached and wants forever?"

He looked up at her, waiting for the rest.

"Then we'll deal with that as it happens," she finally said.

He reached for her, half expecting her to yank her hand out of his, but she didn't. She let him hold her hand, but didn't grasp back, looking down at him. "I don't want to—"

"Shhh." She released his hand and put a finger on his lips. "I understand, respect, and admire you." Her lips curled in a smile. "I also think we got our fortunes mixed up. You need to be a little more mischievous to not be lonely, and I need to…" She gave a quick laugh. "Accept defeat."

He stayed silent, not trusting his voice.

"Good night, Daniel."

He just stared at her.

It *was* wrong. Breaking his vow was wrong. Falling for another woman was wrong. Everything about this was *wrong*.

Except Katie, who was so damn right it hurt to think about it.

He watched her walk out of the garden, seeing a woman he knew could give him pleasure and satisfaction, and he'd easily return the favor. His body screamed for that kind of release. His brain rattled with common sense, telling him they were both smart adults who could not only handle it, but enjoy it.

But his heart. His poor, wretched, broken, bruised heart still belonged to someone else.

Frustrated, he stood, turned, and demanded answers.

"Doesn't it, Annie? Aren't you the only one I should ever be with?"

All he heard was a rustle of wind, a click of the kennel door in the distance, then, after a moment, the familiar bark of a red golden retriever who, if Daniel were to truly be honest, should be moving into his home and room right now. But then he'd fall in love with her. And she wasn't an Irish setter, and that's the only dog he could ever have as his own. It would be wrong to give his heart and home to a dog who wasn't an Irish setter. That's the Kilcannon family dog. That's...

Dumb. That was closed-minded and shortsighted and dumb as dirt.

He walked to the tree in the middle of the garden, closing his fist over a thin, crispy branch, snapping it off with frustration.

"Annie girl, help me." He dropped his head in defeat, staring at the twig in his hand with stinging eyes. He angled it and looked closely. Sure enough, there was a thread of green in there, thin and nearly invisible, but it was...something.

It was hope. It was life. It was the possibility that this tree, dead and dry and withered to the world, still had a chance to grow and thrive. A chance to soak up the sun and provide shade and give a home to birds and bees. This tree's life wasn't over.

Was that what the *gardener* was trying to tell him?

Chapter Nineteen

C assie climbed into Katie's car, barely able to contain the curiosity that had vibrated off her ever since they'd met at Hoagies & Heroes a few hours ago. "Spent the night, did ya?"

Katie gave a soft grunt and questioned whether having Cassie ride with her to Waterford Farm was such a great idea.

"I did." She volleyed back a meaningful glare. "In the guest room, with the sweetest golden retriever snoring at the foot of the bed, not that you for one second would suspect anything else. Can we talk about that restaurant? That layout is almost a replica of the original deli. It couldn't be more perfect for the next Santorini's."

"It sure is," she agreed with what sounded like a sigh of resignation. "And Alex almost had an orgasm at the sight of that brand-new grill top. Speaking of…" Cassie's eyes blazed as she looked Katie up and down as if she could see some physical change. "Just you and the dog and no one else?"

Just the two of them and a few bittersweet tears. "Cassie, please."

"Don't 'Cassie, please' me, Mom. You've spent nearly every waking minute with the guy for a week or more, and last night you didn't come home."

"We painted until well past dark, as I knew we would, so I took an overnight bag. No need to drive back an hour and a half to Chestnut Creek late at night only to turn around and come right back to Bitter Bark. It made sense."

Although, since last night in the garden, nothing made sense anymore.

Not the fact that she had feelings she'd never dreamed she could have again…or the fact that she'd been essentially turned down for being wrong. The wrong woman? The wrong time? The wrong place? Who knew? Who cared? She was…*wrong*.

"Are you okay?" Cassie asked.

"I'm fine." She turned the key and looked over her shoulder while she pulled it out. "It's just…you know." But, of course, she couldn't know.

"Nick. I know."

Katie seized on the obvious. "Today's important, honey. I want everyone to like each other. That'll help when the secret comes out."

"The secret." Cassie dropped against the leather with a noisy sigh, reaching for her seat belt. "It's like living in a soap opera."

"Which I would imagine is your happy place, DQ."

She snorted at the nickname Nico had given his little drama queen long ago. "Not happy, but it's never dull."

"No kidding," Katie agreed. "Was John serious about buying instead of renting?"

"Let's see." Cassie took out her phone to check

texts. "Alex says he won't stop talking about it." She read a text and laughed. "Alex said, 'If the spreadsheet fits, John'll wear it.'"

"So you and Alex text about John behind his back?"

"And vice versa, and I'm sure they grunt about me when I'm not around, and sometimes John gripes about how much money Alex spends on arcane recipes, and I do the same thing with Theo, you know. We all have little subgroups."

"Even Nick?"

She sighed. "It's rare, but we talk to him. John more than anyone. Those two are close."

Katie nodded, understanding the family dynamic and grateful to have Cassie as her insider. "And your brothers are all ready for this gathering at Waterford Farm?"

"Ready? They think the purpose is to meet your new boyfriend."

"Why would they think that?" She sputtered the question. "I haven't given them any reason to think that. It's to help you guys ease into Bitter Bark, maybe get some assistance with the construction and drumming up business. It makes sense for them to help us and..." She glanced at Cassie, who was just smiling.

"And to get to know your new boyfriend."

"Listen, I hate to break it to you, but he's not and never will be my boyfriend. It would be...wrong." Or so he'd said.

"Why wrong? I mean, it would be complicated. Surprising. A little amusing, you have to admit. Occasionally awkward. And..." Cassie reached over and touched her arm. "You've been happier since you reunited with him."

"That's because he's a support system for what I'm facing with Nick," she said.

"Have it your way," Cassie replied, giving up for once, but maybe not for good. "And speaking of Nick who never texts, he actually *did* reach out to me today."

Katie ripped her gaze from the road ahead to look at Cassie. "Everything okay?"

"He's a goner over this French babe."

"Babe? She's an anesthesiologist, Cassie."

"With a Latin phrase tattooed on her hip that says something about bastards grinding." At Katie's questioning look, Cassie shrugged. "I might have stalked her Instagram account."

"Anything good?" Katie asked.

Cassie curled her lip. "Dr. Babe has had a *lot* of boyfriends. One in particular with sixty billion pictures of them in Paris before she went to Africa. I hope she's not a rebound girl."

"Well, people change. And you can't tell anything from social media. What else did Nick say?"

She was quiet for a moment, long enough for Katie to dread what might be coming next, which could be—

"He asked about the Bloodline.com results again."

That. "Really?"

"You know, I think Theo, Alex, and John have completely forgotten about the test. If I never mentioned it again, neither would they. But for some reason, it matters to Nick. No chance he suspects, right?"

"God, no. When I didn't know, how could he?"

"He said this Lucienne's family is weird about being French."

Katie rolled her eyes. "When are people going to learn that your ancestry doesn't matter when it comes to love? For the record, I don't care if you marry a Martian, as long as he's good to you."

"And hot." She threw Katie a sassy smile. "Actually, I don't agree. I want a man who understands my culture, and I don't just mean the difference between pastitsio and baked ziti. I want someone who treasures family and knows the classics and is named after a saint."

Katie had to laugh. "I'm glad your father didn't feel that way," she said. "So what did you tell Nick?"

"A big fat juicy lie." Her voice sounded pained.

"Which was?"

"I told him that his results couldn't be read."

Katie looked at her. "Why did you tell him that?"

"Because you said that happens in one in ten thousand times or some such thing, and it will get him off our case. If he wants to do the test so badly, it'll take time, and by then, we'll have Daniel's results and can tell Nick the truth."

"You hate lying to him."

"More than you know, but he started pestering me for the name of the company and a phone number and how he can get in touch with them. So I cut him off at the pass and…" She shut her eyes. "Pretended the call dropped."

"Oh, honey." Katie turned out of Bitter Bark and headed to the now familiar route to Waterford Farm. "I told you what Daniel said, that they can expedite the results and that they have a division to deal with this stuff."

"I don't want him to know that yet, do you?"

"Of course not." She hit the accelerator a little as they cruised onto a long stretch of road, the engine rev matching her pulse. "I wish we knew what was going to happen and how Nick will take the news."

"Not well."

"And Daniel's family," she added.

"Also not well, especially after they all help us open a restaurant."

Katie practically squirmed in her seat. "Daniel knows them better than anyone. He feels strongly that the bonding will help ease the pain and shock of the news."

Cassie didn't answer, staring out the window in silence, letting Katie's thoughts go back to where they'd been all morning and the night before: Daniel. They stayed there until she pulled into the long driveway, seeing that John and Alex had already arrived and were being greeted by two men she didn't recognize.

"Those aren't Daniel's sons." She squinted at the tall figures with similar dark good looks and wearing matching short-sleeved navy T-shirts with white emblems on the front.

"The firefighters," Cassie said, sliding a look to Katie. "Who are smokin', if you'll excuse the pun."

Katie smiled and almost shared Daniel's thoughts about Braden, but something made her keep that to herself. Cassie wouldn't like being on the receiving end of the Dogfather's matchmaking. "Very nice-looking," she agreed.

"Especially the one on the right." Cassie narrowed her eyes. "Those shoulders. Whoa."

Katie bit her lip and gave a noncommittal, "Hmmm."

"Come on, Mom. You don't have to be under forty to appreciate that." She glanced at Katie. "What?"

Damn her inability to hide anything. Cassie would smell a setup in no time. "Nothing. They're handsome. They're Daniel's nephews, which makes them…" Eligible and single.

"Not cousins," Cassie said. "We're not related in any way, shape, or form, are we?" She dipped her head and gave a playful look. "Although with you and your colorful past, Mom…"

"Stop it." She tapped her daughter's arm and put the car in park, and their arrival made the four men chatting turn to greet them, too. Katie took one quick breath before turning off the car and starting the day. "Do you think this will work?" she whispered, as much to herself as to Cassie.

"I don't know if we'll become one big happy family, but I gotta say this, the gene pool looks like a decent place to take a swim."

On that, they climbed out and began the introductions.

"Hey, Mom, have you met Braden and Connor?" John asked.

Katie came forward, smiling at the two men, finding herself searching for similarities to Nick or even Daniel. She honestly didn't see any, but did notice that both men were handsome, especially the taller, slightly broader one.

"Braden Mahoney," he said, reaching out a hand to shake Katie's, but giving himself away with a second and third glance at Cassie. "Part of what is commonly known around here as the Mahoney cousins."

"Hello, Braden." Her hand was swallowed in his while he blinded her with a smile. No, actually, that smile was directed at Cassie.

"And you must be...Connor or Declan?" Katie guessed.

"Connor." He shook her hand next. "Declan's in the kennels with Uncle Daniel."

"This is my daughter, Cassie," Katie said, putting a hand on Cassie's back.

"Short for Cassandra?" Braden asked.

"Yes, all of us have Greek names," Cassie said. "My oldest brother, Nick, is really Nico. John is Yianni."

"A fact I keep quiet about," John joked.

"Alexander, as in the Great," Cassie finished, pointing to her other brother. "And there's also Theo, which is short for Theodoros. All Greek," she added, her dark eyes glinting with pride and maybe a little bit of a challenge.

"But only one named after a princess and a prophet," Braden said, pinning a dark blue gaze on her.

She inched back and glanced at her mother, unable to hide her surprise. "Why, that's right."

"The prophet no one believed," he added.

Her jaw actually dropped. "Yeah, wow. Someone paid attention in...where did you learn that?"

"I read a lot." There was a hint of humility and humor in the comment that Katie didn't expect from someone so big and handsome.

"He's a literal bookworm," Connor told them. "Just ask the rest of the people at the firehouse. We're cooking, eating, playing video games, or watching movies, but Braden has his nose in a book. And no digital stuff for this dude. He's got an actual library card."

"And you read Greek mythology?" Cassie voice rose with piqued interest.

"I like the classics."

Katie almost choked, the echo of Cassie's list of requirements still fresh in her memory. Good heavens, Daniel was good at this matchmaking thing.

Over Braden's shoulder, she saw the kennel doors open and caught sight of Daniel's silver head of hair among the group of people who walked out. Instantly, she felt her muscles tighten in anticipation of seeing him, hating that she zeroed right in on the man and wanted to stare at him.

"There's Goldie," Connor said, following her gaze.

"Oh!" Katie hadn't even noticed the dog. "Yes, there she is." She felt her whole face light up, but her gaze went right back to Daniel, taking in how broad his shoulders looked in a black pullover, imagining that she could hear his now familiar laugh from here.

"Mom, you're smitten," Cassie teased.

Katie looked away quickly, probably appearing as guilty as she felt. "Well...I...I just have fallen so hard for that dog." With a secret, smug look at Cassie, she gestured to her sons. "Come with me, I'll introduce you to the one who's stolen my heart."

"The dog or the man?" Alex muttered as they walked away.

Both.

Daniel leaned against the kitchen counter, his post-Sunday-dinner coffee warming him almost as much as the laughter and talk that echoed through the entire first floor of his home.

With all of the Mahoneys here, including his sister, Colleen, plus Katie and her three kids, and every one of the Kilcannon clan, the head count reached twenty-six, and the decibel level hit deafening. Gramma's buffet had worked perfectly, feeding the crowd and giving everyone a chance to find a place to eat and mingle.

With dinner over and the last of the daylight fading, some of them had gone out to play with dogs or take walks or offer tours, while others sat in groups talking and laughing. Young Christian led a few of his aunts and uncles to the family room for what sounded like a rousing round of Mario Kart.

"Take her, Dad?" He turned to see Liam's outstretched arms holding nine-month-old baby Fiona. "Andi and I are going to sit down with John Santorini to talk about some of the construction they need done for the new restaurant. Now that they're thinking about buying it instead of renting, she thinks she can easily design the architecture modifications they have in mind."

"As if I need a reason to take my granddaughter."

Fiona's big blue eyes sparkled at the sight of him. With a little drool on the side of her rosebud lips, she reached her tiny hands toward Daniel, greedy for her grandpa.

"Hello, wee Fee," he whispered, kissing her head as he snuggled an armful of sweet delight.

She gurgled and instantly plopped her head on his

shoulder with a sigh of contentment that Daniel knew he hadn't imagined.

"Now she's happy." On his other side, his nephew Declan came closer.

"Now we both are."

Declan laughed, revealing a few crinkles around his eyes and turning his head so the light caught the first few strands of silver at the temples of his nearly black hair. Good God, that was a shock. He still thought of Dec as a fourteen-year-old fishing in the lake or running around with Liam and Garrett playing tag all over Waterford Farm.

But this firefighter captain was closer to forty than fourteen. Maybe Declan should be on the receiving end of Daniel's matchmaking skills, he mused, sliding a look out the picture window to notice that Cassie and Braden were still talking, as they had been since the minute Katie and her kids had arrived. Could his work already be done there, or at least getting started?

"You look as happy as Fiona does," Declan mused, nodding at the crowded kitchen. "Nothing like a full house for your Sunday dinner."

"Nothing like it," Daniel agreed. "And it's been more than a month since you've been able to make it."

He glanced skyward. "Captain's duties. I don't know why I thought this promotion would make things easier, but it seems all I do is work."

"You need time for fun, Dec," Daniel said. "And a woman."

He choked a laugh. "Shane's been warning me I'm next on your list."

"It'll be a rare woman who's got the right heart for you."

He gave a tight smile. "Relax, Uncle Daniel. If you need to be the Dogfather, go to work on Connor, if you can find a woman he hasn't loved and left in a fifty-mile radius. That boy needs some settling down. Me? I'm too busy for a life outside of the firehouse."

Daniel gave him a skeptical look. "No one's too busy."

"Not even you." He gave a pointed look to Katie, who was deep in conversation with Daniel's sister at the kitchen table.

Daniel opened his mouth to deny the suggestion he'd heard over and over again that day, sometimes in subtle ways like this and others less so. But like he had every other time, Daniel closed his mouth and refused to set the record straight. They all thought there was something going on with him and Katie, and that was probably because there was. Just not what they imagined.

Colleen gave a soft hoot, and she and Katie looked at Daniel as if they were talking about him.

"He never knew," Colleen said.

"Never knew what?" he asked, coming closer.

"Something that happened the day I came here for dinner all those years ago," Katie said, the color rising in her cheeks.

"What was it?" He sat down on the long bench facing them, patting Fiona's tiny back.

"You two were caught kissing on camera," Colleen told him.

"What?" Daniel's voice rose in surprise, making Fiona lift her head for a second, before finding her thumb and dropping back onto his shoulder. "No one took pictures that day."

"Not that you knew of." Colleen flipped her long, brown hair over her shoulder, her eyes dancing mischievously. "But Dad bought that Sony camcorder, remember? He couldn't figure out how to use it, so he let me play with it." She gave a toothy grin, suddenly looking very much like the pesky little sister she'd been before she grew into a wonderful woman.

"What did you do?"

"Followed you on that nice long walk you took."

Katie hung her head in pretend humiliation. "I don't think I want to hear any more."

"You didn't do much, just made out like a couple of fools down by the lake."

"And you filmed it?" Daniel practically choked on the words, and this time, Fiona let out a whimper of unhappiness. "I'm sorry, sweetheart," he said, gently guiding the baby's head back to his shoulder, but glaring at his sister. "But your great-aunt Colleen is in big trouble."

"Why?" Colleen asked. "I never showed it to anyone."

"But we saw it, lass." Gramma came over, slipping in from the sidelines where she obviously had been listening to every word. "Seamus and I discovered it when we were watching some family movies one night. Had a good laugh, we did."

Katie put her face in her hands. "And I am mortified."

"No need to blush, lass," Gramma assured Katie. "You didna do anything too terrible, just a whole lot of smoochin'."

"No worries, Katie." Daniel reached over to lift her chin so he could look at her. "It was long ago, and there's probably not a working VCR anywhere in this family."

Gramma sat next to him and peered up over her glasses. "Which is why we had all those old plastic tapes put on DVDs ages ago, before Seamus died. Sometimes I watch them and remember my youth." She gave a yellowed grin at Daniel and Colleen. "And yours."

Once again, Daniel and Katie shared a look at a situation that was both hilarious and embarrassing.

"You want to watch?" he asked her.

"Uh, not with the whole family gathered for a group viewing."

They held each other's gaze during the laughter, and for a moment, it felt like all the noise and family and even the baby on his arm disappeared. And last night in the garden seemed like a million miles and as many second-guesses away.

In her eyes, he saw a reflection of what he was feeling, a need that had practically strangled him since they'd said good night in the garden. As much as he loved this day, surrounded by his family and hers, he ached to be alone with her again. Just for a few minutes, just...alone.

"Want to go see Goldie?" he asked, knowing she was disappointed they'd had to put the dog in the kennels for the day, but the house was full of granddogs that would have tested all of Goldie's lackluster socializing skills. "We could put Fiona in her stroller and take them both for a walk."

"To the *lake*," Colleen teased, cracking them all up.

Katie laughed, too, pushing away from the table. "I'd love to see Goldie," she said. "And, Gramma

Finnie, name your price and I'll take that DVD off your hands."

"Oh, lass, I've no idea where it is."

A few minutes later, he had Fiona buckled up in her stroller and let Katie push it across the driveway toward the pen, where they were both surprised to see Goldie walking slowly near the fencing.

"She's out," Katie exclaimed at the sight of her. "And there are other dogs!"

Garrett waved them closer to where he stood with Alex and two border collies who would be part of a training class launching the next day.

"She's staying to herself, but no aggression so far," Garrett said proudly.

"That's fantastic," Katie said.

"Did you guys do something different yesterday with her? She seems so much more settled."

They glanced at each other, both knowing that the only thing different was that Goldie had slept in the house with Katie, but that couldn't help with socializing, right?

"We had her with us all the time," Daniel said.

"That was a good call," Garrett said. "I got an email this morning from a family in Boone looking to adopt a golden retriever, so I'll tell them we've got the girl they want."

Katie sucked in a quick breath. "Really?"

"It's a good family," Garrett assured her. "They don't have any other dogs and lost a retriever a few months ago. Two kids, big property. I like the fit. You taking her for a walk? Let me go get a leash."

As Garrett walked away, Katie gave Daniel a concerned look. "What about Rusty?"

"What about him?"

"Daniel! Goldie is his girl. His best friend. His comfort."

He let out a sigh. If he let Goldie into his life and heart, she'd never leave. Could he commit to that? He'd sworn Rusty would be his last. There were so many dogs around here and kids, and she wasn't ever going to be *his* dog.

Katie slipped behind the gate and knelt down next to the retriever. "I'm so proud of you, Goldilocks. You're a good girl."

But maybe Katie would change her mind about taking the dog.

"Here you go." Garrett returned with a long walking leash, handing it to Katie, who clipped it on like a dog pro. Yes, maybe she would change her mind.

"Hold off on that call to the family in Boone, Garrett," Daniel said. "Let's be a hundred percent sure about Goldie."

Garrett frowned, obviously not expecting that. "Sure."

All leashed up, Goldie did her happy circles, then trotted over to give baby Fiona a passing sniff before heading down the path. They took a few steps ahead as Daniel got behind the stroller and kicked the brake free.

"You want to keep that dog, Dad?" Garrett asked quietly. "I know she's pretty tight with Rusty."

"I want to…" His gaze shifted to Katie. "Make her happy."

Garrett gave a tight smile and nodded, smart enough not to ask if Daniel meant the dog or the woman. Daniel pushed the stroller and caught up with them quickly.

"Where to?" she asked as they reached the first fork.

"Right takes us to a huge field. Left takes us to the lake."

She glanced over her shoulder. "Should we make sure no one is following us this time?"

"Can you believe my sister?" Daniel shook his head on a laugh. "What a brat."

"What a memory," Katie said under her breath.

Yeah, it was. He put one hand on her back and steered Fiona's stroller with the other. "So what do you think of our family matchmaking efforts?"

"Big success," she said. "You were right to put them together like this to build a bridge. It was genius."

"I don't feel like much of a genius today."

She glanced at him, a question in her eyes.

"I might have blown it last night."

"Nah. You're right. We're better off as friends. I think the paint fumes made me crazy."

He laughed. "I think the way you kiss made me crazy."

Goldie stopped, and so did Katie, turning to look up at him. "I heard you tell Garrett not to call the family about adopting her."

He gave a shrug. "Maybe she can stay closer to home."

"Like inside Waterford?"

"Like in Chestnut Creek."

"You think I should adopt her?"

"I think you two have a great connection, and that

284

way, she'd be close to Rusty. We'd see her every time we see you."

"Which would be how often? I mean, considering this is...*wrong*."

Letting out a little grunt, he closed his eyes to stop the volley about dogs when it was them they needed to talk about.

"I messed up," he admitted. "I never slept last night."

"Lot of that going on," she said.

He stroked her cheek with his thumb, holding her gaze as his heart crawled up his chest and settled in his throat. "I'm confused. A little scared. Uncertain of what to do. For the first time in my life, what's right and what's wrong isn't clear. The only thing that's clear is that I want to be with you."

The corners of her lips hinted at the faintest smile.

"I want to kiss you like I did last night. A lot. I want to hold you and know you and...and..." He lifted her face toward him. "None of that seems the least bit wrong."

"But will you second-guess that decision?"

"I don't want to, but..." He huffed out a breath. "I'm torn. I'm scared. I'm cautious. I'm..."

"I'm none of those things, Daniel. But I do not want you to wake up on our first morning together and drown in guilt or regret. So you have to be sure."

Right that minute, he was so sure. He lowered his face to put his lips on—

"Dad! Dad!"

They jerked apart, spinning around to see Liam tearing down the path toward them.

"What's the matter?"

"It's…Rusty." In the time it took Liam to take one deep breath, Daniel felt his heart stop. "He's having a seizure. Pretty bad. Molly's with him."

He didn't even stop to think except to angle the stroller handle toward Liam and give one quick look at Katie.

"Go!" she said, pushing him forward.

He did, running back to the house so fast the wind whistled past his ears. Screamed at him, actually.

Damn it all!

Was this what happened when he broke his vow?

Chapter Twenty

"She's not exactly a lapdog." Molly came into the den where Katie was tucked into the corner of the sofa with Goldie sprawled over her legs.

"Tell her that," Katie said. "Any news?"

On a sigh, Molly sat down on the other side of Goldie's hind legs, stroking her fur. "Dad's on the phone with Dr. Evangeline Hewitt, who is not only an excellent veterinary neurologist, she was also one of my best friends in vet school."

"Oh, really." Katie sat up a little. The dog experts in the family had been saying that a neurologist was needed but not easy to find outside of large cities. "So she lives nearby? She can see Rusty right away?"

"She works at the N.C. State Veterinary Hospital in Raleigh, and she's a qualified veterinary brain surgeon. She's reviewing the scans we did today. That's all I know, because Dad asked me to come out here and check on you."

"I'm fine," Katie said. "But I don't want to leave him. What's your professional opinion about Rusty?"

Molly took a deep breath as if considering her words. "It could be a tumor, which is my guess, and Dad agrees. Something we can't see on the scans. If that's the case, then it's like any other tumor, either benign or…"

Katie closed her eyes. "I hate cancer in a way that's hard to describe."

"I bet you do." Molly put a sympathetic hand over Katie's. "And we hate to make you even relive a minute of it."

"Don't worry," she said. "At least I'm familiar with the terminology and surgeries."

"Yeah, surgery." Molly sighed. "That's the big question. Is Rusty too old to endure brain surgery? That's what Evie and my dad were talking about when I left."

"The poor man," Katie murmured. "I hurt for him."

Molly nodded with sympathy and glanced around. "I guess most of the troops have disappeared."

"Reluctantly," Katie said. "My kids headed back to Chestnut Creek while you were all in the vet office with Rusty, and Liam and Andi wanted to get the kids home. Garrett practically carried Jessie out of here."

"She's gonna pop any minute." Molly tapped her barely noticeable baby bump. "Makes me wish I could fast-forward to August and join her."

"Do you feel okay? The first three months are so hard."

"I haven't been sick much, but poor Chloe, who's a few weeks behind me, can't even look at food. Speaking of my offspring, where's Pru?"

"She and Gramma Finnie went upstairs to work on a blog."

Molly gave a wry smile. "Code word for Gramma needs to pray, and Pru is probably sound asleep on a mountain of embroidered pillows right next to her, like she's two again."

"They're sweet together."

"Sweet and sassy." She inched back to get a look into the kitchen. "And Trace?"

"He's with…Aidan, I think, and Darcy and Josh. In the kennels with all their dogs." She patted Goldie. "Basically, all dogs have to clear out, or Goldie will bark their heads off."

"It's a shame she has that problem," Molly said. "But my brothers will train it out of her. They've already made good progress."

"I know," Katie agreed. "I just wish she could get good enough to slide into a permanent slot here with Rusty. But Daniel…"

Molly snorted. "That won't happen. He'll never let another dog into his heart."

"Why not?" Katie asked. "Is it really just because she's not a setter? That's so out of character for a man like him."

"Oh, that's what he says. Just like my Grandpa Seamus. The Kilcannon house dog has to be from the line of the 'great Fergus and Enya of County Waterford…'" She grinned at the imitation of her grandmother's Irish brogue, only in a deeper, more masculine voice. "But the truth is, Rusty is Dad's great one."

"His great one?"

"All dog lovers have dogs, obviously. But in your life, there's usually one that stands out. That amazing, one-of-a-kind creature with a soul that utterly connects to yours. For Trace, it's Meatball. For Jessie, it's Lola. For little Christian, well, he'll compare every dog for the rest of his life to Jag."

Katie smiled, knowing the deep connection the young boy had with the remarkably well-trained German shepherd who once saved him.

"No dog will ever reach Meatball's status for my husband," Molly continued. "The great one is a person, really. One that's there with you for the best and worst days of life. Rusty is my dad's great one. He'll love other dogs, welcome them and take care of them and appreciate them. But in his heart? There'll never be another Rusty, and so he says at his age, he doesn't need to start over and try and build that kind of attachment. Doesn't want to. He's had his great one."

Katie stared at her, vaguely aware of the lump forming in her throat.

He's had his great one.

"Well, you're a great one, Goldilocks." Her voice caught, and she cleared her throat and leaned over to put her face in the dog's fur to hide the emotions from Molly.

But Molly put her hand on Katie's shoulder and eased her up. "I'm talking about dogs, you know."

Katie fought a smile and willed her eyes to be dry. "I know."

"Because my dad has been different since you've been around. Happier. Younger. Just…better."

"We both are," Katie whispered.

"That's good." Molly searched her face, no judgment or smile or scorn on her lovely features. Only warmth in eyes that somehow managed to be both brown and green, the same as the eyes of a girl

Katie remembered gazing at Daniel with an unabashed crush. "And whatever happens between you two," Molly said, "you know you'll have our family's full support."

For whatever *happens?* Once again, Katie's stomach dropped with the knowledge that there was so much more that these young men and women didn't know. They would all be tested by the truth soon enough.

"Thank you," she said simply. "And can I just say that you are a carbon copy of your mother?"

Molly's smile grew to blinding. "Thank you. It's my life's goal to be more like her." She leaned forward. "I always wondered about you, you know."

"About me?"

"The one that had to let him go," she said on a laugh. "I mean, the blind date meet-cute is a fun story for us, but Darcy and I would always climb into bed as teenagers and ask each other, 'What about the girlfriend? Wasn't she super put out by the whole thing?'"

"We weren't really..." But they *were* serious enough, as everyone would soon learn. "I told you I was in love with..." But still had sex with Daniel, as they would no doubt realize. "I was fine with it," she finally finished. "We both ended up exactly where we were supposed to spend our lives."

"But your life isn't over," Molly said. "And neither is his. Don't you think it's kind of poetic to reunite after all these years?"

Katie smiled, not sure how poetic any of this was.

"Of course, I say that as a woman reunited with the father of her child," Molly added. "A man, mind you, who didn't even know he had a daughter. And a woman who thought he'd disappeared after one night together."

Katie almost melted into the sofa. "Talk about poetic." And surely this young woman would be sympathetic when she learned the truth. On impulse, Katie reached over and pulled Molly into a hug, not explaining it and not having to. She got hugged right back.

"Good news." Daniel's entrance broke them apart.

"Evie's coming," Molly said, no question in her voice.

He nodded. "She'll be here early in the morning, and she's confident she can operate in our Bitter Bark surgery center. She's bringing a vet van from her hospital, and they have a few bells and whistles we don't, including a mobile MRI that's better than what we have and should help us find that sucker. She's convinced it's a tumor."

"That's good news, Dad."

"She thinks she can find and remove a tumor and firmly believes that it's better for Rusty not to travel to her surgery center in Raleigh. If all goes well, I can take him there after the surgery for a few days of observation and checking to see if..."

If the cancer spread. Katie knew the drill all too well. "And she's not concerned about surgery at his age?" she asked.

Daniel came over to her, his face softening. "I don't have a choice, Katie. If there's a tumor, even if it's benign, it'll grow, and the seizures will get worse, and he'll be in pain. She is adamant that time is of the essence, too. It's our only real option."

"Rusty's strong," she said. "I have faith in him."

That made him smile, the first one she'd seen since they were on their walk hours ago. "Thanks for staying."

He put a hand on her shoulder, the look in his eyes saying he wanted to do more than that. He wanted to hold her, and if Molly hadn't been there, Katie would have obliged.

"I wouldn't dream of leaving."

"I'm going to spend the night in the vet office on a cot next to Rusty," he said.

"We're keeping him on a potassium bromide drip and a heart monitor," Molly explained. "To prevent a seizure in his sleep, although it's still possible."

"Which is why I won't leave him," Daniel said. "The guest room is yours again, though, because it's too late to drive back to Chestnut Creek."

"I'll be in the vet office with you," she said, leaving no room for argument. "And Goldie." She patted the dog. "Who is a *great* source of comfort." She slid a sly glance to Molly, who winked in response as she scooted off the sofa.

"Then I'm going to gather my sleeping daughter and darling husband and go home." Standing, Molly reached up to hug her father. "Glad you have Katie, Dad."

He looked over her shoulder and right into Katie's eyes. "So am I."

A soft moan pulled Daniel from sleep, making him sit up with a jerk to check Rusty. But it wasn't the dog who'd moaned, not that one, anyway.

It was Goldie, who'd given up a dog bed and planted herself on the cold tile floor as close to the special treatment crate where they had Rusty as she could get. His paw had slid out between the metal wires, and Goldie was currently lapping at it with a loving tongue.

Katie slept as soundly as Rusty, curled in a fetal position under a plush throw Daniel had brought from the house, on the lone sleeping cot they had in this office. He wouldn't hear of her staying in the big rocking recliner that Aidan and Josh had dragged over from the trainee dorm, but now that he'd slept on it for a few hours, he wondered if it wasn't more comfortable than the cot.

They'd both crashed not too long after getting situated, which was no surprise considering the stress of the day and night and the fact that neither of them had likely slept the night before. Around midnight, Daniel had dimmed the room to one single light on the corner table, which now cast shadows in the corners of a room that was always blindingly bright for the treatment of sick animals.

But the dim room seemed softer now. Safer. Sweeter, even.

Much like the woman lying on the cot five feet away.

Her face turned toward him, a thick lock of dark hair fallen over her cheek. Her feminine frame rose and fell with each breath. Right then, Katie looked very much like that young girl he'd slept with on a bed not much wider than the one she was on now...so, so many years ago.

The only sound was her breath and the clicking of

Goldie's tongue on Rusty's paw. And Daniel's heart, which for some reason felt like it was cracking. He put his hand over his chest as if that could stop this seismic shift he felt happening inside.

"Are you all right?"

Katie's concerned whisper surprised him and made him realize he'd leaned forward and still had his hand on his chest.

"Yes. I think."

Her eyes flashed as she sat up, all evidence of sleep disappearing except for her tousled hair. "Does your chest hurt?"

"Not like that," he said, putting his hand down. "I just…no. No chest pain." Heartache, but not pain.

She slipped her legs over the side of the cot, her bare feet peeking out of gray sweat pants, with bright-pink painted toes that drew his attention. Had he ever noticed before that she painted her toes? Annie had never done that.

He thought those toes were adorable.

"Are you sure?" she asked, leaning closer. "Something's the matter. Is it just Rusty?" She instantly shook her head. "I don't mean 'just' Rusty, but not your heart."

"It's my heart."

"Daniel!"

He smiled and held up a hand. "Don't worry. I'm fine. I'm…" Not missing Annie.

The realization—the powerful truth of it—stunned him, making him lean back.

"He'll be fine," she said, obviously not reading his true thoughts.

"I know, and if he's not, I will be."

"Are you sure? Because you look wrecked, hon."

The term of endearment damn near did him in. "Long term I'll be fine," he assured her. "Not going to lie and say I'd be stoic if and when I lose that boy." His gaze shifted to Rusty, snoring contentedly as his sweet nurse continued her ministration. "And you're a good girl, Goldie."

Her tail moved left and right to acknowledge the compliment.

"You like her," Katie teased. "Admit it. You are crazy about her."

He laughed softly. "Never said I wasn't."

"But she's not a setter. Not from a long line of Irish perfection. She's something new and different and not quite the same, maybe a little flawed, but still. You like her."

He turned to Katie, the words hitting his heart harder than they should have. "Her only flaw is that she isn't…" *Annie.* "Actually, she doesn't have a flaw," he finished. "She's beautiful, caring, kind, sweet, and has a heart of gold."

"So she's aptly named."

But he wasn't talking about Goldie. "How's the cot?"

"Hard. How's the recliner?"

He pushed to the side. "Big enough for two."

She stood slowly and wrapped the blanket around her like a cape. She opened her mouth, but he held up his hand.

"Don't ask me if I'm sure, Katie."

"How'd you know what I was thinking?"

"You're pretty transparent." He moved farther to the side and reached for her, taking her hand to guide her into the space next to him, where she fit perfectly under his arm. She slid the blanket free and covered both of them in it, turning sideways so she could rest her head on his chest with a big sigh that sounded like pure contentment.

"That's better," she whispered.

So much better.

He cuddled her closer, wrapping his other arm around her as she slid her leg a little over his. "There," he said. "We fit perfectly."

"Who'd have dreamed it?" she murmured lightly.

Not him. Not in a million years would he have dreamed anyone could comfort him when Rusty was this sick. And yet, she did. And right that minute, he didn't want anyone else. No one.

No one.

"Tell me about him," she said softly without lifting her head.

"What do you want to know?"

"Your favorite moments and memories. Cute stories. Things that make Rusty such a great dog."

He didn't answer right away, and she splayed her hand on his chest, right where it felt like it had been cracking before. She pressed lightly, moving her palm in a slow, small circle, warming him, calming him, somehow closing that crack.

"When he was little, he had a toy doll that he had to sleep with. It was all different colors, and we called it Rainbow. All you had to say was, 'Let's go see Rainbow,' and he knew it was bedtime."

"Sweet."

"He was born when Darcy was a teenager, so they were pretty tight. When she went to college, he spent every single day for two weeks outside her bedroom door. Wouldn't move except to eat and walk. We all felt the hit of the empty nest."

"I know it well," she whispered.

"And when Annie died…" He closed his eyes and felt his throat tighten with that familiar lump. "The night I came home from the hospital, I went outside, and he came and found me and…" His eyes stung. "I was on the ground. I don't know for how long. Just…bawling. I wanted to crawl into the earth and never come out. I wanted to die. How could I want anything else but to die so I could be with her again?"

He felt her shift and knew she was looking at him, but he didn't open his eyes.

"Rusty climbed right on top of me and licked my face, over and over and over. Then he nudged me with his nose, making me get up, and walked me back into the house."

"Oh." She reached up and wiped a tear from his cheek that he barely noticed had fallen. "He brought you back."

Very slowly, he opened his eyes, a little stunned to meet her brown ones, as watery as his. "Tonight, when I woke up?"

She nodded, waiting for him to finish.

"I felt my chest split a little."

"Split?" She scooted up. "Are you sure—"

He eased her right back into place. "I think it was making room in my heart for someone else."

"For Goldie?"

"For you."

"Really." She held his gaze for a few long, steady heartbeats, then dropped her head, curled tighter into him, and sighed sleepily. "That's some valuable real estate, your heart."

"But you'll want to redecorate."

"Nope. It's perfect like it is."

Smiling at that, he stroked her hair, and she curled her fingers, her fist still pressed against his heart.

Which didn't hurt at all anymore. In fact, it felt whole.

Chapter Twenty-One

They closed Kilcannon Veterinarian Hospital in Bitter Bark for the day, but that certainly didn't mean the place was empty. The waiting room was filled with Kilcannons, gathered with the seriousness Katie imagined they had when any loved one was in surgery. Pru sat on the floor with little Christian on her lap, the two of them quietly entertaining Fiona in a baby seat while parents Liam and Andi watched. Every few minutes, Darcy tapped texts into her phone, obviously keeping her beloved Josh up to speed, while Gramma Finnie embroidered what looked like a small pillowcase for the baby boy that Jessie Kilcannon would have any day now.

Shane leaned over his wife's shoulder, helping her—mostly whispering jokes—do a crossword puzzle, while Aidan and his fiancée, Beck, flipped through a magazine and discussed plans for their upcoming wedding.

A few were missing, though. Garrett and Jessie had stayed home, only because Jessie had had a bad night. Trace was holding down the fort at Waterford, and Molly, of course, was assisting in the surgery.

Along with Daniel, who refused to be talked out of being in the room while Rusty's head was opened by a brain surgeon.

And that was the reason Katie stayed, even though this was clearly a family affair, and he had more than enough love and support around him. But she had to see him come out of that room happy. She had to. She wasn't ashamed by how much it mattered to her, and none of the members of the family seemed to question that. If they did, they were all far too classy to say anything.

And none of them had arrived with a dog, she noticed, as if Rusty deserved one hundred percent of their attention that day.

She shifted in her seat, her back a little sore after a night in the recliner, but it had been worth it. Sleeping next to Daniel, holding him and sensing the change in him, had made for one of the best nights she could remember in years.

But had it been real? Or was his heart really breaking over Rusty, and what he'd needed was the comfort she gave him? Which was fine, but not enough.

Katie had no issue falling in love with a man who'd loved before—she certainly had loved Nico with her whole heart and soul. But Daniel was far more guarded, and Annie had been lifted to a very high and lofty pedestal.

Katie would rather stand alone than in her shadow.

And they couldn't forget that both their families were about to be changed by more than a romance between Katie and Daniel. There didn't need to be a rush, and she hoped he felt the same way.

The front door opened, getting all their attention,

followed by a chorus of greetings when Declan and Braden Mahoney, both in navy firefighter T-shirts, came in.

"Any news?" Declan asked, scanning the crowd and not at all surprised to see that many gathered.

"Nothing yet," Darcy said, waving them in. "I thought all three of you were on duty today."

"We're on our way in," Braden said, taking a second look around in a way that made Katie wonder if he was looking for Cassie. "And had to get a report. Plus, once Dec heard who was doing the surgery..." He lifted his shoulders and a teasing brow.

"Oh, that's right," Shane said. "Evie's in town. Well, don't go back there and distract her with memories. She's busy."

Pru looked up from the baby toys, frowning. "You know the doctor doing the surgery, Uncle Dec?"

He gave a casual nod, but Shane snorted and Liam gave a secret smile, telling Katie there was much more to that story than anyone was saying. But before she could ask, the door to the surgery center opened and an attractive young woman in scrubs stepped out, looking around the crowd who stared at her, her gaze stopping on Dec.

Oh yeah, more to that story.

"He's out of surgery and doing very well."

She might have had more to say, but a cheer went up that drowned out anything. A few questions started flying, which she held off with one still-gloved hand. "We found a very small meningioma tumor," she said. "Obviously, we'll do a biopsy, but from my experience, it looked to be primary and benign. We made a clean removal, and there's no sign it metastasized, but we want to get Rusty over to my hospital for a few days of tests and observation. We might do chemo for a few months, just to be sure. We'll work up a plan, but right now, we're out of the woods."

Another cheer went up, infectious enough for Evie to lose her doctor seriousness and beam at them. "He did great," she added. "A total trouper."

"Dad or Rusty?" Shane said, and Katie suspected he was only partly joking.

"Both," she assured him. "In recovery right now. Is, uh, Katie here?"

Katie leaned forward. "Yes?"

"Oh, hello. Dr. K asked if I'd bring you back for a moment. Okay?"

"Of course."

Right then, Molly came out through the same doors, her eyes sparkling with success. She smiled from the doctor to the group and dropped her head back like the whole thing had wasted her.

Shane was up in a second to put his arm around his sister. "You okay, Molls?"

"Yes." She blinked, clearly emotional. "It's just that…" Her voice was thick enough that Liam was up next to get on her other side. "Dad is the strongest man I know." A tear rolled down her cheek as everyone murmured comments of full agreement.

Katie stood slowly, taking her jacket and handbag to follow the doctor, smiling at Molly as she passed and slowing down to hear the rest of what she said as Dr. Hewitt led her through the door.

"You guys, we have the best dad in the world. Never forget it."

As she finished, Katie turned to look over her

shoulder, witnessing the group hug, the love, the support, and the palpable *family-ness* of the group.

And all she wanted at that moment was to be in the arms of her own.

"Right here," the doctor said, gesturing to a door. "Go on in."

Katie stepped into a softly lit room where Daniel, also in scrubs, leaned against an oversized pen attached to the wall. Rusty was asleep behind the open gate, his head shaved and bandaged.

"Hey."

He turned, and his face lit with a slow smile, and Rusty's eyes fluttered open in a silent greeting. "We made it."

"I heard the report." She came to his outstretched arms, taking the hug and giving it back. "As good as could be expected."

"Better, really. We got it early, and best of all, Rusty sailed through anesthesia. Right, bud?"

His eyes closed.

"He'll be on pain meds for a while, and Cordell, our vet tech, is going to ride with him in Evie's medical van back to Raleigh."

"And you're going?"

"Oh yeah. I'm going home to pack, but I'll be staying there with him." He tipped her chin and brought her face up. "Not exactly a romantic getaway, but would you come with me?"

She considered it—had already considered it, to be honest—and shook her head. The disappointment in his eyes was a tiny bit gratifying, but not enough to change her mind. "I think we both need to take this time to think."

"I've *been* thinking," he said gruffly, still holding her chin and angling her face as if he was about to take the kiss they purposely hadn't shared last night. "I thought all last night while I held you in my arms. And during this surgery, in the back of my mind, I wanted you to be the first person I saw when it was over."

Her heart tripped at the words she'd been longing to hear.

But...he'd had his great one.

"You need to think some more, though."

"I don't need—"

She silenced him with a fingertip to his lips. "I won't settle for less than...everything."

He held her gaze, the slightest flicker of fear in his, but it disappeared quickly. "Exactly what I want. All night, all—"

"All of you," she said. "That includes your body *and* your heart."

He let out a breath. "Okay."

Okay? She wasn't sure it would be that easy. "So that's what I want you to think about."

"I will. Can I think about it with you?"

"Think about it with Rusty," she said. "And, if I may, I'll keep Goldie for the week, so I have someone to talk things over with, too."

He gave a slow smile, obviously liking that. "Sounds like a plan, Katie."

"Oh, and when you get back, your living room should be almost finished. The floors are being done this week, and the shutters will be installed, and I'm coordinating a one-day furniture delivery from three different places. I should be there for all of that."

His shoulders dropped ever so slightly, as if the last thing he cared about was furniture. But he nodded, inching back. "All right. We'll both think." He leaned closer to her ear to whisper, "But don't be surprised if I call you in the middle of the night."

"Call anytime," she said, smiling. "I'll be there."

He took her chin one more time and brought her face to his so they could look at each other. He didn't say a word, but lowered his head and kissed her on the lips. A long, sweet kiss full of promise and hope and a whole bunch of things that would keep Katie warm until he returned.

Daniel skipped the coffee his mother offered and said only a few words to Garrett, who had the most questions since he'd spent the morning with Jessie. After answering them and accepting all of his family's comments, hugs, and words of support, he slipped out with the excuse that he needed to pack and head out to Raleigh.

Then he climbed the staircase to walk the hall to his bedroom. Tense, uncertain, and tired, he pushed the door open, took a breath, and waited to see if anything was different.

Would the room where he had slept with his wife, then mourned her, then slowly crawled out of his black hole, seem different now that he wanted to be with another woman?

Different but the same. Different because he was different. The same because...

God, look at the place.

He hadn't even bothered to get a new comforter in four years. They might be different sheets, but only the housekeeper would know. Either way, he couldn't share them with Katie. Couldn't get on that mattress or sit by that fire or cuddle on that sofa. Yes, Molly and Gramma Finnie had helped him remove all of Annie's belongings many months after she died, but it was still *their* room. What was he going to—

"Dad?"

He turned to see Liam outside the door, a cup of coffee in his hand, a look of concern on his face.

"You okay?" his son asked.

"I'm…yeah. Wiped out, but relieved it's over."

He searched Daniel's face as if looking for something he wasn't finding. "They sent me up to check on you."

Daniel chuckled. "Of course they did. What makes you think something's wrong, other than the obvious? My dog had a brain tumor removed this morning."

Liam gave a classic thoughtful nod, but it was also a silent request to be invited in. "May I?" he asked when Daniel didn't make the offer.

"Of course." He stepped to the side. "You're always welcome."

"In here?" Liam frowned. "Not without an invitation. Not since I was a toddler. And not unless you had something important to say to me."

Daniel couldn't argue. He and Annie had established the room as a sanctuary, utterly and completely private, and when the kids were brought in, it was usually for a serious talk.

"Well, nothing important to say today," Daniel said. "Except that I have to pack."

"You sure, Dad?" Shane's voice came from the hall, making Daniel shake his head.

"You need backup?" Daniel asked Liam.

"We're concerned about you." And Aidan was there.

"Well, why don't you all march right in, sit down, and talk to me while I pack?"

And, son of a gun, they did. All of them, no spouses or dogs in tow, though. Six kids, wearing various looks of concern and love, walked into the room, suddenly making it feel small and crowded.

Even Molly was there, changed from scrubs and here to work at the Waterford Farm office today. Darcy's blue eyes scanned him carefully, and all four boys stared.

"What the hell is going on?" he asked.

"It's not like you to run off," Darcy said, getting closer to him. "You didn't drink any coffee and didn't even notice that I picked up a box of Linda May's raspberry croissants."

"I'd have brought you one," Molly said.

"But no food in Mom and Dad's room," Shane said, lowering his voice to teasingly mock Daniel.

"That was Mom's rule," Daniel said. "If I had the occasion to eat up here, I would." He added a look to Darcy. "So feel free to get me that croissant. I'd love it."

"What else would you love, Dad?" she asked.

"Coffee."

She lifted one of her pretty brows. All of them, in fact, were staring pretty hard, confusing him, but touching him, too. They wanted to help. They just didn't know how. And God, he loved them all for it. But could they handle it?

He took a long, slow breath. "It's this room," he told them. "It does have a lot of rules, like Shane said, but the biggest one is that I...I..."

"You live here," Garrett said.

"But you can't *live* here," Molly added.

"And you know we're all for you living your life, Dad." Darcy put her arm around his waist. "So how can we help?"

He just smiled at her, at all of them. "You can't, unless you want to help me move that life into a completely different room."

"Why don't you change this one?" Aidan asked.

"Yeah, maybe I will." It was time, and he knew it. "When I get back, I'll move some stuff and paint. Maybe put the bed on that wall so I can see the sunrise."

"Or get a new bed."

He gave a look to Garrett. "Maybe. And get rid of that sofa."

"Then Rusty *will* die," Shane whispered.

Daniel smiled at the comic relief. "I do appreciate that you all care so much."

"The thing is, Dad," Liam said, "we like Katie."

Kind of from left field, but he nodded. "So do I," he told them. "Very much." He waited a beat, taking in all of their faces. "So you all came up here to give me a taste of my own medicine?" he guessed. "A little pep talk? A reminder of what's important in life? Some direction if I appear lost?"

"Look, we know you don't need our permission or pep talks." Shane took a few steps forward. "But I *have* had a few talks with you in this room that changed my life."

"We all have," Aidan added.

"You gave me Mom's ring to give to Andi in here," Liam reminded him.

"The oldest son," Shane quipped, "gets the goods."

The oldest son. For a moment, Daniel looked at Liam, studying the set of his jaw and the direct gaze of a man who went through life stoic and strong. Good God, he had a surprise coming.

He put his hand on Liam's shoulder. "I remember that day," he said. "And Andi wears that ring as beautifully as your mother did."

Liam's smile grew tight as he nodded.

"Basically, we came to tell you we love you." Darcy hugged him again. "And we know today's been tough."

"Thanks for that," he said.

"We want you to be happy, Dad," Garrett said.

"You know a child is only as happy as their least-happy parent," Molly added, making them all laugh at her twist on Annie's favorite saying.

"Well, here's the thing, kids. I am happy. And things in my life—and yours—are going to change, and not all of that change will be easy." He looked from one to the next. "But I happen to know you are the strongest, smartest, most amazing family a man could dream of having, and you'll survive and thrive."

"How does he do that?" Shane asked. "He always manages to turn this stuff into a life lesson."

They all laughed, the moment passed, the sentiment appreciated.

While Daniel packed for his trip to Raleigh, he mentally redecorated his entire room and swore it would be the first thing he did when he got home.

Chapter Twenty-Two

Daniel had been true to his word, calling Katie not only in the middle of the night, day, afternoon, and morning from Monday through Friday, especially on Thursday, which happened to be Valentine's Day. They texted, too, and planned for their first date when he came home late Saturday afternoon.

He was thinking, all right. And she liked the direction of his thoughts.

For the first time in years, Katie Santorini felt giddy over a man. Dying to get a fresh mani-pedi and have her hair done. Shopping for clothes—alone, because if Cassie saw her mother walk into Victoria's Secret, it would all be over. Falling asleep—with Goldie snoring softly at the foot of the bed—with a silly grin on her face and waking up with it still there.

And every time her phone rang or buzzed, her heart took a little leap of joy.

Saturday couldn't come soon enough, but the week had been consumed with her project at Waterford, including supervising the refinishing of the hardwood floor in the living room and the installation of the shutters.

Today was the final furniture-delivery day, and that had her humming as she and Goldie pulled into Waterford early that morning. But as soon as she made her way down the long drive, she sensed something was off.

It was…empty.

There were a few people in the pen with some dogs. Trainees, she guessed, but none of the Kilcannon men. No sign of Trace Bancroft and his service dogs or Darcy moving her grooming clients from kennels to salon. And no cars in the driveway, which was usually lined with the various vehicles that they all drove to and from and all around Waterford.

She parked and walked to the back door, holding Goldie back as she barked in expectation of seeing Rusty. They were both a little surprised when it opened before she arrived.

"Mornin', Miz Santorini." Crystal, the white-haired housekeeper Katie had met on more than one occasion, beamed at her, a look of unbridled excitement in moss-green eyes. "Big day for the Kilcannons."

"It is?"

"Miss Jessie's water broke about two hours ago."

Her jaw dropped wide. So it had been Daniel texting her on the way over from Chestnut Creek. She reached into her bag to find the phone she'd ignored while driving.

"That's fantastic news. So everyone's at the hospital?" She had no doubt a Kilcannon baby was a family affair.

"Oh yes, and I only work a half day on Fridays, but I've been packing up lunches and dinners I've made for everyone. I'll be here a bit longer, then no one'll be in the house."

Katie made a face. "Furniture's being delivered from three different places. Would it be okay if I stayed?"

"Of course. Gramma Finnie told me you might be coming and to tell you to make yourself at home and give you the guest room if you need it. She's staying at Molly's tonight, since it's closer to the hospital, so there won't be anyone and no dogs." She grinned down at Goldie. "'Cept this one."

"And what about Daniel?" she asked, as much to herself as the housekeeper. "Will he be back in time for the birth today? I know Dr. Hewitt wanted to keep Rusty until tomorrow."

"I don't know, but come on in, and we'll figure it all out."

Goldie leaped forward, bounding into the house and starting her search for Rusty, destined for disappointment.

Katie soon realized it hadn't been Daniel texting while she was driving, but the furniture and rug stores confirming delivery. In fact, he hadn't answered her texts or calls that morning. She hoped that didn't mean something was wrong with Rusty...but maybe he was so consumed with the new baby, he'd forgotten about her.

She actually didn't think him forgetting about her was possible, but as the various trucks arrived and she dragged some of the art and lamps she had in her car into the house, Katie was too busy to worry about it.

At around one in the afternoon, she finally stopped and looked at her handiwork, unable to keep the smile from her face. This living room was totally transformed, from the gleaming white plantation shutters to the beautifully refinished hardwood floor. It was covered with a pale blue faded country rug with a farmhouse-style coffee table. The wingbacks were gone, and now a sleek sectional invited entertaining and talking around a fireplace. The Comfort Gray walls had the perfect amount of framed art, with some floating shelves for knickknacks and dried flowers.

The only thing unfinished was the "wall of fame," which was painfully empty. But it wouldn't be for long, she thought, when she could—

A car door slammed outside, and instantly Goldie launched from her place near the fireplace with a loud bark. In fact, she barked furiously all the way into the hall, through the house, and toward the kitchen.

Only one creature on earth could make her bark like that...which meant Rusty was home. And that meant the one creature who could make Katie feel breathless with anticipation was with him.

She came around the corner as Daniel entered the house, and they both froze for a second, as though the impact of seeing each other literally knocked them back a bit.

"You're home early," she said.

A slow, sexy smile tipped his mouth. "Not a minute too soon." With two long strides, he reached her, pulled her into his chest, and lowered his head to kiss her like they'd been apart for a year.

But Goldie's wild barking killed the moment, making Daniel pull away reluctantly. "Let's get the patient, who is doing magnificently." He started to step away, but looked at her again and pulled her right back for another kiss, making her laugh. "Speaking of magnificent."

She reached up to touch her hair. "I really wasn't expecting you until tomorrow, but—oh! The baby. Any news?"

"She won't deliver anytime soon. They're taking shifts, it's all covered, and…" He looked around. "It's just us?"

"And your brand-new living room."

He grinned. "Let's get Rusty before Goldie breaks the window and has her way with him."

They walked out arm in arm, which felt like the most natural thing in the world, to find Rusty looking magnificent indeed, except for the plastic cone around his head.

"It's really to protect the incision from anything touching it," Daniel explained. "He can sleep without it."

"Hey, big guy." Katie approached him tenderly while Daniel held Goldie and showed her the same kind of love. "We missed you, Rusto."

He looked up at her with enough spunk in his brown eyes to make hers fill with tears of gratitude. "He looks great," she said to Daniel, who was crouched down, rubbing Goldie's head.

"He's amazing. And there's not a sign of other tumors, but I am going to start chemo, which is just a pill, for a month or so. There are risks, but I think it's the right thing to do. In fact, I couldn't be happier." He angled his head, squinting at her in the sun. "Well, I take that back. I could be happier."

"How?"

"You shouldn't have to ask."

She laughed as she led the dogs into the house, and he brought his bag in behind her. "Let me take this upstairs."

"Then straight to the living room to see my handiwork."

"Deal." He lifted the suitcase off its wheels and wrapped an arm around her, walking her through the house and planting a kiss on her head. "I was so glad Evie released Rusty a day early."

"You wouldn't want to miss that new grandson."

"Yeah, that, too." He turned at the stairs and reluctantly let her go, taking them two at a time as if he were floating on air like she was. When he disappeared into the hall, she turned back and started walking toward the living room, stopping when she heard him call her name.

"Yes?"

He didn't answer, but appeared at the top of the steps, a look of abject confusion on his face. "When did you do it?"

"Do what?"

He gave a dry laugh. "I mean, I love it, but... how?"

"What are you talking about?"

"My..." He shook his head. "You didn't do my room?"

"Do what to your room?"

With a flick of his fingers, he beckoned her closer, and she headed up the stairs, moving slowly as she tried to figure out what he could be talking about.

Silent, he took her hand when she reached the top

316

and led her down the hall she'd only ever been in once, when he'd first given her the tour of the house. At the end, his double bedroom doors were open and...

"Oh my God." She stood in the doorway and stared in shock at the soothing blue-gray walls, the washed-wood headboard, the cool-teal comforter, and the geometric rug she'd loved when she'd first seen it. "Oh...my... This is right out of my website and the stuff I sent to your Pinterest board."

"Darcy," he whispered.

"She did this?"

"She had the password to that account, and you sent pictures."

"She replicated the picture of a room I posted and added accents that were on the board. Like those pillows. And that rug."

He took a few steps in, as stunned as she was. "She didn't do this alone."

He put his hand to his chest and turned slowly as they both took in the ambient light, the subtle colors, the whole new placement of the bed, the sleek love seat, and the sheer curtains that lightened the room by indescribable measure.

"Do you like it?" Katie asked.

He looked like he needed to catch his breath. "I love it."

"You're not mad at them for overstepping?"

"When my kids rally for a cause..."

"It's a thing of beauty," she finished. "In every way."

He finally shifted his attention from the room to her, reaching out to pull her in again. "This is for us, you know."

"I had a feeling." And realizing that made her treasure his children in a way she hadn't thought was possible.

"So you know what we have to do?"

She looked up at him, her eyes bright with anticipation. "What?"

He stepped back, closed the door, and locked it. "We have to tag all this furniture with new memories." Lowering his face to hers, he covered her lips with a kiss so long and sweet and tender, she almost swayed in his arms. "Starting with that bed."

Chapter Twenty-Three

Everything was new. The silky handfuls of hair sliding through his fingers. The sweet taste of a kiss that hovered between demanding and tentative. The smell of peaches on her skin and fresh paint on the walls. A sultry whimper he'd never heard before. And when they descended to the bed, the fluffy new comforter sighed as if it had been waiting for Daniel and Katie to fall.

All new, but not entirely unfamiliar.

Daniel eased her under him, clinging to her arms and shoulders as if she might somehow disappear if he didn't hold her, while Katie whispered his name. Even her voice sounded new to him.

He lifted his head to look at her, to see her dark hair half on her face, half on the bed, and even the expression in her eyes was something he'd never seen before. Wait. He had. Many, many years ago on a dorm-size bed in Gillespie Hall.

"Why are you smiling?" she asked, reaching up to stroke his face.

"Take a wild guess."

"You've missed me?"

"For forty years."

Her eyes widened. "I know that's not the truth. You never missed me in that time."

He didn't answer right away, tracing her face with his gaze, taking in her lashes and brows and sweet lines that showed she'd laughed more than cried in this lifetime. "You look like Katie Rogers right now, and I was thinking about our first time, on that dorm bed."

She bit her lip. "You fell out once."

He dropped his head, laughing. "My knee hit the floor, and it hurt so *freaking* bad."

"You didn't tell me."

"I didn't want to stop." He kissed her lips. "Don't want to now, either."

She closed both hands over his cheeks and angled his head one way, then the other, as if deciding where he'd taste best. "This time will be better," she whispered. "You won't fall out. I won't hit my head—"

"Oof." He cringed. "Forgot about that."

"And we certainly won't fail with a condom."

He eased back an inch and reached into his back pocket, pulling out a wallet and tossing it on the nightstand. "They're in there. Bought them in Raleigh, to be honest."

"You did? So you knew this would happen?"

"Oh, I knew." He dragged his hand along the column of her throat. "It seemed like the gentlemanly thing to offer. Plus, practice what you preach and all."

She sighed and let her eyes close. "You are nothing if not a gentleman."

"Yeah, yeah, yeah. Can you forget that for a second? Actually, for a few hours?"

"Mmm." She dropped her head back in surrender. "Make me."

Very slowly, he lowered his head and settled his mouth into the hollow of her throat, flicking his tongue lightly, then suckling his way back to her mouth. With each heated kiss, his need for her grew until they were rocking their bodies in a natural, heavenly, ancient rhythm that might not be new, but didn't feel quite like anything he could remember.

She turned her head, offering more of her throat and inviting him to kiss lower, while her hands explored his arms and shoulders and slipped under his T-shirt to burn his skin. He sat up and pulled it over his head, tossing it to the side as he looked down at her.

Her chest rose and fell as her breaths grew sensual and strained, the outline of her breasts beautifully visible in the thin T-shirt she wore. His gaze stopped there, taking her in, drinking in what he'd just surreptitiously enjoyed over these past few weeks.

Silently, reverently, he tugged at the top to slide it over her stomach and reveal a thin, lacy bra that he could see right through. Her body was sloped and soft and, once again, completely new to him.

"Katie." His voice was thick and gruff. "You're beautiful."

"But I didn't get to show off my brand-new Victoria's Secret underwear. I thought you'd be home tomorrow."

"You went to Victoria's Secret? For me?"

Biting her lip, she nodded, the look sexy and sly, and the idea that she'd anticipated this was downright arousing.

"Let's get rid of this one, then." He reached under her and unsnapped the bra, drawing it off her as he lowered his head to kiss this entirely new treat in front of him. Arching her back, she let out a moan that told him it felt as good as it tasted, which only made him want more. And more.

But not quickly. If one thing would be different from the first time they'd made love, he planned to take all day. So he moved over her like she was covered in honey, drawing out every kiss, every caress, and every sultry, whispered word.

But as clothes fell off and the comforter came down, and they were naked and sliding on crisp, unfamiliar linens and a brand-new mattress, neither one of them could slow down. Their breathing hitched and caught in quick, aching pants for more. Their hands locked in place as they found the perfect place to hold. Their legs wrapped and squeezed and opened for each other.

There was no fumbling this time, no one's head hit the fancy new headboard, and Daniel didn't slide off the mattress. Instead, they moved like two people who were somehow completely comfortable with the act of making love, yet giddy over the sensations they'd long ago forgotten.

As he rose above her and lifted her hips to take him, Katie's gaze traveled down to where they were about to be connected, and his followed. For a moment, neither one of them moved, frozen at the sight of their bodies and this age-old connection that somehow felt damn near virginal. They stared at themselves for two, three, four crazy heartbeats before looking into each other's eyes.

For a second, he thought he saw doubt in hers. Or that same shadow of fear he'd seen when they first met.

"Are you sure?" he asked gently.

"Not only am I sure," she whispered, blinking against the damp corners of her eyes, which right then could have been sweat or tears, "I'm…crazy about you."

He laughed. "You just sounded exactly like that girl in Gillespie Hall."

"'Cause you make me feel like her." She reached up and pulled him closer, bowing her back enough for him to know exactly where she wanted him. "What a gift it is."

Yes, it was. A second chance to lose himself in the heart and soul and body of a woman. As he eased into her, Daniel lowered himself so that they could kiss as their bodies joined. He tasted her mouth as their tongues tangled with the same urgency as their bodies.

With each stroke and breath, with each push toward the edge, with each agonizing, torturous, heavenly, thrilling sensation of his body in hers, Daniel felt everything disappear. Time, space, grief, life, the whole world.

There was only Katie, warm and willing and as lost as he was. A woman whose heart he adored and whose body fit his perfectly. As the thought and pleasure rocked him, he clung to her, pulled her up to press against him so no two parts of their bodies weren't touching. He turned his head to flatten their cheeks to each other, and only then did he realize they were soaked with tears. His, hers, and theirs.

She realized it, too, and gasped softly. Maybe laughed. Maybe cried. He didn't know. All he knew was that her nails were digging into him, and every move was pure, pure bliss.

He heard his name. Pressed his mouth into her shoulder. Burned his body into hers. And finally lost himself completely.

She was right there with him, out of control and fully satisfied when she fell back onto the pillow with a half laugh of disbelief and a murmur of, "*Wow.*"

Wow was right.

He went with her, easing himself down gently, waiting for what he knew was inevitable.

He squeezed his eyes shut as the aftershocks rocked him into her, making her groan with satisfaction.

Where was it? The buzz of remorse. The sting of guilt. That bitter taste of knowing he'd broken a promise he'd made with every intention of keeping.

But not one of those unwelcome sensations rolled over him. All he felt was right and comfortable and completely at home.

Katie drifted in and out of sleep, vaguely aware that the afternoon had slipped into evening when she heard Daniel's voice, far away, in the kitchen.

She shot up, shaking off dreamy satisfaction to seize panic. Family?

In the distance, she heard him laugh, and even that sound made her smile. Then silence, so if someone was down there, they were quiet. Gramma Finnie? Hadn't Crystal said she wasn't coming home? One of the kids?

She didn't want his kids to know…

That was ridiculous. First of all, they were all adults. Second of all, they didn't redecorate this room because they wanted their father to have a nice place to sleep. Everyone knew why change had been necessary.

But then she looked around and couldn't help a sigh of contentment and a smile of admiration. Someone had a great eye and really had dug into Daniel's Pinterest account. The room didn't even look like it was in the same house, let alone the same room as before. It might have been Annie's room once, but—

A familiar bark outside the door startled her. "Goldie!" She pushed the covers off, then froze, realizing that she didn't wear a single stitch of clothes and couldn't very well open the door naked.

Looking around, she grabbed the first thing she saw, which happened to be a gray Waterford Farm T-shirt. The large shirt fell over her hips and grazed her thighs, so she snagged her panties from the floor and stepped into them before heading to the door. Which was currently being scratched by a dog who demanded to be let in.

"I'm coming," she muttered, turning the lock and opening it slowly, spying not one but two dogs, one wearing a handsome-looking cone. "Hello, you two. Come on in."

Goldie launched in, spun in a joyous circle, and jumped up to greet Katie like they'd been apart for three weeks instead of a few hours. She scratched the dog's head, but turned to Rusty, who stood still except for his coned head as he looked from side to side. If a dog could be shocked, he was.

"Do you have the dogs?" Daniel called from what sounded like the foot of the steps. She hoped that meant they were still alone and he'd been on the phone or maybe talking to the dogs.

"I do. And you better get up here and do some explaining to Rusty."

"On my way."

Rusty took a few steps toward the bed and barked once. Then again. Then let out a low rumble in his chest as he stared at the unfamiliar comforter.

"He's not a big fan of change," Daniel said from outside the door, which opened as if it was being pushed by something. Then he stood in the doorway, wearing gray sweatpants, no shirt, and carrying a tray with some food, a split of champagne, and two stemless glasses.

"Oh," Katie exclaimed. "Nice room service."

"Nice room...mate." He looked up and down at her immodest and unexpected outfit, a slow grin growing. "That's a great look for you, Kate."

She peered over the tray and spied a selection of cheese, crackers, and olives. "And you cooked," she teased, plucking a square of cheddar and popping it into her mouth.

That made him laugh, but then he realized Rusty had moved to the new love seat that was in a wholly new place, and the growl had grown to an actual snarl.

"Bud, we got a nice new room. Relax."

He barked and put a paw on the seat.

"Just get up on it and make it your own," Daniel told him, setting the tray on the small coffee table. "New room, old rules." He walked around the table and guided the dog onto the seat, and instantly Goldie loped over to join him. "And now my little sofa or settee or whatever you call this is once again a place for a dog."

"Plural."

"Dogs," he corrected. "Because Goldie's welcome whenever you're here, which I hope will be often."

She eyed him. "I didn't adopt her. I'm fostering."

"You're a foster failure. I know one when I see one."

She didn't answer, but smiled at Goldie. "She is…a great one."

"Yep, failure." He laughed and reached out to wrap her in a hug. "Which is good, because her feelings for Rusty will have you over here very often."

She tipped her head back and studied him for a moment. "I'd like that."

He kissed her to seal the deal, sliding his hand around her neck and under her hair with a soft moan. "Oh." He pulled back and widened his eyes. "The family got bigger about forty minutes ago. You were sleeping when the call came in, so I went downstairs."

"Jessie had the baby?"

"Patrick Garrett Kilcannon, seven and a half pounds, twenty-two inches. Mom and baby are doing well. Dad is on cloud nine."

"Don't they wonder where you are?"

He made a face. "I might have given them the impression I was still in Raleigh, guaranteeing that Gramma Finnie will stay with Molly and we are alone until morning."

She gave a noisy fake gasp. "Daniel Kilcannon, you're a liar."

"No, I'm a..." He pulled her closer for a kiss. "Goner."

"And a grandfather again."

"Does it make you feel weird to make love to a grandfather?"

She laughed. "'Weird' is so not how I'd describe the things you made me feel. About the grandfather part? What I feel is flat-out jealousy."

"Then let's get working on those kids of yours." He gestured toward the bed. "Climb back in, and I'll bring the tray. Champagne's for the new baby. And the new room. And the new..." He gave a slow smile. "Light in my life."

"Aw, you're sweet. But crackers in bed?"

He started to answer, then stopped, catching himself from whatever he was going to say. "Yes. We have crackers in bed, you and me." He gathered up the tray and walked it closer. "Let's make another memory on this new bed."

She scooted over, smoothing out the comforter so he could find a place for the tray. "I'm still reeling from the first one," she said softly.

As he situated the tray, he leaned over to kiss her again. "Reeling is one way to put it."

"Floating on air would be another."

He slipped under the covers next to her. "We're good together, Katie," he said simply, as if no more words were needed. Instead, he pointed the small champagne bottle in the other direction and twisted the wires that held the cork.

"Do not get those bubbles on this new comforter," she warned. "You'd have a lot of explaining to do to your amazing, secret decorating team."

The cork popped, and he expertly managed not to drip a single bubble as he filled the glasses.

"Your family would do the same," he said. "There are a lot of similarities, don't you think? Which is why once Alex and John and Cassie are here for the restaurant, we can get to work on grandchildren for you." He handed her a glass. "Toast to the matchmaking skills of the Dogfather and company?"

She clinked his glass, but felt her smile fade before she took a sip.

"No?" he asked, immediately reading her expression.

"We don't ever talk about Nick."

"What do you mean?" He blinked at her, putting down his glass. "We *only* talk about him. But recently, last week, we talked about us, then Rusty. Then we were focused on other things, but we can talk about him right now. You know it's my favorite subject to hear every detail of his childhood."

She thought of a million things she wanted to say about her son, but sighed. "I guess it's premature since we don't have that confirmation yet."

"You're not still holding out hope that the results are wrong, are you? They told me that wasn't possible, but we'll know for sure in less than a month."

She picked up the champagne, but put it back down again.

"Hey." With a hand on her chin, he lifted her face to him. "What's the matter?"

"I forgot about it, that's all. I got all lost and happy and made love to you, and I totally forgot that we have this big thing hanging over us, and now...now..."

"Now?" he urged when she didn't finish.

"Now what's going to happen when he finds out we're..." She threw a sideways glance to encompass the bed.

"Lovers?" Daniel shook his head, a little hard to make his point. "What difference does that make? In fact, I think it's good."

"None of this is going to be 'good' to him."

"It shows solidarity. We're together, we care for each other, we have each other's best interests in mind. I can't wait to tell him that. I can't wait for him to see how I feel about you. I think that's going to go a long way toward easing the transition."

"Transition? He's not *transitioning* to a new father."

Daniel held up his hand. "Wait. Stop. Don't."

She looked at him, not sure what she wasn't supposed to do or say.

"Do not ruin this memory or this day or this wonderful new thing with an old discussion we've had already." He took her hand. "We'll work it out. We're all mature, loving, sane adults. Don't you think it's possible he'll actually like me?"

"Maybe. Eventually." God, how she wanted to believe that.

"Then we'll weather the storm until he does. And he'll see how I feel about you."

She searched his features, looking for clues. "Which is?"

For a long time, he didn't say a word. He locked on her gaze and held her hand and sat very, very still. Then he brought her knuckles to his lips to kiss them.

"You've made me forget all the pain, Katie. You've made me realize that vowing to be alone when there's a woman like you is crazy and wrong. You've made me feel like a whole new man, emphasis on whole."

"Oh. That's…"

"That's the truth. And at the risk of sounding like something my mother would embroider on a pillow, let me say that love conquers all, Katie Rogers Santorini. You know that. I know that. And Nick will know that."

Love? He meant that in the broadest possible way, of course. Family love. General love. Not *love* love.

Because he might break a vow and sleep with her, but he'd never—

"Katie?"

She nodded. "I hope you're right," she finally said.

"I *am* right. I know it in my bones. I feel it in my gut. Trust me on this." He took a sip of champagne, then his eyes flashed as he realized something.

"What is it?"

"If Nick marries this French girl, and they have a child…"

"We'll be grandparents together," she finished.

They just stared at each other as that sank in. Then they clinked their glasses, chugged the champagne, and laughed like they were teenagers in college again.

Chapter Twenty-Four

"**G**randpa! You're not wearing green!" Pru stood at the bottom of the steps, hands on her hips, reprimand in her eyes. "It's Saint Patrick's Day. The wearin' of the green, lad!"

He laughed at her dead-on imitation of Gramma Finnie's brogue and glanced down at his slate-blue pullover. "I grabbed the first thing I found because Katie texted that they're pulling up to Waterford."

"Change before everyone else gets here," she said. "Now, come and look at the shamrock centerpiece spray!" Pru seized Daniel's hand as he came down the stairs and tried to drag him toward the dining room. "Cassie had it hiding in her event closet, which sounds like a place I might enjoy."

But he eased her toward him instead. "I can't see anything but those pretty pearly whites."

She graced him with a blinding, braceless, full-mouth smile, fluttering her fingers on either side of her face with unabashed pride. "I feel like a new girl."

"Well, I hope the old one's still here to run this party tonight." Because he'd literally handed the whole thing to her, and Katie had enlisted Cassie's help, too. Giving Katie and Daniel more time to be alone. Well, not entirely alone. Goldie was a constant, and Rusty was lumbering through his recovery with more bad days than good.

"No worries, Grandpa. We got this. Alex and Cassie are like master caterers, and since our party is also the announcement of Santorini's in Bitter Bark, the food is a mix of Greek and Irish. All the Greek gets a green touch, though. And there are fifty people on the RSVP list!"

He had to laugh. How could he do anything but? The last month had flown by as the fastest and best that he could remember in years. Four years, to be precise.

Trace came around the corner. "There you are," he said to Pru. "Your mom wants pictures before everyone gets here. Let's go, gorgeous."

"Gorgeous beats brace face," she quipped. "Uncle Shane will have to come up with a new nickname for me."

"Yes, gorgeous," Trace reiterated. "But it doesn't change the fact that you can't date until you're thirty-five."

She giggled, sounding much younger than she looked with her newly straightened teeth. "I'm not worried. When I'm ready, Grandpa's going to find me my one true love."

Trace narrowed his eyes at him. "Twenty years, Daniel. Not a moment before."

"Oh, speaking of true loves." Molly joined them, sporting green ribbons in her hair that brought out the emerald in her eyes. "Katie's here. And the rest of the Santorinis are pulling into the driveway."

Daniel just looked at her, still processing *true loves* and *Katie* in the same sentence.

At his stunned expression, Molly tugged one of her ribbons. "Too much?" Then she looked at Pru. "I told you it was—"

"They're adorable, Mom. I'm going to get mine now. All the girls are wearing green ribbons, even Cassie."

As she took off, Molly followed, slipping her hand around Daniel's arm to bring him along. "Thanks for letting her take ownership of this, Dad," she said. "It's meant the world to her to organize this party, because she's missed it so much."

He nodded. "It's high time we celebrate Saint Patrick's Day again," he agreed.

They found his mother in the kitchen, wearing her own kelly-green ribbons that matched a brand-new button-down sweater purchased for the event. "And we even have our wee Patrick Kilcannon, who is one month and two days old," she added to their conversation. "It couldn't be better, lad. Thank you."

"I just hope the whole plan is a success," he said, peering out the kitchen windows at the small gathering around the Santorini's catering van that had pulled up. "I want this to be a great opportunity to showcase Alex's talent and help them launch this new endeavor in April."

"Considering all the people coming, that should work," Trace said, handing Daniel a small digital camera. "Molly is using this to document the entire nine months. Can you get a picture of the three of us before we go out?"

"Of course." Daniel waited for Trace, Molly, and Pru to link arms and smile for the camera.

"Technically, it's the four of us," Pru corrected after he snapped the shot and the three of them headed to the driveway.

Daniel lingered for one moment, though, watching the scene unfold outside, unable to wipe the smile from his face as he watched his kids and Katie's gather together on the driveway. He was vaguely aware that his phone was vibrating in his pocket, but he made no effort to interrupt the pleasure of this moment when anyone he really wanted to talk to was out there.

The Mahoneys had arrived, too, piling out of Declan's truck to greet the others. Goldie, who for the past month had spent any night Katie wasn't at Waterford in Chestnut Creek with her, was already out of the car, spinning in circles and on the hunt for Rusty. Molly, Trace, and Pru headed out to join all of the others, as a group of fifteen or twenty seemed to organically grow in front of him. All of them bathed in a late afternoon golden glow, but maybe that was just the way Daniel was seeing the world now. Bright and beautiful and full of hope.

On an impulse, he lifted Molly's camera and snapped a picture through the window as Garrett and Jessie joined the group, holding a shaded baby carrier together. "She'll like that one," he said.

"Aye," Gramma whispered, coming up next to him. "Family makes the prettiest picture, lad."

"It sure does."

"Even if her lad is making green tzi...tza..." Gramma shook her head.

"Tzatziki," he finished for her, as his phone quieted.

"I speak Gaelic, not Greek." Then she smiled at Daniel. "But I'll learn for you, lad."

He looked down at her, full of love for this tiny woman and her gigantic heart. "I know you will."

She inched up on her tiptoes to whisper, "I've been studying some Greek sayings."

"You have?" he asked as he finally pulled out the phone, but the call had gone to voice mail.

"For next year's Christmas pillows," Gramma said.

The smile that gave him disappeared the minute he read the name on the missed call.

Hannah Stavos, Bloodline.com

He stared at it, vaguely aware that his mother did, too. After a second, he looked up to meet her gaze. "I guess the verdict's in."

"Oh, Danny boy." She put a spotted, aged hand on his arm. "You already know what it is. One look at your uncle Paddy, and we had no doubt."

"None," he agreed, shoving the phone back into his pocket. "And if I call her back now, this whole evening will be different. I'll have to tell Katie, and she'll fret about how we tell Nick. I don't want anything to change this party. I'm afraid that once this is out—"

His mother squeezed his arm. "Courage is knowing what not to fear."

He frowned, vaguely recognizing the quote. "Oscar Wilde or James Joyce?"

"A little lad named Plato." She grinned. "Thought I'd start at the top of their food chain, if you get my drift."

He chuckled and hugged her. "God, I love you. Come on, let's show these Greeks how Kilcannons celebrate Saint Patrick's Day."

"Aye. Someone should be dancing a jig before the night is up."

"Or a...what's it called?"

"Sirtaki," Gramma supplied. At his surprised look, she shrugged. "What? I did a little googlin', 'tis all."

"You really think..." He shook his head. "It's because of Nick, right? You want to establish a bond with him someday."

"Aye, and I will, but we also have a new lass, and she comes with a big family that we have to respect and embrace." She reached up and patted his face. "I found that old videotape that Colleen took, by the way."

"You did? Do I want to see it?"

"Only if you want to know that you and sweet Katie had something special even way back then." She paused for a moment, stroking his cheek with a mother's touch. "I know you loved Annie, Daniel. We all did. And we miss her so terribly. But God has sent you a second chance at love, and that rarely happens. Don't let anything get in the way, no matter how difficult it seems."

"I don't intend to," he told her, the declaration coming out more forcefully than he'd expected. "And I don't intend to miss out on my fifth son, either."

"I have all the faith in the world in you, lad."

Together, they headed outside to a shower of greetings and hugs and one sweet kiss from Katie, who joined the fun with a little green ribbon of her own. He took a couple more pictures with Molly's camera, then handed it to her.

"Right there, Dad," Molly said, pointing at him and Katie. "Toss those Irish ribbons, Katie! Say green!"

They slipped their arms around each other's waists and smiled for the camera, and after the picture was taken, he flat out leaned over and kissed her on the mouth, not caring who saw or what they thought.

But chaos reigned as trays were passed and jokes were shared and Goldie barked insanely.

"Where's Rusty?" Katie asked, looking around. "He's the only thing that'll calm her down."

"Inside. Come on." They heard another car peeling into the driveway, so they tugged her by the collar before any more people got her riled up. In the kitchen, Goldie took off on her hunt, but Daniel and Katie stopped for a proper kiss.

"I missed you last night," he murmured into her mouth.

"Mmm. I ended up staying at the restaurant late with the kids and helping them get ready for this event." She leaned back. "They are Kilcannon fans."

He gave in to a slow smile. "Our first matchup is a bona fide success." He heard Goldie barking at the other side of the house, so he put the tray down. "Let's get her and Rusty set up in my room for the night," he said. "There'll be dogs in and out of here all evening, and they can keep each other company."

"Is he doing better?"

"He's tired. Not eating. But passes all the tests. Whined in his sleep last night, but right now? He's as happy to see his girlfriend as I am to see mine."

She slipped her arm around his waist and dropped her head onto his shoulder. "Girlfriend. Who'd have ever thought it?"

"My mother, it seems."

His phone vibrated again, making him slow his step. Should he take the call? Get the news right then and there, with Katie at his side? As Goldie rushed off to bark at Rusty, he slid the phone out of his pocket only to realize it wasn't a call this time but a text from Hannah Stavos.

Please call me. ASAP URGENT. Not what you think.

Not what he thought?

"Daniel? What is it?"

He looked up from his phone to meet Katie's concerned eyes and every cell in his body froze.

Not what he thought?

Was it possible that after all this, Nick *wasn't* his son? A punch of disappointment slammed so hard, he actually grunted.

"Daniel?"

He blinked at Katie. Would everything change? Would he lose her? Would they care for each other as much? Could he let go of this new fantasy he'd built?

"It's…" He frowned. "What's that noise?"

"Goldie," she said, heading toward the wide hall and living room. "Who is losing it."

"No, that's…someone at the front door."

A hard, insistent pounding at a door had them both rushing around the corner, the two earsplitting sounds of Goldie's out of control bark and a furious knocking at the door making it impossible to even talk.

"Open the damn door!" a man bellowed from outside.

"Who's that?" Daniel asked.

"Oh my God."

He barely heard Katie's whisper as he strode to the door and flipped the lock, only able to see the shadow of a man behind the leaded glass.

"Open the door right now! I know you're in there, Mom!"

Mom? Which of her boys...

"Oh my God, it's Nick."

What? Daniel dragged open the heavy mahogany door without a second's hesitation to come face-to-face with a man who was his size and height, with dark hair and eyes that were both foreign and familiar.

This was Nick? His son? His firstborn? Unless—

His fist came at Daniel so fast he barely registered until knuckles cracked his jaw and sent him reeling backward.

White lights popped in his head, and before he took his next breath, the hall started to fill, Liam leading the charge, jumping on Nick, and pulling him back, Shane on the other side, and Aidan coming in to close ranks.

"Who the hell do you think you are?" Liam demanded.

Nick scowled. "Who are you?" he asked.

"I'm his son," Liam said, gripping the other man's collar.

Nick snorted. "Get in line, pal, 'cause so am I."

Everyone went speechless. For a long, stunned moment of shock, the only sound was Goldie's incessant, demanding bark, then chaos broke with questions, demands, gasps, and...

Daniel turned to Katie in the living room. Leaning against the empty wall where pictures of his perfect life had once hung, she stared at Nick as tears poured over cheeks he'd just kissed.

"I know everything." Nick ground out the words, sizable shoulders rising and falling with ragged breaths. "Everything."

That's what the text meant. Nick…knew.

Nick took a few steps forward, coming face-to-face with Daniel, meeting him inch for inch, eyeball to eyeball. "I don't care what it says on some piece of paper. I don't care what science says. You will never be my father as long as I'm alive and after I'm dead."

Daniel rubbed his chin and held the younger man's gaze, vaguely aware of the eyes full of confusion, distrust, dismay, and questions pinned on him from three families that had gathered to celebrate, only to find out…

Like this.

"Nick, I understand—"

"You don't understand *anything*." Lightning bolts of fury cracked in his dark eyes, his voice low and controlled and barely audible over Goldie's barks behind him. "But I understand you're sleeping with my mother. *Again*." He jutted a square jaw as if daring Daniel to deny it. "My brothers and I text. One of them mentioned your name…a name I was already painfully familiar with when I got my results from that DNA site." He threw a look over his shoulder at his younger brothers. "So I guess I'm not surprised that I pulled in here today to see a Santorini's catering truck in the driveway."

"Listen, son." Daniel reached out his hand, only to have Nick knock it away.

"Do not ever, ever call me that. You are a shadow of my father. A dismal, pathetic, miserable—"

"Stop it!" Katie launched forward, her face soaked with tears. "You don't know him. You don't know anything about him."

"And I don't want to."

"Nick! Give us a chance to explain. Take a breath and listen before you—"

"I've taken my breaths, Mom. I breathed when the results came back. I breathed when I took leave and spent two days flying back. And I breathed all the way over here to find you." He glared at Daniel. "And tell you to go straight to hell, you son of a bitch. Is that clear?"

"Hey!" Liam was on him again, fire in his eyes, as he whipped Nick around and pulled back to prepare a punch.

"Stop." Daniel grabbed Liam's arm before it launched and used his other hand to quiet everyone, except Goldie, who'd become frenzied with the conflict.

"Please," Katie said on a sob. "Please, all of you. Let us try to explain."

"No." Nick leaned closer to her. "You have to make a choice. It's him or me. You can't have us both."

Daniel almost choked, stunned by the demand, not sure he really understood. "Don't—"

"Stay out of it," Nick ordered. "This is between my mother and me. Him or me?" he repeated. "Simple choice, and you have to make it. There will never be any other choice."

Then the only sound was Goldie, who'd replaced barking with a high-pitched whine that echoed the emotion etched on Katie's face.

"Oh, Nick." She let out one long, battered sigh as if the choice made even breathing impossible.

But really there was no choice. And even if there could be, Daniel would never force her to make one.

You're only as happy as your least-happy child.

He'd never let this dear, good, wonderful woman be that unhappy. That would be selfish and wrong.

Daniel leaned in to make his point. "I love her too much for that," he said simply.

Nick's dark eyes tapered to slits of distrust and agony. "If you loved her, you wouldn't have gotten her pregnant in the first place."

Daniel just closed his eyes, kicking himself for being such a complete optimistic, idealistic, blind fool. Had he really thought it would be easy? That they'd all just shrug their shoulders, throw back a few Jameson's, and do a jig for joy?

Fool. Blind, stupid, desperate fool.

And had he really thought loving Katie was *right*? He needed no more proof of how wrong it was. He couldn't do this to them. To *her*. She shouldn't have to make such an untenable choice.

"She's yours, *son*." He couldn't help hitting the last word as hard as that fist had hit him.

"Dad? Dad!"

He didn't know which of his kids was calling him. A few, since it sounded like Molly and Shane and Garrett, too. Did they want him to fight for her? Didn't they see it was wrong to separate a mother from her son? He'd tell them later. Now, he wouldn't take his eyes off Nick Santorini for one second, making sure he understood his position.

"Grandpa, please." Pru grabbed his arm and pulled

it like she was a little girl again, desperate for his attention.

"Not now, Pru."

"Dad." Molly got right up next to him. "Something's wrong with Rusty."

He jerked around at the words.

"Really wrong." Her face was dead-set serious, the face of a vet who knew…

"Oh God." Behind her, Trace and Shane were picking up Rusty, Garrett holding back a crazed, jumping Goldie.

"I think he's had a heart attack," Molly said. "We have seconds. Literally." She didn't wait for him to answer, but followed Trace and Shane, passing Liam and Aidan on the way. "Stay with Dad," she ordered. "And for God's sake, remember you're Kilcannons. Act like it."

In that one moment, she could have been Annie reincarnated.

Paralyzed, Daniel watched them break into a run and felt his whole body tear in two with the need to stay here and fix this and go there and fix that. But right then, Daniel Kilcannon's life was too shattered to fix *anything*.

"Go," Katie said softly, as if she'd read his mind. "Take care of Rusty. He needs you."

"So do you."

"I have…Nick. My family."

Of course she did. And that was right. He nodded and gave one more look at Nick, wondering, for a fleeting moment, if he'd ever see the man again. Maybe not. And that hurt more than his throbbing chin and his broken heart.

Without a word, he headed out. As he passed Pru, he heard her whisper, "I'll call everyone and cancel the party, Grandpa."

And that, more than anything else, made a tear roll down his face as he ran across the grass to save Rusty, praying that a heart attack didn't take his best friend away *again*.

Chapter Twenty-Five

She's yours.

Of all the outrageous and agonizing things that had just transpired, those two words cut Katie the deepest. She backed into the blank wall, her fingernails digging into the fresh paint that she herself had applied, as if she could possibly erase the power and presence of the woman who'd come before her.

Obviously, if Daniel was that quick to give her up, Katie had been very wrong about...everything.

She closed her eyes, inhaled deeply, and focused her attention where it mattered—on the broken and battered families in front of her.

"Let's go," Nick said to Cassie, Alex, and John, managing not to look at Katie at all. "Let's all get out of here."

"Whoa, whoa, whoa, *whoa*." Alex stepped next to his brother, his much-darker eyes glinting. "No one is going anywhere until everyone in this room understands what the holy hell is going on."

Nick looked at her, along with every other person in the room. The Kilcannons and Mahoneys were silent, as though the warning from Molly had hit home.

Finally, Gramma Finnie stepped into the middle of the room, by far the smallest adult there, but giant in her stature and respect.

"I don't think it takes too much explainin'," she said. "You all know their history and can figure out what happened."

"How could you?" Nick ground out to Katie.

"How could I what?"

"How could you not know? How could you not tell me? How could you...you...take up with a man who is my biological father?"

She let out a breath, studying him, seeing Daniel in a way she never had before, but plenty of Nico's hot temper, too. "If you shake off your selfish moral outrage for one moment, Nick, I'll tell you everything, which you don't know even though you claim to."

He averted his gaze at the chastisement, giving her a moment to turn to the others.

"The fact is, I've known this, Cassie and I have, since I first arrived in Bitter Bark. Believe me, I had no idea before that. And my dear, departed husband went to his grave thinking, as we all did, that our reunion when I left Vestal Valley College resulted in Nick's conception. I could have easily gone my entire life with that...misconception."

No one smiled at the bad pun, but Gramma Finnie took a few steps closer, reaching her hand out to Katie.

"No one blames you for the mistake, lass."

Her heart folded a bit, as it did every time she received this woman's unconditional love. "Of course, I blame myself, but life went on, and quite well. Two very healthy, strong, beautiful families formed, eleven kids between us and nearly eighty combined years of happy marriage."

A few of the men shifted from one foot to the other, and some of the women wiped away tears, while Katie mentally reviewed Nick's questions.

"I told Daniel as quickly as I could, which obviously wasn't easy," she said. "He was rocked by the news."

"Why didn't he tell us?" Liam's question held an uncharacteristic amount of emotion, enough that she noticed he glanced around for Andi, but Katie suspected she'd whisked Christian out of the room and away from the drama.

"We wanted one hundred percent confirmation from the company that did the analysis, and then, if correct, we were planning to tell Nick first."

"Then how does she know?" Nick glanced at Gramma, and behind him, a few of the Irish tempers bristled at the *she*, but they remained quiet.

"If I show you a picture of my brother, laddie, you'll know, too." She gave the smallest, slyest smile. "There's plenty of Brennan in your blood, whether you like it or not. I'm guessin' not."

He just closed his eyes. "I don't need to see pictures. It's confirmed. I did my own test and got a call from the company a few days ago, and I took leave to…to…"

"To punch his lights out," Aidan murmured.

"The DNA company called Daniel this afternoon," Gramma Finnie said. "But he didn't take the call. He didn't want to ruin tonight's gatherin'."

Shane snorted softly, the irony of Daniel's decision not lost on any of them.

"What else do you need to know, Nick?" Katie asked, then stopped him from answering with a raised hand. "Oh, I remember. How I 'took up' with this man." She didn't answer, but gave a wistful smile to the Kilcannons and Mahoneys, the realization that this meant she'd lost them, too, choking her up. "Friendship and a shared challenge at first," she said. "A couple of dogs. Some magic. It's the Dogfather recipe for…" *Love.* "Romance." Her throat hitched on the last word.

She's yours.

"Mom." Cassie came right up to her and slid her arm around Katie's waist. "You don't owe anyone any more than this. I really think we should go and let this family, and ours, pick up the pieces in private."

"I need to check on Rusty," Darcy said, stepping away. "And Dad."

"Good God," Liam mumbled, spinning around. "Dad. Rusty."

"What the hell's wrong with us?" Aidan took Beck's hand. "Dad needs us."

They started to leave, one by one, not one demanding more information than what they had. Just…loving. Only Braden Mahoney lingered as the group started to pour out of the living room. He came closer to Katie and Cassie, no smile on his handsome face, but no judgment, either.

"I hope you don't give up on Bitter Bark or this family," he said. "We've all weathered worse."

Cassie looked at him and sighed. "I have no idea what's going to happen, Braden."

"What's going to happen is that we're leaving," John said, gesturing to the rest of the Santorinis. "All of us," he added, narrowing his eyes at Nick. "In fact, I'll drive with you."

"Okay, but first..." Katie glanced around the now empty room, her whole being longing to rush to Daniel. The need was palpable, strong, and breathtaking. She didn't want to give him up. But—

"Mom will drive with me," Nick said. "We have a lot to talk about."

Like why he'd made her *choose*. "Not until I say goodbye," she said. "I'll meet you in the driveway, and you will wait for me as long as I damn well please."

Without waiting for an argument, she walked through the empty room, taking one last look at that wall, which gave her a gut punch. Oh well. She could return all those photos, and he could hang them right back up like they'd been.

In fact, Daniel could easily slide right back into Life Before Katie.

She's yours.

The words echoed as she hustled over to the small crowd gathered outside the clapboard building that housed the Waterford Farm vet offices. Some were in the small waiting room, some under the overhang that covered the porch, and Garrett stood off to the side, holding Goldie by the collar and talking to Jessie, who swayed with the baby in her arms.

They all stopped talking as she approached, except for Goldie, who let out a noisy demand to be let go. At Katie's nod, Garrett released her, and she ran to Katie, looking for love and, like all of them, some answers.

She stood with the dog, taking in all the familiar faces of Daniel's family. Shocked faces. Disappointed faces. Bewildered and uncertain and even a few sympathetic faces.

"I'm so sorry," she managed to say. "None of this…" She quieted Goldie with one hand and rooted for composure she didn't feel. "You're a wonderful family and didn't deserve—"

Daniel walked through the door, and everyone turned to him, silent and breathless.

"We managed to save him," he said on a deep and agonizing sigh.

No cheer went up this time, probably because there was no joy in Daniel's expression.

"For now," he added. "I think the chemo may have affected his heart. But he made it through this one. Barely."

The last word was a whisper, eliciting soft moans from almost the whole family.

"Katie." He took a few steps past them and down the porch to where she stood. "Can we talk?"

She nodded as he came closer and led her toward the path they so often walked with Goldie and Rusty. In a moment, they reached one of the many benches around the property, this one well out of earshot and sight of the families they'd left behind.

Daniel went to the bench and dropped down with a sigh, and Goldie instantly ran to him, jumped up, and put one paw on his leg. Katie held back and watched them for a moment, memorizing the sight of a man she'd fallen so hard for being comforted by a dog who'd managed to worm her way into his heart no matter how much he hadn't wanted that to happen.

When he rubbed his fingers along an angry bruise on his jaw, Katie came closer.

"Does it hurt?"

"Not as much as everything else," he said dryly.

"Oh, Daniel." She sat on his other side. "I knew it would be tough."

He gave a rueful laugh. "Tough? We made a hot, holy mess."

"Nick made it," she said. "We let it happen."

He looked at her, a stark pain she'd never seen before turning his eyes to an ice blue. "You need to go to him. He needs as much comfort as I do, maybe more. His father has died all over again, and as much as I want to help him, I…"

"You can't right now."

"He doesn't want me." The words sounded like they poured out from a hollow, numb heart.

"He's in shock, Daniel. Remember when you first found out?"

He nodded, looking past her to the horizon. "Go to him. Explain it as best you can. Like you did with me."

"So you want me to leave?" she asked, unable to hide the hurt in her voice.

"I want you to…" He turned to her, looking as if he was fighting the urge not to hold her. Sadly, he won that fight. "Be happy."

She had been happy. For one blissful month in his arms, she had been happy. "Do you think that's possible?"

"Right now? No. But maybe someday."

"So you're just going to give up?"

"Give up?" He snorted. "That man I just met wants no part of me. I can't force him to accept me. And I will never, not as long as I live and breathe, try to take you away from him."

"So I'm not worth fighting for?"

His eyes flashed. "Am I worth losing your son?"

She didn't answer because...she couldn't. She simply didn't know the answer because the question was so unfair.

"I didn't think so." He put his hands out, as if trying to push her away without actually touching her. "Katie, nothing—nothing in the world—comes before your children. I know you believe that, and you know I do, too. No matter how old we are, they are the priority. Nick is your priority."

"Nick is a grown man living in Africa who has to accept this card that life has dealt him."

His eyes narrowed with doubt. "And when he and the French girlfriend have a baby and you are cut out of knowing and loving that child because of me? How would you look at me in a year or two or five?"

She swallowed, not even able to fathom the idea of Nick cutting her out of his life. But that look in his eyes? The depth of his feelings? The agony of this betrayal to his whole being? "I would hate that," she whispered.

"No. You'd hate me."

In the distance, she heard a horn honk from the driveway. "There he is," she said on a dry laugh. "Calling me home."

"Where you belong," Daniel said, taking both her hands. "With your family, with your children. God knows, he's had enough pain in his life. Choosing me over him would be wrong."

And she knew better than to try to argue with Daniel Kilcannon when he thought something was wrong. And just like that, she gave up, too.

"All right then." She pushed to a stand, having no desire to sit here and beg for a way to work this out. "I'll go pick up the pieces of my jigsaw puzzle and put it all back together again."

He tried to swallow, but managed only a nod.

"And Goldie?" She looked down at the dog. "Rusty needs her."

"I know Rusty needs her, and I love her," he added, taking Katie's hand and urging her back down on the bench. "But I also love..." He touched her cheek tenderly, as if it might be as sore as his. "I also love..."

She held her breath and waited. If he said it, she'd stay. If he loved her, she'd make it work. If he gave her his whole heart, she'd never break it.

But he shook his head. "Rusty needs quiet and rest if he's got a prayer. It's better if you take her, really. She's yours."

The words sliced her heart right in half.

With a whispered goodbye, she gestured to Goldie, who jumped off the bench and trotted to her, as if she understood every word. As they walked up the path, Katie longed for Daniel to call her back, but she wasn't the least bit surprised when he didn't.

"C'mon, Goldilocks," she whispered. "Let's leave the men we love and soldier on, girl. You're a Santorini now."

Chapter Twenty-six

"**C**an they not read in Bitter Bark?" Cassie blew out a disgusted breath at the sound of someone knocking on the closed and locked door of Santorini's. "Does 'Open for business in one week' on our snazzy new blackboard mean nothing to these people?"

Alex gave her a light elbow, bending over to peer through the stainless-steel pass that blocked her view to the front. "I think you want to answer this one, Cass."

"No, I don't. I want to finish making this list of potential corporate customers I can call on for catering your amazing food when we open and make this place into *Butter* Bark, home of Alex Santorini's famous kourabiedes."

"No one ignores the *fire department*," he replied.

"What?" She jerked around to follow his gaze. "You mean, like the fire marshal? Checking on our seating capacity?" But even as she said it, she knew he hadn't meant that. He'd meant one particularly smokin'-hot firefighter.

Yep. One look through the front glass at a man

with spectacular shoulders and a Bitter Bark Fire Department emblem stretched over an equally spectacular chest confirmed that. "Well, what do you know? Einstein's here."

"Einstein?"

"There's a big brain in that big...body." As she walked through the nearly complete dining area, Cassie took a breath and brushed some hair back that had fallen out of her ponytail. It had been three weeks since that fateful Saint Patrick's Day party. The worst of the wounds had started to form scars. At least, they had in the Santorini family. She couldn't speak for the Kilcannons, since none of them had had contact with Cassie or her brothers, and certainly not with Mom.

But she and her brothers had already carried a mortgage on the property and had gone too far on the renovations to back out. So they continued as planned with the Bitter Bark location, getting the restaurant prepared for an April opening as planned.

But there'd been radio silence between the Hatfields and McCoys. Cassie, for one, missed the colorful clan. All of them. Even the one standing outside her door. Especially him.

She flipped the lock and inched it open. "And here I thought you were such a great reader." She pointed to the sign. "No spanakopita for you."

He gave her that slow, sweet smile that did stupid things to her insides. "I need a table."

"We're open in—"

"A table for about twenty." He beckoned her with two fingers, which was somehow enough to make her step through the doorway and look to her left at...

"Holy cow." They were all there. The whole stinking lot of them, including little Gramma Sweetcakes and the teenager who was more mature than most thirty-year-olds.

She squinted around, but no Daniel, the one Cassie really wanted to see storm Santorini's.

But it was still a crowd, so big and beautiful and Irish, she half expected one of them to hand her a pot of gold. "We're not serving food, but…" She settled her gaze on Darcy, who really had potential to be a great girlfriend. "Something tells me you're not here to eat."

"Cassie." Braden reached for her with his big, strong, fireman's hand that made her arm look tiny when he touched her. "We want to sit down with you and your brothers and present an idea."

"Feels…Mafia-ish." She lifted a hand and gestured to them. "So no shooting, okay? Well, Nick's not here at the moment, so I guess we're safe."

Her joke made a few of them laugh as they passed her, each and every one giving her a warm greeting. Some hugged, some asking about the restaurant they'd all worked to help complete. Gramma hugged her and whispered, "We miss you, lass."

And all the Mahoneys were there, even the spiky-haired Ella, whom Cassie had met only a few times, but totally appreciated as a fellow drama queen.

Molly was last, taking Cassie's hands in hers and holding them tight. "How's your mom doing?"

"She's okay, I guess. Nick extended his leave from Africa and is staying with her, and I guess they're working things out."

"That's good."

"How's Rusty?" Cassie asked, bracing for bad news.

But Molly gave an encouraging smile. "Better than his master," she said. "He does have some heart issues, but he's done with chemo and is cancer-free. We've got him on meds, and he's hanging in there."

"And Daniel?" She peeked over Molly's shoulder, hoping against hope he was here, too.

"He's the reason we're here."

"Come on," Cassie said, bringing her inside. "I'll get my brothers."

In a few moments, the dining room was half filled, the entire crew taking a bunch of tables and booths, but all close enough to easily talk. John and Alex had come out and exchanged greetings, but the whole thing was just this side of weird.

"So..." Cassie said when things quieted to an awkward silence. She was sitting at a four-top with her brothers, but looking at the new arrivals. "We meet again."

At the soft chuckles of the group, Liam stood at his table and cleared his throat, looking very much like the de facto leader of this pack. "We have a proposal for you."

"A proposal to get a proposal," Shane cracked.

Cassie and her brothers shared looks, but stayed silent.

"As you no doubt know," Liam continued, "we call our dad the Dogfather for many reasons, not the least of which is that he, like the Godfather, is a bit of a master manipulator."

"In a really good way," Darcy added, reaching to hold her fiancé's hand. "So people find love."

"We've heard the folklore," Alex replied.

"Well, we want to return the favor," Molly interjected. "God knows we've tried on our own, but every effort failed until…"

"Until your mother came along," Shane continued, uncharacteristically serious. "We thought he managed to find his match all on his own, but then…"

"Disaster struck," John piped in. "We were all there. Have the shrapnel to prove it."

"It wasn't a disaster," Garrett said. "It was a setback."

Cassie leaned forward. "A setback? He let her go."

"But she left," Darcy said.

The statement silenced everyone.

"'Tis a bit of a kerfuffle." Gramma Finnie stood, and even though she didn't tower over anyone, she had their attention. "And I can tell you this. I haven't seen my son this miserable in a long time."

"And our mother is moping," Alex said. "But does he love her?"

"Because if not," Cassie added, "we're not helping you. Because I know my mother, probably better than anyone in this room, and that woman loves that man."

Molly and Darcy reached their hands together and squeezed them, the silent gesture telling Cassie the answer to Alex's question. And giving her a ridiculous amount of hope.

"I think he does," Liam said. "And the reason I can say that is because he let her go so she would be able to keep your family together."

Because Nick forced his hand. Cassie looked down, still ashamed of what her brother had done, but fully understanding how the news that he wasn't Nico Santorini's son had affected him.

"So what do you need?" Alex asked.

"A well-timed meeting, a mutual cause, and…a dog," Pru said. "That's kind of his foolproof formula."

"A dog?" John asked.

"Works for him," Molly said, smiling at Trace.

"Okay, okay." Cassie stood, already seeing the possibilities. "But what about Nick?"

"What about me?"

Every head in the room swiveled toward the kitchen door when Nick stepped into the dining room. And no one, not a single person, said a word for what felt like an eternity. He stood leaning against the doorjamb, wearing a washed-out blue button-down with his hair nearly grown out over the collar. He hadn't shaved much lately, and the shadow of whiskers made his hollow cheeks look rough and sinister, like a man who really didn't give a hoot about anything anymore. Cassie knew this news had hit him almost as hard as Daddy's death.

Liam was the first to stand and approach him, slowly, with an outstretched hand.

"Hey, man," Liam said. "Good to see you."

For a moment, no one moved. Everyone just stared at Nick and waited to see how he'd respond. *Come on, Nicky. Show them what Santorinis are made of.*

He lifted his hand and took Liam's. "How's it goin'?" he said casually, but both men held the other's gaze, and there was nothing casual about it.

Cassie almost melted with relief.

"I've been listening," Nick said, glancing at them. "My mother told me…" He gave a dry laugh. "My mother told me a lot in the past month. A little more than I wanted to know, to be honest."

Everyone in the room either laughed softly or shifted uncomfortably in their seats.

"And I know I was wrong to make her choose, but I..." He closed his eyes. "I don't know how to undo what I've done."

"We do." That from at least five Kilcannons, in unison.

"Yeah," Nick said. "She told me all about this... this matchmaking crap."

"It's not crap," Aidan muttered.

Nick held up a conciliatory hand. "Turn of phrase," he said quickly. "Everything I heard about your...about *him*...has been..." He searched for a word, shaking his head. "Flattering? Impressive? Familiar?" He shrugged as if all of the descriptions were true. "But mostly, she's made me see that I acted like a complete ass that day and I should probably get my act together and do some damage control."

They all stared, no one quite sure what that meant.

"Can you help us?" Liam asked.

For a long moment, Nick stared at him, the two men face-to-face. A blind man could see the resemblance. Not like Alex and Nick, of course, but... it was there.

Brothers.

Cassie steadied her breath as the realization truly hit home.

"I think I can help you," Nick said. "I've got your mutual cause in the back of the truck John's been letting me drive. You guys handle the timing of the meeting. And, trust me, we've got the dog. Let's do this."

For a moment, maybe two, there was dead silence in the room. Then the whole group got up to follow Nick when he waved them back through the kitchen to the parking lot to see what he was talking about.

One look at it, and everyone was high-fiving and talking at the same time. All but Molly, who pulled out a little digital camera and asked Nick, "Do you think I could add one more?"

Then they put their collective heads together and made a plan.

Rusty was moving slowly that morning, but Daniel refused to give up on the croissant run. Yes, they were later than usual. But Linda May would have saved him at least one pastry, and it was better to go in the store when it was less crowded.

Just as he reached the bakery, he looked up, sensing movement in the windows above the store, where Andi's office was. Inching back, he frowned into the reflection of the windows, certain he'd seen her where she often stood while she was on the phone. But he must have been mistaken.

He pulled the door open and inhaled the buttery goodness, seeing Linda May's warm smile the minute he walked in.

"Hey, stranger," she called. "Don't worry. I have two left."

He smiled back as he headed to the counter, letting Rusty sniff his way over and waiting while Linda May packed the pastries in paper and poured his coffee.

"How's our old boy doing today?" she asked.

"He's holding steady."

"And your dog?" she added, making him laugh.

He waited for the croissants, taking his coffee to the side counter for sugar, and just as he was putting a lid on the cup, Rusty started to bark. Hard. He tore across the little bakery, bounding to the window, practically plowing into the person sitting at the table next to it.

"Whoa, bud, whoa!" Daniel launched after him. "I'm so sorry," he said to the man who'd narrowly escaped a coffee spill.

But Rusty's face was smashed up against the window, his bark bellowing louder than Daniel could remember hearing for a month. "What is it, boy?"

And then he saw—well, heard—the other dog barking. And his heart definitely skipped a beat, which meant poor Rusty's was probably doing dangerous things.

He bent down to calm him, face-to-face with Goldie on a leash, lapping at the windowpane as if she could lick her way to Rusty.

The moment he looked up from the dogs, he saw Katie. And everything in him, every cell that made him human, every chemical that made him alive, every ounce of blood that pumped through his fractured heart, suddenly felt alive again.

She struggled with the leash, and next to her, her son Alex helped by easily getting Goldie by the collar.

For one split second, they all looked at each other, and Daniel knew it was wrong to keep these two dogs apart. And even more wrong to go one more day in misery when fate had just handed him everything he wanted.

"Linda May, I'll be right back," he called, heading to the door, a hand around Rusty's collar.

"I'm not holding my breath, Daniel," she replied with a knowing laugh.

Because everyone knew what he was going through. Everyone except the one person who had to know.

Rusty rushed outside, and instantly the two dogs collided, pawing each other's necks, biting playfully, and barking hysterically, until Goldie dropped to the ground, rolled over, and let Rusty poke his nose in her belly.

The display of affection made them—and a few bystanders—laugh, easing what could otherwise have been an awkward moment.

"I think we've kept them apart too long," Daniel said, reaching for Katie's hands to bring her in for what he hoped was a casual hug. Even though imitating Rusty would be a better way to show his true feelings. "Hey there," he whispered into her ear.

"Hi." She added a little squeeze as if she just couldn't help it.

"And, Alex, good to see you." Daniel extended his hand for a shake. "How's the restaurant going?"

"We open in a week." He sounded a little surprised Daniel didn't know that, but then, Daniel had gone well out of his way to avoid that section of Ambrose Avenue, even rounding the square the long way so he wouldn't bump into a Santorini.

"Oh yes, I heard that at the Economic Development Committee meeting," he said. "That's good. I know things will go well for you here. And…" He looked down at Katie, hating that his heart was slamming against his chest. "How's everything?" Why not ask what was important? "How's Nick?"

"He's still here," she said. "He's been staying with me and we've been talking."

"Oh, that's great." If only he were talking to Daniel. Maybe someday…if he got things right today.

"It looks like Rusty's doing well," she said, smiling at the two dogs as they finally settled down to happily pant in each other's faces.

"Better now," he said. "He's been pining." But then, who hadn't been doing that?

"So…" She tilted her head expectantly. "Did you…like it?"

He frowned, having absolutely no idea what she could be talking about. "Like what?"

"Oh shoot, man!" Alex snapped his fingers like he'd just remembered something. "I never took it out to Waterford Farm. Nick brought it in yesterday, and I completely forgot. It's still in the catering truck, if you want to get it."

"What is it?" Daniel asked.

"A surprise," Katie responded. "But I'll have to figure out some other way to get it out and installed." Then she gave a mother's look to Alex. "I can't believe you *forgot*."

"Mom, I'm up to my ass opening a new restaurant."

"It's fine," Daniel said, dying to know what the surprise was. Nothing could be much better than the one he was experiencing now. "Whatever it is, I can get it now. My Tahoe's right over there. I can drive it to the restaurant and get…whatever it is."

"No, the van's right there," Katie said. "Alex

parked there to go…" She frowned. "Why did you park over here again?"

"So I could…" He glanced down the street. "Stop at the hardware store," he finished as if he'd just remembered. He added a laugh. "Honestly, my brain is scrambled eggs this week. Come on, let's get it, and the two of us can carry it to your car."

"Two of us?" Daniel asked.

"It's kind of heavy," Katie said. "And it will take at least two people to install."

Daniel put a hand on her shoulder, mostly because he had to, but also to ask a very serious question. "What *is* it, Katie?"

"Just something I promised you."

He searched her face, thinking of all the promises she'd made and so many that he never got, but still wanted. "I'm sure curious."

While he and Katie got the dogs, Alex walked a few feet ahead. Just as Daniel clipped a leash on Rusty, he noticed Alex looking up at the windows above the bakery and could have sworn he nodded. But when Daniel followed his gaze, he didn't see anyone.

"It's good to see you," Katie said softly as they started to walk.

"It went pretty far past *good* the minute Rusty barked," he joked. "I might have howled a little myself."

She laughed at that, looking up with a gleam in her eyes. "Yeah," she whispered. "Same."

With that one word, Daniel felt more hope than he'd known in weeks.

Alex was already at the back of the white Santorini's van, opening the back door to reveal a massive brown box about five feet long and three feet wide. He stepped aside and pulled out his phone, while Daniel peered at the box, mind whirring.

"My pictures?" Daniel guessed.

"What?" Alex's exclamation interrupted Katie's chance to respond. "Cassie, you've got to be kidding me. Now? Okay, okay. Do not let them leave. I'll be there in five minutes." He tapped the phone and shoved it into his pocket. "How far's your Tahoe, Daniel?"

"Right there." He pointed to the small lot where he always parked, no more than twenty feet away.

"Let's roll. Our first major catering client just arrived at Santorini's, and I totally forgot I was supposed to be there."

"Oh, you didn't mention a meeting, Alex," Katie said.

"Told you." He tapped his temple. "Scrambled eggs. Let's move, please."

"But I can't dump this on Daniel to get home and—"

"Come with me," Daniel said as he helped Alex pull the box from the back. "Whatever it is, we can install it together."

He noticed Alex's gaze intent on his mother, as if he was waiting with the same bated breath that had caught in Daniel's chest.

She hesitated a nanosecond before nodding. "I'd like that," she said. "And I'm sure Goldie would, too."

By the time they reached Waterford a little while later, Goldie and Rusty had settled down. And so had Daniel. As if by silent agreement, Daniel and Katie avoided the tough subjects on the drive there, slipping back into the easy conversation and frequent laughs that he'd missed so damn much.

As they pulled in, Garrett and Shane came over from the pen, even though they were in the middle of a training session, greeting Katie as if they weren't that surprised to see her. That helped alleviate any awkward explanation, and before Daniel even finished asking for help with the box, they were headed to the back of the Tahoe to offer an assist.

It was as if they knew what he wanted before he did.

They took the box in the front door at Katie's request, making him even more certain it contained his family pictures, although she teasingly had refused to answer.

And then his sons were gone as fast as they'd shown up. In fact, the entire house seemed deserted, he realized as he went to the mud room to get a knife and the toolbox Katie had said he'd need. The kitchen was empty, with no sign of Crystal or his mother or the family and staff that marched through there during the workday at Waterford.

But none of that mattered as he knelt down and slid a knife along the side of the box that Goldie and Rusty sniffed with vague interest before they curled up next to each other by the living room hearth.

"I feel like a kid at Christmas," Daniel said. "Can't remember the last time I was this excited about a present."

She put her hand over his before he lifted the lid. "I almost didn't do it," she said. "I almost sent the bins back with all your pictures because…"

"Because I hurt you."

She looked at him. "Life hurt us."

"No, no." He dropped the knife and took her face in his hands. "I could recite a litany of excuses for my behavior that day. But none of them would be good enough."

"No, no—"

"Shh. Let me tell you something else," he insisted. "Let me tell you that for twenty-two nights, I have paced the floor of my newly decorated room and second-guessed every single moment of that day. I know what I did, why I did it, and how much it disappointed you."

"You didn't want me to have to make a choice."

"I didn't *let* you make a choice," he said, his voice rough against his throat. "Because I was too damn scared that you wouldn't choose me. Yes, yes, I believed I was doing the right thing by taking the decision away from you, by protecting you, by letting you have Nick and not me. But deep inside, I thought that if I fought for you, I would lose."

She stared at him. "You could never lose me, Daniel."

He huffed out a breath that felt like he'd been holding it for damn near a month. "Thank God."

"But the fact is, I don't have to make a choice," she said softly. "Nick has accepted the truth, and we've talked and cried it out together."

He inched back. "Then where have you been?"

"In the same place as you."

"Really? 'Cause I haven't seen you on those miserable nights, except in my imagination."

She smiled. "The same mental place," she said. "I was scared to fight for you because I'll never be..."

She swallowed noisily as her eyes filled. "That great love of your life."

"Oh, Katie." He pulled her into him. "I'm not scared of anything anymore except waking up without you."

She leaned back, holding his gaze and gesturing to the box. "You better open your present before you make any pronouncements."

He hesitated a moment, then finished with the lid, opening it slowly, then lifting packing tissue to reveal…a large, metal puzzle piece.

"It's a puzzle?"

"A jigsaw puzzle," she said. "Of your life."

For a moment, he couldn't breathe, taking in the bronze frames of all different shapes and sizes, each somehow perfectly fitting with the next one. Some framed one or two or three different images, but altogether there were about fifteen puzzle-piece-shaped frames, each meant to be hung next to the one they fit with.

"I'm speechless."

She laughed. "At the amount of hammering you're about to do?"

"At the creativity and meaning and perfection of this." He turned to her. "All the pictures are here?"

"Every one, from your wedding day to Molly's sleigh ride in a bridal gown in January. It was quite an undertaking. But Nick helped me. We did a few every day, talking the whole time, and working things out."

He looked at her, then back to the frames. "He did this with you?"

"It helped him," she whispered. "It helped him to understand who you are and how we got to this place."

He lifted each individual frame and started laying the shapes on the floor, seeing how perfectly they fit next to each other, still unable to put his emotions into words as the jigsaw puzzle of his life took shape.

"I still can't believe this," he said as he lifted one that held pictures of Fiona and Liam, both as babies in the same christening gown. There were kids of all ages, dogs of all sizes, and at least ten of Annie at various stages of her life.

He eventually came to the bottom of the carefully wrapped piles. "No one has ever given me a gift like this."

"There are a few extra puzzle pieces that are empty, so you can add more," she said. "And be sure to look at the last one. Nick made it for you."

He closed his eyes for a moment, then reached for the frame that held a collage of four pictures, all of Nick. One as a very little boy, one as a teenager holding a basketball, one in a cap and gown, and one in scrubs, laughing.

"Katie." The word came out thick with emotion. "I have to thank him for this."

"I think he'll let you do that," she said, putting her hand over his. "I think he's just about ready."

"What's this one?" he asked when he moved Nick's puzzle piece.

"No, that's all."

"There's one more." He lifted a frame that held only one five-by-seven photo, with space for more. A photo of…

"That's us," Katie said, kneeling to come closer. "That's you and me on Saint Patrick's Day."

He recognized it immediately—it was the shot Molly had taken when Katie had first arrived that fateful day. "How did you get this?"

"I didn't get it." She dropped back to the floor. "But somehow someone did. Nick or Alex or…"

"Molly or Liam or Shane…"

"Or *all* of them."

For a moment, neither said a word, but stared at the picture that fit perfectly with the puzzle piece next to it.

"I don't understand," she said. "I didn't have that picture, and only Nick knew what was in the box."

"And I went to Linda May's late today, but Andi could see from her window…"

"And Alex insisted on parking on that side of the square, even though…"

Daniel turned to look at the two dogs nestled together by the hearth as a knowing smile pulled at his mouth. "We've been Dogfathered," he murmured, fighting a laugh. "By our own kids."

They both sat there and laughed until the only thing they could do was slide into each other's arms and kiss all the hurt away.

A few hours, about twenty nails, and several dozen more kisses later, the puzzle wall was finished, and it was an absolute work of art. By then, after a text from Gramma Finnie and hours of silence in the rest of the house, Daniel was pretty sure they were strategically and certainly alone for the night.

"Let's celebrate," he said, heading to the Jameson's decanter and glasses that now sat on a brand-new floating shelf that was decades more modern than the bar cart. He poured two glasses and brought one to Katie on the sofa, where she admired their work.

"To jigsaw puzzles?" she guessed.

He sat next to her and held out his glass. "To the pictures we haven't taken yet, the years we haven't lived yet, the matches we're going to make together, the grandchildren we can't even imagine yet, and the great, great love we haven't even begun to enjoy together."

"Oh, Daniel." She closed her eyes and put the glass down as if she didn't trust herself not to drop it.

So he did the same, taking her face in his hands. "I love you, Katie Rogers Santorini. And you are the only woman I want to love for the rest of my life."

"I love you, too." She pressed her hands over his. "Thank you for giving me Nick. For taking me to Nico and for letting me back into your life."

"Where you are going to stay."

"Yes," she whispered as he closed the space and kissed her.

Epilogue

Bushrod's was packed…with Kilcannons, Mahoneys, and Santorinis.

On the sidelines of the party that had started as Nick's going-away dinner at Santorini's in Bitter Bark and then turned into a family-wide bar hop to the biggest dance floor in Bitter Bark, Katie could actually feel her face hurting from laughing. Watching Cassie, Alex, John, and Nick try to teach a dozen Irishmen and women how to dance the sirtaki was flat-out hilarious.

It was late enough on a weeknight that most, but not all, of Bitter Bark's locals had left the place, though some stuck around to witness the impromptu dance lessons.

"One, two, sweep, *extend*." Cassie rolled her eyes, making the circle of family around the dance floor laugh as she teased Braden. "It's not that difficult, Einstein."

But Braden shook his head and held out his hands. "I am not Zorba the Greek."

"No kidding." Cassie gave Braden's strong shoulder a squeeze. "But we'll make a Greek dancer out of you yet."

As John started up the familiar mandolin music on the sound system, nice and slow for the non-Greeks, Cassie called out the steps for the line dance. Taking it all in, Katie leaned back into the man who stood behind her with his arms wrapped around her waist. Next to them, Goldie and Rusty were tucked under a table, both sound asleep despite the noise.

"You sure you don't want to try?" she asked.

Daniel's chuckle rumbled from his chest into her back. "I want them to get good and involved, so no one will notice we've slipped out." He planted a kiss on her head. "I have plans for tonight, sweet Kate."

She turned to look up at him. "You have to say goodbye to Nick."

"I will." He looked over her head, his gaze landing on the man at the end of the line who might not be Greek by blood, but had obviously danced to this music a thousand times in his life. "We've come so far these past few weeks."

Katie sighed in happy agreement. They'd started slow, with no big confrontation and no massive breakthroughs. The times that Katie and Daniel had spent with Nick had been more quiet than anything, with simple conversations about work, Africa, life, dogs, and family. The only time it got serious was when Daniel offered a copy of his results from Bloodline.com, and Nick had perused them, nodding.

The truth was out, the shock had subsided, and now they all had to figure out how to move ahead. The going-away party had been Cassie's idea, and they'd closed the restaurant for a private dinner Alex cooked for all the families. When it was over, Garrett had driven Gramma Finnie home to babysit the

youngest kids, and the rest of them—including Pru—
had moved to everyone's favorite bar to take Cassie's
bet that they couldn't learn the sirtaki.

They stumbled through one more time, and a few
of the dancers peeled off to grab drinks and let the
ones who were getting the hang of it try it at a faster
speed. Nick said something to Cassie, who nodded,
reached up, and hugged him and kissed him on the
cheek. Then he headed toward Katie and Daniel,
shaking back his long hair as he strode across the
dance floor.

"Time for old people to go home," he said as he
reached them.

"I hate to think what we are if you're calling
yourself old, Nick," Daniel joked.

"You are…" He looked from one to the other.
"Very happy."

Katie let out a sigh. "Yes we are."

"I guess you're going to Waterford tonight?" Nick
asked Katie.

She nodded. "I am, but Cassie and John and Alex
are staying in town at their apartment." The three-
bedroom unit in Ambrose Acres had been a godsend
in a building owned by Josh, Darcy's fiancé. They got
the apartment for a song, and it meant that they could
easily work at the new restaurant without driving back
and forth to Chestnut Creek. "You could stay there,"
Katie suggested.

"And sleep on a couch?" He shook his head. "I
haven't had anything to drink, and I'm good to go
home. I have a lot of flights and connections to make
to get back to CAR. If it's all the same to you, I've
said my goodbyes. I'm ready to hit the road."

"You'll be missed," Daniel said simply.

Nick met his gaze and gave a slight nod to acknowledge the words. Then he looked over his shoulder at the dancing, laughing crowd. "It's good to be around family."

"Bitter Bark could always use a top-notch doctor," Daniel added, lifting his brows with the suggestion.

Nick regarded him for a moment, no smile, but the anger and hate had evaporated. Yes, it would be a long time before Katie could hope Nick would feel anything like love for Daniel, but they'd reached mutual respect, and for the moment, that satisfied her.

"Don't tempt me with regular hours and a lack of bloody skirmishes."

Katie winced. "When you and Lucienne are ready to settle down, honey, you know where your family is. Safe and sound."

A shadow crossed his face, one that Daniel might have missed, but Katie saw it. "Is everything okay?" she asked.

He shrugged. "Let's just say I need to get back."

She searched his face for clues, but he wasn't giving any. Instead, he reached out a hand to Daniel, but before they could shake, a woman Katie didn't know sidled up to them. No, she *did* recognize her, Katie realized. The cat lady.

"So these are all yours?" the woman asked Daniel with a flirtatious grin and a sideways glance to Nick.

"Some are mine, some are Katie's, some are..." He and Nick shared a look, the closest thing to a connection she could remember the two men having. "Bella Peterson, you know Katie Santorini."

"Everyone does now," she said on a laugh.

"And this is Nick, her...my..." He hesitated, uncertain where to go with that, but the smile grew a little on Nick's face as he extended his hand to the woman.

"Nick Santorini," he said, shaking her hand. "I'm..." He swallowed and glanced at Daniel. "I'm Daniel and Katie's son."

Katie sucked in a soft breath of surprise, but Bella gasped so noisily it was surprising the dancers didn't hear it.

"What? Excuse me? Did you say..."

But Daniel was looking right at Nick with amazement in his eyes.

"I don't understand—"

Daniel put a hand on her shoulder. "Long story, Bella. But thanks for stopping by."

Her eyes sparked as she got the not-so-subtle message and backed away, looking from Nick to Daniel and back again.

"Well, you've done it now," Daniel said on a laugh. "The Bitter Bark rumor mill is about to go into overdrive."

Nick shrugged. "I believe in telling the truth," he said. "It's the right thing to do."

"Yes, it is," Daniel agreed, reaching out to pull Nick into a quick, fatherly hug. "We'll miss you, son," he said softly.

Nick gave his back a pat and pulled away. "Take care of my mom," he said.

"I will."

"Hurt her and you die."

Daniel laughed. "And I'd deserve to."

Nick turned to Katie, leaning over to hug her and add a kiss on the head. "I love you, Mom."

She couldn't get the words out, because her throat was so thick, so she kissed his cheek, and he got the message.

A minute later, he was gone.

She turned to Daniel, her eyes swimming, still speechless. He cupped her face and leaned close. "Let's take the dogs for a walk and get some air."

With a quick glance at the group having too much fun to miss them, she agreed while he got Goldie and Rusty out from under the table, and the four of them slipped out into the warm spring air.

"Want to walk through the square?" she asked.

"Yes, but..." He glanced at her, thinking. "Actually, I have a destination in mind."

"You do?" Intrigued, she curled closer to him, taking Goldie's leash and walking arm in arm as the dogs led the way. As always, when one dog stopped, so did the other. When Rusty slowed, so did Goldie.

"They're so good together," Katie mused, watching them.

"She's changed his life," Daniel said, looking down at her. "Like someone else I know."

Her heart snagged on the statement, though it wasn't the first time she'd heard it. She still couldn't get used to this euphoria of love. Sometimes, she looked at him and remembered that there were days that she'd been convinced she'd never be truly happy again.

But she'd been so wrong about that.

They walked under the lights in the trees, past the statue of Thaddeus Ambrose Bushrod, the town's founder, pausing along the path where Rusty had gotten sick and she'd confessed her secret.

Then they stopped for a kiss at the spot where they'd decided to go their separate ways and follow their hearts to Annie and Nico. But after that, he led her out of the square completely.

She had no idea where they were going until they reached the perimeter of the Vestal Valley College campus.

"So, your car's not parked in the vet school lot anymore," she mused. "Where are you taking me, Daniel Kilcannon?"

"First night."

She frowned as they crossed the street, looking up and down. "I can't remember where that apartment was when I found you feeding pretzels to a dog."

"Nope, not that part of the first night."

"Then where..." She slowed her steps as they reached the red brick walls of Gillespie Hall. "Ah, the scene of the crime."

"Right up there." He pointed to a window on the second floor, dark now, as it had been the night they'd conceived a baby. "You remember the first night."

"Like a woman could forget a kiss like that."

"I believe you once described it as 'kissing the holy hell and common sense out of you.'" He looked down at her. "I was thinking I'd try that move again."

"Please do." They reached the side of the building, still in deep shadows, as they had been that night when he'd walked her home. Far away from any people or dogs, they dropped the leashes and let Rusty and Goldie take in the smells of a new place.

Then Daniel slowly backed her to the wall, looking

down at her with the same heated expression she remembered from all those years ago. Decades disappeared, a lifetime of love and family and separation melted away, and all that mattered was this moment. This man. This…kiss.

She tasted the now familiar mouth that she loved so much, closing her eyes, enjoying the rush of love that washed over her every single time they kissed.

"Katie Rogers," he murmured into her mouth.

"Yes?"

He drew back, just enough to look at her. "Anything could have changed," he whispered. "You could have picked another girl for our double date or not left Bitter Bark that night. And the course of our lives would have been completely different."

She sighed. "All different children, different memories, different lives."

"But that wasn't what fate had in mind," he said. "Do you remember that night I took you to Chestnut Creek and you told me, 'You can't fight fate'?"

"Did I say that?" She narrowed her eyes, thinking back on the conversation. "It's true, I guess. Fate had other plans for us."

"Or did she want us to wait?" He smiled and tipped her chin. "So that we would be right here again, different people than we were, but still, somehow, the same?"

She studied the lines of his face for a moment. "What brought on all this existential thinking, Dr. Kilcannon?"

"We've come full circle," he said. "Right back to where we started, making me wonder if fate or God or the universe or two really clever angels guided us to where we were always meant to be."

"I don't know." She nestled closer. "But I thank them all."

"You were right," he said. "You can't..." He kissed her forehead. "Fight." Her nose. "Fate." Her lips. "She'll win every time."

She moaned into the kiss, melting the same way she had on that very first January night.

"I love you, Katie," he whispered into the kiss.

"I love you right back, Daniel."

He inched back. "I love your grace and goodness."

"I love your moral compass."

"I love your family."

"I love *your* family."

"I love your dog."

She looked to the spot where Goldie sat, one paw on Rusty as if she was constantly monitoring his well-being. "And she loves *your* dog."

He laughed. "I love your heart and humor and ability to take something dreadful and dead and bring it back to life. Like you did with me."

"You were never dreadful."

"I was on the inside."

She squeezed him. "And I was still bleeding inside, too."

He searched her face, quiet as his expression changed. "You know, we've lived full lives. Wonderful lives. But we're not even close to done."

"There's so much left to do," she agreed.

Slowly, holding her gaze, he lowered his whole body to the ground until he was on one knee.

This time, her heart didn't catch. It stopped altogether.

"Katie Rogers Santorini, I know I'm not the first great love of your life. But I would be so honored and humbled and happy if I could be the last great love of your life. Will you marry me?"

She tried to breathe, but couldn't. Tried to answer him, but was speechless. Tried to think of a single reason not to spend the rest of her life as Katie Kilcannon and couldn't come up with one.

"Oh yes, Daniel." She reached to bring him up for another teary kiss. "Yes, I will marry you and be the last great love of your life."

When he kissed the holy hell and common sense out of her again, with the bricks of Gillespie Hall against her back, Katie knew that all the puzzle pieces of her life had fallen exactly into the places they belonged.

Who's next for the Dogfather?

The Mahoneys and Santorinis must all find love and in fact, Daniel's already started pulling those strings!

Watch for *Hot Under the Collar,* when Cassie Santorini and Braden Mahoney join forces for a cause. There's a crazy ex-girlfriend, a firefighter bachelor auction, and one adorable service dog school dropout.

Be sure to sign up for my newsletter for release date information. And join the Dogfather Reader Group page on Facebook for daily updates and excerpts, and a vibrant community of dog and book lovers discussing "tails and tales."

facebook.com/groups/roxannestclairereaders/

Author's Note

Dear Readers,

I want to share something with you now that you've finished **Old Dog New Tricks**. Three days before I wrote Chapter One, I lost my darling dog, Pepper, to cancer at age thirteen. Not only was she my first dog, but she was also the one that transformed me from a person who was uncomfortable around animals to the doglover I am today. It was all Pepper. She was, as Molly said, a great one.

I struggled with the book, writing very little as I grieved. Pepper had more personality than a lot of people, and was the backbone of our family. Most of all, she was my husband's spirit animal and her death broke his heart.

After a few months of writing the book, I was far behind schedule. The story was good, but not amazing. Something was missing. And then I got a call from Alaqua Animal Refuge, where all of my covers have been shot using their rescue dogs. The owner had rescued a two-year-old "mixie" who had been deemed "unadoptable" by the county shelter because she wasn't well socialized. But Laurie Hood, who runs Alaqua, felt this dog might be a good fit for me.

My husband was adamantly opposed and still grieving Pepper. But he agreed that I needed another dog, and my daughter and I made the ten-hour round-trip drive together…and I fell instantly in love. Rosie is unlike any dog I've ever seen or known—a little terrier, a little doxie, a little Corgi, and lot of pure sweet love.

From the day she arrived until the moment I wrote "The End," my whole feeling changed about the story. I started over and introduced the character of Goldie and almost typed "Rosie" every time I wrote her name. (It really worked because the dog on this cover is technically a red golden retriever, not an Irish setter. When we shot the covers, it was the closest rescue we could find to match Rusty. Now, this dog even makes more sense. That's Goldie!)

But most importantly, as I witnessed my husband's heart melt to our new arrival, I was able to weave all those emotions into Daniel's love story. Yes, there can be more than one great one. For that reason, the book is dedicated with all my love to Rosemary Ruth, the newest member of our family. She has attached herself to my husband's side and won him over heart and soul.

Thank you for reading my books, for sharing them with friends and fellow romance readers and doglovers, and for visiting the wonderful world of Waterford Farm again and again. Stick with me, there will be many more love stories and great dogs, I promise!

xoxo
Rocki

The Barefoot Bay Series

Looking for more books by Roxanne St. Claire? Take a trip to Barefoot Bay! On these sun-washed shores you'll meet heroes who'll steal your heart, heroines who'll make you stand up and cheer, and characters who quickly become familiar and beloved. Some are spicy, some are sweet, but every book in the fourteen-book Barefoot Bay series stands alone, and tempts readers to come back again and again. So, kick off your shoes and fall in love with billionaires, brides, bodyguards, silver foxes, and more...all on one dreamy island.

Secrets on the Sand
Scandal on the Sand
Seduction on the Sand
Barefoot in White
Barefoot in Lace
Barefoot in Pearls
Barefoot Bound (novella)
Barefoot With a Bodyguard
Barefoot With a Stranger
Barefoot With a Bad Boy
Barefoot Dreams (novella)
Barefoot at Sunset
Barefoot at Moonrise
Barefoot at Midnight

Find them all at roxannestclaire.com/barefoot-bay-series/

About The Author

Published since 2003, Roxanne St. Claire is a *New York Times* and *USA Today* bestselling author of more than fifty romance and suspense novels. She has written several popular series, including The Dogfather, Barefoot Bay, the Guardian Angelinos, and the Bullet Catchers.

In addition to being a ten-time nominee and one-time winner of the prestigious RITA™ Award for the best in romance writing, Roxanne's novels have won the National Readers' Choice Award for best romantic suspense three times, as well as the Maggie, the Daphne du Maurier Award, the HOLT Medallion, Booksellers Best, Book Buyers Best, the Award of Excellence, and many others.

She lives in Florida with her husband, and still attempts to run the lives of her young adult children. She loves dogs, books, chocolate, and wine, especially all at the same time.

www.roxannestclaire.com
www.twitter.com/roxannestclaire
www.facebook.com/roxannestclaire
www.roxannestclaire.com/newsletter/

Made in the USA
Lexington, KY
30 May 2019